Now or Never . . .

It's the last chance for Cynthia Brightly, the *ton*'s most bewitching belle. Driven out of London by a secret scandal, she *must* find a grand husband at the Redmonds' house party before word of her downfall spreads all over England. Unfortunately, someone at Pennyroyal Green is already privy to the whispers of broken engagements and dueling lovers: Miles Redmond, renowned explorer and—thanks to his brother's disappearance—heir to the family's enormous fortune.

Miles set his sights on Cynthia once, at a time when the ambitious beauty thought herself too good for a second son. But now he's heir apparent, relishing his control. He strikes a bargain with her: he'll keep Cynthia's steamy secrets and help her find a husband among the guests—in exchange for a single kiss.

What could be the harm in a simple kiss? Cynthia is about to discover that it's enough to unleash fierce passion—and that Miles Redmond is most certainly like no other lover in the world.

By Julie Anne Long

SINCE THE SURRENDER
LIKE NO OTHER LOVER
THE PERILS OF PLEASURE

Like No Other Lover

Julie Anne Long

An Avon Romantic Treasure

AVON

An Imprint of HarperCollinsPublishers

AVON BOOKS
An Imprint of HarperCollins*Publishers*
10 East 53rd Street
New York, New York 10022-5299

Copyright © 2008 by Julie Anne Long
ISBN 978-0-06-134159-5
www.avonromance.com

First Avon Books paperback printing: November 2008

Avon Trademark Reg. U.S. Pat. Off. and in Other Countries, Marca Registrada, Hecho en U.S.A.
HarperCollins® is a registered trademark of HarperCollins Publishers.

Printed in the U.S.A.

10 9 8 7 6 5 4

For Sammy

Acknowledgments

My gratitude to May Chen for her cheerful support, sharp, insightful editing, and the extremely heart-gladdening smiley faces in the margins; to the amazing, hardworking Avon staff, including Tom Egner for the *beautiful* cover; to all the friends who keep me sane and grounded—Karen, Kevin, Melisa, Josh, Toni; and as always, to my marvelous, preternaturally patient agent, Steve Axelrod.

Like
No Other
Lover

Chapter 1

"You've gone an alarming shade of russet in the face, Redmond."

This observation from Mr. Culpepper, Pennyroyal Green's resident historian, ended a pronounced lull in conversation, which had begun when the door of the Pig & Thistle swung open, admitting a rush of damp air, a rustle of laughter, and three people. One of the people was Miles Redmond's sister Violet. As Violet was invariably emphatically *Violet*, she bore watching. Particularly because the person best at goading Violet, his brother Jonathon Redmond, came in the door beside her. The third person . . .

The third person was responsible for Mile's russet color.

Miles watched Cynthia Brightly—of all people, *Cynthia Brightly*—pull at the fingers of her gloves until her hands were free of them, hang up her cloak on a peg near the door, and say something to Violet that caused his sister to tip back her head and laugh merry peals calculated to draw looks.

Every head in the pub drifted helplessly toward the sound the way flowers turn to the sun.

Normally Miles would have rolled his eyes.

Instead he watched, riveted, as Miss Brightly took a general look about the pub: at the table full of laughing Everseas, at Miss Marietta Endicott of Miss Marietta Endicott's Academy for Young Ladies having supper with what appeared to be two concerned parents and one sullen young lady. At him. Her remarkable blue eyes neither brightened nor darkened in recognition when they brushed his—why would they?—and her faint smile, the aftermath of laughter, remained unaltered. He might well have been the pillar or a hat rack for how *seen* he'd been.

Whereas the brush of her gaze left Miles buzzing like a struck tuning fork.

What in God's name was she doing in *Sussex*? In Pennyroyal Green? With *Violet*?

"I would have said he's gone more of a *claret*," Culpepper said to Cooke. He threw the words down like a gauntlet. He was irritable this evening, as Cooke had won three chess games in a row, and Culpepper hungered for a controversy, any controversy.If none other was forthcoming, Miles's complexion would have to do.

The two scholarly gentlemen had known Miles since he'd been born, and they'd been particularly proprietary about him since he returned from his now renowned South Seas expedition two years ago. He'd in fact thrilled them into silence when he confided he was in the midst of planning a much grander return expedition and offered them an opportunity to invest in it.

Which was when the door opened and Miles had apparently changed color.

His bloody sister had a gift for controversy, but he never would have anticipated this.

He found his voice. "I've gone claret? Perhaps it's just that we're too close to the fire."

Across from him, two pairs of furry brows dove in skeptical unison. At the Pig & Thistle, Culpepper and Cooke and, by association, Miles, were *always* close to the fire, as this was where the chessboard lived.

Miles gave what was meant to be an illustrative good-heavens-isn't-it-warm-in-here tug at his cravat. He was surprised to encounter the hard thump of his pulse in his throat.

This, too, was Cynthia Brightly's fault.

He dropped his hand flat to the table and stared hard at it, as though he could read in its veins and tendons the reasons for his response. The scientist in him wanted to know *precisely* what it was he felt about the woman. Strong emotions visited him so seldom—he could hardly blame them, as he was hardly a hospitable host—it was difficult to know whether it was anger or something else.

Certainly anger was a part of it.

He recalled that help was literally at hand. He closed his fingers around his tankard and poured the rest of Ned Hawthorne's famous dark brew down his throat with long inelegant gulps. It was both cure and courage.

He swiped his mouth with the back of his hand.

"What color am I now?" He asked defiantly.

It was, in a way, the fault of his first South Sea expedition that he'd noticed Cynthia Brightly at all.

It happened at a ball. The guest list for the enormous annual Malverney affair ranged in pedigree from Prinny to far less discriminate choices. Miles, as second son of the staggeringly wealthy and influential Isaiah Redmond, wasn't certain where he fell in the ranking, and didn't care.

Miles's ship had docked in England again so recently his complexion was still fading in degrees from tropical brown to a proper English shade of parchment, and had reached the sallow stage. He was still too thin for his large frame;

fevers, bad food, and a long ocean voyage did tend to strip flesh from a man. Roasts of beef and Yorkshire puddings were replenishing his.

He'd taken a ragtag crew on a barely seaworthy ship to a swollen, pulsing, fever dream of a land: brilliant flowers the size of parasols tangling with vines thicker around than a man's arms; snakes as supple and long as the vines themselves; beetles the size of St. Giles rats; ants the length of thumbs. Noisy rainbow-feathered birds and iridescent butterflies the size of Chinese fans spangled the air; duskyskinned women as entangling as the flora shared his bed at night. *Everything* was abandoned, moist, outsized and excessive. He learned to move slowly, languidly; he learned he would never be dry or cool, regardless.

Death was as surprising and thickly everywhere as the life, hidden and overt: scuttling through the undergrowth as tiny scorpions, emerging from the trees as a tribe of cannibals with whom he successfully negotiated for his life, as a tenacious fever that nearly killed him anyway.

Miles wasn't immune to awe, but the strangeness and dangers of Lacao never frightened him. Fear was usually rooted in ignorance, and he'd long ago learned to vanquish ignorance with preternatural patience, and acute observation and tempered-steel determination. And he recognized beauty, but he never exalted it. He understood the purpose of beauty in nature was to attract mates or prey—which, he'd decided dryly after more than two decades of observing his parents, his family, and the *ton*, was, in fact, its purpose in every society.

And for this reason, he had never, for God's sake, challenged anyone to a duel, written terrible poetry, climbed balconies (as Colin Eversea had once been rumored to do), or otherwise *embarrassed* himself over a beautiful woman.

Miles quite sensibly and discreetly satisfied his formidable sensual appetites in the arms of the ton's aristocratic widows, who considered him their best-kept secret.

He would return to England to write the first of what would become a series of books about his adventures. This book would eventually earn him great notoriety, first among scientific circles, which rippled concentrically outward to encompass fashionable circles, until he was avidly sought for lectures and salons and envied by men possessed of less fortitude or who were leg-shackled by wives and broods of children.

This bemused Miles.

He simply couldn't see his voyage as courageous or mythical when his nature gave him no choice in the matter: he was driven by a simple but quietly ferocious need to *know* things. Negotiating with cannibals for his life simply seemed a quite logical conclusion to the trajectory he'd been on since he was soundly thrashed for taking apart his father's gold watch when he was seven years old. He'd had all the tiny glittering pieces laid out before him, analyzed and understood their relationship to one another, and was *just* about to reassemble it when he'd been caught.

The thrashing did nothing at all to detract from the giddy triumph of finally understanding at last how the bloody thing *worked*. It was, however, a very important lesson: the quest for discovery was often a dangerous one.

But all of this notoriety was a year away.

For now, he was simply happy to be home again among family, roasts of beef, low uncluttered green landscapes, and discreet, randy aristocratic widows clothed in layers and layers of fabric that could be peeled or coaxed off. He was even happy to attend a ball, and he loathed balls. It just seemed a decidedly, blessedly English thing to do.

But Lacao seemed to be relinquishing him only gradually, the way a dream dissolves into wakefulness. And suddenly, as Lord Albemarle stood at his elbow and pressed him for stories of warm-blooded women of easy virtue, it happened: the heat of the ballroom crush became tropical; the fluttering of silk fans in the hands of women became fronds and butterflies; the rustle of silk and muslin and coats became jungle foliage. His two worlds kaleidoscoped into one.

Which was why he reflexively turned when a flash of iridescence caught his eye. His first thought was: *Morpho rhetenor Helena.* The extraordinary tropical butterfly with wings of shifting colors: blues, lavenders, greens.

It proved to be a woman's skirt.

The color *was* blue, but by the light of the legion of overhead candles, he saw purples and even greens shivering in its weave. A bracelet of pale stones winked around one wrist, a circlet banded her dark head. The chandelier struck little beams from that, too.

She's altogether too shiny for a woman, he decided, and began to turn away.

Which was when she tipped her face up into the light.

Everything stopped. The beat of his heart, the pump of his lungs, the march of time.

Seconds later, thankfully, it all resumed. Much more violently than previously.

And then absurd notions roman-candled in his mind.

His palms ached to cradle her face—it was a kitten's face, broad and fair at the brow, stubborn at the chin. She had kitten's eyes, too: large and a bit tilted and surely they weren't *actually* the azure of calm southern seas? Surely he, Miles Redmond, hadn't entertained such a florid thought? Her eyebrows were wicked: fine, slanted, very dark. Her

6

hair was probably brown, but it was as though he'd never learned the word "brown."

Burnished. Silk. Copper. Azure. Delicate. Angel. Hallelujah. Suddenly these were the only words he knew.

He stared. She didn't notice. Nor did anyone else, such was the crowded ballroom and Mile's lifelong ability, despite his considerable height, to be more scenery than seen when he chose.

Moments later this grave female disturbance to his peace of mind was swept by the gentle tide of her friends into the ballroom proper and lost to his gaze.

So it wasn't just a mere poetically excessive expression after all: a woman *could* literally take one's breath away. Apart from the four intimate, athletic rounds he'd gone two nights earlier with Lady Dovecote—who was at this moment signaling a subtle but unmistakable suggestion to him with her fan on his peripheral vision—no woman had ever before left him breathless.

Miles ignored Lady Dovecote. He remained pointed toward where the woman had last been, like a compass needle quivering toward north.

"Who is the girl in blue?" He took pains to sound a mere quarter turn past bored. He directed this question to Lord Albermarle.

Albemarle was foxed and garrulous and pleased to be able to enlighten Miles. "Oh! That would be Miss Cynthia Brightly. She's a bit fast, so I've heard, and it's no doubt ungentlemanly of me to say it, but there you have it. The belle of the season, and it would be duller for lack of her, though there's Violet this year, thank God, and God *save* us, my apologies, Redmond. Please don't call me out over your sister. Miss Brightly has no fortune and no family, one hears, but she has . . . everything *else* . . . as you can see, and it is quite fashionable to be in love with her."

Ah. So this phenomenon had already been discovered. The scientist in Miles was displeased.

"Care for an introduction?" Albermarle concluded. "My sister can probab—"

But Miles had already vanished.

He remembered that passage through the ballroom now. He'd no doubt been acquainted with most of the people he brushed past, but so focused was he on his objective that he was incapable of recognizing any of them. He smiled very slightly all the way through that silk and muslin jungle as though his smile was a passport, a lantern, an apology for the fact that his elegant English manners were only now returning to him along with his English complexion, in degrees.

All the while some internal blacksmith took great clanging strokes at his heart.

At last he saw again that flash of iridescence—surely that dress was fashioned of fairy wings? He was too enthralled to be appalled at his own metaphor. Perhaps one thought in geysers of clichés when one fell in love.

His pace slowed. Was this extraordinary confluence of reactions *love*?

It wasn't entirely pleasant, if so, he mused. But it was definitely interesting, and Miles appreciated "interesting" more than nearly anything else in the world.

He was close enough now to see that her profile was designed to do dramatic things to hearts: stop them, steal them, break them. Her bottom lip—a pillowy, pale pink curve—inspired decidedly earthier thoughts, all of which communicated with immediacy to his groin. Her complexion was burnished in chandelier light and flushed from the heat; a few streamers of hair trailed from her coiffure, specifically, it seemed, to draw attention to her long, long neck and the bosom creamily, philanthropically displayed by her daringly low neckline.

And then he heard her voice. He would never forget that first sound of it: lilting, feminine, surprisingly mature and confident. She'd lowered it; the woman she stood near—a Miss Liza Standshaw, Miles thought—had looped a familiar hand through her arm and leaned her head into Cynthia Brightly's: the better to hear secrets.

Unfortunately, he had remarkably good hearing.

"Lord Finley has thirty thousand pounds a year and golden hair, but his mama is a harridan. Still, such a small price to pay for *thirty thousand pounds*, don't you think, Liza? He's a bit dissolute but quite a lively dancer. He's claimed two of mine already—waltzes! The Earl of Borland has a wen, but it's something a girl can overlook given the title and the money and the various castles, don't you think? And Mr. Lyon Redmond is exceptionally handsome and wealthy, isn't he? The Redmond fortune puts that of Croesus to shame, or so I've heard. I've heard he's eyes only for Miss Olivia Eversea, quite moony over her, in fact, but the families are about as cozy as the Montagues and Capulets, and I'm certain their papas will never allow a match, so let's do put him on the list. I shall want an introduction."

"Miss Olivia Eversea will be no match for you, Cynthia," her friend maintained stoutly. "We shall get you that introduction. There's Mr. Miles Redmond here tonight. The second Redmond son. He's eligible, too. Will you want an introduction?"

"Mr. Miles Redmond . . . Miles Redmond . . . Oh! The towering dark chap with the spectacles?" she sounded aghast. "He does whatnot with insects, does he not? Lud, Liza, are you *mad*?" Cynthia Brightly gave her friend a playful rap on the arm with her fan. "Why should I settle for a dour *second son* when I could have an actual heir? Or an *earl*?"

They giggled. A sound as musical and icy as the spring thaw.

Miles backed away smoothly, unnoticed. One step. Two steps. Three steps.

Until he bumped gently against a short pillar supporting a Grecian-style sculpture: Hercules, he noted. Doing something heroic with or to a lion.

For a moment he unconsciously mimicked the statue's absolute stillness.

The shock, when it arrived, was unnatural and nasty: as though a butterfly had landed on his wrist only to sink fangs into it.

It gave way moments later to a distant sort of amusement. He'd been a simpleton about women, really. Somehow he'd never dreamed such a coldly mercantile heart could beat inside so delicate a breast. He was impressed and unnerved and fascinated and, in a peculiar way, grateful; from that moment on, he saw every woman anew, sought evidence in their eyes of the tick of their minds, danced with them as if holding little grenades. They all became much more interesting for what he suspected they didn't say to him than for what they did say.

Only later would he realize that the tectonic plates of his pride had shifted that day. The rumble in his character was low and deep, but he was permanently changed:

Miles Redmond did not like being dismissed.

Last year, if anyone had told Cynthia Brightly she would actually be grateful to spend part of a Saturday evening in the *country* in a drinking establishment named for a farm animal and a weed, she would have laughed hard enough to snap her stays. At the very least, she would give the person in question a gentle pat and suggest they might like to make the cup of ratafia in their hand their last one for the evening. Because last year, *all* of her evenings had involved an excess of everything, ratafia included.

She'd always had more luck than her fair share of luck. And luck this time had appeared in the unlikely friendship of Violet Redmond: beautiful, charming, restless, and surprisingly unsentimental, Violet possessed a gift for creating mayhem at unpredictable intervals—a gift Cynthia rather admired, as she herself was no stranger to mischief. Violet had once threatened to cast herself into a well over a disagreement with a suitor, and she'd gotten one leg over the edge before she was pulled back by the elbows. She'd allegedly once challenged a gentleman to a duel. The great majority of the time her manners were exquisite, and though she'd made it clear that she hadn't yet met the man she could *conceive* of marrying, it didn't prevent her from encouraging London bloods to jockey for her attention.

So when the rest of the *ton* had dropped Cynthia with teeth-jarring finality, unsurprisingly, Violet had invited her to her family's home in Sussex for a fortnight's house party.

Cynthia was certain the invitation represented two parts friendship and two parts mischief, but she was in no position to care, and had every intention of making the most of it.

Her instinct for gaiety instantly located the table in the pub containing Everseas: two dazzlingly handsome men, one of them, Colin, infamous and newly wed—*so* newly the broadsheets were still agog about it—the other, judging from the way he was listing a bit in his seat, well into in his cups. A sleek black-haired woman—Colin Eversea's wife?—smiled at a slim girl who paused by the Everseas'

11

empty plates and tankards and gathered them up in that deft many-armed way barmaids seem to possess. The girl conspicuously did not smile in return.

And then Cynthia watched the girl slip behind the bar, where an older man gave her braid a tweak and handed her a broom once her hands were empty again. *He* earned a smile. And his smile was the same size and shape and brightness as hers. Father and daughter. Cynthia turned her head away, suddenly feeling *immersed* in families. It was like a language she'd never learned, for she had no family at all.

"The Hawthornes," Violet told her, seeing the direction of her gaze. "Ned and his daughter Polly. The Hawthorne family has owned the Pig & Thistle for nigh on centuries now." She pretended she hadn't seen the Everseas, and ignored the ironic hand lifted in greeting by Colin and slapped down by his brother.

Violet steered Cynthia away from the implied delights of Everseas to a much less promising table. At this sat three men: two older men, between them a chessboard with black and ivory pieces neatly rowed, and a younger man—large, dark, dour, bespectacled.

Ah, yes, of course. Violet's older brother. Mr. Miles Redmond.

He's . . . something to do with insects, Cynthia recalled vaguely.

Miles watched his sister inexorably approach with Miss Brightly, and was motionless again.

He'd never seen Cynthia again after that night, and naturally had never said a thing about what he overheard. But that season she was ever a feature of gleeful *ton* gossip, always in the ceaseless ambient conversation in clubs and salons: he heard of reckless, predawn phaeton races, the triumphant winner earning all of Miss Brightly's waltzes at Lady Murcheston's seasonal do; about the volumes of terrible poetry written on the subject of her complexion and her eyes; and oh, the wagers—whimsical and desperate and inflammatory wagers that allegedly caused men to come to blows—recorded in the betting books at White's concerning who would finally win her hand.

In short, many, many men had foundered on the iceberg of Miss Cynthia Brightly's heart.

And she *encouraged* all of it, or so it was whispered, half in censure, half in awe.

He'd been drinking at White's the day he'd learned of her engagement to the Earl of Courtland's enormously wealthy heir. Nearly two years ago now. And though the news had nothing at all to do with him, it had knelled peculiarly. He'd gone still, puzzled and heavy.

And then, ever the gentleman, ever quick to do the right and gracious thing, Miles had joined everyone in drinking to Courtland's good fortune. He'd continued drinking all night long, in an attempt to fill that peculiar resounding emptiness, but ever pragmatic, had given up before they needed to carry him out of White's.

Violet and Miss Brightly were upon them now. He saw his sister drop a familiar hand on Miss Brightly's wrist. He stared at Violet's hand. He still couldn't seem to resume thinking clearly, and normally thoughts poured through him the way his blood did: ceaselessly.

Though it seemed he *could* stand: his breeding was tugging him to his feet. They all stood: he and Mr. Cooke and Mr. Culpepper.

He didn't yet look directly at Miss Brightly. He *did* manage to send a speaking look at his intractable sister.

"I can't lie to you when you look at me like that, Miles," Violet had once complained. "It's like looking at my own conscience."

He'd laughed. He had a good laugh, and his siblings liked to make him do it.

But he was very nearly the only person on the planet who could make Violet rue something. His father indulged her, and she loved and feared him; Lyon had spoiled her, and she had worshipped him; Jonathan goaded her, her mother despaired of her. Miles was the one who watched over her.

Watching over the things he cared about was his particular talent.

The mischief in Violet's eyes faltered a bit.

Ah, that was better.

"Good evening, gentlemen," she said prettily and a trifle less spiritedly than she might have before Miles fixed her with a disciplinary stare. "I should like to introduce you to my dear friend, Miss Cynthia Brightly."

Miles refrained from snorting at the "dear."

The admiration on the faces of the two old chess foes was unabashed and touching. They were fond of Violet—they'd known her since she was a baby, and loved hearing of her exploits—but Miss Brightly was new. They gazed at her with wordless delight for a moment before offering a pair of courtly bows and polite greetings to both young ladies.

Miles thought dryly: beauty confers a sort of royalty; it commands reflexive obeisance; it inspires awe and resentment and obsequiousness all at once. Everyone wants a role at its court, regardless of how we feel about its bearer. But she isn't a *true* beauty, he told himself. Her eyes were too large, her lips too full. Her face *not* an oval.

Unfortunately, analysis failed to vanquish whatever was happening to his body.

Because it was required of him, he, too, finally bowed over Miss Brightly's hand.

When he was upright again it struck him again how odd it was that he didn't so much see as *feel* her: like a brush against the short hairs at the back of his neck, like a hot breath in his ear, as a low hum in his solar plexus, as a knot in his throat. His skin felt singed.

They regarded each other. She betrayed almost no recognition. But he felt it, almost as though it spun from her to wind him in a cocoon: that indefinable thing known as *charm*.

He understood at once he was the deliberate object of it. He was a man, but he was hardly a fool. If Cynthia Brightly was in Sussex, in Pennyroyal Green, in the *country*, without a husband or a fiancé . . .

Something untimely must have happened in London.

His realization must have done something cynical to his eyes, for something uncertain subtly shadowed hers.

He reminded himself that he genuinely did not like her. The realization restored his breathing and senses to something resembling normal. And he was a Redmond, after all: his manners were as fine as cognac, as instinctive as breathing. He would say something innocuous and polite now.

"I must leave," he said, and turned and did just that.

Four mouths dropped into O's behind him.

Miles was just as surprised as everyone else. He felt a peculiar sense of vertigo, as though he'd given a push on a pendulum and it had swung instead right at him and knocked him flat.

But he never paused as he deliberately wended his way through the drinkers and diners at the Pig & Thistle. He passed his youngest brother, Jonathon, who had lingered near the bar. Jonathon had said something to Polly Hawthorne to make her giggle, which was a good sound, as Polly Hawthorne, like nearly every women in Pennyroyal Green between the ages of seventeen and eighty, had been in love with Colin Eversea and was taking the matter of his marriage rather personally. She was at an age where *everything* was taken rather personally. She'd taken to sending dark, wounded looks at Colin Eversea's wife, Miles had noticed.

Apparently, Polly wasn't pulling Jonathan's ale fast enough to suit him, because he was patting the bar with an impatient hand. And then he turned, and something he saw in Miles's face made him raise his brows comically high in a question.

Why? Miles asked, with a curt gesture of his chin at Miss Brightly as he took his greatcoat from the peg near the door.

He hesitated when he saw her cape hanging there. It was an ordinary cape—gray wool, clearly not new—but it seemed imbued with a peculiar charisma.

He stared at it. He frowned darkly.

Jonathan, being a man, understood the gist of Miles's question. He accepted his ale from Polly and rose it to her in thanks, then took a long noisy draught before answering Miles'. He lowered his voice to do it. "Can't say for certain why she's here—Violet don't know, either, and I escorted the two of them here from London—but I *heard* there was a duel. 'Twas kept very quiet, as it was the Earl of Courtland's heir she was engaged to, after all. All I know is the engagement was broken and she seems untouchable in London—heard everyone's dropped her, but *no one* seems to know quite why, and I reckon it's ungentlemanly to discuss it. I certainly haven't asked. I like her. She's lively enough company," he added carelessly. "I warrant Violet lured her here to cause mischief and to have a go at the rich eligible bloods at the party. Have a care, old man! Miss Brightly's come for *you*," he said, cheerfully ghoulish.

Jonathan mimed a fishhook with his forefinger, inserted it in his mouth, tugged it up and bugged his eyes out.

And at this Miles flung the pub door open, let it swing shut to the sound of his brother's laughter, and plunged into the familiar rolling, soft dark of the Sussex downs.

He was suddenly nostalgic for the somehow more comfortable dangers of a Brazilian jungle.

Chapter 2

When he reached home, Miles handed his hat and walking stick to one of his mother's expensively liveried footman, and as he stood there over the chessboard-patterned marble, he paused to imagine something: all of the moods and circumstances under which his ancestors must have come through that door—foxed from a night at the Pig & Thistle, giddy or guilty from an assignation, triumphant from battle, perhaps grieving after a funeral held at the town's little church, or newly married and filled with lust or trepidation. One ancestor had allegedly come home and put a pistol to his head.

This occurred to him because for the first time in his life he had no idea what *he* was feeling. Mysteries were his lifeblood and nearly an affront: he routinely quietly, ruthlessly, methodically unraveled them.

But he'd never before been a mystery to *himself*.

He eyed the stairs. He could swiftly take them, instruct his valet to pack a light trunk, and then bolt for London—where he kept rooms—before the rest of the houseguests arrived in the morning. He took two swift decisive steps toward the stairs when the prospect of the imminent arrival of Lady Middlebough slowed him. Lush and brunette, mar-

18

ried and bored, discreetly enough connected to learn of his repertoire of skills and the formidable appetite with which he applied them, sophisticated enough to signal her intent to him all but wordlessly at a recent ball, clever enough to secure an invitation to this house party from his mother—the very promise of her held him motionless for an instant. She was *precisely* the sort of woman he enjoyed.

He hesitated, and his hand slowly, involuntarily, curled, as if in anticipation of wrapping it around Lady Middlebough's soft white thigh.

This reverie proved to be a grave mistake. It gave his mother, Fanchette Redmond, an opportunity to sweep into the foyer and intercept him with this horrifying bit of news:

"Your father would like to have a conversation with you, Miles, dear."

He froze. The reverie popped like a soap bubble.

His mother put up her cheek for his kiss, and her son unfroze long enough to dutifully plant one on her soft lilac-scented cheek. And then Fanchette Redmond surprised Miles by kissing him on both cheeks, as though apologizing for the fact that he would have to speak to his father.

Because Miles baffled his father.

Whereas many bored wealthy young men dabbled in the natural sciences, to his father's utter bemusement, Miles had set out to *become* an entomologist. "Insects and whatnot," is how Isaiah Redmond referred to his life's work. And Miles knew full well that if he hadn't gone on a long journey involving dangers, privations, fevers, people who allegedly ate other people, and affectionate women who wore nothing for clothing above their waists all day, his father would have thought him less of a man than he ought to be.

And before Lyon disappeared, this hadn't mattered in the least.

His father had steadfastly refused to present the idea of funding Mile's next, grander expedition to his formidable investment group, the Mercury Club, for this very reason. But Miles had never once failed to accomplish something he'd set out to do. He'd begun shamelessly rooting out every possible funding source, even resorting to enchanting old Culpepper and Cooke with the idea. Still it was all taking rather longer than he preferred, and desperation—just a hint—encroached.

"He'll be up to greet you in the library in a moment," his mother added.

Leaving him to wait was very like Isaiah Redmond, too.

"One other thing, dear. As you know, we've a number of guests arriving, but your father and I have been called away to deal with some business on my side of the family, and I fear we must leave first thing in the morning. It involves a will, you see, and money and property, and your father absolutely insists upon seeing to it straight away, as you can imagine. I've arranged the seating and the meals and the entertainments and the like. You need only ensure the guests enjoy themselves until we return."

Miles was speechless. Why, why, *why* did he suddenly feel as though it would be infinitely preferable to be the guest of hungry cannibals than host of this house party? He had nothing at all against *people*, per se. He had beautiful manners and a command of every kind of conversation.

"Of course, Mother," he said calmly. Fooling his mother not at all.

She gave him a pat, not doubtful at all that he would do his duty—unlike, in the end, Lyon, who had allegedly been brought low by love and subsequently vanished.

* * *

While Miles awaited his father in his father's study, Cynthia and Jonathan and Violet returned from the Pig & Thistle. Cynthia now stood in the center of the room she'd been assigned, taking the measure of it.

It had been so passionately cleaned and polished that every piece of furniture—the walnut dressing table and matching mirror above it, the wardrobe where Violet's obliging abigail had tenderly hung Cynthia's gowns, the tall posts of a bed that could fit three of her across and six of her down—seemed to have its own halo. But no carved acorns or vines decorated the hearth. No friezes enhanced the walls. The legs of the dressing table and bed and chair were unturned rectangles. The carpet possessed no discernible pedigree.

Quite a contrast to the furniture she'd seen downstairs: gilded, delicate, haughty refugees from the French revolution, no doubt purchased cheaply from fleeing aristocrats by an opportunistic Redmond (was there any other kind?) at some point during the last century. The carpets, she knew, were Savonnerie and Aubusson: thick and soft as pelts, colors rich despite their advanced age, fringe luxuriant.

In other words, Mrs. Isaiah Redmond was making an eloquent point by assigning Miss Brightly this room.

Cynthia smiled as though an entire ballroom of guests was watching her at this very moment. If one thing could truthfully be said about her, it was that she was equal to a challenge.

She was startled when one of the curtains began to shimmy; the window was open. And though this room was doubtless one of the smaller ones in the house, it still seemed to take a quarter of an hour just to cross to the window to close it.

21

Before she did, she hesitated. Then parted the curtains wider to look out.

Millions of stars crowded the Sussex sky, and below it and beyond it was a vast soft dark punctuated by the woolly dark shadows of trees. For a dizzying moment she was a little girl again, shivering between her parents atop a cart in the dead of night grinding over a rutted road to a new home in Little Roxford, leaving behind the noise and crowds of their rooms atop the Jones family in Battersea in London—such a *lot* of rambunctious boys the Jones's had. And when London at last gave way to the endless skies and endless dark and ringing silence of countryside, she'd looked up to see a shooting star arcing across the sky.

It had struck Cynthia as odd that an event so startling, so unnervingly beautiful, should also be silent. It was something the entire world could see all at once but would miss if they blinked. And she'd thought at the time a funny thing to call it—a shooting star. It didn't so much shoot as *bolt*. As though it had seen an opportunity to escape its place in the firmament and taken it.

Then again, perhaps it had been *ejected* by its fellow stars, she thought dryly.

She knew a thing or two about bolting from firmaments. And about ejections.

A minute twitch of motion caught her eye: a little spider was shifting in its web in the corner of the window.

Cynthia reared backed in alarm.

The spider reared back in alarm.

Cynthia leaned forward to slide the window closed and then dropped the curtains abruptly. It had been years since she slept in a room where a spider would be allowed to build a home. Since Battersea, and the room above the Jones's.

She rubbed the fine hairs on the back of her neck, where a bit of fear pricked.

When she was younger, after her parents had gone, she often woke in terror from a dream of falling, falling, falling through an impenetrable blackness. Just like that star. Once awake, she would knot the sheets around her fists as if to anchor herself to the bed, and turn her face into her pillow to stifle her gasps so the vicar and his wife wouldn't hear them. It wasn't so much the fear of striking the ground, which is what she'd always halfhoped would happen in the dream. That, at least, would have been an *ending*—albeit, granted, not of the happy variety. It was the nothingness; it was the not knowing; it was the possibility of flailing alone for eternity.

Cynthia restlessly turned to the mirror. What she saw there cheered her immensely. She was an optimist, after all.

But she'd done something uncharacteristic as a talisman against the flailing: through an acquaintance in Little Roxbury, she'd learned of a certain savage old woman in Northumberland who spent the entirety of her days in a bath chair and was always in need of a companion, as she exhausted the goodwill of companions very rapidly. A Mrs. Mundi-Dickson.

Cynthia had written inquiring about the availability of the position and given the Redmond address. It was an admission that straits were dire, indeed.

The very idea of Mrs. Mundi-Dickson drove her to the wardrobe to restlessly do what had become a habit over the past few weeks: she fished her reticule out and gave it a little shake. It still scarcely clinked. It wasn't as though her few remaining shillings would mate and create pennies that would grow up to be other shillings when she wasn't looking, after all. Still, that pathetic jingle—and the fortnight duration of this house party—was all that remained between her and destitution. And Mrs. Mundi-Dickson.

She could, perhaps, parlay those remaining few pounds into more by suggesting a card game among the members of the house party—

No. She was to be *good*. Testing her luck was how she *found* herself in this position.

She suddenly realized her palms had gone damp.

She shoved the reticule back into the wardrobe and sat down abruptly to test the bed. Soft. She gave a bounce: no creaks. She peeled back the counterpane and slid a clammy hand underneath: cool, smooth, very fine sheets, ironed by one of the battery of maids she'd seen scurrying for other parts of the house like mice for their holes when she entered with Violet and Jonathan.

She felt more cheerful. As long as such a bed was hers to lie in at night—as long as she was a *guest* and not an employee, and not, heaven forfend, a *mistress*—there was hope.

In particular, there was hope in the form of the Redmond heir.

Though admittedly her first encounter with him had been brief, and she'd seen more of his back than his front as he stormed out of the pub. Hardly promising.

Violet had assured her this was an aberration. "Good heavens. I must apologize for my brother, though I believe it would be the first time I have *ever* apologized for Miles. His manners are usually so beautiful, Cynthia."

Cynthia had shrugged lightly, and silently regretted deeply he was not an Eversea, which would be have been *delightful*, or the dashing, proud, center-of-everything oldest Redmond, Lyon, who had done the extraordinary and disappeared a year ago, allegedly out of thwarted love for the most inappropriate woman possible. Leaving dour Miles as the heir.

"He felt unwell," the older gentleman called Mr. Cooke had volunteered, stoutly defending Miles. "He'd gone a claret shade in the face." His eyes slid sideways to his friend.

"Russet," Mr. Culpepper said quietly.

Something had glinted in Miles Redmond's dark eyes as he stood over Cynthia. It wasn't just admiration—this she invariably saw in the faces of men, and she most definitely saw it in his. It was something she couldn't quite identify. Her hand had almost seemed to hum as she took it away from him.

She reflected again upon Miles Redmond's big, dark, retreating form, threw herself back on that comfortable bed and beamed up at the ceiling. She would have rooms in the family quarters one day, she was certain of it.

Because, really. . . how much challenge to *her* charm could that dour, bespectacled man possibly pose?

While Miles waited, he gazed out the window into the dark upon a darkened view of the vast Redmond park overhung with millions of stars, because he preferred that view to the deceptively calm colors of his father's study: the browns and creams, the velvets, the soft scrolls over the carpet. Little that was *actually* mild or calm ever took place in this room. It was where Isaiah conducted any meeting he considered of import, such as scathing disciplinary lectures, or where he retreated in order to ponder new ways to build the family's fortunes ever higher.

Miles turned when he heard his father's footsteps. Isaiah Redmond: very tall, lean where Miles was broad, still conspicuously handsome in the way that Lyon was. So nearly the twin of Lyon it sometimes startled. Green eyes, clear as gems.

Miles was fond of his father. He even sympathized with his father that he didn't happen to be Lyon. Not enough to attempt to be anyone other than who he wanted to be, of course.

"Good evening, Father."

"Good evening, Miles. Your mother may have told you that we must away to Cambridgeshire to see to a property matter concerning the Tarbell side of the family—one of your mother's cousins left a fortune, no will, and a squabble."

Miles had no doubt that his father would find a way to neatly, legally, fold the fortune into his own.

"She did. I shall be happy to step in and see that the house party goes smoothly."

They spoke to each other politely, which was how any Redmond would speak to someone who felt rather like a stranger.

"Very good. I wanted to speak to you of a business proposition, and as time is rather of the essence, I needed to speak to you about it before we departed."

Miles went still. Isaiah had never wanted to speak to him of a business proposition in his life. And the last proposition Miles had brought to *his father*—the financing of his extraordinarily expensive second journey to the South Seas—had been met by incredulity and cold dismissal.

"Very well, sir," Miles said cautiously.

Isaiah strolled over to his polished walnut table, gestured a question with one hand to the brandy decanter. Two crystal glasses so clean they were nearly invisible flanked it. Miles gave his head a shake.

"Have you given any thought to marriage?" His father said this evenly, his back turned, decanter in hand. Expensive brandy gurgled into a glass.

Miles refused to allow his surprise to show. But this was Isaiah Redmond, after all. This was not a casual query.

"A thought or two," Miles said dryly. "A man does when he reaches my age." Nearly thirty.

His father turned slowly around, brandy glass cupped in his hand. He hesitated.

"May I ask if you already have a particular bride in mind?"

The hesitation amused Miles. No doubt his father thought visions of bluestockings danced in his second son's head. Wait—a bluestocking wouldn't dance. They would *march*—march with baskets of food hooked over their arms for the poor.

"No. I haven't a particular bride in mind," Miles said calmly. "Though I should like her to have a brain in her head, a good family, a fortune, a pretty face."

A pause that seemed inordinately long ensued. Miles wondered which part of his sentence troubled his father. No doubt the brain part.

"Do you . . . do you need to be in love?" his father asked grimly, at last.

Miles stopped himself just in time from gaping. He *did* dig one of his fingernails hard into his palm to prevent laughter. Dear *God*. He wasn't to have a conversation with his father about *love*, was he? He could not imagine anything less bearable. Not scorpion stings, nor overhearing cannibals discussing his fate.

But all at once he recalled that "love"—for Olivia Eversea, that was—was what had allegedly caused Lyon to cast all reason to the wind and disappear, presumed dead or never to return, leaving Isaiah with the far-less-comfortable-for-Isaiah Miles for an heir. Lyon, victim, perhaps, of the unfortunate legendary curse: once per generation, an Ever-

27

sea and a Redmond were allegedly destined to fall in love with each other.

Doubtless Isaiah wondered if he harbored any similarly fatal romantic flaws.

Suddenly, unbidden and vivid, came the image of a homely gray cloak hanging from a peg in the pub. Miles inhaled sharply.

"Love," he declared with quiet and absolute conviction, "of the sort you're suggesting, is absurd. I don't need love in order to marry."

Isaiah regarded his second son, the shadow of a frown touching his forehead. His mouth parted, stayed parted briefly. He seemed in a state of indecision about what next to say.

But then he nodded crisply and said, "Very good." As though this were a meeting of the Mercury Club and the two of them had just put the notion of love to the vote.

"May I ask if *you* have anyone in particular in mind, sir?" Because now Miles was curious, and knowing his father, Isaiah most certainly did.

"Georgina Mossgate, Lady Rutland, is a lovely girl, and she has been invited to the party." His father didn't even pretend to issue this statement casually.

"Hmmph." The name surprised Miles because he'd known the Mossgates for most of his life. Her father, Rutland, was an avid amateur naturalist and had taken to corresponding with him. But what did he know about Georgina? As a child she'd worn a long braid; as an adult, she invariably wore her pale hair wound into a coil so perfectly symmetrical it reminded him whimsically of a henge. He'd once conversed with her about the ants of Sussex and their habits, about which she knew a surprising amount, and her gray eyes had been soft and attentive and alert, and never once moved from his face. She had a quiet but not retiring way about her, and her bosom—Miles never failed to take note of a bosom—was remarkable. He approved of the way she'd turned into a woman; he'd danced with her more than a few times over the years; she intrigued him not at all.

This struck him, suddenly, as a very peaceful and desirable quality in a wife.

"And as you know, I've wanted Rutland as a member of the Mercury Club for years now."

It took Miles less than a tick of the clock to know precisely where this conversation was heading. The neatness of the solution was exhilarating, brilliant, cynical, and utterly typical of his father.

In short: he and his father would both get what they wanted most.

His heart thumped. He revealed nothing. He simply waited for his father to spell it out.

Isaiah wasted no time. "If you and Georgina were to wed, Rutland will at last consent to become a member of the Mercury Club. And with Rutland's support and extraordinary resources, I'm convinced it will be a simple and swift enough thing to persuade the group to finance your voyage to . . ." He frowned faintly.

"Lacao, Father," Miles said calmly. By now, most people in England knew the name of the place he'd written about so extensively. Not his bloody father, however.

"Yes. Lacao." His father never asked about the place. Isaiah had always been more comfortable with what to him were the infinitely more compatible and practical sensibilities of Lyon, who had the making of money in his blood. There *was* money in writing and talking about Lacao, and Miles had become modestly independently wealthy as a result of it. But the making of money had been rather inadvertent and serendipitous and beside the point.

He stayed silent.

"You're amenable to the match, then?" Isaiah said finally.

"I'm amenable." He saw no reason to object.

"Very good," his father said crisply again. "Georgina will be in attendance this fortnight at the invitation of your mother, and was expected to arrive this evening. Your mother has arranged various entertainments for the fortnight, dinners for the neighbors, and dancing, and so forth. So dance with the girl. Talk with her. Make yourself agreeable by—"

Oh, for God's sake.

"You may be relieved to learn you needn't tell me how to make myself agreeable to a woman, Father," he interjected dryly. Or *any* woman, he didn't add. But anticipation twinged when he considered making himself *agreeable* to Lady Middlebough. Georgina was a bit of a complication, but Lady Middlebough's stay would be brief and she wanted only one thing from him, which should be a simple enough thing to arrange.

His father gave a short placating laugh. "Yes, of course. Forgive me, Miles. It's simply that your mother and I are invested in ensuring that our children are well and appropriately matched in a way that does credit to the family. We cannot countenance matches of any other kind."

The faintest, faintest whiff of a warning was contained therein.

The warning was unnecessary. Miles could not imagine an instance in which he would be tempted to make an inappropriate match. Marriage was perhaps the most important business arrangement a man would ever make. He knew by "do credit to the family" Isaiah meant "increase the family fortunes and expand its already outrageous range of influence," and Miles had no real philosophical objection to this, either.

"I understand your concern, sir," he said gravely. "And a match with Lady Georgina would be expeditious for all of us, and I hope for Lady Georgina as well. I'm certain we shall manage to suit."

Isaiah went curiously quiet for another moment. At last he nodded.

"Speaking of concerns, Miles," his father continued dryly, "I have another of them. Your sister has made the acquaintance of a certain Miss Cynthia Brightly. She has invited said Miss Brightly to our home for a fortnight's stay."

It was as though his father had uncorked a bottle containing a genie. Those two words uttered side by side in his voice—"Cynthia" and "Brightly"—brought her so suddenly and vividly into the room that the muscles banding Miles's stomach tightened in response. He couldn't breathe to speak.

"Yes?" he at last managed calmly enough,.

His father hesitated. "Word has reached me about Miss Brightly."

"What sort of word?"

His father produced a humorless smile. "Does it matter?"

No, Miles supposed it did not: "word" reaching one about a young lady was often sufficient warning that the young lady in question was far too interesting. For instance, "word" often reached one about the Everseas, though word had rather reached a crescendo with the recent events surrounding Colin Eversea, and the broadsheets had been rather quieter on the topic of them since then. With the Everseas, however, it was always simply a matter of time.

One did not find Redmonds in the broadsheets. Good and scrupulous breeding, and the judgment his father described, and money for bribing all manner of officials, took care of that.

"And Miss Brightly is . . ." Miles invited his father to complete the sentence with a list of objections. He was suddenly rabidly curious to hear what his father might know of her, and why she was here. Isaiah Redmond did have a way of knowing things.

"This is all I know so far: she's far too pretty and charming for someone with no money and no family, very likely ambitious beyond her right to be, surrounded by a cloud of rumor that cannot be substantiated—though I have *certainly* tried—and in light of this, not at all a suitable companion for Violet or for any of the Redmonds."

And thus was the only woman who had ever stopped Miles's breathing summarized and dismissed by his father.

Of course, he knew that his father wasn't at all wrong about Miss Brightly.

"I imagine Violet wishes to be controversial and has befriended Miss Brightly for this reason," his father continued, sounding weary and rote as he said this; Violet generally endeavored to be controversial, and managed both to charm and alarm in the process. "What do you know of Miss Cynthia Brightly, Miles?"

I know she makes my thoughts explode into poetry the way butterflies burst from cocoons. And see? It's already happening. And if we keep discussing her, I'm liable to begin speaking in the sort of metaphors that will embarrass both of us. And have I mentioned that the curve of her bottom lip is perhaps the most carnal thing I have ever, ever in my life—

"I think perhaps an engagement was broken." He made Cynthia Brightly's engagement sound like an urn toppled by reckless horseplay. "I find it impolitic to speculate."

He didn't mention that he'd seen her once that evening already. He knew his father would approve of the use of the word "impolitic." Redmonds *lived* to avoid being impolitic.

"Doubtless your sister knows what happened," his father said.

"Doubtless." Though according to Jonathan, Violet did not.

"Regardless, I mention this because, given her choice of guests, I think Violet bears watching during this fortnight. If we must extend our hospitality to Miss Brightly, we shall, but only for the fortnight of this party, not beyond, and undue warmth is probably not necessary." He added dryly,

Irritation plucked at Miles again: Violet *always* bore watching, in large part because of the way she'd been indulged by her father.

"Your mother has invited Lady Windermere for a stay," Isaiah continued, "and Lord and Lady Middlebough, as you know, will also arrive, though I believe his wife will precede him. I'm expecting Milthorpe, who will be disappointed to find me gone, no doubt, and Mr. Goodkind, who wishes to enlist me in a financial partnership. Nevertheless, I do think your sister bears watching."

"Leave your concerns in my hands, Father." It was a list of people he knew well.

"Thank you, Miles," Isaiah said calmly. "I know everything will be well with you in charge. With luck, we'll return inside a fortnight and enjoy the final evening of the party."

And Miles almost felt the transfer of responsibility physically.

There was a silence.

"How goes the scientific studies?"

A surprising question from his father, and not an earnest one. He was about to take a sip of the brandy.

33

"Very well. There is talk of putting me forward as president of the Royal Society when Sir Joseph Banks retires."

His father's brandy glass froze halfway up to his mouth.

Isaiah Redmond spoke the language of status. He knew Sir Joseph Banks. *Everyone* did. Friend of the king. Famed naturalist and adventurer. A learned, respected, influential man.

It was precisely a measure of the respect in which Miles was now held that the notion of his stepping into Sir Banks's shoes had even been discussed among his colleagues.

Miles learned long ago not to care what his father thought of him, as there was little he could do about it. But the reaction was nevertheless gratifying.

"Very good," Isaiah said finally, calmly.

Miles simply nodded shortly.

"Good luck with the house party, Miles, and with Georgina."

It was his dismissal.

"Thank you, Father. Have a safe and prosperous journey."

Isaiah acknowledged this wryness with a smile. He, for one, had no doubt it *would* be prosperous.

A footman liveried in bold blue slipped quietly into the room to refill the brandy decanter, and moved to the window to pull closed the sable velvet curtains with gloved hands.

And Miles suddenly saw heart-stopping blue eyes, and the footman's hands in the velvet became his own hands, lifting a mass of shining sable hair. He was riveted.

Christ. It was like a return of the fever.

He frowned darkly at the footman, whose back was turned.

Then he bowed and left the room quickly, to savor the fact that his dreams had just been handed to him on a shining Redmond platter.

Chapter 3

⌒⌒⌒

The following morning, Cynthia made her way downstairs to find breakfast lying beneath shining tureens on a sideboard, and a few houseguests already seated before plates at a long table. Introductions were made, conversation began haltingly and politely, and then gained momentum as eggs and kippers and coffee took away reticence and sleepiness, and social stations were gradually, subtly revealed, so that everyone knew how to talk to one another.

There was a Lady Windermere, a widow invited by Mrs. Redmond who was brisk, stout, handsome, and hungry, judging by how rapidly she forked the eggs into her mouth. Cynthia, still a little sleepy, found the motion of her arm soothing and practical; it was like watching someone shovel coal. Breakfast for Lady Windermere was clearly fuel. The restless glint in her gray eyes implied that she enjoyed herself rather more than widows her age typically did.

Next to her sat a woman of perhaps about thirty years of age, Lady Middlebough, who was "regrettably" (her word; interestingly, she didn't sound regretful) without her husband at present; he was to meet her here in a day or so, and they would travel on to Kelham Cross east of Sussex to visit relatives there. She was very pretty in a round, lush, blunt way, with shining dark hair she wore piled and pinned. She was wealthy, if her clothes were any indication: spotless, multiply flounced, crisp, and current in deep green. Her sleeves were long, her neckline deep, her bosom impressive. She seemed restless, too, but without Lady Windermere's eye glint. Her eyes were bright but her overall demeanor was distracted, and she pushed and stirred her food about as if she hoped she would uncover something else of interest on her plate. At intervals she sent glances toward the door.

Cynthia wondered where Miles Redmond was. She wanted to observe him for a time to decide whether he was truly as humorless and lurching as she suspected. One needed to tailor one's approach, after all, to one's quarry. It helped to observe the quarry in his native surroundings first, to see him perhaps interact with others of his class and genus.

This comparison amused her; it was one that she thought Miles Redmond would appreciate, given that he was a lover of insects.

She'd worn white muslin that capped her lovely shoulders sweetly but *not* demurely and was ribboned beneath her breasts with a band of blue that matched her eyes. She'd done up her own hair, then drawn down a few calculatedly wayward spirals to play about her chin. She was devastating when she looked innocent but a trifle mussed.

At least, one of the poems written to her had said as much. She could not recall the name of the poet now. Lord . . . something.

"Where did Miles get to, d'you know?" Jonathan stifled a yawn.

"Oh, Miles was up with the birds and went out riding for some reason known only to him," Violet said vaguely. "I don't know how he manages to rise so early. He was at the pub last night, too. He doesn't drink as much as he ought for a man his age."

"Violet!" Jonathan admonished, as she had so clearly said it so someone would admonish her. Everyone looked very interested in this remark.

"It was the South Seas, you see," Violet explained. "He was there for a year, and he fell terribly ill with a fever, and now he seldom takes drink at all. He's become staid."

So Miles Redmond was a staid, nondrinking near-invalid, to judge from the way Violet described him. Cynthia felt her cheery mood waver.

Lady Windermere paused in her shoveling. "Plenty of debauchery to be had in the South Seas," she said sagely. "Native girls and whatnot. He's probably just grown bored with that debauchery nonsense."

Jonathan laughed, and Violet looked fascinated, and Lady Middlebough murmured something that sounded like, " . . . not what I heard about Redmond." She sank small teeth into a piece of fried bread, slowly tore a strip away, and chewed it as if chewing would be her only scheduled activity for the day and she needed to make it last.

Cynthia looked at her sharply. *Could* one grow bored of debauchery? she wondered.

Was Miles Redmond *capable* of debauchery?

"Oh, never fear, sister mine. I drink enough for both of us," Jonathan proclaimed cheerily. He hefted and bolted his cup of coffee, then waved for a footman to refill it.

Cynthia liked Jonathan, but he was not an heir, was too young yet to consider marriage—though he was probably her age—and was clearly thoroughly *enjoying* being young too much to be leg-shackled. A bit of a pup all the way round, she had decided. Though, in his dark way, he promised to be every bit as handsome as the wayward brother, Lyon Redmond.

Just then a young woman appeared in the doorway and paused diffidently.

Lady Middlebough glanced up quickly then glanced away and tapped long fingers against her teacup, like a flautist playing a jaunty tune. Lady Middlebough seemed to be expecting someone and was continually disappointed. Her husband?

"Georgina!" Violet sprang up out of politeness. "Goodness, when did you arrive? Everyone, allow me to introduce Georgina Mossgate, Lady Rutland. Please do have some breakfast, before Jonathan eats two pigs worth of bacon."

Everyone, uncertain what to do, began to stand in order to deliver curtsies and bows.

"Oh, goodness. Please don't get up," Lady Georgina said, sounding flustered to have made something of an entrance. "I arrived very late last night, and everyone bar the footmen seemed asleep. It's a lovely day, isn't it? My room is quite beautiful. I've a view of the lake. Quite blue, the lake. As is the sky today, isn't it?"

She was nervous. She was babbling. As well she ought. Several females were studying her with curiosity, not all of it benign.

Lady Georgina was a woman, not a girl—her figure swelling out of her pale striped muslin walking dress made this very clear—but she had the open, innocent face of someone who had never wanted for much or been deliberately hurt, and so found the world altogether peaceful and pleasant and could not imagine it otherwise. There was a serenity about her—that smooth brow, clear gray eyes, eyelashes and eyebrows only a shade darker than her complexion—that Cynthia wanted to rumple. She recognized the impulse as uncharitable, and forgave herself, as it was also probably natural. Unbroken surfaces must invariably be broken: the spoon eventually dipped into the pudding, the sheet of new-fallen snow trod upon eventually, and satisfaction could be had in all of that.

Lady Georgina probably *was* a lovely person and not remotely interesting.

"Our families have been close for lo on a decade now." Violet provided this explanation for Lady Georgina, after everyone else at the table had been introduced and explained *to* Lady Georgina ("dear friend of my mother's" for both Lady Windermere and Lady Middlebough; "dear friend from London," for Cynthia). Jonathan apparently required no explanation; he rose and bowed anyhow.

Cynthia waited, a trifle tensely, for recognition to light Lady Georgina's eyes when the new arrival heard her name. Perhaps her eyelashes and eyebrows and forehead were so very pale that subtleties of expression could not be seen from the distance of a few yards and the width of the kitchen table. Emotions that typically writ themselves large on features via a dropped jaw, perhaps, or bulging eyes, ought to be visible, however, and Cynthia comforted herself with the possibility that Lady Georgina hadn't yet had a London season, or a well-connected gossiping relative or neighbor, to inform her all about Cynthia Brightly.

A chair was slid out for Georgina by a footman and she joined the table.

"That's nearly all of us, then, but for the gents. Argosy ought to be here by noon. Sent word from the inn in Monkton. Milthorpe is even now stabling his horse. He'll be disappointed to find Father gone, that's for sure," Jonathan said with perverse relish.

"We've planned a salon for everyone to greet each other

this afternoon," Violet said sweetly. "Everyone should be recovered from their journeys by then."

Miles felt a trifle guilty about avoiding breakfast—because "avoided" was precisely what he'd done, and he wasn't proud of it—by taking Ramsay out for a long ride over his land. But it turned out to be the wisest thing to do, as the ride and the weather did marvelous things to his mood, and his mind soared across the sea to Lacao as he galloped the length of the park, up to the rise over which he could see the other ocean, the Atlantic, undulating soft and gray in the distance. He thought of the ships that Lord Rutland's money would finance, and the hopeful letters sent to naturalists, men he admired greatly, the country over.

And when he had his replies, he relished being able to tell them he could make it happen easily and soon, on a scale and scope none of them had dared dream of before.

Once he married Lady Georgina, of course.

He returned Ramsay to the stables and walked back to the house, arriving happily dirty and perspiring and resolved. He gamely swabbed his torso with hot water and soap to ensure he smelled as little like horse as possible, submitted to a ruthlessly clean shave at the hands of his valet, dressed in a spotless, flawlessly cut coat and crisp cravat and shining boots, replaced his spectacles on his face, and prepared to step further into his future.

The salon was held in a wide room too stocked with furniture and carpet to echo much despite the fact that the ceilings might as well have been the cliffs of Dover: they soared, high and white. Curvaceous settees striped in cream and brown sprawled amidst prim chairs propped on gilded legs. Two enormous fireplaces intricately carved in harvest motifs—nuts and vines, plump vegetables and fruits—were brilliant with fires, and conspired along with Isaiah Redmond's modern gas lamps, globes of soft light balanced on tables, to cast the entire gathering in a painterly light. Molding echoing the harvest motif encircled the top of the room like a great cuff, and two chandeliers of twisting brass birch twigs had been lit for the occasion. An extravagance of wood and fire, but then again, the Redmonds had the money to pay for all of it.

The room exhaled Redmond wealth and history and comfort; the way a church always seems to exhale peace and prayers.

But it was also the room, Miles recalled, where he and Lyon had played at soldiers by ducking behind the settees and aiming fireplace poker muskets at each other, and where they had pretended that the vast spreading carpet—scrolled in interlocking roads of cream and brown and oxblood—was instead a great sea of boiling lava (this was Miles's idea; he had read of volcanoes and lava), which meant they couldn't walk on it. They were instead compelled to traverse the room by leaping from chair to settee to table to settee to chair again, which is what they'd been doing before they were caught. Naturally, as a result of all their leaping, a marble bust— some somber blank-eyed, anonymous, quarter of a man— Miles never could understand the purpose of busts—crashed to the ground and had not, sadly, bounced. It shattered.

They hadn't been thrashed, interestingly. His father instead decided to make it their first lesson in commerce: he'd explained the cost and provenance and fragility of every single thing in that room, what those things meant to the family, and what it meant to be a Redmond. And even then Miles had felt the weight of his own history and the duty to the name encase him like armor.

Now strangers and old friends clustered toward one end of this familiar room. A late arrival was Lord Milthorpe, a Sussex neighbor, member of the Mercury Club and friend of his father's who had come to stay for a few days to discuss investments with Isaiah. As his father had predicted, he looked decidedly uneasy, almost as if all that carpet really were lava and would ultimately lap up over his ankles. The poor man had expected manly company and manly conversation with Isaiah Redmond; instead, he'd been dropped into a party filled with chattering women and handed a teacup half the size of his hand.

An earlier arrival was Anthony Cordell, Lord Argosy, heir to a viscount and another longtime friend of the family, and a particular friend of Jonathan's. Indolent from centuries-old money, he'd virtually been born bored. To his credit, he hadn't yet done anything *untoward* to rectify this—just the usual gambling, women, pugilism, and shooting. Argosy was not unintelligent, and it was entirely possible he might develop character if given any reason at all to do so. He could not yet be described as dissolute, but only required a nudge or so, really, in that direction. He needed an occupation, Miles thought. But Argosy was none of his concern, unless he intended to lead Jonathan into mischief, or Violet, for that matter.

And then there were the four women: Violet, whom he needed to watch; Lady Middlebough, whom he very much wanted to speak to privately; Lady Georgina, who looked impossibly fresh and round and who was politely pretending not to be scandalized by whatever Violet happened to be saying. He ought to begin charming her. It wouldn't be difficult, he decided, looking at her now. And then the one whom . . .

He went still. One simply . . . wanted to warm one's hands over her.

Her dress was a deep shining green, cut simply: a rectangle neckline and short untrimmed sleeves. It would have in fact been surprisingly severe but for the overlay of mist-fine net in which little sparks seemed to be caught. Miles was not a modiste. He couldn't have said precisely what caused the little sparks. He could, however, say quite definitively that the effect was like watching the mist pull back from the Sussex downs in the morning in response to the first rays of the sun, and oh dear *God* he was thinking again in poetry.

He frowned darkly to scare away his own thoughts.

As though she'd heard a rumble of thunder, Cynthia Brightly looked up, saw his frown, and smiled. It was a demure smile, but warm. A soft *ray* of a smile, that could send mist receding and then heat the downs so that the scent of warm spring grass rose—

The damned girl was much too certain of her own charm.

With effort, Miles reduced his frown to a socially neutral expression and turned his head ever so slightly to make it appear he'd been looking beyond her, at his sister Violet, who had just said something to make Lady Georgina laugh.

Undeterred and unaffected, Miss Brightly turned her head slowly away from him, taking with it that smile. She said something to Violet, who laughed and touched Cynthia affectionately on the arm.

Miles began to frown again. He caught himself. And did what he always did when he felt uncertain: he observed.

Miss Brightly wasn't fully involved in that conversation, though he was probably the only one who noticed. She seemed to be casually touching her eyes on things and people in the room, watching them, in fact, in the way that he normally took in a room: Milthorpe, Argosy, Jonathan, the chandeliers, the furniture. He imagined her registering

43

everyone and everything present the way his father's man of affairs kept books: compiling neat columns of assets and liabilities, performing the math, arriving at conclusions, deciding upon where next to invest her charm.

And then she gracefully stood.

Miles took a step toward Milthorpe. Cynthia had begun a sort of drift toward him.

And Miles seemed unable to move any farther than that. He waited. And then she looked up, lovely face mildly surprised to find him in her path.

Ah, very good acting, indeed.

"Good afternoon, Mr. Redmond. You were missed this morning at breakfast."

Very direct, very disarming.

If he *could* have been disarmed, that is.

"Good afternoon, Miss Brightly. I hope you are enjoying your visit so far. What makes you think I was missed?" He matched her tone so flawlessly it was very nearly mockery.

If she'd noticed, she did an admirable job of disguising it.

"I *am* enjoying my visit, thank you." Her face glowed up at him. "Your home is beautiful. And a number of inquiries were made after you at the meal, which is how I drew my conclusions about your presence being missed. Suggestions were made that you had tired of South Sea island debauchery and embarked upon a life of wholesome abstinence."

It was so very *alive*, her face. Delicious, playful wickedness flickered through her innocence like those sparks caught in the net of her dress.

And granted, hearing a word like "debauchery" emerge from lips like hers generally held a good deal of appeal. If another appealing woman had uttered it—perhaps Lady Middlebough—he might have attempted to steer the conversation down promising byways of innuendo.

Instead he said: "This room must feel rather like Tattersall's to you, Miss Brightly. What an interesting variety of eligible men are represented. However will you pick one out?"

Miss Brightly went rigid.

A tick of fraught quiet went by between them.

And then she tipped her head slowly up to him, as though balancing a scalding cup of tea atop it. Aware of a grave, grave danger.

And she looked—*really* looked, for probably the first time—into his face.

What she saw there caused wary reassessment and comprehension to cut across the blue field of her eyes as swiftly as a pair of hunting falcons. They were there and gone as though they had never been, leaving her eyes once again blue fields of innocence.

So she was not entirely a fool. This was a bit vexing, as he would have preferred her to become *less* interesting, rather than more.

"I hope you'll forgive me, Mr. Redmond, but I'm not certain I take your meaning."

"Oh, come, Miss Brightly," he jollied on a murmur. "I *am* one of your hosts, after all. I must insist you share with me. You're here for the eligible men, are you not? Why else *would* you be here in Sussex? Perhaps you even have your eye on one in particular?"

Her features were entirely still. Her eyes, however, seemed even more vivid, as though she'd focused her thoughts entirely on him, and it was a potent look, indeed. He thought he detected a rustle of nervousness. Ah, yes: a glance told him that one of her hands had burrowed surreptitiously into one of the folds of her gown.

"If you'd care to share the name of the fortunate gentleman, perhaps I can provide some insight into his pedigree?" He was as solicitous as a shopkeeper. "As host, I feel it's my responsi—"

"*Mister* Redmond." It sounded like a warning. Rather as though she wished to protect him from himself. "I would very much like to participate in a conversation with you, but I must confess to feeling excluded by my own confusion. Your conversation has taken a turn I do not understand."

Her face was innocent. But her eyes burned. She understood *very* well.

He sighed heavily. "Very well, Miss Brightly. Forgive me, but I'm about to bore both of us by telling you things you already know, but do keep in mind that you have forced me to do it. Things such as: you are not without charm, but you *are* at present attending a country house party without a husband or even a fiancé. While you were in one possession of a rather grand fiancé last I heard—the heir to an earl? Courtland? This leads me to believe something rather unfortunate happened in London to end the engagement . . ." He cast his eyes toward the ceiling rosette. "A duel, perhaps?"

He returned his eyes to her.

Before his eyes, her jaw slowly set; storm clouds gathered across her gaze, and the blue went very, very dark.

Cynthia Brightly was officially angry. Unsurprisingly, anger suited her. Perversely, her anger suited *him*.

"I see I've assessed the situation correctly," he said cheerfully. "Shall I go on?"

"Mr. Redmond—" Her eyes darted left then right, then fixed with a momentary flash of longing on the footman strolling through, bearing a tray of tiny glasses with splashes of sherry glittering in the bowls. He wondered whether the sherry or the fact that the footman was leaving the room appealed to her.

"Now, now, Miss Brightly. You did ask for clarification. As I am a man of science, I dislike cursory explanations. So let me be thorough. I imagine whatever scandal you left behind in London, if it's the sort of the magnitude that ended an engagement, will follow you here to Sussex soon enough, for foul weather *does* have a way of traveling the land, and I don't imagine Sussex will be spared it. You are, then, one step ahead of it at the moment. I suspect you wouldn't be here at *all* if Sussex didn't represent your last hope for a respectable marriage, as doubtless your reputation is growing, shall we say . . . rather threadbare." He added with confiding relish, "Goodness knows you've certainly taxed it over the past season or so."

And now her frown drifted into something like puzzlement. Her fine brows nearly met over the bridge of her nose. Those blue eyes scrutinized him like a jeweler bent over a suspect diamond with a loupe. Searching for provenance, character flaws, authenticity, motive.

Miles allowed her the silence; he allowed her the inspection.

He didn't know how he'd expected her to respond, though he was thoroughly enjoying confounding *her* expectations.

He'd almost given up hope of her responding when she did.

"You're opposed to ambition in a woman, Mr. Redmond?"

His head went back a little at the words. Stunned.

And then . . . peculiarly thrilled.

He'd never dreamed that right here, in the middle of his father's grand Harvest Room, surrounded by cheerful guests, he would engage in the socially unthinkable:

A genuinely honest conversation with a woman.

He rewarded her with a nod, as though she were a pupil who'd passed an exam. "Oh, on the contrary," he said softly, conspiratorially. "I applaud ambition, Miss Brightly. It's all I've ever known. And marriage is in essence a business alliance, is it not? And the wisest among us approach it as such. We should *all* aspire to make the very best marriage our born assets and gifts will allow us to make. Wrapping it in the folderol of love and romance is a recipe for disaster. Or disillusionment. *Quite* unnecessary. Wouldn't you agree? Something tells me that you do."

A shadow of uncertainty passed over Miss Brightly's brow, followed by a flicker of cautious optimism. He could see that she was wondering whether agreeing with him wholeheartedly might very well aid her pursuit of him.

He relieved her of suspense.

"It's just that I'm on a bit of a hunt for a marriage myself, you see, and I thought it might be companionable for the two of us to compare notes while we're about it. For instance, Lady Georgina is the most suitable partner for me, as she has a staggering fortune, a fine family, and a grand title, and an alliance with her would please my parents and permanently connect two great families. And as Redmond heir, I cannot *possibly* marry anyone other than a woman of the very finest family, fortune, and character without risking my position in my family and dishonoring my father's wishes. Though certainly, as clever as you undoubtedly are, you already know that. Hence, we are free to compare notes upon our quest for matches this fortnight, as I'm quite out of the question for you."

She understood. Her mouth had gone white at the corners from the strain of maintaining that smile; her breathing was shallower. Her blue eyes were dark with a very pure anger.

She turned her head away from him slowly.

A moment later she swallowed.

For a second or two, as laughter and chatter rustled around the two of them, they comprised a perfect island of stillness. He suspected she was beginning to hate him.

Hate, he told himself, was better than indifference. And she was most *decidedly* seeing him now. Tension banded his stomach muscles. He had the peculiar sensation he was drawing back a bow throughout this conversation, and now it quivered taut in his fingers.

"*But*, Miss Brightly . . . I could tell you things about all of these other gentlemen that would facilitate your quest for a very respectable match. I could . . . oh, help you narrow your choices. Focus your attentions. Deploy your *assets* most effectively, if you will, in order to help you achieve your aim."

She turned her head back quickly toward him. Her gaze was flinty with cynicism.

"And you'll do all of this out of the goodness of your . . . heart . . . Mr. Redmond?"

She enunciated the word "heart" doubtfully. Pointedly calling into question whether or not he possessed one.

He appreciated this with a nod and a pitched brow.

"I seldom do things simply out of the goodness of my heart. For where is the logic in that? I am a man of logic, of purpose, of planning, of objective. I suspect you of all people understand that, Miss Brightly."

She was catching on; cynicism hardened her soft features. "I see. And what do you require in exchange for your valuable information, Mr. Redmond?"

Tension snapped; the arrow flew.

"A kiss."

Chapter 4

Well, then. Judging from how still Miles Redmond had gone, he'd shocked himself as thoroughly as he'd shocked her.

But he didn't unsay the words, or apologize. He watched her.

Cynthia took the measure of her tormentor: broad-shouldered and formidably framed; not lean like his brother Lyon, but not awkward with his size, either. His hands were large; his fingers long and quiet against his thighs. Most men, she'd learned, betrayed internal preoccupation with fidgets, by fingering a coat button or drumming fingers against their thighs even as they mouthed words meant to charm her. This man was still, but not unnaturally so. It was the stillness born of focus. *She* was his entire focus. His attention was enveloping. It created a world of the two of them.

And then there were the spectacles, which she often found absurd on men. But the dark eyes behind his spectacles had that quality unique to doorways into mysterious darkened rooms: they beckoned, they disguised; they invited and un-settled. His face was long and his nose was . . . *significant* was unfortunately the word that seemed most apt—and his jaw a join of lines so elegantly articulated it could have been drawn with a protractor. Hair dark and fine and longer than it ought to be dropped softly down over a brow high enough to contain what *surely* must be his multitude of tremendously important thoughts.

She'd gone sarcastic in her thoughts out of self-defense.

But his mouth . . . It was a sensual tourist in that face: firm, wide, finely drawn. Like his eyes, it implied things. Specifically, it implied Miles Redmond skillfully used it for purposes besides tasting food and tormenting his guests. She thought about native women and debauchery.

He interrupted her scrutiny. "Am I correct in assuming that you have been kissed before, Miss Brightly?"

There went the mouth again: tormenting. Yet no footman extending a platter of sweetmeats had ever sounded more blandly deferential.

This must be why she never spoke to men who wore spectacles, she thought darkly. Some instinct for self-preservation. For this . . . *scientist*—she turned the word into a pejorative in her mind—this wealthy, indolent *heir*—this last word she faltered over, hesitating to turn it into a pejorative, as it had been one of her favorite words to date—had sniffed out unflattering truths about her.

She halfadmired it. There was something heady, a peculiar *relief*, in being understood.

But then she thought: if he can see it, who *else* can see it?

She turned her head away briefly from his dark-eyed, windowed gaze. An attempt to rally her composure. His gaze seemed to linger in front of her, the way an image lit by the glare of the sun hovers before your eyes after you close them.

She decided then: only him. Only *he* sees.

She would need to tread very carefully here.

"Rumor has it that you are a gentleman, Mr. Redmond. A . . . man of honor." She hoped to flatter him into helping her in exchange only for the pure pleasure of helping her.

He dashed her hopes.

" 'Rumor' does?" He sounded amused. "Oh, I hardly think I have ever inspired anything so intriguing as a *rumor*, Miss Brightly. Particularly regarding *honor*. Please don't be tiresome. We were doing so well. Say all that you mean to say and we shall continue our negotiation."

She sighed, and took pains to sound bored. "Very well, Mr. Redmond. *This* is what I mean to say. I question your motive in offering to help me. My confusion lies in the fact that we've just established that you are most decidedly *not* of a romantic or whimsical temperament. And a single kiss as payment for information strikes me as a rather romantic— even quaint—notion."

His smile took its time forming; slowly it spread; it settled in faintly. His head tipped up a little.

"Quaint." He repeated the word as though it had an unfamiliar taste and a texture. A whimsical one.

He returned his eyes just as slowly to her. "You have never kissed *me*, Miss Brightly."

Cynthia stopped breathing.

Their eyes met and held. His words were low, matter-of-fact, comprised entirely of a terrifying confidence. His voice matched his eyes. She felt it peculiarly at the base of her spine; it had an edge that scraped pleasantly over her senses, like ragged silk or the bristly beginnings of a beard brushed against her cheek. She wanted to hear more of it, even as it said appalling things. Her breath rushed out.

And now she was afraid. For the reason she could make comparisons between Redmond's voice and the beginnings of beards was that she'd *felt* bristly short whiskers brush her tender cheeks late, late at night, after balls, when young men trembling with eagerness and worship had pressed kisses upon her. But the reason Cynthia was stingy with her favors was twofold: a beautiful penniless girl could keep a man at arm's length and hope for a good marriage only as long as her virtue was known to remain entirely intact.

And Cynthia did not precisely dislike being kissed.

But no kiss had yet been a match for her bone-deep pragmatism and sense of self-preservation.

She felt fury welling. Despite the spectacles, the verbal fencing, the penetrating observations, the fortune, and the superciliousness, this one was like all the others beneath the skin:

He simply wanted to kiss a beautiful woman. He wanted to kiss *her*.

And no doubt no beautiful woman would *freely* consent to kiss him.

She was about to call his bluff.

"Before I kiss you, I shall need proof, Mr. Redmond, of the quality of your information."

Mr. Redmond froze as though her words were a thrust between his ribs.

Ha! She knew a moment of triumph.

But then he inhaled thoughtfully, exhaled on a nod of agreement, and gestured subtly with this chin to a ruddy, expensively clothed man so rawboned and rectangular he made the teacup he held seem crushable as an egg. He was pretending to enjoy the conversation of Lady Windermere, whose wide rubbery mouth moved and moved and moved animatedly.

"Lord Milthorpe"—Miles Redmond's voice was quiet, laconic—"is the Marquis of Blenheim—an ancient title.

Twenty thousand pounds a year." He paused briefly, as if to allow Cynthia's heart to skip a beat over the majesty of the figure. "Clever investor—a member of the hallowed Mercury Club—arrived expecting to find my father here, and will stay until my father returns. A widower. Two vast estates, one in London, one in Sussex. Not adverse to another marriage. A bit suspicious of fortune hunters, however. Prefers the country to the city. A blush would not go amiss. Mention dogs."

He snapped his head back toward her with predatory swiftness.

Just in time, she knew, to see the astonishment and hope and hunger fleeing her face.

Bloody man.

This—*this*—was precisely the sort of thing she needed desperately to know. How much easier her task would be if she was armed with this kind of information.

They both watched Lord Milthorpe cast the china cup a wistful glance, as if he knew he was bound to crush it eventually and was issuing a silent advance apology.

"When *was* the last time you blushed, Miss Brightly?" Miles asked suddenly, sounding genuinely curious.

"Blushing," she was snappish with nerves now, "is the province of naive fools."

His brow furrowed and he nodded as though she'd said something Socratic.

She desperately wanted something to do with her hands, and cursed the fact that she'd left her own cup of tea atop one of those tiny shining tables, well out of reach. Across that thick, languidly patterned, aristocratic carpet was another small world, a world where Violet Redmond was laughing gaily about something unimportant, where the worthy-of-Miles-Redmond Lady Georgina sat looking untouched and demure, where Lady Middlebough, for some reason, was watching Miles Redmond with big dark eyes.

And where a smoldering-eyed, golden-haired man was pretending not to look at Cynthia. Lord Argosy.

Ah! Her interest perked up. She wondered what Miles knew about *him*.

Bloody hell.

She returned her gaze to her tormentor. Who looked intolerably amused. He'd seen the direction of her attention.

"I do not want to kiss you, Mr. Redmond." She was appalled to hear her voice had gone threadbare.

"But I think you will kiss me anyway."

More of that soft, secretly amused, bloody, *bloody* confidence.

Walk away, she told herself.

Unfortunately, her feet and her brain were not in communication at present.

She looked up at him wearing a mask of a social smile. Eyes, spectacles, nose, mouth, height: the sum of his appearance meant that in another circumstance she would not have given Miles Redmond another glance. But this, too, she realized now, had everything to do with his self-possession. She understood now that if one did not notice Miles Redmond, it was simply because he did not wish to be noticed.

"I can give you such a list for every man in this room, Miss Brightly. Just *imagine* the use someone like you could put it to." He was still diabolically, quietly cheerful. "It seems like such a waste not to share it. I've stated my price for it. Nod your assent and we shall seal our bargain straight away. Shake your head, and I shall abandon it altogether, and wish you happy hunting."

Cynthia's heart was kicking painfully now. Her mouth had gone dry.

One kiss. One kiss could help her secure her entire future, or permanently shatter her reputation if the man could not be trusted to stay quiet about it. She thought of her slim purse upstairs, and the angry woman in the bath chair in Northumberland, and her own pride, which refused to accept the idea of a post in Northumberland or to abandon the idea of a grand marriage.

Miles took one small, impatient, warning step away from her.

She had promised herself she would be good. She would not foment mischief when brilliant opportunities for mischief arose. She would be very careful not to encourage men to shoot each other over her. She'd promised herself she would no longer gamble with her future, regardless of past successes, as she had so very little left to gamble with. Literally and figuratively.

But was it her fault if gambles continually found *her*?

Don't do it. Don't do it.

She sealed her fate with a duck of her head.

"Alcove," he said instantly. The word was a low command. And he turned and melted from the room.

Well, then.

His large frame rounded the corner, which she knew opened onto a hallway off which lay other rooms.

So smooth had been his departure, no heads turned to witness it. Lady Windermere talked on and on. Lord Milthorpe's chin was slightly turned toward the window like a weathervane, as though his body very much would have preferred to be outside. Violet giggled at something her cousin said, mercifully oblivious to the fact that her brother was about to kiss her guest.

And Cynthia slipped out of the room to follow Miles, her heart knocking inside her chest with woodpecker ferocity.

She saw him nowhere.

But suddenly she heard a throat clear from the aforementioned alcove, a halfcircle carved for the situation of a statue that had been removed for cleaning or whatever wealthy people did to statues. He fit into it like a statue himself.

With a peculiar sense of observing herself do it, Cynthia went to him.

Paused before him.

He loomed both like shelter and an encroaching storm: dark hair, dark eyes, dark coat, large hands, and she was momentarily confused, like a vole finding sunlight blotted by the shadow of a hawk.

He hesitated not at all. One of his large hands came to rest, very lightly, at her waist. She steeled herself. And put her face up as Miles put his face down.

Miles almost laughed.

What on earth was he *doing*? He didn't recognize himself in this . . . *maneuvering*. What did he hope to prove or gain, precisely, by kissing a woman who did not want to be kissed by him? When so many others *did* want to be kissed by him?

But given that he'd just proved that Cynthia Brightly was willing to use kisses as currency, backing away now perversely seemed dishonorable. Or so he told himself. He'd better do it, and quickly.

So he came at the kiss like diving into cold water and swiftly touched his lips to her.

Oh, God.

Soft. Soft. *So soft*.

He was ashamed of how inadequate the word was.

His eyes closed against a breath-robbing spike of desire; his hands on her waist. His lips hovered against the undreamt of vulnerability of lips; her breath, soft and warm, rushed over his. He couldn't lift his head again. Somehow this kiss had created its own gravity, and he was at its mercy.

Realization finally caught up with impulse: he thought of his father's watch, and how the relief of conquering that mystery had been worth the consequences. He wanted to take Cynthia apart, to discover whether a woman's heart ticked inside her. If he understood her, solved the mystery of her, then she would cease to torment him.

And he knew the power of a kiss to unravel a woman.

I don't want to kiss you, Mr. Redmond.

She would forget even how to speak when he was done with her.

And so he took another kiss. His mouth was a feather, a mist, a whisper over hers; again, and softly, softly, he brushed it over hers. Showing her that a world of sensation could be had from just his lips meeting, caressing hers; implying a universe of sensation lay everywhere in her body. She sighed, that involuntary, irresistible sound that signaled the brink of surrender. Her lips slipped apart; her breath mingled with his. Her hazy blue eyes disappeared behind her lids.

Oh, God.

He wanted to devour her. He thought of softness, darkness, and wetness: her tongue twined in his, her wet, plum-sweet mouth, the musky damp gathering between her legs, the silk give of her breasts in his hands and the ruched silk of her nipples, her round thighs. *Take, take, take.* His hands were greedy; they wanted; they urged him. His cock swelled, ached. He was mad.

The one bit of sanity left to him somehow knew that way lay quicksand.

And though he wanted, wanted, *wanted*, he did nothing but softly kiss her.

Their lips danced and breath danced over each other; still, he did not breach hers with his tongue. His hands remained, just barely, within his control, resting at the nip of her waist.

But now no space remained between their bodies. She was all he breathed, all he felt; his world was soap, musk, female, heat, supple, soft. Her belly beneath the fragile muslin of her proper day dress brushed against the ferocious erection confined by his nankeen trousers. Bliss knifed him; her rib cage jumped; her gasp of pleasure met his. He heard himself, absurdly, between kisses, murmur her name: *Cynthia*. Insanity, insanity.

Her head tipped heavily back; his lips slid from her lips to the silk of her throat, where her pulse drummed. Her breath, hot, swift, rushed over his hair, his ear, and oh God, it began to seem sensible to take her now in the alcove, to hike her dress and plunge into her.

This was when Cynthia's hands opened and hovered like butterflies between them for a second. Then landed flat, very lightly, against his shirt.

Undecided, it seemed, whether to touch him or push him away.

Doubt was an agony; it drove a stake into him. It tore him to the surface of sanity.

He yanked his head up, lifted his hands and kept them airborne as though she were a highwayman robbing him at pistol point, and stepped back until the wall of the alcove supported his back.

Slowly, he lowered his hands to his sides.

And breathed. In and out. In and out. Every new breath brought him closer to equilibrium and further away from oblivion. And this he both welcomed and resented.

He refused to look at her yet. It occurred to him then that minutes could have passed, or an eternity; he would not have known. Instead, with his instinct for order and sense, he sought out clues to the passage of time. Conversation still hummed in the room nearby. He craned his head and saw Lord Milthorpe looming like a solar eclipse against the salon window, still imprisoned by Lady Windermere's monologue. Miles could see fragments of darkening blue sky through that lacy overhang of trees outside the window. Still daylight, then.

With a single practiced movement he managed to disguise the still formidable bulge in his trousers with a swing of his coat, and he retrieved his watch from his pocket. He fumbled it open with still-awkward hands, hands resentful that they were no longer touching Cynthia.

He stared at the dial as accusingly as he would a bold liar.

The hands and Roman numerals claimed less than a minute had passed.

He finally risked a look at Cynthia.

A faint puzzled frown made two little dents between her brows. Her eyes glittered between her lowered lashes as she turned her head toward the sounds of the gathering—deliberately avoiding his gaze. Her hands, moments just moments ago raised to either touch or push him, were now hidden, curled tightly in her skirt like bashful children.

She seemed to be holding her body very still. Gingerly. As though she no longer trusted or recognized it.

Cynthia turned back toward him then and blinked, as if the force of his gaze was physical. They stared. Miles raised the backs of his fingers to his face, absently showing her where hot color smudged her cheekbones.

Unconsciously she mirrored him, her hand drifting upward to touch her face. She frowned more deeply, as though the heat of it puzzled and shamed her.

His confusion made him say something ridiculous, and he said it politely and gravely.

"Thank you, Miss Brightly."

Oh, for God's sake.

Her eyes widened. But then . . . damned if his words didn't little by little restore a certain amount of . . . *mischief?* . . . to her gaze.

It *had* been a ridiculous thing to say.

And for an unnerving, magical instant, they shared smiles, and in that moment Miles felt as though the ground beneath his feet had opened up, and below and above and everywhere was endless brilliance.

"You're welcome, Mr. Redmond," she finally said, softly.

Their smiles broadened. Some instinct made Miles look abruptly away. Because suddenly her smile was nearly a physical pain. And there was another silence.

"Well. I shall look forward to hearing information about the other . . . gentlemen . . . present this fortnight, Mr. Redmond."

He watched her curtsy—and what an ironic curtsy it was—twitch her shoulders as if shaking off a scratchy cloak, and turn to rejoin the guests.

When she slipped out of sight once again, back into that room full of people with widely varying desires and agendas all disguised by polite conversation, he felt a strange, faint echo of the panic he'd felt when he watched her disappear into the ballroom proper the first time he saw her. As though something in him would be imperiled if he never saw her again.

He raised his knuckles and pressed them to his lips; they were still hot.

He'd meant to take her apart with a kiss. How, then, did *he* wind up in pieces?

Thoughtful, strangely weary, he remained in the alcove, knuckles against his lips, until every bit of the heat of that kiss had faded.

Chapter 5

Cynthia drifted back into the salon and paused before a handsome James Ward portrait of a white horse. Her smile felt as immobile and separate from her as a masquerade mask. And still that kiss continued, as no other kiss ever had: in the flush of her skin and the beat of her heart.

A few deep breaths would take care of that. She studied the horse and took deep breaths.

Violet looked up curiously, saw Cynthia's fixed smile, gave her one of her own, returned to her conversation.

Breathing steady, heart steady, Cynthia directed her peripheral attention to Lord Milthorpe, the Earl of Blenheim, and studied him.

Lord Milthorpe was composed of stark lines: his shoulders a long vertical shelf, his spine midden-mast tense, his hair lank, steel gray, trained to stay behind his ears. The only soft thing about him was his belly, which was round and sat in his lap as though independent of his torso. His buttocks mistrustfully occupied the very edge of his spindly chair; he was quite sensibly poised to leap to safety should the spidery thing collapse into kindling beneath his bulk. One of his hands twitched atop his knee like a hairless creature in the throes of sleep; the other, curled into a loose cylinder, appeared to be gripping the stock of an invisible musket.

Cynthia felt certain he felt nude without a dog and a gun, and hadn't the faintest idea what to do with his hands in the absence of them. She sympathetically imagined it would be difficult to converse casually when one felt nude.

She wondered what had become of his teacup. It was missing now. Perhaps a footman had taken it away, concerned for its safety.

Twenty thousand pounds.

It was time to test Miles Redmond's stinging, informative list of facts. She took a sustaining breath. Turned ever so slightly.

And resolutely glowed in Lord Milthorpe's direction.

Lord Milthorpe froze as though a hunting horn sounded in the distance. He frowned faintly.

And then he cautiously rotated his head, scanning the chattering social forest for the source of whatever disturbed his awareness.

He gave a start when he found himself fixed in Cynthia's beam of radiant interest.

Cynthia instantly cast her eyes down. She let a crucial suspense-building second pass before she demurely, *oh* so tentatively, cast her eyes up again—ah, but not all the way up: instead she aimed her gaze at him through the fluffy lowered awning of her lashes.

This look alone had in the past inspired three entire poems.

Lord Milthorpe's frown vanished and his lips slipped apart.

He was officially transfixed.

Good, and good. What next? A blush, she thought quickly. A maidenly wash of color in the cheeks would not go amiss, Redmond had said. How to blush . . .

Miles Redmond slipped back into the room just then and showed no sign of noticing her at all. She watched his broad back proceed across the room toward his sister. She felt again Miles Redmond's mouth hard on hers, the hard swell of his erection pressing against her belly, her nipples just brushing the buttons of his coat—

Whoosh. Her entire body instantly caught flame. Heat roared along her limbs and into her cheeks. Her *eyes* actually felt scorched.

Well, that had obviously been a terrible mistake. No doubt she was scarlet and blotchy, which would more likely terrify Lord Milthorpe than charm him.

Lord Milthorpe did looked puzzled by her sudden and dramatic color change; his unruly brows dove.

Cynthia studied the fetlocks of the horse in the painting, rendered in delicate, affectionate precision, and willed her face to cool.

When she glanced up again, Milthorpe's mouth had parted a little again, as though he meant to speak. It stayed that way, like a transom opened to admit air. He closed it again. He leaned forward, toward her, and opened it again. Then closed it again.

Oh, for heaven's sake.

She rescued him. She closed the distance between them in a few steps. Startled, he made as if to stand, but she gestured him back into his chair with a "please don't bother!" little wave, and settled into the spindly chair next to him.

"I wondered, Lord Milthorpe," she said in a voice scarcely more than a whisper, "if I might trouble you for an opinion."

When she sat, he turned his head away from her. As if to look directly at her would singe his retinas. He seemed to be quivering the slightest bit.

"Of house parties?" He said finally, with such grimly humorous fatalism and disregard for the niceties usually considered necessary to the occasion that Cynthia began to like him.

She covered her mouth with the tips of her fingers to disguise a smile. "Oh! Do you find house parties . . ." She wrinkled her nose a little. " . . . *tedious*?" Her voice was a mischievous hush, the last word a whisper, an invitation to confidences. She leaned toward him; her bosom, at that angle, issued an invitation to ogle.

He bravely returned his eyes to her. His gaze bounced immediately to the pale generous swell of her breasts and was flung instantly back up into her face.

It was *his* turn to blotch beneath his ruddiness.

"Not any longer." The words were graceless but delivered with a crooked smile. It made his meaning unmistakable and the moment triumphant:

Lord Milthorpe was officially *flirting*.

"*I* find house parties tolerable, as well. Now, that is." Her eyes twinkled up at him.

Lord Milthorpe's smile vanished. He looked stricken and bewitched.

"But of all the people present," she added pragmatically, "I thought you might be able to advise me best on a particular matter. I hope you don't mind if I beg a bit of practical advice from you, sir."

"I should be delighted to be of any assistance in any regard, Miss Brightly," he said with quiet fervor. His eyes crept downward again to her snowy bosom; he tugged them back up to her face again, like a dog on a lead.

"Well, it's this, sir. I thought I might like to have a . . . well, I'd like to have a dog. And you struck me as the sort of gentleman who knows the country and knows dogs and might be able to suggest what sort of dog a girl such as myself should have."

Lord Milthorpe's narrow blue eyes flew open wide. Then he cast a brief look skyward, perhaps issuing a silent thanks for an answered prayer, sighed happily, and committed his buttocks emphatically to the chair by scooting back to claim the entire seat. The chair gave a long and frightened groan. Milthorpe didn't seem to notice.

"A dog? Are *you* a country girl, then, Miss Brightly? Forgive me for saying so, but your manners are so fine and your skin so fair you look as though you've never set foot on the downs before or held a gun or a bow and arrow. Do you shoot?"

A throat was cleared near the window. She knew who it was even before she turned.

It seemed Miles Redmond had managed to separate Lady Georgina—she of the staggering fortune, shy smile, appropriate pedigree, and cornsilk worn in a plait around the top of her head like an accursed halo—from the other women, and maneuver her into the window, his head bent over hers attentively. Lady Georgina was animated, white hands fluttering in front of her, little pink mouth moving rapidly. Everything about Miles Redmond's posture implied solicitous attention. Cynthia knew how Lady Georgina must be feeling: enclosed in the entirety of that attention. Light glanced from his sleek dark head. He raised his hand to gesture: in that instant she thought she could still feel a handprint of warmth on her waist, and her breath snagged.

It occurred to Cynthia that calling Miles Redmond "handsome" would not in fact be absurd. The realization struck her as trickery. As something unfair he'd perpetrated upon her, a power he could flex or sheath at will.

She forced herself to address Milthorpe's question. She could not in truth have said what sort of girl she was anymore. She'd lived in the country; any bright memories of that time were limned in darker ones. She'd loved her time in the city: the giddy social whirl, the heady sense of her own power.

Mostly she wanted peace and certainty and permanence and a reticule that jingled healthily, and she'd take them wherever she found them.

"I've . . . I've spent a good deal of time in the country, Lord Milthorpe. But life finds me ever in London, and— London is ever crowded and noisy, wouldn't you agree?" She darted a look about the room, as though she didn't wish the others to overhear for fear of offending them. "I thought it would be a pleasure to have a fine dog as a companion."

A tiny flash of light caught her eye: sunlight bouncing glare from spectacles. He *was* listening. Miles Redmond was. The angle of his shoulders had scarcely changed, but his spectacles had given him away. And the back of his head seemed peculiarly alert.

Lord Milthorpe was talking. " . . . oh! But she's a bonnie bitch spaniel—Eleanor, her name is. Named her for Eleanor of Aquitaine. The sire has gotten three fine litters on her, and I've two pups left of it. Both little bitches."

He directed this to Cynthia's earlobe. He still seemed to be acclimating to her startling loveliness only in fits and starts.

Which was just as well, as her mind had suddenly filled with disconcertingly vivid images of Lord Milthorpe's spaniel "getting litters on" Eleanor of Aquitaine the spaniel. Her features had been entirely unprepared for it, and she froze.

A throat cleared again.

She'd recovered by the time Milthorpe looked at her again. "Puppies are delightful! I congratulate you, sir. How fortunate you are."

He beamed at her. One of his front teeth was entirely gray, like a little headstone in the churchyard. She tried not to stare at it. At least he had a full *complement* of teeth.

His eyes retreated to the relative safety of her earlobe again.

"I should be . . . I should be pleased to give you a pup from Eleanor's litter, Miss Brightly."

"Oh, would you *do* that?" she breathed, then leaned the minutest amount toward him. She paused, reached a hand out as if to touch his arm, and pulled it back abruptly, because this caused him to go as motionless as a rabbit before a lunging wolf. His eyes flitted to her cleavage again then fled back to her face. "If you did—if you did—I should be pleased to name it for you. I could name it Lord Milthorpe."

There was a pronounced cough over near the window. Cynthia cast a glance in the direction in time to see Miles Redmond put a fist discreetly to his mouth.

She knew it! The bloody man had stifled a *laugh*.

And hell's teeth, she suddenly needed to stifle one of her own.

She kept her rapt attention on Milthorpe. Talk of dogs had him feeling comfortable, and her cleavage had made him cheerful, and now he was brave enough to look her full in the eyes. What a large face he has, she thought. As large and English as Gibraltar, and nearly as rectangular as his body.

He could not truthfully be described as homely. Nor was he handsome. He had kind eyes.

And twenty thousand pounds a year.

"Perhaps you'd consider naming a dog Monty, instead, Miss Brightly." He'd lowered his voice for this bold and hopeful jest. "Monty is my given name."

Good for Lord Milthorpe, she couldn't help but think warmly. He was clearly out of practice, but he was doing a reasonable job of flirting. She approved.

"Oh! I'd happily name it . . . Monty . . ." She ducked her head shyly over the use of his given name. "As long as you don't mind a—a—" The word did not trip as easily as she would have preferred from her tongue. "—b-bitch frolicking about with your name. For didn't you say all the pups were bitches?"

Milthorpe seemed dumbstruck. And then he opened his mouth, and out came a rasping bark of a sound. It took a moment for Cynthia to recognize this as a laugh rusty from disuse.

"That's right! By *George*, Miss Brightly. Only little bitches left!"

She giggled to encourage him, which caused every head to turn just a little their way, because she had an étude, a minuet, of a giggle, and it made everyone who heard it restless to be near her.

And as nothing essential ever escaped Cynthia's notice, she saw that Lord Argosy's gaze lingered upon her speculatively. And that Miles hadn't turned to look at her at all, and Lady Georgina was still talking. But he'd gone very, very still.

Lord Milthorpe sighed with happiness. "Oh, Daisy will do, Miss Brightly. If you take away one of my pups, you can name the bitch Daisy or some such name. Perhaps one day soon you would honor me with a visit to Milthorpe Crest to see the pups."

Ah. This was *very* bold of him. Very promising for her. But here was where she was required to manage the situation like a conductor standing before an orchestra with a baton. It was not quite time to bring the violins to a swooning crescendo. It was time once again to retreat into stammering shyness.

"I . . . think I should like that . . . Monty."

He went even ruddier when she used his name. His hands had gone a little quieter. He was less lonely when he was talking with her. For some reason this pleased her.

"We can get in a bit of shooting here at Redmond House in the parklands, if you like, Miss Brightly. I'll speak with Miles and we'll take a party out for target shooting. You do shoot, yes? Last year I took a party out and we shot so many grouse they heaped nearly as high as a haystack."

Her smile froze. Men are so eager to shoot things, she thought. Grouse. Each other.

"As high as that? You must be a gifted hunter, indeed. Shooting would be a pleasure." She cheerfully ignored the question of whether she *was* a shooter. One lifted, pointed, and pulled a trigger. How difficult could it be? She'd managed any number of tricky situations in her life. She would manage, should she be required to shoot in order to charm Lord Milthorpe.

There was a sharp movement: Miles Redmond's back straightened as abruptly as though a puppeteer had pulled him upright. She could practically *see* incredulous hilarity radiating from the back of his head.

Lady Georgina had tipped her head very fetchingly and seemed to be listing something as she spoke—perhaps her very favorite things about herself—judging from the way she was using the finger of one hand to count on the other. Her eyes were clear and charmingly abstracted.

I'll name my spaniel bitch Lady Georgina, Cynthia thought.

"Lord Milthorpe, I fear in the sheer enjoyment of your conversation I've neglected my hostess, Miss Violet Redmond, who is a dear friend. Will you be so kind as to excuse me? I thank you so much for your advice. I do hope we shall speak more of dogs during this fortnight. Perhaps on the morrow, during the picnic."

"I hope we shall." He smiled. The gray tooth, she decided optimistically, merely served to make all of his other teeth look whiter. "It will be a pleasure, Miss Brightly."

Cynthia ducked her head demurely, exquisitely curtsied to Milthorpe, and made her way over to Violet, who was standing near Lord Argosy. Who was fixedly regarding her progress across the room through excitingly lowered lids.

By contrast to Milthorpe, Lord Argosy's dark eyes were all lazy confidence, his posture easy grace, his smile as loose and sensual as the spirals of dark blond hair spilling over one brow. *He* had no trouble at all looking at her. Argosy was the sort who was quite at home at house parties. Or anywhere, really. His sort quite firmly believed he would be welcomed in any home, under any circumstance, and he moved through the world with the comfortable manners born of this conviction.

Very appealing, very oblivious, very maddening.

Cynthia pretended not to see him. Which was precisely what one did with the Lord Argosy's of the world. It was like a razor strop for their interest.

Intrigue them and leave them wanting, she thought. And if at all possible, avoid tempting the men into wanting to kill each other over her.

She thought of shy Milthorpe and his pile of dead pheasants and of other men aiming pistols, and her arms pricked up in gooseflesh.

Chapter 6

They trod out en masse in the late morning, ladies covered in a variety of stylish bonnets against the heat, gentlemen already genteelly sweating in their coats, footmen behind swinging the hampers full of food, napkins, and plates that clinked just a bit inside.

The party's destination was a stream that ran through the Redmond property and at some point was rumored to empty into the Ouse. It also allegedly joined streams that then meandered over Eversea lands. The symbolism of this was not lost on anyone who lived in the ancient town of Pennyroyal Green, Sussex, as Everseas and Redmonds had blended their histories since the Saxons met the Romans. Sheltering shade trees were promised, however, and Cynthia could see them in the distance, bunched like bouquets: enormous oaks and beeches, walnut and ash, lacy willows lining the water. And should the thick heat bring down rain, as Miles predicted it would, shelter could be had beneath them or in the various follies scattered about the property. It was generally agreed that a rainstorm would be romantic.

Cynthia was in silent but vehement disagreement.

The rest of the company present had the financial wherewithal to replace boots and bonnets and clothes should they become splashed and muddied or otherwise ruined. She did not. She *did*, however, have the use of Violet's abigail for the duration of the party, and the girl was talented. She'd sponged spots away from her hems, revived lethargic lace, and restored brightness to some of her white things.

But the abigail could do very little about her walking boots. She'd begun to feel the ground through them. Perhaps she could insist upon being carried in a litter. Like the savage woman in the bath chair in Northumberland.

Ah, but that could never happen. Not to *her*. It was easier to tell herself this during the day. Last night her old dream had awakened her, and in the mirror this morning she'd seen the aftermath in the pale violet of her eyelids, and the faint blue shadow beneath her eyes.

Now, as they walked, the pale gold head of Lady Georgina bobbed in front of her. The neatly coiled braid pinned to the back of her head resembled a target, Cynthia decided. She entertained herself by imagining her gaze as a dart, and conceded this was unfair. She told herself she would be happy to like Lady Georgina if there had been anything *to* like. Last night, after dinner, Georgina's conversation had primarily consisted of admiring things: dresses, coiffures, witty things said by the other women. She spoke primarily when she was spoken to. She listened a good deal. She was so polite and shiningly nice it was difficult to gain a purchase on her personality.

Next to Lady Georgina, the significantly taller Miles Redmond strode confidently, elegantly, easily, as though the world, and this property, was a coat sewn just for him. Beneath his hat, his hair was long enough for the breeze to lift. Lady Georgina, a blossom in a white muslin walking dress, struggled to keep up with him.

It hadn't quite become Noah's ark, however, with paired-off men and women walking alongside each other; the group trundled over the grass in a casual configuration, like a scattering of billiard balls after the first shot was taken. But subtle jockeying for various positions was taking place. A shadow came up behind Cynthia, and the sun blotted briefly as the rectangular Lord Milthorpe overcame handsome young Lord Argosy, who had been casually coming up on the outside in an attempt to catch up to her. She'd seen him from the corner of her eye, and she had rooted for him, but alas Milthorpe was first.

Nonchalance, she could have told Argosy, does not pay.

Argosy was forced to drop back a little to join up with Violet and Jonathan, who were laughing gleefully at something while thoughtfully keeping company with the widow, Lady Windermere, who trudged over the grass as solidly as a four-wheeled cart, and the lushly handsome, married Lady Middlebough, who glided over the lawn in a flattering maroon day dress like a finely sprung barouche.

"I've been giving some thought to just the right dog for you, Miss Brightly," Milthorpe ventured.

"Have you been thinking of me, sir? That is, of a dog for me, that is?"

His ruddy cheeks flushed to a mulberry. Ah! Very good. So both statements were clearly true. But he maintained his aplomb. Dogs, for Lord Milthorpe, were a serious topic.

"There are so many splendid breeds, but I believe a dog should be well-matched to one's personality. And where you are concerned, Miss Brightly, I cannot decide," he thrust his hands into his pockets, "between a Sussex spaniel . . . or a greyhound."

Ahead of her, Miles Redmond slowed his pace to point to something perched on the leaf of a shrubbery. And then he stopped, drew in closer to it. Lady Georgina peered where he pointed and made an O shape with her mouth. "Mr. Redmond! That's so *interesting*," she piped.

What was interesting? A worm? A fly? A spider?

" . . . mating," was the one word that came to her of the all the words in Miles Redmond's reply to Lady Georgina.

Cynthia returned her focus abruptly to Lord Milthorpe, feeling warmer.

"How did you narrow it to the two breeds, Lord Milthorpe?" she asked

"Well." He cleared his throat. "The spaniel rather reminded me of you, as it has handsome, long, silky—"

This sounded promising!

"—liver-colored ears."

Startled, Cynthia's hand flew up to her ear.

Milthorpe didn't notice. He was warming to his subject. "In fact, the Sussex spaniel has long, liver-colored hair *everywhere*. Feathery hair, on their chests and sterns. And a short handsome tail."

Cynthia heard a peculiar strangled sound up ahead. The sun glancing off Miles's spectacles gave him away. The bloody man was listening, and the strangled sound was laughter killed before it could escape him.

Her own eyes began to water a little. Hysteria or hilarity? She could not have said.

"They have a very sweet and loyal nature, spaniels do, Miss Brightly. They're small and compact and limber. And they have *lovely* shiny eyes."

Cynthia wondered if *she* had a loyal nature. She wondered if Lord Milthorpe considered her compact and limber.

Miles Redmond's shoulders had gone back as abruptly as if he'd been struck by a bolt of hilarity.

"Spaniels sound *lovely*," she said more loudly than necessary. She decided she did have a loyal nature: given an opportunity, she would be as steadfast a companion to the right husband as any spaniel. *Gratitude* would ensure it.

They'd come upon Redmond and Georgina, which was when Miles magically finished examining whatever crawling thing had taken up residence on the leaf and moved on rapidly and suddenly. Georgina puffed to keep up.

"What was your other choice, Lord Milthorpe?"

His expression was dignified and triumphant. "This might strike you as a bit daring, but that would be the greyhound, Miss Brightly. Elegant, sleek, noble animal. They want a bit of winning over, do greyhounds. But they're wonderful friends when they've been won over."

He was more insightful than she had credited him. She looked over at Lord Milthorpe and tried to picture decades stretched out alongside him in bed at night. He would snore, she was certain of it. She shied away abruptly from the thought of sleeping next to him for the rest of her life and focused on the moment.

Milthorpe's fingers twitched at his thighs, then curled into a cylinder. They felt empty, no doubt. All this talk of dogs was making him yearn for a gun and a dog the way a sot aches for the wineskin.

"I must say, sir," she said softly. "Both comparisons flatter me. I hardly know which to choose."

"On the contrary. The comparisons do not do you justice, Miss Brightly. But it was the best I could do upon considerable thought and our short acquaintance."

Cynthia smiled. She was unaccountably touched when she pictured Milthorpe carefully reviewing a parade of dogs in his head last night. All for her benefit. She began to feel that nearly any man could become charming given the right encouragement.

Lord Milthorpe saw her smiling, and his entire body seemed to straighten and bloom as though she were the rays of the sun.

He would never be handsome. He would never be young. She doubted he would ever really be interesting.

But he would be kind.

"What say you, Redmond?" Milthorpe called out to Miles, full of the bonhomie and confidence that comes from enjoying the undivided attention of a lovely girl.

Miles Redmond halted mid-stride and turned sharply, smiling politely. He had all of his teeth, they lined up very neatly, and they all were, blast him, quite white.

"What say I, Milthorpe? You're in need of an opinion? I have opinions to spare. Ask away."

"You were country bred. What manner of dog ought Miss Brightly to have? I've narrowed it down to a spaniel or a greyhound."

"Hmmm . . . a dog for Miss Brightly?"

Miles Redmond looked at her directly for the first time that day, and she tensed as though absorbing a small shock. There passed a silence longer than perhaps was wise. A silence people could notice.

Miles straightened his shoulders, clasped his hands behind his back and looked away from her.

"Well, the way I see it is this, Milthorpe. Spaniels flush *small* game—waterfowl and the like—and then retrieve it once it's killed. They're small dogs, rather low to the ground, can get in and out of shrubbery and undergrowth. While greyhounds . . . ah, greyhounds are an aristocratic breed. They're used for coursing, typically. Do you enjoy coursing, Milthorpe?"

"Aye, old man. Oh, if anything involves *hunting* I enjoy it. I don't own a greyhound presently, but Custley out in

Shropshire has written to me of his new pups, and I have every hope of going off to choose one to bring home."

"One can never have too many dogs," Miles said somberly.

Cynthia stared at him suspiciously.

"Never," Milthorpe agreed fervently.

Miles continued. "As for greyhounds . . . well, coursing is a more . . . ambitious sport. Requires quite a reach on the part of the greyhound, wouldn't you say? And whereas spaniels are useful for the smaller game, greyhounds can pursue larger, more impressive game and a wider *variety* of it . . .." Miles swiftly touched looks upon Argosy, who walked yards behind them flanked by Jonathan and Violet, and Milthorpe. To Cynthia, this was as obvious as a gesturing finger. " . . . and they do it in the open, over wide-open ground . . . where anyone can see. And greyhounds can most often be found with the aristocracy and the nobility."

Miles looked at Cynthia a speaking second longer, then turned abruptly and began striding on again.

"Definitely the greyhound for Miss Brightly," he said over his shoulder.

She wished she had something to throw at his back.

"I believe I prefer a spaniel," Cynthia said instantly to Milthorpe. Tightly.

"Both grand dogs," Milthorpe allowed diplomatically. He looked a little puzzled, watching Miles's retreating back.

"Pomeranians are lovely!" Lady Georgina turned around and said encouragingly. She was mercifully ignorant of the great cloud of innuendo that Miles Redmond had sent up. "I should like a Pomeranian!"

"Ah, but I've heard that Pomeranians bite, Lady Georgina," Miles said with deep concern, and "we wouldn't want you bitten."

Lady Georgina's giggle was more excited than it ought to have been, given that what he'd said wasn't funny.

Was *I* ever such a ninny? Cynthia wondered. She supposed she'd never had the luxury of being a ninny. And yet, there weren't many years between her and Lady Georgina, if any.

And then they all walked past—or rather, around, since Miles pointed it out so they wouldn't go blundering through it—a small but beautiful spiderweb linking two shrubberies.

Miles stopped to admire it, and suddenly Cynthia and Milthorpe were clustered before it, too. Behind them, they heard Violet squeak a protested, "Jonathan!" Being mercilessly teased by her brother.

"I've a spider in my room," Cynthia said suddenly.

"Please do send it my regards when you retire," Miles said dryly. Not looking at her.

She wasn't entirely certain he was jesting. "Would you know what sort of spider it is?"

"Oh, no doubt a nursery web spider. She can't harm you. She just—"

"She?" This charmed her.

He didn't notice. "—wants shelter, and the corners of windows are wonderful, safe places to trap tiny flying or crawling things. Spiders are marvelous housekeepers."

Cynthia had never thought of spiders as housekeepers. Housekeepers usually attempted to prevent spiders from doing things in houses.

"Be kind to the spider. It's simply working hard to be itself. And don't tell the maids," he added wryly.

She stared up at him, for an instant, struck.

Working hard to be itself.

He broke the gaze suddenly and strode abruptly for-

80

ward to catch up to Georgina, who had unwittingly gone on ahead.

"He does like to lecture, but he's a good sort," Lord Milthorpe told her. "Do you truly enjoy hunting, Miss Brightly? Mr. Redmond seems to think you do."

She hesitated. "I have not yet tried coursing," she said carefully. It wasn't quite the answer to his question, but there was nothing untrue about it.

Milthorpe's head went back in preparation for rhapsodizing. "One day, perhaps, you'll know the pleasure of a lean dog racing over open ground—"

Violet caught up with her with a bound then. "Cynthia is a *wonderful* huntress," Violet said earnestly. With a sly sidelong look at her.

"Oh, then *very* good!" Milthorpe brightened. "I see you were just being modest, Miss Brightly. It's settled, then. I'll have a word with Miles and we'll get up a target shooting party tomorrow. Will you be joining us, Miss Redmond?"

"I think I shall," Violet said speculatively, in a way that could bode no good for any hunting party. Cynthia gave her a surreptitious pinch, and Violet mouthed *Ouch* insincerely.

Up ahead they heard Miles's voice lecturing to Lady Georgina, " . . . 'tis the season for mating for this particular species, and the eggs will hatch in August."

"Oh, for heaven's sake. Miles is always speaking of mating and whatnot," Violet half apologized to Cynthia. "It's what insects and animals do."

"And native girls do," Cynthia muttered. "Rumor has it."

Miles spun and turned his head with fixed interest in her direction and pointedly did not look away for a good one . . . two . . . seconds.

Enough for her to remember that a prelude to mating was a kiss, and enough for her to picture it, and for her cheeks to flame, and heat to rush over her limbs.

Then he turned around again.

She fanned at her cheeks with one of her blue bonnet ribbons and trudged along the ruthlessly barbered grass. She thought she could feel damp upon her stocking, which meant the boot stitching was at last giving way. Her whole life seemed to hang on fragile, strained threads.

Milthorpe had fallen back to talk to the boys, Jonathan and Argosy, and they all quickly became very animated. Doubtless talking about things with four legs and killing.

"Well, that is," Violet expounded on her earlier statement, "that's what insects and animals primarily do, after all. Mate, eat, kill. If you ask Miles, that is. The whole of his conversation is about that."

Hearing his life's work summarized thus by his sister, Miles shot a wry look over his shoulder.

"They're rather like people in that regard." Cynthia's voice rose slightly. The business of mating and killing were far, far too closely related in her mind since the end of her engagement to be amusing.

But her remark resulted in a ripple of chuckling and elbow nudging. Lady Windermere, a de facto chaperone for the younger ladies, looked uncertain as to whether she could continue to allow such talk, and irritated by the very notion that she might be called upon to pass judgment upon it.

She decided to fall back and speak to the footman.

"Is there any port in yon hamper, good man?" Cynthia heard her ask in a lowered voice. "Perhaps we can stop and open it up just now?"

Lady Windermere, it appeared, was about as appropriate a chaperone as the Wife of Bath. This cheered Cynthia.

"Actually," and Miles stopped, and his voice rising to a stentorian lecturing volume. Accordingly, the party instantly fell silent, since Miles was allegedly a renowned adventurer, and one was required to be fascinated. "When the male of the *Pisauridae,* or nursery web spider, is in the mood to mate, he brings a gift—perhaps a fly—to the female spider. Which distracts her long enough for him to get the mating done. But he has to make a quick job of it, because if she finishes her gift before he finishes the job, she'll turn right around and eat *him* with no compunctions."

There was a shocked and total silence.

"As for me, I generally like to bring a good brandy," he added mildly.

There followed an explosion of laughter so unanimous it sent birds scattering like shot from the trees and shrubberies.

"Sweets! I like to bring sweets!" Argosy yodeled.

"Posies!" Jonathon declared. "Hothouse posies! Distract 'er!"

"A quick job of it!" Lady Windermere had seized upon this part delightedly. "How *like* a man!"

"Not like Redmond, I've heard," said Lady Middlebough, in a voice meant only for Lady Windermere, and they nudged each other.

Cynthia turned to look sharply at the handsome married woman again, but she was laughing with Lady Windermere. And as she wasn't laughing, a sound in the midst of the merry uproar reached her and stood the hair on the back of her neck on end:

"Haw! Haw! Haw!"

What the *devil* was that? It sounded like . . . could it be . . . two donkeys angrily mating? A rusty gate flapped vigorously? Avenging crows descending to peck out

83

their eyes and steal the picnic? She spun, looking for its source.

"Haw! Haw! Haw!"

She flung her hands up over her head in case she needed a defense from above and risked a look up into the trees. Nothing stirred up there apart from leaves, as the birds had been frightened away by the laughter. She pivoted left, pivoted right.

"Haw! Haw! Haw!"

And then she saw. Oh. Oh, *no.* That. . . *sound.* . .

Was coming out of Lord Milthorpe.

His head was tipped back, his mouth open the width of a village well, and *haw haw haws* roared out of it. Over and over and over.

She was riveted.

Milthorpe paused to draw in a wheezy accordion breath, bellowed, *"Brandy*, Redmond! By God, that *is* rich!" gave his thigh a hearty slap, and then: *"Haw, Haw, Haw!"*

He could have confidently approached the walls of Jericho with a laugh like that. Joshua could have dispensed with the trumpet had he been accompanied by Milthorpe.

Rattled, she looked away from Milthorpe as the collective laughter continued and saw Miles pointedly watching *her* and grinning so broadly his eyes seemed to have vanished.

She wondered if he'd seen her fling her arms up over her head.

Bloody man.

Lady Georgina, from the shelter of her large bonnet, looked troubled, too—she was peering at Lord Milthorpe with some of the concern that had plagued Cynthia at first. Or perhaps she was embarrassed by the ribald joke. Or perhaps she didn't understand it. Or perhaps she was transfixed by a fantasy of Miles Redmond bringing brandy to her and getting the job over with quickly.

"Now, now, *Mister* Redmond," Lady Windermere admonished as she wiped her eyes. "Perhaps I should now remind you that we are not in the tropics, that we are in England, and that perhaps certain topics are not proper for mixed company."

It was another halfhearted attempt at chaperoning.

"Oh, I'm absolutely certain brandy and spiders are a proper topic for mixed company," Miles said soberly.

"Well, when put like that," Lady Windermere capitulated happily.

And in this state of giddy bonhomie, they all finally came upon a lovely, broad silver snake of water lined by dense clusters of crack willow, ash, and alder trees.

This, apparently, was to be where their picnic was held.

Chapter 7

Miles said something to the footmen. They settled their burden, and one flipped open the woven hamper lid, bent into its depths and removed a folded rectangle of fabric. They billowed it outward and began to smooth it over the ground with the aid of the other footmen.

Miles stepped over to help them smooth one corner, which brought him nearer to Cynthia. He murmured, "He *loves* to laugh. Nearly as much as he loves dogs. And shooting."

She resisted the urge to tread on his instep.

He stepped away in time, anyway, perhaps sensing the impulse.

The removal of things to eat from the hamper went on for quite some time: stacks of plates and silver, dark bottles of cider and ale, cold chicken and whole golden loaves of bread swaddled in linen napkins. The unpacking slowed when a footman staggered under a half wheel of white cheese, but he was propped up by a quick-moving Miles. Slices of seed-speckled cake were fanned on plates, and strawberries, blueberries, and currants spilled into bowls.

As all the talk of mating and killing and the heat of the day did something to whet appetites, they all fell upon the food like hungry jaguars. A comparison Miles provided, straight from the jungles of Lacao.

They were attended at intervals by tiny flying and crawling interlopers—all of which Miles Redmond identified for everyone by lengthy Latin names.

Some attention had been paid to tending the lawns up to the stream bank, but native Sussex flowers had sprung up: blue-purple rampion and bladder campion nodded on stalks over the stream like bystanders at a boat race. Betony fluttered on stalks; lavender self-heal hid in the long feathery grasses at the bank.

Iridescent dragonflies patrolled the stream and buzzed over them to see what the fuss was about. A butterfly loped by in the air. It, too, was blue-lavender, in keeping with the floral theme of the stream bank.

"Polyommatus icarus," Miles told everyone. "The common blue."

"Do they really have butterflies that eat people in Lacao?"

Jonathan asked this, mostly to make everyone gasp. He knew full well it isn't true.

"No, but they have plants and people who would happily eat men," he told his younger brother.

This *did* elicit a gasp.

And suddenly Miles had everyone's attention, and he talked of Lacao, and she saw him ease out of his coat, out of his hat, roll up his sleeves, and enter, through words, the world he'd explored and loved, the world that had made him famous.

And despite herself, Cynthia was interested, and then rapt. She listened to him field questions—about snakes and flowers, about weather and customs, about dogs (Milthorpe) and cannibals, about poisons and the variety of deaths that could be had from them at the hands of animals and natives, delicately skirting, she guessed, the more prurient and more frightening, and she sensed there was a good deal of that to be heard as well.

And she felt shyer, suddenly: he'd gone and *discovered* with no compunctions, he'd seen things no one else here would ever see, he'd been ill near to death and survived, and this, she suspected, was what gave his eyes and voice that depth and resonance, his bearing that confidence. He contained worlds. The more he knew, the more he wanted to know.

For a moment she thought she could happily listen to him forever. A moment later she blamed the wayward thought on the heat.

After lunch had been devoured, a boat race involving twigs for boats was contrived for the stream. Cynthia was about to happily head for it when Miles came around the other side of a crack willow and intercepted her. The man was bloody quiet and subtle.

She didn't for a moment think the meeting was accidental. He had a motive, and she was certain she was about to learn it.

Everyone else collected at the stream, and she gazed after them with a certain longing.

"So a spaniel will be the dog for you, Miss Brightly?" he said lightly.

"Lord Milthorpe says spaniels call me to mind," she said neutrally.

"Because your stern is covered with silky liver-colored hair?"

She bit the inside of her lip to stop her smile, tempted to tell Mr. Redmond he would never get a look at her stern.

Be good.

"And will you name it Lord Milthorpe?"

"Ah, Mr. Redmond. I see you were listening my conversation yesterday. Which leads me to believe your own conversation was less than riveting, because you otherwise would not have been so very rude as to *eavesdrop*."

"Quite to the contrary. Lady Georgina shares my interests."

"Ah. Does she? The way I share Lord Milthorpe's interests?" she said innocently.

This gave Miles pause. "Do you even *like* dogs?"

She considered this. "Probably," she admitted.

"Probably?"

She looked sideways at him but said nothing.

"You would like a wild boar for a pet if it meant twenty-thousand pounds a year, wouldn't you, Miss Brightly?"

The look she turned upon him surprised and confused him: it contained pity and the minutest measure of contempt. He was disconcerted into momentary silence.

"I've never had a pet," she said.

"Of *any* kind?"

She flinched. He hadn't meant to sound incredulous. It was just that animals—all creatures, really, furred, hooved, carapaced—had been so integral to the way he lived his life.

She shrugged, and sent an eloquent look toward the stream. Perhaps if she said nothing at all he would go away. Then again, she conceded that Miles had never once been boring.

Nor, one might argue, were brushfires or earthquakes or tornadoes.

"I like him," he said suddenly. It sounded like a quiet warning. "Milthorpe."

Her head jerked up instantly, wary. "I like him, too."

Another silence. She looked away from him toward the rushing trickle of the Ouse. She would have liked to race a twig boat, too.

"Do you?" Very ironic, his tone.

She turned her head slowly. "What is this, Mr. Redmond?" She took pains to sound bored. "You think me unkind? That I'm a siren, and intend to dash him on the rocks of my charms? You've placed enormous faith in my powers, then, if so. He's a grown man. A widower. Perhaps he's simply enjoying my company. How do you know what will make him happy?"

Miles didn't answer this for a long while. He simply leaned up against the willow. It might have been his cousin, that tree: they both had the same dark stolidity.

"Milthorpe doesn't offer to give his dogs to just anyone," he said finally.

"Then I shall account it a great honor should I receive a dog," she said evenly. "Any kind of dog."

More quiet from the quiet man. "He is what he appears to be, you know."

And now she was angry. "Meaning I am *not*?"

"He's kind. He loves the outdoors, and hunting and dogs and horses and his land. He likes a bawdy joke and laughing too loud at things that are only a little funny. He loves ale and making money, which is how he became friends with my father. He's a good sort. A *simple* sort."

"I'm puzzled, Mr. Redmond. Do *you* object to any of these things? Are you under the impression that *I* object to any of these things? I find nothing objectionable at all about them. Make your point."

He uncrossed his arms, and she watched. His arms were brown and hard and sinewy from use. She saw crisp copper hair over them, the trace of pale blue veins.

She imagined brushing her finger across that coppery hair. She saw again, felt again, his hands on her waist.

Rattled, she looked up into his face. Which was hardly safer.

"I am simply wondering, Miss Brightly, who *you* are. I feel some responsibility for your presence here at Redmond House, as I am your host. I feel responsible for your conduct insofar as it affects my guests. I rather unleashed you upon him, and I shall take it hard if he comes to some hurt."

She felt her face go cold. Anger whitened it. How *dare*—

"Oh, please do make certain you count the silver at night, Mr. Redmond. I may steal it and go tearing off with the Gypsies. Or rob your guests of their watches and necklaces in the night."

He spent a moment in apologetic silence.

"Gyspies *are* camped outside Pennyroyal Green. They always are this time of year. Wouldn't be difficult to join their ranks." He was attempting lightness.

She rolled her eyes and fanned her cheeks with her bonnet ribbon, then stopped herself, as it bordered on fidgeting.

"And then there's the matter of my sister."

"What of your sister? She's amusing. Intelligent. Much more *interesting* than most of the females of the *ton*. I like *her*, too. She invited me because I will prevent her from being bored." She flashed a sudden smile at him, all mischief.

"Precisely my fear," he said.

She turned abruptly, preparing to stalk away. Then changed her mind and whirled about to face him again. "Why do you feel you have the right to gravely insult one of your own guests by questioning her provenance and behavior? You, who are so allegedly so concerned about the *welfare* of your guests?"

He inhaled at this and straightened abruptly. She watched his chest rise and fall with that breath.

"You're quite right, Miss Brightly. It is just that you are . . . an unknown quantity, shall we say. I know nothing of you or your family, and suddenly you are an intimate of my sister. And Violet can be . . . willful. If anything, she has become more so in recent years. I am responsible for her well-being."

Interesting that he didn't say *we*. That he and not his father was responsible for Violet.

"You distrust the judgment of your sister so completely, Mr. Redmond?"

There was a silence.

"No," he admitted. "Not *completely*."

It was an admission that she might be something other than a stranger, and they both began to smile.

"I'm so flattered."

She could not, however, deny the logic in his concern. She in fact reluctantly respected it.

She tamped her pride. "What will reassure you, Mr. Redmond, that I am not a thief or murderess?"

"From where do you hail? Who are your people?" he said quickly.

Cynthia turned her head toward the stream, as if imagining a boat upon on it, taking her away from here. A tense twig race was taking place. Milthorpe seemed to be captaining the enterprise. He was shouting nautical-sounding orders and waving his arms, and Jonathan and Argosy were kneeling on the bank, as the ladies clustered and cheered them on.

"Do you have any dogs here at Redmond House?" she asked suddenly.

"Of course. Why? Did you wish to practice liking them?"

She smiled again. "I thought Lord Milthorpe might enjoy the company of one."

"Really? What makes you think so?"

They both smiled at this. And again this exchange of smiles somehow made the world seem dizzyingly large, and made it strangely, deliciously, difficult to breathe.

But then Miles watched as Cynthia shifted restlessly, as if drawing that opened-up world closer about her again.

He waited. He didn't think for a moment she'd forgotten his question.

"Has it occurred to you, Mr. Redmond, that it might be difficult for me to speak of my family?"

"Yes," he said promptly. "I suppose I never imagined, however, that you were afraid of difficulty."

Admiration for this gambit made a rueful smile slowly light her eyes and then her entire face.

Oh, her smile. He felt it like a sharp, shining half-moon in his chest.

He looked swiftly at Lady Georgina, toward her pale gentle colors and curves, to remind himself of his future, of his passion and ambition and duty. And at Lady Middlebough, to remind him of what he allegedly desired. To distract himself from the uncomfortable, baffling intensity of . . .

. . . joy.

The word frightened him.

No. That couldn't be right. He was *never* frightened.

"Very well." She sighed. "You asked about my people . . . well, my mother is dead. She died when I was young. I haven't

93

seen my father since I was five years old. He left us. I imagine he's dead now, too. I am two and twenty now. Allegedly, my family was related, in some distant way, to a baron." She punctuated this with a faint ironic smile. "But I know only what I was told, and I don't know the name of this baron. I hail from Little Roxford by way of Battersea, in London; we moved to the country—I suspect we fled debtors or something less savory since this happened in the dead of night—when I was six years old. When my mother died, I was taken in by the vicar of Little Roxbury and his wife. They were very kind. I had a penchant for mischief, it seemed, and she found me a pleasant challenge." A wicked little uplift of the brow here. "But the vicar's wife died when I was eighteen years old, and the vicar's new wife . . ." a faint twist of the mouth here. " . . . wanted little to do with me. She cast me out. The Standshaws befriended me. I went with them to London." She spread her hands as if to say: and that is all.

Dead, dead, dead. Each time she said the word, she enunciated it very clearly, from *d* to *d,* as if punishing herself or punishing him for asking. It was such a heavy word, an *ending* of a word. How had she gone from being turned out by the second wife of a village vicar to becoming the toast of the ton, the fiancée to the heir of an earl? How had it all come crashing down?

How *true* was any of this?

A common blue flapped by on its way to, he suspected, taking nectar from a self-heal, into which it would nearly blend as it feasted. Nature was clever that way. Beautiful and terrible and practical.

He remembered his first look at Cynthia: her face turned up into the chandelier light, the bemused, encompassing delight on her face. He could imagine why now. And the sheer *determination* of the girl. What mischief this orphan had stirred in the ton that season. No one, he suspected, had ever enjoyed popularity more.

Beneath her eyes were faint blue semicircles. Nearly the color of the wings of the common blue.

She wasn't sleeping well.

He felt his feet shift restlessly.

The sun beat down even through the trees, warmed his arms. A bead of sweat began the journey from his collarbone down his chest.

"A *vicar*?" He was quietly incredulous. This was the part of her story he decided to take up.

The question emerged sharper than he wished it to. Because he cared more than he wanted to.

Her mouth smiled. Her eyes did not. "Test me on scripture, Mr. Redmond."

"Luke 12:15." He whipped out the verse like a rapier.

"And he said to them, 'Take heed, and beware of all covetousness; for a man's life does not consist in the abundance of his possessions.' Very witty, Mr. Redmond, as usual. I expect nothing less of you. But if I wanted to invent my past, I might have concocted a more imaginative tale. Russian royalty, perhaps. I did *not* invent my past. It's precisely as colorless as I paint it. I hope to, however, invent my future. As you well know."

She looked evenly at him. Blue eyes dark with challenge.

He leaned back against the tree thoughtfully. They were quiet together.

The common blue decided instead to flutter about Miss Brightly, perhaps confusing her for a nectar-bearing flower or another butterfly.

She smiled at its confusion. "Beautiful color, I've always thought. Seems unfair to call it a *common* blue." She held out her hand, as if hoping it would alight. Alas, the butterfly came to its senses and hied off to drink from the self-heal.

"I would never have seen you at all if not for a butterfly." The words had emerged from him with no warning, as though he'd fired them from a bow.

Her head jerked up. She stared at him.

"Morpho rhetenor Helena." He smiled a little, made those Latin words sound like an incantation. "Native to the South American jungles. It's large, iridescent, beautiful—blues, greens, violets in its wings. It was the Malverney Ball, two years ago. Your dress. I . . . I thought your dress . . ."

Abashed, he trailed off. She was staring at him so wonderingly.

And he couldn't speak, he *wouldn't* speak, when he could simply drink up the blue of her eyes with his own.

They were both aware of the trickle of the river, the other voices. The sounds might have emanated from another universe.

She'd been wearing a blue dress that night. She'd been wearing green when he'd kissed her. In Tudor times prostitutes wore green dresses so the grass stains wouldn't show on their dresses when they were taken ferociously outdoors.

He thought she was fortunate indeed to be wearing white muslin right now.

He wanted to sink into her. He felt a white hot desire that stole his breath again. He glanced toward Georgina, the key to his other passion, to his whole life. To calm his breathing, a search for sanity.

And then suddenly the intensity of Cynthia's gaze flickered with a hint of trouble. "A . . . blue dress? I wore a blue dress?"

He could see her reaching for the memory of the ball, for a memory of him.

He closed his face abruptly, guillotining the moment. "You once had a fiancé?" he said abruptly.

She blinked at the abrupt change. "Yes, Mr. Redmond. I had a fiancé," she said quietly, ironically.

"Did you tell him about your past, your family?" He was distantly aware that she had begun to feel restless and cornered, but the questioning seemed to have acquired an impetus.

"I did."

"And is this why he cried off? Or did *you* cry off?"

"No," she said curtly. "It is not why he cried off. It mattered little to him." She fixed him with one of those enigmatic looks. Faintly cutting, almost pitying. "Though I bear responsibility for the reason he cried off, I did not end the engagement. Why on earth would I, Mr. Redmond? He *was* an heir. *Very* wealthy, too."

She cast a quick gaze around the vast green sea of the Redmond estate, as if assessing it against her erstwhile fiancé's wealth and thinking it perhaps paled. It worked precisely as she'd meant it to: he felt a swift surge of combativeness.

"Then what happened, Miss Brightly?"

She sighed. She turned away from him slowly, as though the conversation had made her weary. Tipped her face up to the sun, drawn by the warmth of it, perhaps, or instinctively seeking out pleasure in the midst of his uncomfortable questioning.

Then she changed her mind and put her face down again. Freckles and brown skin would not do, particularly since her beauty was her particular asset.

"Nothing that does me any credit," she said evenly, almost wryly. He was aware of a tension in her: she found the words difficult to say, and he knew them instinctively to be honest. "And nothing that will unduly discredit your

97

family should you learn of it, as it was nothing out of the ordinary, even if it was unpleasant. I comprehend this matters greatly to you—the safety and honor of your family. I promise you, I seldom lie. Something about being raised by a vicar. Shouldn't you be speaking with Lady Georgina? She will be feeling neglected."

A glance showed Miles that Lady Georgina was being shown how to make a whistle from a reed by Jonathon and Lord Argosy, and Violet was speaking with Lady Windermere and Lady Middlebough and Lord Milthorpe.

He wondered if the two women could be counted on to remember that Violet was an unmarried woman, and refrain from saying anything too fascinating—or, in the case of Lady Middlebough—too incriminating.

"Scarcely a minute or so has passed, Miss Brightly. It's entirely possible Lady Georgina will survive my absence."

Interesting how the two of them seemed to create their own time inside of time.

"Yes, but I'm not certain I will much longer survive your presence, Mr. Redmond. I am, as ever, interested in self-preservation."

He smiled then. He touched his fingers to his head as though his hat sat there, though his hat sat upon the picnic blanket with the hats of all the other men, and strode abruptly off to join Lady Georgina and his sister, who welcomed him with smiles.

Cynthia leaned back against the sustaining trunk of the crack willow and exhaled.

It was decided soon after to leave for the house, as rain was an ever-increasing likelihood, and so the carnage of their meal was bundled, the hamper packed, and the trip undertaken at a swift clip.

On the way back, Milthorpe accidentally crashed through the grand spider's web. Cynthia saw it: a sad, fluttering tatter from the hedgerow.

"Demmed spiders," Milthorpe muttered cheerfully, and trudged onward.

Cynthia almost felt the destruction personally. She wondered what had become of the spider. She paused, stared at the flutter.

And suddenly Miles was next to her. "She'll rebuild it," he told her. He'd interpreted her troubled expression correctly. "She won't think anything of it. It's just a part of her life. Sewing her world back together again, sometimes even daily."

He said it lightly. It sounded as though he were reassuring her.

Peculiarly, she did feel reassured. *Just a part of her life.* The savage tearing down of what looked to be an enormous undertaking would simply be taken up again, and would reappear in the morning as a new, complicated, fragile little net. It was the spider's nature.

Cynthia looked up. From this angle she could see the underside of his elegant jaw, shaved spotlessly clean; she could see where his glossy dark hair touched his ears below his hat. It wanted scissoring. She knew a shocking rush of tenderness. She wanted to touch it. Was it crisp? Or feathery, like the wing of a bird? Or silky, like a spaniel?

She turned her head away with some difficulty. Unnerved.

Ahead of them, the handsome Lord Argosy's curls beneath his own hat contrived to be both mussed and deliberate as one of those ruthlessly trimmed Redmond hedgerows or the slim cypresses arrowing up to the sky.

Everywhere, those trees created neat walls and divisions within the property, partitioning it in such a way as to perhaps make everyone feel more secure within its sheer grandeur, like aristocratic sheep in a very grand pen. Providing an illusion of order, and hinting that a certain amount of captivity—to fortune, to family name, to history, to duty— was also involved.

"Will she start the web over completely?" Cynthia was surprised to realize she was genuinely interested in the spider's fate.

"She'll use the half already made to build it, and it will be stronger than before, if not quite as symmetrical. More interesting, however. Did you know that spider silk is stronger in some ways than steel?"

Hmm. Perhaps *not* so fragile a net, then. And if this were indeed true, she wished that spiders were in the business of repairing shoes. She glanced down at her own.

Felt her resolve solidify again. She looked at the solid back of Milthorpe in front of her. She knew he was the man she should be walking alongside. Or Argosy.

"But it looks so delicate there, moving when the wind moves it." She still sought reassurance from Miles.

"Perhaps that's its strength. The flexibility. The fragility. Appearances . . ." He paused. ". . . are often deceiving."

She was silent. Was this an apology? Was *she* being complimented obliquely? The thought disarmed her. Because if it was *indeed* a compliment . . .

It was quite simply the best she'd ever received. No one had ever before admired her for the things she liked best about herself. Because she was very careful to never show that part to anyone.

Strand by strand Miles Redmond was unwinding the cocoon she'd spun for herself out of observation, charm, and ambition. It was both compelling and extraordinarily unfair.

It then occurred to her that he might simply be speculating aloud about her the way he would any small, shiny exotic creature with legs. He wanted to understand her; he was hoping to coax more clues from her. After all, he was forced to host this gathering in the absence of his parents, and it was hardly a South Sea island, was it?

Well, he could bloody well put Lady Georgina beneath his microscope.

She took two quick strides forward. It was enough for her to fall into conversational parallel with Lord Argosy, a much more familiar, less unnerving specimen to *her*:

The London blood.

"Do you dance, Miss Brightly?" Lord Argosy asked without preamble. As though he'd been expecting her all along. He slid her a sidelong glance, then slid his gaze away again. His smile was secretive, pleased and inclusive. *We know we're the best-looking people here*, is what it said. *Let's enjoy being young and beautiful.*

"But of course," she told him easily. As though they were just picking up a conversational thread.

"Do you play?"

She paused, wondering if an innuendo lurked in the word.

"The . . . pianoforte?" she guessed, carefully.

"Yes! Please say that you do not. Or that you *will* not. I could not abide another indifferent recital, and I know if it rains this evening it's what we will have. I have five sisters you know. *Five* of them," he said glumly.

"Oh, no one would be able to dance while I play. Or, rather, a good deal of wincing would take place simultaneous with the dancing, and eyes would therefore be shut more often than open, and the dancers would collide with one another. I play quite, quite badly."

"I'm relieved to hear of it. But perhaps I'll request a song for the pleasure of hearing you botching it."

Cynthia laughed, and he laughed, and his laugh was mercifully ordinary: merry and deep and male. Lord Argosy was pleased with himself but not insufferably so; life was good to him and doubtless always had been. And besides, all young aristocratic heirs were pleased with themselves. He was charming.

And he might very well be one of those lords who possessed a splendid title but was in need of a fortune to support everything that came with the title: lands and castles filled with spoils of ancient battles.

She would need to know more about Lord Argosy.

She threw a glance over her shoulder, toward the person who would tell her the things she needed to know about him. For some reason, she'd wanted to see if Miles had heard and was wondering about her laughter. Lord Milthorpe might possess comic possibilities. Argosy was a different matter altogether.

She saw two heads lowered in what appeared to be easy, quiet conversation: Miles Redmond and Lady Georgina, who "shared his interests." Very dark, very light. He'd adjusted his pace to match her shorter legs, and they were strolling in tandem.

"Mr. Redmond! How very *interesting*," Lady Georgina was saying enthusiastically.

And suddenly Cynthia was blindsided, weakened, by an urge to know what this was like: easiness and openness and quiet. Not flirtation and strategy and bartered kisses and hectic laughter.

She simply wanted to be courted again. She did not want to need to *court* the courting.

Ah, well. She hadn't been born a Redmond, or any sort of

aristocrat. And when she thought of how far she'd come entirely on her own, fleas came to mind: how their tiny bodies could leap astonishing distances, distances equivalent to miles beyond their size. She was merely resting between leaps, she told herself.

Why on earth did all of her metaphors suddenly include insects?

She squared her shoulders, as if shaking off the notion of them, and of the man who made her wonder about them.

And because she'd promised to be good and she thought she'd done a fine job of it for the day, she rewarded herself with a moment of imagining a distant future that included walking quietly side by side with a husband over some grand property. They would both have gray hair, and the green trees and lawns as far as their eyes could see would belong to them, and perhaps a spaniel named Lady Georgina would frolic about their feet.

She had a fortnight's worth of hope of this particular dream still available to her.

"I do believe Lady Georgina plays well, however," Lord Argosy was saying.

Of course she does, Cynthia thought.

"She will play, then, and *we* will dance," Cynthia said defiantly.

Lord Argosy languidly stretched up his body and dragged his hand through a low-hanging branch of an ash tree. The glossy leaves rustled like pound notes. He might have been dragging his hand through the long, long hair of a woman.

Cynthia hid a smile. She knew he'd done that so she could admire the lean length of his body, and because his sensual urges had spilled over in her presence and he could not very well touch *her.* Yet.

Ah, the language of flirtation.

He had a dimple in his chin, a feature she generally found devastating. Such an interesting little addition to a face. A good square English jaw and a straight nose and dark eyes that were not extraordinary but did not cross or squint and were not disguised behind spectacles, and his teeth were splendid. He was symmetrical and expensive in every visible way. Centuries of handsome people mating with other handsome people had produced Lord Argosy.

"Do you *dance* well, Miss Brightly?"

"I dance *very* well," she told him.

This *was* an innuendo, and Lord Argosy appreciated it with a smile.

Chapter 8

C ynthia returned from the picnic to find no letter from Northumberland.

Which was both a relief and a disappointment.

So she dressed for the evening with particular care: a dress with a coppery sheen that echoed the shine of her hair. A neckline just shy of scandalous, showing a half circle of snowy skin and much of her very good bosom. Hair coiled up high to expose her long neck, streamers of it pulled artlessly down.

Mrs. Fanchette Redmond had arranged for two large dinners to bookend her house party, inviting two dozen or so members of Sussex gentry to each. The first dinner, on the heels of the picnic, went flawlessly: the household staff scrupulously trained, the cook and staff was gifted, the courses multiple. Miles and Violet and Jonathan possessed exquisite manners and had known these people their entire lives. Even Violet said nothing unduly scandalous.

But because the seating had been arranged in advance by Mrs. Redmond, Cynthia was seated between two voluble elderly widows, one of whom nodded off over the soup.

And once dinner was concluded and the business of separating the ladies and gentlemen had come and gone, Lady

Georgina was settled before the pianoforte with sheets of music, which Lord Milthorpe volunteered to turn for her. Lady Windermere was elected caller of dances.

One of the neighbor girls had unfortunately claimed Argosy first, but she had spots on her face and hairy arms, so Cynthia was not at all concerned about losing his interest to her. But because destiny has a black sense of humor, she found herself facing the prospect of a reel with Miles.

The music began. Jaunty, irresistible, demanding.

And they both had what appeared to be a simultaneous realization: they would need to touch each other.

Oddly, never had anything so innocent as a reel seemed so fraught.

They stared at each other for an absurd moment while all the other dancers began the steps.

And then Miles took her arm as though it were a fragile, breakable thing.

She frowned faintly.

Gently, he placed her arm upon his own. And began to move her in the steps that Lady Windermere called.

Neither of them seemed able to speak. His hands meant something different to her now, his arm, which she now knew was brown and covered in copper hair and strong, seemed to burn through his coat, through her glove, and she was excruciatingly aware of the man beneath it.

This was *ridiculous*.

It occurred to her to listen to the music. Lady Georgina *did* play very well.

Lady Georgina, the woman intended for Miles Redmond. *Ah, sanity.*

"I shall need to know about Lord Argosy," Cynthia said immediately.

They parted from each other in the figure called by

Lady Windermere. When they came together again, Miles said, "He's very wealthy and unmarried. Isn't that what matters?"

It felt as though his irony drove them apart, though dancers everywhere in the room backed away from each other, as required by the dance.

And came together again. Cynthia coaxed, "Don't be tiresome."

His smile was small and tight. And they circled each other, in the steps Lady Windermere called out like two wary cats undecided as to whether to fight or mate. Eyes locked.

"Very well, Miss Brightly." He began another of his helpful, scathing lists. "Argosy has thirty thousand pounds a year. He's an heir, as you know. I've not heard of any terrible debts or vices. He does very little of anything at all beyond amusing himself in various male ways. Horses, pugilism, women, hunting, gaming. He doesn't seem particularly inspired to improve himself in any way. But of course this wouldn't *matter*—"

The requirements of the dance parted them. They backed abruptly away from each other, and Cynthia was left in clenched-jaw suspense until they approached each other again.

"—to you. So forgive me for digressing. He does have two titles, several enormous properties entailed to him, and—"

"—five sisters," Cynthia completed.

"Ah, so you and Argosy are confidants already?" His voice was curiously even.

"I've learned a thing or two about him. Do go on."

But the next called figure required Miles to take her hand.

They faltered, began to lose their place in the dance, and

it would soon become obvious. She felt herself flushing. Her hand rose; she gave it to him hesitantly.

He took it as though she'd handed him a rare artifact. As though puzzled to be handed such a precious thing, he gently closed his fingers over it. Then firmly, decisively claimed it.

And led her in the figure the dance required.

Conversation was forgotten. The world was comprised of the place where their fingers knit.

Cynthia felt suddenly she danced not on carpet, but on clouds. The thought shook her. She glanced over at Argosy, deliberately, and her feet felt the floor once more.

Miles noticed, of course. Because noticing is what he did best.

"Argosy has never wanted for anything," Miles said, sounding quieter, conciliatory. "He therefore, I imagine, would find it stimulating to want what he cannot have."

Cynthia nodded; she understood instantly, and knew precisely what to do. "Does he have any peccadilloes? Predilections?"

"You would make use of a *peccadillo*, Miss Brightly?" He sounded genuinely curious. "How so?"

"One never knows what will be useful, Mr. Redmond, as you should know. I don't know why you should be the only person allowed to ask questions."

Oh, God. Lady Windermere called a figure that required them to rest their hands on each other's shoulders.

Time slowed, even as the music did not. Cynthia watched their arms rise, and then his hand was resting on her shoulder. She saw how small her own hand looked there. If they walked two steps closer, they would be in each other's arms. It seemed ironic, unfair, that the requirements of the dance should simultaneously link them and keep them apart.

His eyes were dark and fierce. And as their bodies rotated

slowly in the dance, he spoke, his voice so low, so close to her, so resonant, that it called up gooseflesh along her throat.

"Miss Brightly, what do *you* want?"

Heat washed her limbs. She ducked her head so he couldn't read her eyes, and her eyes wanted to close so she could shut out all sensation apart from his hand upon her shoulder and the smell of his linen and his clean warm body, so she could imagine his hands on the rest of her, relive the feel of his hard arousal pressed against the frail fabric of her gown.

But she wasn't a ninny. She breathed in.

"I want you to answer my questions, Mr. Redmond," she said with some strength.

She forced her head up then, forced herself to casually look away from him. Outside the line of the dancers she saw the clean profile of Lady Georgina as her fingers jumped over the pianoforte keys in a facsimile of the dance. Lord Milthorpe looked up, catching Cynthia's eye as he turned a page of music for Georgina. One dim tooth and one bright tooth side by side in his smile.

She reflexively gave him a smile of her own.

Miles's hand tightened on her shoulder. She felt the humming tension of the muscles in his arm beneath her hand. She looked from her hand up into his face too quickly and shaken, saw that everything about his face, every bit of it, was simply *right*.

"Here is something," he said suddenly, finding his voice. "Argosy is superstitious. He's drawn to the supernatural. I know he has visited a mesmerist more than once in the *ton*; he has also attended more than one séance held by a madame, and swore that he has spoken with the spirit of his dead mother more than once."

Good heavens. "Heavens" was particularly apt, since

Argosy apparently sought conversations with those living in the afterworld.

"His mother is dead?" she said softly. This was something she had in common with Argosy.

"He was raised by a stepmother. A friend of my mother's. She's a pleasant woman, quite handsome. Then again, his father wouldn't countenance a homely woman. I'm certain Argosy won't, either." He said this with mock reassurance.

"You know a good deal about Argosy, Mr. Redmond."

"People talk to me, Miss Brightly. I'm not certain why."

"And I assure you I can shed no light on that particular mystery, either, Mr. Redmond."

And at that he laughed. She'd surprised it from him. It was a glorious sound, and at once she felt strangely floating and formless, unaccountably delighted.

They danced in a sort of détente.

"I have a question, Miss Brightly. If you could choose a mate—if you could choose one by *design*—what qualities of character would you choose?"

She stiffened instantly. "I find such speculation pointless and frivolous."

"I'm curious whether—"

"Yes, yes, I know: you are *nothing* if not curious, Mr. Redmond. But *I* find speculation a waste of my time. As you noted earlier, marriage is a business arrangement. I would *prefer* a man of character—"

"What sort of character?"

"—and despite the pleasure I take in music and—"

"You take pleasure in music? What kind of music?" he demanded instantly.

"—other pastimes. I am a practical woman to my bones, and I do not wish to—"

"What kind of character should a man have?"

"—speak about this *further*. Particularly to *you*."

He raised his brows again. Her vehemence merely inspired him, of course.

He gave another of those Socratic nods, as though he knew it was only a matter of time before he'd extracted all of her secrets. Perhaps he would publish a scientific paper, and travel the country to give lectures about them.

"Why the *urgency* for a match, Miss Brightly? Is it something more than ambition? Or greed?"

It was a lash. A sign of his own frustration.

She lashed back. "I did you the honor of assuming you were a man of your word, Mr. Redmond, when I . . . You promised to help me in exchange for . . . in exchange for . . ."

"For?" He raised his brows, daring her to produce the word.

She gave her head a rough shake. "Please do not *ever* think I did such a thing lightly."

Such a thing, of course, meant kiss him—and kiss him and kiss him—in the alcove.

It was as truthful and as complete an answer as she wished to give him.

The music came to an end with a flourish. Dancers began to bow and curtsy and disperse in search of new partners.

And it was his turn to go silent. He frowned faintly, in the way he did when he was ferreting information away to the laboratory of his mind to decide what it meant to him. Or to formulate another question.

"Why does it matter, Mr. Redmond?" she asked. It was almost a plea.

Here was a question, at last, it seemed he couldn't answer. He glowered at her in silence.

"Because everything matters," he said tersely at last.

And he left her abruptly.

Just as Lady Middlebough was being persuaded to change places with Lady Georgina at the pianoforte.

And Lady Georgina clapped her hands delightedly together at the prospect of dancing, and acquired, to her visible pleasure, Miles Redmond as a partner.

Chapter 9

W hile Cynthia at last acquired Lord Argosy as a dancing partner.

He appeared before her with a sense of quietly triumphant expectation: not arrogant, but absolutely, peacefully certain she wanted him there. He didn't appear taxed by the last figure of the reel, which he had danced with Lady Middlebough: his cheeks were scarcely rosy. And again, he offered a secretive little smile.

Fortunately, Cynthia had never been naive about secret smiles, and she could supply one of her own. And did.

He bowed, she curtsied, and another reel leaped into the room from the pianoforte—Lady Middlebough was less accomplished than Lady Georgina, but she played the notes in the right order and with aggressive vigor.

It felt almost peculiar to dance with the slimmer, smaller Argosy, as though she were accustoming herself to a less substantial conveyance, one that could be blown over in the road in a stiff wind.

"Are you enjoying your stay with the Redmonds, Miss Brightly?"

Ah. So he was to begin with clichéd pleasantries.

"I am, thank you. Are you, sir?"

"Indeed. I find myself in pleasant surroundings and among pleasant company."

"Will you next compliment my dress? I should like to be prepared with the proper response." She was teasing him.

He laughed. "Forgive me, Miss Brightly, if I err on the side of banal conversation. I am out of practice with English girls, you see, as I have been traveling in France and Italy for lo these last few months, and my knowledge of pleasantries in those languages is limited. I must ask you something. Have we met before this week? I feel I most certainly would have remembered you. And yet I cannot shake the sense that your name is familiar to me."

Oh *no.*

"Oh, no doubt my name seems familiar because it's an adverb," she said lightly. "Perhaps you've used it before in a sentence? 'The stars shine brightly.' Something along those lines?"

He laughed again. "I can think of all manner of sentences in which I would like to use the words 'Miss Brightly.' But I think they would make you blush."

Oh, this was *very* good! Last season she would have taken a statement like that and spun from it an entire delicious, naughty web of innuendos, and she might have included a mention of Lord Milthorpe, perhaps, just for the pleasure of inciting competition.

But she knew the dangers in that. And alas, she was endeavoring to be *good.*

"Then, Lord Argosy, perhaps you oughtn't to say those sentences aloud. Do, however, feel free to *think* them."

He laughed *again*, delightedly. Good! She intrigued him. She knew it was necessary not just to charm but to intrigue someone like Argosy.

114

They dutifully hopped, clapped, and turned as the reel required, and when they faced each other again, he said:

"And you are unmatched, Miss Brightly?"

She decided to misunderstand him. "Good heavens, Lord Argosy. I do thank you for the compliment."

He laughed again. Peculiarly, it was almost wearying to charm someone *so* easily. It was a bit like playing tennis with a wad of feather down. One wanted a bit more *resistance*.

She glanced over at her source of resistance. Just as he was glancing over at her.

She jerked her head away.

"Though that statement is very likely correct, Miss Brightly—you are indeed matchless in *this* room, Violet notwithstanding"—Argosy said this with a pretty gallantry she approved of—"I did wonder whether you were unwed. I think perhaps my French and Italian are battling with my English for expression, and so my question emerged oddly. I have not made so bold as to ask anyone the question, though I assumed it was true, and I confess . . . the question has been pressing upon me."

He confided this last in the low and ardent fashion she had come to know and expect during her glorious London season. *Pressing* upon him, indeed.

She knew precisely what to do about this: she ducked her head shyly for a brief second. Then cast up at him her patented through-the-lashes gaze.

Argosy parted his mouth with fascination. Then clapped it closed, and his jaw tensed with burgeoning yearning.

Splendid!

"I don't find your question at all bold, sir. For those of us of marriageable age, it is an *important* question, is it not?" Lord Argosy nodded his head vigorously. "I am not yet wed. I am tremendously particular, I am afraid."

She made it sound as though she were simply *spoiled* for choice.

"Are your parents ambitious for you, Miss Brightly?"

A very good and circumspect question. He was not a fool, Lord Argosy.

"Well, that's precisely it, you see. I do believe they would have been, but . . . my parents are . . ." She took a risk. "My parents are deceased. I lost my mother when I was quite young, and my father even before her. I know my mother would have preferred me to marry a man of the finest character and fortune, and it is often difficult to be certain of someone's character or fortune without a long acquaintance. I so often wish I knew what the future held. If only there were a way to know! I so *often* wish I could benefit from the advice of my mother."

Argosy stumbled for an instant. He forgot to clap his hands. He stared at her.

He recovered himself neatly in a few nimble movements. "Oh, Miss Brightly. As do I . . ." He sounded almost breathless. " . . . as do I wish I could communicate with my mother, that is."

"*Do* you?" She matched his breathless tone.

"I lost her when I was young as well. I so wish I could contact her, as she hid from me one of my favorite toys when I misbehaved. I should like to know where it is."

Well, then. So much for Lord Argosy missing the warm words and advice of his sainted mother. Imagine a wealthy young lord missing his favorite *toy*. More charitably, she considered that the toy might represent a lost fragment of his childhood, something of his mother to remember.

"It's a wooden duck one pulls about on a string," he continued. "Family lore has it a fortune in rubies is stuffed inside." He said this pragmatically. "*I* think not—I think they were stolen long ago by an unscrupulous guest of my uncle's—but wouldn't it be better to know?"

So much for maternal longings.

"Goodness. I can see how you might like to have the duck, if that's the case. Do you know, Lord Argosy . . . this may strike you as a frivolous or unusual idea, but . . . oh, I cannot say."

"Please do feel free to share your idea with me, Miss Brightly. I have had *many* of my own unusual ideas in my day." He gave her one of his secret little smiles.

Cynthia was suddenly both curious and a little worried about Lord Argosy's unusual ideas, but she stopped herself just in time from encouraging him to launch into a series of innuendos regarding them. It was imperative she remain single-minded about her own agenda.

Single-mindedness reminded her of a large, bespectacled man who at this moment was dancing with a small blond girl with every appearance of deference and pleasure.

Did he put *Lady Georgina* under the lens of his questions? Perhaps the very fact that the girl didn't seem to have acquired any real *faults* as of yet—no angles of character under which hid secrets, nothing interesting to *expose*, for that matter, as far as anyone could discern—made her as soothing to Miles Redmond as that spreading green surrounding Redmond House.

She was certainly pretty. If tremendously, monochromatically blond.

Cynthia inhaled deeply and jerked her head away.

"Well, here is my idea, sir," she confided to Argosy. "I have learned of a Gypsy encampment on the outside of Pennyroyal Green. And as I have longed for some time to—" She stopped; the dance drew them apart briefly. When they were together again she said, "Oh, I cannot say. You'll think me foolish."

She ducked her head again shyly, and turned it away from him again just in time to see Jonathan dart an arm out, tap his sister Violet on the shoulder, and dart it back to his side again. He remained straight-faced. Violet swiveled her head to and fro, puzzled, started to frown and stopped herself, as Violet lived in dread of frown lines encroaching.

Cynthia bit back a smile. She would have loved to have brothers to look after and torment her.

"Nonsense!" Lord Argosy was saying eagerly. "I think I know what you're about to say, Miss Brightly. You would like your fortune told!" He presented this conclusion to her with a patronizing triumph: *Feel free to bask in the rays of my insight.*

She rewarded him with awe. "Oh! How did you *guess*?"

"You see, I, too, have always wondered what the future might hold. And the Gypsies—they read tea leaves and the like, and see portents in the shapes of them, and I've heard many of their predictions are eerily accurate. My dear friend Mr. Geoffrey Woolsey once visited a Gypsy who saw a wheel in the tea leaves. Three days later, Woolsey lost a wheel from his barouche!"

"You don't say!" Cynthia breathed.

Argosy nodded his own awe. "And the Gypsies will throw the tarot—fortune-telling cards, you know, with symbols upon them that tell a story about your future—and look at your palm and read things in it about ocean voyages and marriages and children and the gaining and loss of fortunes."

She knew this much about Gypsies, but she allowed Argosy the thrill of informing her. "Gypsies sound quite accomplished. Do they do all of this out of charity?"

"Good Lord, no. We shall need to pay them. Do you know whether these are the kind of Gypsies who tell fortunes? Or do they paint sorry horses and try to sell them as good ones? Unsavory lot, on the whole, Gypsies are, but they excel as entertainers. We must be careful. I shall protect you."

"You are too kind, sir. I'm not certain what manner of Gypsies these are, these Gypsies in Pennyroyal Green. That is, if they are the fortune-telling variety. Perhaps—"

"I'll ask Miles," Argosy proclaimed. "He knows everything about these parts. He'll be able to tell us."

Cynthia wasn't eager to see the mirth on Miles Redmond's face when he learned they were on a quest to have their fortunes told. He would know precisely how that had come about. And Cynthia had no real illusions about the Gypsy ability to tell her future.

She would, however, be willing to pay one of her remaining five pounds to a Gypsy to ensure that Lord Argosy's future included her.

"Perhaps we can arrange a visit to the camp, if they *will* tell our fortunes," she said. Arriving, at long last, at her objective.

"I would very much enjoy embarking upon an excursion with you, Miss Brightly." He smiled again. He had the kind of smile that turned *everything* into an innuendo. She wondered if perhaps it was something he was born with and couldn't help.

She returned his smile. She would need to be warm, but not *too* warm, with Argosy.

She did wonder why he should be concerned about the future. But perhaps his future struck him as so endlessly *certain,* he would have liked to know if anything at all of interest could ever occur.

"I do marvel that we have a certain amount of serendipity in our favor, sir. Imagine the two of us meeting here unexpectedly at Redmond House, the two of us longing to know the future! Only to discover that the keys to the future may lie but a few miles away, hidden in tea leaves or in our own palms. It's as though it was meant to be."

These last words suffused Argosy's face with a celestial light.

"Meant to be," he repeated dreamily.

When Lady Georgina curtsied as part of the dance, it was clear to Miles that her modiste had shamelessly glorified her finest assets: her low, silver-trimmed neckline bisected a bosom as plump as two loaves of unrisen bread, and her stays lifted most of it up out of her dress. A man could happily lose himself in there for days.

And yet he wanted to go somewhere to hoard the lingering sensation of Cynthia's hand upon his arm.

He began to move in the reel, reflexively. Cynthia seemed happily immersed in her conversation with the lordling; she was smiling. Argosy's laugh could be heard over the music. A pleasant enough laugh. Certainly not like Milthorpe's.

Nevertheless, it grated over Miles's sense like a hoe dragged over cobblestones.

"You dance very well, Mr. Redmond," Georgina said. As he'd forgotten to speak.

"And you lie very prettily," he said. "I dance passably at best. I'm much too large."

"Oh!" Georgina colored adorably, and he was momentarily charmed and distracted. "Forgive me. I only meant to compliment you. I am no expert on dancing."

"Forgive me. I should not have teased you. And I *was* teasing you."

Oh, for heaven's sake. And he'd told his father he could make himself agreeable to a young woman. He *could*, in fact, given fertile ground for flirting: a sparkle in the eye, a tilted head, a clever word—tinder to his match, if you will. And yet he'd felt less like a suitor than a tutor today as they strolled through the grounds of his home.

A girl with her handsome face and appealing bosom ought to be able to flirt, for God's sake.

He heard Argosy laugh again.

For some reason it made him want to rush over and kick the man.

Pulled like a compass needle, his head turned. He saw Cynthia's back as she rotated with Argosy touching her. Her dress fell in fluted Doric folds. Her hair was swept up high, leaving a rectangle of luminous bare skin exposed above the line of her dress, which was closed in the back with tiny buttons. He imagined what it would be like to touch his tongue to each pearl of her spine, to touch his lips to the nape of her neck and see the gooseflesh rise, to know her nipples were peaking—

Mother of God. He sucked in a breath.

"Your home is very beautiful, Mr. Redmond. I'd forgotten just how beautiful."

With a Herculean effort, he returned his eyes to Georgina. He stared at her. It seemed impossible that someone should be saying something so politely banal to him while Lord Argosy was touching Cynthia Brightly. "How long has it been since you've last visited Redmond House?"

"Five years, three days last spring." She added with unconvincing nonchalance, "I believe."

"Ah. I remember now. Your hair was in a braid down your back." *Not wound up like a henge.*

"You remember!" She went pinker. "You raced your brothers across the park on horses. You came in second. Lyon was first. Your horse was brown with white stockings."

"Ah. Did we race?" He was bemused. He'd been forever racing his brothers then. Coming in second sounded about right.

"Yes. You rode so *well*."

She said this with such baffling fervor that he didn't know what to say after that. It occurred to him that she was awkward because her father had ordered her to view *him* in a new context. Or perhaps she *already* viewed him in that context. This was an intriguing possibility.

He really ought to teach the girl to flirt.

Argosy laughed again.

Miles jerked his head in that direction as violently as if the man had struck him.

He blinked when he met a pair of brilliant blue eyes aimed straight at him. Held them for a second.

They both whipped their heads back to their partners.

Lady Middlebough worked out her impatience over the keyboards, thumping them soundly. Never had a reel been so very passionate and expressive.

He would go straight to her after this dance and be between her thighs before midnight. He felt his mood begin to ease.

"I find I am very interested in ledibopreta, Mr. Redmond." Georgina sounded a trifle desperate.

Miles was startled into giving her the entirety of his attention. He'd never heard that particular word in his life.

Ah. Then he understood.

"Lepidoptera?" he guessed. Perhaps she'd had wine with her dinner? "Butterflies?"

"Yes. Lep-i-dop-te-ra." She gave every syllable careful attention. "Butterflies." Her eyes were aglow. "You spoke of them today at the picnic. A common blue came by."

It was undeniably pleasant to be looked at by glowing eyes. If a little puzzling.

Certainly this was a place to begin flirting. "Oh, they've *beautiful* butterflies in the jungle, Georgina." His voice acquired an intimate storytelling timbre. "Bigger than your fan. Brilliant as"—*Miss Brightly's eyes*—"summer skies, or rampion in bloom."

She giggled helplessly.

He almost sighed. If he could compare Georgina to a butterfly, which one would it be? Not a tropical butterfly: it would be an English one. A dingy skipper, or a brown argus. Uniform in shade, ideally designed to blend into their woodland surroundings.

"My father is terribly interested in all of these things, too," she said.

Miles was acutely aware of this. "Your father is a man of great intellect and discerning tastes," he said shamelessly. If only he could teach the man's daughter to *flirt*.

"I saw a butterfly in our garden the other day and I could not identify it, and nor could Papa. I thought perhaps that you could."

Argosy laughed again.

Miles's vision focused on Argosy's hand on Cynthia's arm. An unpleasant sensation sizzled along his spine. Like a flame touched to a fuse. He felt a metallic taste in his mouth.

"Perhaps you could describe it to me?" Miles said, scrupulously polite.

Georgina opened her mouth to reply, but Lady Middlebough ended the reel with a great crash of passion then.

Miles didn't even bow. He left a startled Georgina and strode across the room straight for Lady Middlebough.

And then, to his own astonishment and hers, and to

anyone else who witnessed it, he walked right past her and kept walking until he was out of the front door of the house.

The dancing continued past midnight, and the neighboring guests boarded their carriages happy and rosy and disheveled. But given that Miles was host of the event, his startling departure from the festivities had not gone entirely unremarked.

"He . . . might be feeling unwell," Violet said quietly to the few who inquired discreetly. "The tropical fever returns now and again, you see. He'll be right as rain soon, straight away."

The fever hadn't done anything of the sort in the entire time Miles had been home in England, but everyone nodded sagely and sympathetically. If one was to be unwell, one might as well have a glamorous complaint.

And then Cynthia and Violet went up to bed, and Jonathan, Argosy, and Milthorpe convened over billiards—Milthorpe having assured Cynthia that he'd discussed the target shooting party with Miles.

She hesitated on the threshold of her room. Then ventured over to the window and peered into the corner of it. She knew a peculiar relief that the web was still there and still intact.

Such a fragile way to sustain a whole life: on a web one weaves for oneself.

Then again, it wasn't much more certain than the way she'd built her own.

She blew gently on the web; it fluttered. The spider scurried forward and then stopped and waved two arms at her, like a gentleman hailing a hackney or a shopkeeper railing at a thieving urchin.

"Sorry to disturb you, Susan." It pleased her to give the spider a pretty name. "Good night."

Susan the spider quieted and seemed to regard her for a moment. Then she backed up into her corner and perhaps nodded off. It was difficult to know, given that she was a spider.

Mr. Redmond would likely know.

Cynthia had watched him stride from the room that evening, and she'd felt it almost physically, as though he were pulling her along with him. She pictured him today, steering people away from that grand web.

And she went still, breathless with a rush of understanding: she suddenly saw that Miles Redmond saw the world as little worlds *within* worlds. Everything—spiders, people, plants that ate animals—were both separate and connected, living the intricacies and beauties and violence of life, woven together like a web.

And this, too, was why, even when he was quiet, when he was still, he seemed to contain worlds. To feel *vast*.

Because everything *matters*, he'd said.

Before he'd abruptly left her.

Cynthia gave her head a toss to scramble him from her thoughts. He'd no right to pry, no right to be angry, no right to touch her as though she was something precious and wondrous and *aflame*, and she couldn't allow her body to long for him, for she was proud and that way lay disaster, the end of her dreams.

By way of disciplinary action, she went to the wardrobe and took out her reticule. She gave it a shake: it still, of course, scarcely jingled. She reached in her hand to finger her last few pounds.

It was a very effective way to strengthen her resolve.

She squared her shoulders, sat down upon the bed, and

like a general reviewing plans for a campaign, trained her thoughts upon Argosy and his fortune and eagerness and flawless good looks and their plans for a visit to the Gypsies, and Milthorpe and his fortune and sincerity and his bray, and considered the shooting party she unfortunately had somehow managed to inspire.

They were scarcely a day into the house party, she thought optimistically. There were almost two entire weeks left. Surely she could captivate *one* of them. She'd captivated Courtland, after all. The richest prize of all.

And because she'd been good and strong, she surrendered to a moment of encroaching weakness.

She closed her eyes and savored for a moment a particular man's hands on her in the dance this evening, angry and intimate, devastatingly gentle, precise and wondering. She suspected everything he was, everything he thought, everything he felt, was in the way he touched her. In the way he'd kissed her.

Oh, God.

She rested her hand on her own smooth shoulder, as if to recreate the warmth of his hand there. To feel what he might have felt. She felt her eyes burning with a want she'd never before known, and knew she could never, ever afford to indulge.

She took her hand away from her shoulder gently, as surely as if it were his.

Then got into her night rail and burrowed beneath the blankets.

She suspected she had no hope of sleeping the night through.

Miles was as surprised as everyone else that he'd left the party. He'd gone straight for Lady Middlebough with one very specific intent—had he bowed to Georgina first, or said thank-you, or anything of the sort? He couldn't recall now—and moments later he'd found himself outside, at the mercy of another intent.

He'd crunched his way in the dark over the vast circular drive, generous enough to accommodate a battalion of carriages—his mother had visions of the ball to end all balls when Violet was finally wed, and in his youth he'd seen the drive filled before with all manner of conveyances: a ball held for his parent's twenty-fifth wedding anniversary, a ball held in honor of Lyon's majority. Coats of arms of the finest families lined up as far as the eye could see, carriages and cattle washed to a gleam for the occasion, a rainbow of livery on the attending footmen.

There would no doubt be another such ball when he wed Georgina.

He looked up: the rain clouds had dumped their contents and were now parting like curtains on a stage, revealing an achingly clear blue-black sky and a tipped saltcellar's worth of stars. He thought instantly of brilliant blue eyes gone midnight dark with anger, and a net studded with tiny sparks laid over a dress, and a homely gray cloak and a curtain opening on a performance. Hers.

Every bloody thing made him think of her.

He gulped in the air, hoping it would be cold enough to hurt and to distract him. Whenever he thought of Cynthia Brightly, breathing became both a struggle and a piercing pleasure.

He spared a thought for Lady Middlebough now, but he couldn't make his thoughts linger there, because he was on a mission driven by a compulsion he didn't understand, and he was a man of singular focus.

It was a long walk to the outbuildings, and his valet

would cluck over the condition of his boots when he returned, because the pounding rain had turned the earth to mud and he'd track much of it back with him. The stables were, of course, dark. Soft stable boy snores chuffed in the tack room; one of them must have dozed off over the rubbing of oil into saddles and halters. A spaniel—spotted, this one, not liver-colored—that should have barked upon his approach remained stretched like a small snoring rug on the straw between rows of stalls.

It sensed him, lifted up its fine head, thumped its feathery tail cheerfully three times, and flopped again with a contented sigh.

Miles was terribly glad he was so terrifying.

He gave the dog the benefit of the doubt and decided he'd been recognized; he was here just this morning, after all. He thought of Milthorpe, and Cynthia's kindness to him, and then shied away from the thought, because it made him feel unaccountably fierce and tender.

He decided the dog could earn his keep tomorrow.

He felt about at the stable entrance for the oil lamp he knew hung from a wall hook. With a flint, he lit the wick; it flared instantly into almost too lively a light. He cupped a hand around to filter it and keep the stable boys asleep.

Ramsay whickered softly. Miles raised the lamp to illuminate his horse's delicate head, those soft wide-set Arabian eyes; he offered a whispered greeting, gave his smoke-colored coat a pat. But he wasn't here for a midnight ride.

It was the loft he was interested in.

Because of his height, he needed only scale two steps of the ladder steps to peer into the loft. He stared at the heap of straw, and then did what he did best: waited patiently, and listened, and observed. Miles was brilliant at waiting, brilliant at watching, brilliant at listening. The most fascinating things happened when one was quiet and simply watched without appearing to watch. He often saw falling stars, for instance. He saw animals and insects conducting the quiet business of their lives, learned their habits and customs. And he'd once seen an expression—so fleeting he could have imagined it but knew he did not—on his father's face when he'd glanced up at Isolde Eversea in church. She was the mother of all those other Everseas, including Colin, who'd nearly been hung of late for allegedly murdering the cousin of a Redmond.

The expression had been so like pain.

It had confused Miles then. He thought he understood it now.

At last he heard rustling. He stopped breathing; held his body very still and scanned for the source of the sound. For a time the world was just his breathing and the breathing of the animals below and the dark.

Until at last he saw the faintest stirring of straw.

He leaned forward and parted the straw gently with his hands. Peered. And smiled.

He reached into the crackling nest and lifted out what he'd come for.

Chapter 10

~~~ ◦⟋⟍◦ ~~~

Cynthia awoke—for the second time—to the sound of a maid building up the fire and to the smell of steaming chocolate. She remembered waking the first time, when she recognized the tangled nest she'd made of her sheets and blankets.

Blast.

The dream of falling had visited with ugly force last night. The slamming of her own heart against her breastbone woke her, and she lay, sweating in the dark, resigned, breathing into the deep silence, waiting for her heart to slow. Furious that everything she controlled and channeled so beautifully during the day could simply have its way with her during the night.

The maid, having coaxed the fire into life, paused before she left.

"Miss . . . you should know . . . there's a . . . basket . . . for you here. Outside the door."

The maid sounded skeptical and a little concerned, which puzzled Cynthia. Was it or *wasn't* it a basket?

"Would you bring it in, please?"

The maid brought in a small handled basket in with a

130

hinged lid, left it gingerly in the middle of the carpet, offered a shallow curtsy, and backed out of the room quickly and closed the door.

Cynthia rolled out of the bed, reached for her chocolate, blew gustily at it until she surmised it was a drinkable temperature, then bolted half of it. The rich taste rolled her eyes back in her head in bliss, but it only nudged her slightly closer to full alertness.

It would have to do until she was able to drink an adult-strength coffee downstairs.

She pushed her hair out of her eyes, found it lank because the nightmare had made her perspire. She would order up a bath today, she decided. Have a long wallow in a large bathtub with the finest of Mrs. Redmond's soap.

She eyed the basket with idle curiosity. Then set the chocolate aside and dropped to her knees on the carpet before it. She began to reach for the lid to lift it—

A dark, furry . . . *arm* . . . shot out of it.

Cynthia shrieked and toppled backward on the carpet. "*Sweet Mary Mother of—*"

She was certainly awake *now*. Her heart drummed sickeningly.

The furry arm waved around a bit. As if searching for her hand to snatch.

Cynthia stared at it suspiciously. Then crawled on her hands and knees toward the basket and peered. On closer inspection, the furry arm proved to be a paw. A *miniature* one. Dark gray and feathery-looking, with tiny white curving nails at the end of it.

The furry arm waved around a bit more, then disappeared back into the basket. Almost reluctantly, as though disappointed it hadn't snatched her.

Cynthia gingerly lifted up the lid and peered in.

She found herself staring right down the little pink gullet of a kitten.

"*MEEEEE!*" it bellowed.

She jumped back again, dropping the basket lid. What the *devil*?

She opened it again, and looked down at the wee thing.

"*MEEEEEE!*"

"Good heavens, you are *loud*," she told it. "I thought cats were supposed to say 'meow.' There are *two* syllables in meow."

"*MEEEEEE!*" It corrected vehemently and with great singularity.

She carefully plucked it up out of the basket. Its four little paws flailed the air before it settled into her palm. It had a tiny, full round ball of a belly and little birdlike ribs she could feel when she dragged a finger softly across its body. Its fur was puffy soft, like the down of a baby bird or bread mold, and it was the color of rain clouds but for its eyes, which were gray blue and perfectly round. It was, in fact, a comical little thing, all candy floss roundness and triangles: two isosceles triangles for ears, a funny little furry erect pine tree of a tail, minute pointed beads of white for teeth, miniature claws that pricked and itched her palm.

"My goodness," she said to it softly.

Its whole body instantly vibrated with a deafening purr.

She held the buzzing little animal in her hand and felt it vibrate her entire body. Clearly, this particular kitten did nothing by halves.

She was in awe of it. Enchanted breathless.

"Where did you come *from*?" she said to it.

It struck her then that she already knew. Because she'd only told one person she'd never had a pet.

"Meeee!" it said. And resumed purring.

Her heart felt as though it might burst open.

She used one tentative finger to rub the kitten's forehead. Her finger sank into the puffy fur there. It closed its eyes.

First, she eliminated the options she knew were unlikely: Milthorpe would not have given her a cat, of all things. Argosy would not have thought of it . . . would he? A jest from Violet?

No: she knew. She peered into the basket and saw was a folded sheet of foolscap.

She placed the kitten down before her and shook out the folded foolscap with trembling fingers.

Miss Brightly,

Sadly, as no wild boars were available in the stables, I was forced to settle for this. You'll note that its stern is covered with silky gray hair. It is male. And loud.

Yrs,
M. Redmond.

She held the note in her trembling hand and traced with her thumb, absently, *Yrs.*

The kitten pounced on the hem of her nightdress, and then danced sideways, back arched, tail puffed, and pounced again, looking for a way under. She lifted her nightdress to allow the kitten beneath, and its furry body ricocheted for a time around her ankles. It was having a wonderful time in the wilderness comprised of her nightdress and her long legs.

With a yelp, Cynthia plucked it out again before it could climb her thigh with its pointy little claws.

It blinked its tiny round eyes in the light. It vibrated madly again.

Oh. She was in love. She thought her heart might very well break.

"Spider," she told it firmly. "I'll name you Spider."

She was wholly breathless. Both by the living, purring gift, and at the implications of it. It was the very opposite of a dog, some might say. And perhaps this was the point. And it belonged to *her*.

It was, of course, an absurd gift. And so perfect she felt her eyes burn ridiculously, and she felt fiercely angry again. Had Miles Redmond meant for her to fall in love? With something, with anything? Did he mean for her to look at something she loved and think of him?

How *dare* he.

He had no right to give her gifts. No right to remind her she was alone by ensuring that she was not. No right to test whether she had a heart. No right to court her, to please her, or to do whatever he bloody well might be doing by giving her a kitten.

She held the little cat up to stare at it fiercely. As though it were Miles Redmond himself.

It laid a paw on her nose.

Cynthia did not go down immediately for breakfast. She didn't just yet want to see Miles Redmond, or anyone, for that matter.

She wanted to be alone with her pet. *Her* pet. Hers.

She asked for coffee to be sent up to her and for a bath to be prepared, and then availed herself of a small brick of Mrs. Redmond's good lavender soap and soaked luxuri-ously. She washed her body, slowly, languorously, every slim pale curve and angle and hollow of it, and then scrubbed her great length of dark hair, and savored the entirety of her bath ceremoniously. In one week she might *be* the one fetching baths.

Oh, for heaven's sake. She gave her head a toss, like a spirited mare flicking away a fly. That was no way to think. She was *Cynthia Brightly*, after all. She would prevail.

And while the fire and the sun pouring through the window dried her hair to a fluff twice its usual size, she played with her kitten, learning that kittens thought *everything* could be played with, particularly fingers. And then she tamed her hair by dragging it through her fists three or four times—the kitten also played with her dangling hair—and she pinned the whole mass of it artfully up, and managed to get herself dressed without assistance. She chose the white muslin for shooting.

Funny: even though she'd told herself she wouldn't foment mischief simply because an opportunity presented itself, she'd promised herself she would good, that she wouldn't take undue risks—in the span of a few days, she'd managed to kiss the family's heir, receive a cat, and now she was going on a shooting expedition in order to impress another wealthy man and she hadn't the faintest idea how to shoot.

It was true: risk sought *her* out.

She pulled out her brown leather walking boots and began to slip them on, then hesitated. She gingerly turned them over to press with a delicate finger at a soft place where the sole of one was thinning.

She felt that prick of fear again at the back of her neck. Her bravado wavered. Bloody hell. *This* was about as productive as shaking her nearly empty purse.

She deliberately turned to look herself in the mirror, as if assessing her armory: She saw a satiny glowing complexion, brilliant eyes, lustrous hair, and her lovely slim young body with generous bosom swelling up out of innocent white muslin. Long white arms. Hatched with a few fine kitten scratches now, granted. But graceful nonetheless.

She squared her shoulders. She would go down now. She could face all of them, even Miles.

But what to do with Spider while she was out?

She rang for the maid.

"Oh, I've instructions to look after the wee cat, Miss Brightly," the maid told her. She glanced down warily at the little creature, who was bouncing over the counterpane like a flea, attacking invisible prey. No doubt the maid was surprised to have received such instructions from Mr. Miles Redmond, master of the house as long as his father was absent, as cats belonged in the barn, as far as the maid was concerned. And she knew for certain how Mrs. Redmond would feel about a cat anywhere in the house.

Cynthia did, too. This only added another frisson of pleasure to the gift.

Cynthia found everyone except Miles still at breakfast, and some powerful hybrid of disappointment and relief held her motionless for a moment. But there was a new addition to the house party seated at the table as well, which made her forget Miles and her gift for a moment.

Everyone, in fact, seemed to be watching the new addition rather balefully.

He was a handsome gentleman in his middle years. Crisply dressed in a dark brown coat and a cloud-white cravat. Face weathered in a pleasing way that suited his age. His hair had all but relinquished tenancy on his tall, noble scalp; a palm-sized scrap remained up top, like a rug in the middle of a polished wood floor.

Interestingly, his expression was serene and distant

and slightly . . . pitying? As though he was possessed of some greater wisdom than the rest of the guests and entertained no real hope that they would ever reach his level of enlightenment.

And then he noticed Cynthia, and the gentlemen immediately stirred themselves and shook and preened a little.

"Mr. Goodkind," Jonathan introduced Cynthia. "A business associate of my father's. "Miss Cynthia Brightly, Mr. Goodkind."

The man stood and bowed to Cynthia, who offered him a pretty curtsy, and was offered a chair by a footman and accepted gratefully the hot coffee poured for her.

"I came here to discuss an opportunity to invest in a publishing matter with Mr. Isaiah Redmond, when I discovered he was not at home," Mr. Goodkind explained to Cynthia. "I am abashed to intrude upon a party in progress, but I confess I am pleased to find myself in such pleasant company anyhow."

Well. This sounded promisingly charming.

Though Cynthia could have sworn that Violet rolled her eyes. She glanced that way quickly, but Violet's visage was bland again.

"My father maintains that little money is to be had in publishing," Jonathan said rudely. Forgetting that his brother Miles had made a small fortune from his own writing.

Goodness. Cynthia stared at the youngest Redmond son. Goodkind must have said something to cause Jonathan to lose his manners. She was immediately intrigued.

Mr. Goodkind simply offered a serenely dismissive smile that managed somehow to include everyone and no one.

"Mr. Goodkind was just telling us that drinking is the quickest route to hell," Jonathan volunteered evenly to Cynthia.

Ah. *Now* she understood.

"And that joining the army would have made a man of me," Argosy volunteered laconically. "Because it made a man of him."

Implying, of course, that Argosy needed to be *made* into a man. As he wasn't yet one.

What an eventful breakfast it had been. Pity she hadn't arrived earlier.

She gave Argosy a little smile meant to reassure him that she thought him every bit a man, but knew she didn't dare make her allegiance seem too pronounced until she knew more about Mr. Goodkind and his fortune.

She simply couldn't afford to eliminate any options.

"And . . . and that shooting is a frivolous pastime." Milthorpe sounded quietly amazed. His posture was rigid and incensed. He nearly stuttered.

Goodkind sat peacefully as antipathy eddied around him.

"I think I shall read something inspirational while your party . . . shoots," he said pleasantly. He managed to make the word "shoots" sound like something both comical and pitiable.

Which was when a great screech went up as chairs were scraped back in unison. Everyone was in a hurry to escape from Goodkind.

The unfortunate, bloody, misguided, ridiculous shooting party—as Miles had begun to affectionately refer to it in his thoughts—was to take place on the south lawn. Since he was the house party host and responsible for the safety and enjoyment of his guests, he'd enlisted footmen and a few stable boys to help set up targets—apples atop crates—and from there his guests, including Miss Brightly, apparently, would waste perfectly good musket balls by turning perfectly good apples into smithereens.

This absurdity had come about because Milthorpe wanted to impress Cynthia, who allegedly enjoyed dogs and shooting, and Cynthia wanted to impress Milthorpe by shooting something, though he *sincerely* doubted she could. And he was helping set the stage for this farce.

He began to dislike Milthorpe for being so easily and *obviously* smitten.

He disliked himself for disliking a man he generally quite liked.

And his mood was due in no small part to the fact that he'd slept badly, mostly because he'd never before given a woman a kitten.

A *kitten.* Why, in God's name . . . ?

It was just that the need to give her *something* had been overwhelming. He'd wanted her to have a pet. And now he felt uncertain and raw and off balance and absurd, and he could not recall the last time he'd felt any of those things. Whimsy seldom survived the scalpel of his mind. The South Seas had made a nearly unshakable thing of his confidence.

Striding back to the house to meet the amassed guests, he decided it might be rather pleasant to shoot something into smithereens, after all.

And there they were, clustered before the house waiting for him, the women airy as clouds in pale muslin, bonnets on snugly and ribbons fluttering beneath. There was Lady Windermere, and Lady Middlebough—

Good *God,* Lady Middlebough!

She intercepted his hardly flattering startled gaze: she wasn't a fool. She knew she'd been entirely forgotten last night. Hopefully, she'd attribute it to the absent-mindedness of a scientific man, and not quickly and discreetly spread word of his inattention throughout the *ton*.

He gave her a smile, a quick one, one that contained promise and apology, and if he lingered on the promise of her long enough he knew he could cheer himself up and thoroughly enjoy her.

It was a smile she understood. One of her eyebrows twitched upward, her lovely mouth curved, and then she turned casually back toward Lady Windermere, whose company she seemed to be enjoying.

Cynthia was standing behind Jonathan, who had Redmond height, too. Almost as though she was hiding.

Miles went still when he saw her. He felt his cheeks warm. For God's sake.

She saw him, and went still, too.

Absurdly, he seemed unable to speak. He glowered instead. Then caught himself. He was not a coward, he was a man of truth and fact, and what he had done would need to be addressed. Explained away, or apologized for, or otherwise acknowledged. A *kitten*.

"We're set up on the south lawn," he told everyone easily. And with a gesture waved them to follow him. Once he had the guests moving in the proper direction, he fell into step beside Cynthia. By some sort of tacit agreement, they fell back several feet from the others.

And walked in silence for a time.

"You gave me a *cat*, Mr. Redmond," she finally said lightly. Her voice quite soft.

He tipped his head back, pretending that he was trying to remember whether he had, in fact, given her a cat. "Why, so I did."

She smiled. Oh. Slowly, truly, a smile of the purest pleasure and amusement.

And suddenly he couldn't feel ground beneath his feet.

They walked on in silence. He, for the first time in a very long time, could not think of anything to say. They watched the backs of very different people walking ahead of them: the lush sway of Lady Middlebough; the brisk and sturdy Lady Windermere; the twin images of grace, Violet and Georgina; rectangular striding Milthorpe; slim, proud Argosy and Jonathan, the latter two of whom routinely engaged in pastimes much more frivolous than shooting apples from crates, because that's what young men invariably did, and thought nothing of it.

"And how do you like the cat?" His words were casual. But his heart thumped like South American surdo drums.

She held out her arms. They bore tiny scratches.

He knew a moment of terrible worry that this was her way of saying she did not—

"Oh," she said dreamily. "He's a very good gift, indeed." And then she looked up at him, and her face was luminous as a star. "I cannot begin to say what . . . he's . . . he's perhaps the very best gift I've *ever*—"

She stopped herself abruptly. Too full of emotion, clearly, and rendered inarticulate.

The radiance in her face seemed to flood him. "I don't often give gifts that draw blood."

She laughed. "It's only a little blood," she said practically. "It doesn't hurt much at all. You should see how his little tail puffs! He has the *softest* fur. And he purrs . . . good heavens, he makes such a *racket*. It's extraordinary."

"The creature *is* loud." Miles was as proud of choosing that cat for her as if he had indeed been chosen president of the Royal Society. "Knows its mind, I've noticed. What did you name him?"

She hesitated. "Don't laugh," she warned.

"I won't promise anything."

She pointedly didn't look at him. "Spider."

He felt a smile creeping slowly over his face. "*Did* you now? You named him Spider?"

She frowned abruptly, which was obviously an attempt to stop his smile from becoming enormous. "Because it seems to have twice as many legs as a usual cat. And it walks sideways to pounce. He looks . . . like a spider." She said this mildly defensively.

"He has four legs," Miles said firmly. "I counted them before I chose him. I wanted to make sure you had a complete one."

She laughed again, that sound so like music, that sound that made people restless. It turned heads toward them.

Miles thought: if I hold my arms out straight, the breeze will bear me straight away.

Yet another bloody poetic notion. But in the moment, it didn't seem at all ridiculous.

They walked on. Said nothing. Happy chatter lilted around them in bass and treble notes. They heard none of it. The silence between them grew denser and denser, acquiring the snap and vigor and portent of the air before a thunderstorm.

It broke.

Her words rushed breathlessly out. "Why did you give me a kitten?"

"Because the very first time I saw you I thought you had a kitten's face."

He'd said it just as quickly, his voice low and tense. It sounded for all the world as though they were arguing.

They'd stunned each other.

She stopped walking. He stopped walking.

As though they were linked and he could not go on if she didn't.

Cynthia stared at him. Her eyes were huge, dark with amazement. Her mouth had parted a little. Her chest rose and fell with agitated breathing. Her hand rose to her face briefly. And then she dropped her head in confusion.

He followed her gaze. Her walking boots were worn at the heels, too, he saw. He felt peculiarly restless when he saw that. He felt his hands curling at his sides. As though they were desperate to touch her, and desperate to prevent him from doing it.

He looked up and saw that Violet and Lady Georgina had glanced back toward them. He saw the vivid flash of Violet's eyes. He felt puzzlement coming from her almost in waves.

And when Cynthia finally looked up, she asked the question he dreaded. So softly. Her words very measured, as though she herself feared the answer and hesitated to frighten him away.

"Why did *you give* me a kitten?"

He measured out his words, too. They sounded like a quietly furious accusation.

"I . . . don't . . . know."

Hot color rushed into her cheeks. Her head turned abruptly away from him. Her fine, dark brows drew close in a puzzled frown. She'd buried her hands in her skirts again.

He was instantly reminded of the moment after he'd kissed her.

And that's when Miles abruptly abandoned her.

In three strides he was parallel with Lady Georgina and his sister, both of whom were happy to have him, and his sister looped her arm through his, and he felt anchored.

He wasn't fleeing, he told himself. He'd never run from anything in his entire life.

* * *

Cynthia watched him go, her thoughts spangled and agitated and peculiarly angry, too, and watched him easily merge his stride with Georgina's and his sister's.

He was nearly big enough to provide shade for both of them, she thought.

I don't know. She was certain the admission cost him. After all, he was renowned for knowing so *very* many things. She took a deep breath, filling her lungs with clean Sussex air and willing her face to cool and her heartbeat to steady.

There was some pleasure in knowing he was as confused as she was.

His anger, however, was unwarranted and unfair. She tossed her head. She had an objective, an urgent one. She could not allow a difficult, inscrutable man to divert her from it.

She was soon taken up by Jonathan and Argosy and Milthorpe, all of whom had been walking abreast some ways ahead, and all of whom were delighted to have her among them.

And this was of course as it should be, she thought.

She was buoyed by their admiration and simplicity, and quite felt herself again, and if she didn't think of it, she didn't even feel the ground beginning to press through the sole of her boots.

The south lawn proved to be a monotonously, brilliantly, scrupulously trimmed sea of green. On the west flank of it, beyond the arranged targets—red apples glowing atop a line of crates—marble sculptures were arranged. A replica of Michelangelo's *David* mingled with Hercules and Mercury, and appropriately enough, Diana, the goddess of the hunt. All frozen in graceful contortions and glaring whitely in the sun.

Now that the group was there, they clustered together and waited to hear how Miles thought everything should proceed.

Milthorpe was happy to be holding a musket, it was clear. "What were you and Redmond discussing, Miss Brightly?" he said to Cynthia. "Was he regaling you with more tales of the South Seas?"

It was an interestingly proprietary question. Still, she would have to be careful, as all the men here were holding guns.

"Cats," Miles said shortly, answering for them. Gripping his own musket as though he'd like to use it as a club.

Cynthia looked at him sharply. *Everyone* in fact looked at Miles, whose face was stern and whose tone had been startlingly terse.

"Cats? Cats ain't pets." Milthorpe thought this amusing. "They're for mousing."

As if in adamant agreement, they heard an exuberant *woof!* in the distance.

They all whirled. On the far edge of the lawn, a footman was bent, leading by the scruff the feathery spaniel from the stables, who was clearly desperately eager to be with them, judging from the way he was straining against the footman's grip and from the mad blur of his tail.

Milthorpe went still and looked positively radiant at the sight. His delight was a pleasure to behold.

Cynthia turned slowly to Miles. She was astounded. She knew he'd done it for Milthorpe. Which meant he'd done it for her.

He'd listened. He'd remembered. And this made it yet another gift to *her*, somehow.

And just then the dog broke loose and launched itself forward, its four legs scarcely touching the ground on its way to

145

them. It came to an abrupt stopbehind Cynthia and inserted his nose into her arse.

"*Oh!*" she squeaked.

Helpless giggles exploded among the guests. The dog sat back on its haunches and wagged up at her, smiling in a bright-eyed doggy way.

"Don't goose the young lady, there's a good lad!" Milthorpe said, not the least embarrassed. He patted his thigh to get the dog to come to him. "You know dogs, Miss Brightly. One must often surrender one's dignity around them."

"Of course." She knew that *now*, anyway.

Milthorpe talked to the spaniel in gruff country squire tones, which the dog seemed to enjoy, and the dog's delight and Milthorpe's delight was contagious.

Cynthia glanced at Miles. But he had gone to stand proprietarily next to Lady Georgina, who was clustered among the other women who had been sensible enough not to incite a shooting party. The girl looked up, flushed and pleased and awkward, as usual.

On the far horizon, near the lawn behind the statues, Mr. Goodkind came strolling into view, very, very slowly, so slowly he looked as though he were moving through a pudding. His head was lowered over a small book cupped in his hands, and the book even from this distance had a pious look to it. Perhaps he wanted to set a very obvious good example for the shooting party. Instill a bit of guilt.

"There's Goodkind," Argosy said dryly.

"Probably psalms in that book," Milthorpe said grimly. "Why don't you shoot first, Redmond? As you're the host."

Miles didn't have to be asked twice. He stepped forward, slung his musket up to his shoulder, and murmured, "Stand back, Miss Brightly. It kicks. But then you know that, don't you? As you are such an experienced shooter."

She'd just taken that precautionary step back when there was an explosion, and a cloud of smoke, and the glint of sun on the musket stock jumping backward in Miles's hands from the force of the shot. A tiny red apple shattered into millions of pieces.

It had been such a quick, casual motion. Fluid, natural, and deadly.

Cynthia was peculiarly shaken. What an interesting skill to possess. To walk around with the ability to shoot some distant thing into tiny bits.

Everyone was silent with admiration for a moment.

And then they applauded enthusiastically. Miles had just set the bar.

He threw her an enigmatic look, then stepped back and began swiftly and deftly reloading the musket, tearing the paper in his teeth, ramming in a ball, locking it.

"Your turn . . . Monty," Miles said without looking at Milthorpe.

Milthorpe spared him an odd glance. But he was buffered by happiness, and his attention was really all for Cynthia. "Well, Miss Brightly. Ladies, that is. Shall I impress you now?"

"Oh! Please do," Cynthia encouraged, beaming. "I'm certain you shall."

Milthorpe smiled. And like Miles, he shouldered the musket, eyed his target, and in a moment there was another boom, another great cloud of cough-inducing smoke, and another red apple became smithereens.

Milthorpe turned around and beamed again, particularly for Cynthia. Everyone applauded him happily.

Men. They're so pleased about *shooting* things, she thought again desperately.

"Why don't you have a go, Miss Brightly," Milthorpe suggested, aglow from his success and the applause.

She hesitated. But then Miles, with mocking ceremony, held out to her the musket he'd just loaded. And levered, ever so slowly, one of his brows.

She hesitantly took it in her hands and promptly nearly dropped it.

There were a few gasps and a muffled "Goodness!" from near the ladies.

Good *God*, why hadn't she known how heavy guns were? Men made them look as though they weighed nothing at all.

Milthorpe looked troubled. "You . . . hold it like so?" he said politely, as if hating to remind her of something she supposedly already knew how to do. He demonstrated with motions of his hands the raising of a musket to a shooting position.

All eyes were on her in total and silent fascination. Which helped not at all.

"I'll catch you, dear, if you fall," Milthorpe vowed. "This 'un has a good kick. Watch your shoulder."

The prospect of catching a falling Cynthia galvanized the men. They all—save Miles—scrambled for position behind her. She could hear the happy, overly familiar spaniel panting noisily and hotly somewhere down around her ankles, released in Milthorpe's jostle to help catch her.

The women had all gone quiet. She couldn't resist a glance in that direction.

Miles remained protectively near the ladies, arms crossed, legs planted apart, an unholy glint in his eye behind his spectacles: *See what you've gotten yourself into, Miss Brightly.*

Well, no one was more aware of that than she was.

She took a deep breath. Raised the gun to her shoulder. Closed one eye into a squint in order to properly aim at that shining red sphere in the distance. Held the pose for a moment to accustom her body to it, and began to feel more confident. Perhaps she *wouldn't* shame herself.

She took a deep breath.

And pulled the trigger just as the dog inserted his nose into her behind.

She leaped, squeaked, and there was a boom and a shattering *pling* as the musket ball struck the statue of David's penis and hurtled it westward toward Mr. Goodkind.

"*Duck,* Goodkind!" Miles screamed.

Mr. Goodkind threw himself to the ground instantly: he'd been in the army, and he did not think of waterfowl when he heard the word "duck."

The penis of David slammed into Goodkind's hat and sailed away across the lawn with it. The shooters heard a faint yelp. Cynthia staggered on the recoil, and about six arms flew out to prevent her from falling and to set her upright again.

Mr. Goodkind remained flat on the lawn, motionless, arms folded over his hatless head.

Oh, God. I've killed a man with a marble penis.

Perhaps there was a horrible sort of poetry in this, she thought. She was trying to impress one man and killed another. *I'm a terrible,* terrible *person.*

The shooting party stood as frozen as the statuary, staring at Goodkind.

A bird tra-la-la'd merrily into the silence.

There was a noisy, collective exhalation then. Goodkind's hands began to crawl about his head experimentally, making sure it was still intact. And then he pushed himself to his hands and knees.

And then he stood up, and gave a cheery wave indicating all was intact and unwounded.

Then he put his hands on his hips and shook his head sadly, slowly. As if to say: *See? If you'd all had the good sense to read psalms, you would not have shot a penis off a statue.*

It was questionable, however, whether Goodkind knew what had knocked his hat off.

Perhaps he was better off not knowing.

"Well *done*, Miss Brightly," Argosy said with all sincerity.

Milthorpe turned to study Cynthia. His expression was grave. Judging from the temperature of her cheeks, she was scarlet with shame. She darted her eyes sideways toward Miles.

His face was fulsome with mirth. His eyes had nearly vanished with it.

Cynthia cleared her throat. "I've . . . I've never shot a fowling piece quite so fine as this one before," she faltered. "I'm unaccustomed to the aim."

This was undeniably true.

"I thought it was a very good shot!" Lady Georgina, ever full of admiration, enthused. "*I've* never shot anything at all!"

"What *sort* of fowling pieces have you shot before, Cynthia?" Violet had returned, with all apparent innocence.

Cynthia sent her a quick ferocious warning glare.

Lord Milthorpe still looked troubled. He dropped one hand on the head of the spaniel and stared at the maimed statue with something akin to surprise, as though he could not fathom how anyone could possibly shoot so very, very badly.

Off in the distance, Goodkind had retrieved his hat, which he'd shoved back onto his head. He was now walking bent over, searching the grass for the missile.

He found it, plucked it up; they saw it glowing whitely in his fingers from a distance. He hefted it in his palm in a mystified fashion and turned it this way and that.

"Well, just goes to show all of us that one needs strong nerves and strong arms to hold your weapon under all manner of circumstances," Milthorpe said finally. "Even if . . ."

The delicately uncompleted part of that sentence was: *a spaniel inserts his nose into your arse.*

Cynthia could say nothing. All around her, eyes were brilliant, glistening, watering with hilarity.

"But everything improves with practice, Miss Brightly," Milthorpe finally encouraged jocularly.

"Not *everything*," Lady Middlebough muttered. Lady Windermere gave a cynical snort of laughter.

Cynthia decided to smile at Milthorpe.

Ah, this was good. He visibly basked in her smile for a moment; he seemed helpless not to. She was sorry he was disappointed. He'd clearly been hoping that against all odds, in the most unlikely of places, he'd stumbled across the woman of his dreams: beautiful, worshipful, charming, a lover of dogs, a dead shot.

This was when Miles stepped briskly forward and slid the musket from her grip. She looked up at him cautiously. His expression wasn't entirely readable.

"I'm afraid I'm calling a halt to your involvement in this shooting party, ladies," Miles said firmly. Miles dared Violet to protest with a flick of a dark gaze. His sister's mouth remained closed. "We'll have grouse or some such for dinner, no doubt." All the men nodded sagely. When it came to killing, it was better to do it in the company of men only. "If you would be so kind as to escort Miss Brightly safely to some other pastime, Lady Windermere? I don't recommend anything involving weaponry."

No desert had ever been dryer than that last sentence.

He touched his hat to them all, but in particular spared a soft apologetic smile for Lady Georgina, who doubtless never would have attempted to shoot a musket.

The women and men parted and walked in opposite directions on the property, the women toward the house, the men toward the killing of delicious things.

"D'yer shoot tigers in the South Seas, Miles?" Cynthia heard Argosy ask curiously and bloodthirstily.

"Now, why would you want to shoot a tiger, Argosy?" Miles sounded patient once more. "When clearly apples are much more dangerous game."

Much masculine laughter echoed after them.

Chapter 11

"What do you know about Mr. Goodkind, Violet?" Cynthia asked resignedly as they walked back toward the house. Thinking she had better expand her options, now that she'd disappointed Milthorpe.

"Goodkind," Violet told her firmly, "is difficult to like. He was a soldier, but he returned from the war . . . well, as you see him now. Insufferably pious. But my father tolerates him because he's respectable and very wealthy—at least as rich as Milthorpe, from what I understand. And he's clever enough to belong to the Mercury Club along with my father, and I know they only allow in men with lots of capital and cleverness. And . . . well, he isn't homely, is he?"

She added this last part almost gently. And noticeably didn't look at Cynthia when she said it.

Cynthia glanced quickly at Violet, who was still looking innocently straight ahead. She'd never confided the entire desperation of her circumstances to her. Had Violet sensed them?

Her pride gave a great, unpleasant throb.

What must it be like to be a Redmond, with choice abounding? With safety and certainty a constant? With brothers to look after and tease you? Cynthia squelched an unworthy rush of envy, because she knew in truth Violet was attempting to be kind.

"No. Not entirely homely," she agreed.

They smiled together.

"Cynthia, where will you go when you leave the house party?" Violet sounded carefully disinterested, which only further abraded Cynthia's pride.

"Oh, I shall be a companion to a nasty old woman called Mrs. Mundi-Dickson in Northumberland," she said lightly.

Violet went utterly silent. "It will never come to that." She was so aghast her voice was a hush.

Cynthia produced a laugh. "I was jesting, Violet! Can you *imagine*?"

"Not for even a second." Violet shuddered.

Ahead of them, the two cynical married ladies had sandwiched Lady Georgina, and all were talking pleasantly of mutual acquaintances in Sussex. As long as they don't start talking about the *ton*, Cynthia thought.

Cynthia and Violet were quiet together for a moment.

"I wonder if Miles is experiencing a return of his fever," Violet said to her, sounding a trifle worried. "They do come back now and again, you know—the tropical ones. So I've heard. It's just that he's been so odd lately. I hope he hasn't been rude to you yet again. I saw his face when he spoke to you earlier today. He can be very strict, you know. Rank is very important to him," Violet added, obliviously cruel. "It is to every Redmond. And ever since . . ." She hesitated, as though the word was difficult to pronounce still. " . . . Lyon left, I know Papa relies on Miles to do just the right thing. Miles has *always* done the right thing."

Had Miles been *rude*? Cynthia wasn't certain it was the word she'd choose.

"Perhaps he's just preoccupied with thinking about his next expedition," she offered.

"Oh!" Violet lowered her voice. "You could be correct. And possibly his nuptials too. That could make any man jumpy, I suppose," she said blithely.

"Naturally." Cynthia matched Violet's tone. But suddenly she felt as though she'd swallowed a brick.

She glanced at Lady Georgina. Would Miles willingly spend the rest of his life with that colorless girl?

For heaven's sake. Be practical. Cynthia took in a deep breath. Kitten or no, she must be *practical.*

"I think I should apologize to Mr. Goodkind," she told the ladies, and Violet gave her a knowing and encouraging glance.

Cynthia made her way back over the green toward where Goodkind was last seen, putting her feet down lightly in an attempt to spare her boots.

The rest of the shooting party was now long gone from view. In the distance she heard the throaty boom of a musket, saw smoke drifting upward, thought of a grouse plummeting to the earth, and shook off the thought. She found grouse delicious enough, when it came to that.

She found Mr. Goodkind hatless and admiring a bank of heavy-headed damask roses. Their scent was powerful. Those roses would need to be topped soon, she thought. Only a week or so left before they were done for. Just like me, she thought with some grim amusement.

When she was closer, she saw why he was hatless: he was holding his hat in one hand, and it featured a large dent.

He turned. He was visibly surprised to see her, but visibly pleased, too. "Why, Miss Brightly!" The dark scrap of hair on his head lifted and fell in a mischievous breeze like a trapdoor.

"I've come to apologize for the mishap, Mr. Goodkind. I do hope you're uninjured."

"Quite sound. Quite sound. Thank you for inquiring, Miss Brightly. But why do *you* need to apologize?"

"I fear I am entirely responsible. You see, I had never before shot a fowling piece quite like that one, and I missed." She'd decided it wise to omit the bit about the dog and the nose and precisely *what* had struck him in the hat.

"Well, I'm quite all right, and given that no harm was done, doubtless a valuable lesson was learned. Women should never be handed firearms. I don't know what Redmond was thinking. I'll have a word with his father."

It struck her as ridiculous that anyone would have a word about a man like Miles Redmond with his father. And she'd heard of women in America being armed with muskets, but thought it unwise to begin a debate on that particular subject.

"You are very likely correct, sir," she said diplomatically instead.

He nodded, satisfied. "Do you happen to know what struck off my hat? Looks like a bit of statue." He held up a white fragment.

You were struck in the hat by a great marble penis.

"Yes, part of the statue of David, I believe. Mr. Redmond assures me, however, that it wasn't valuable. The statue. It was a replica of some sort."

"Ah, well. The damage to the statue will linger as a reminder not to hand firearms to women."

You've already made your point, Cynthia thought. She began to suspect Violet was quite correct about Goodkind. Whereas Argosy was self-satisfied and Milthorpe was by turns shy and blustery, one's first opinion of Mr. Goodkind was . . . *pompous.* A nice juicy word, she thought, all those bouncy *p*'s in it, like the cushion in that extravagantly gilded coronation carriage.

Then again, she supposed everyone would come home from the war differently. Mr. Chase Eversea, of the delightfully controversial Pennyroyal Green clan, had come home with a limp, Violet had told her, and seemed to be drinking a good deal more than he ought. One ever found him, she'd once said, darkly satisfied, in the opposite corner of the Pig & Thistle. Sometimes completely alone. Here was another Eversea on his way to dissolution, she seemed to think. And wasn't Chase an ironic name for a man who couldn't run?

Violet could be cutting on the subject of the Everseas.

And then Cynthia recalled that the famous poet known as the Libertine, the Earl of Rawden, had returned from the war to write poetry.

She decided—for Goodkind's sake and her own—to give him the benefit of the doubt.

"You were very absorbed in a book when we were shooting, Mr. Goodkind."

"Do *you* read, Miss Brightly?" Mr. Goodkind seemed a tad condescending and resigned, as though he fully expected her to ask him what on earth "reading" might be.

"Oh, at every opportunity, sir." Which was *partially* true. The gaiety of the past few years had left very little time for reading.

Mr. Goodkind produced the little dark book from his coat. It looked like a well-thumbed prayer book. Piety required constant maintenance, apparently.

"I ask, you see, because I am publishing—at my own expense, unless I obtain funds, though I do have the cooperation of the very reputable London printer Withnail & Son—a book of essays on proper behavior for young men and women. I've been at work on it for the past year or so. I do feel the subject is timelier than ever. I have been recently in London among society, and it is . . . iniquity." He took his time over the word's syllables, relishing it. "Sheer *iniquity* among the young there. The close dancing, the horse racing, the gaming."

She stared at him cautiously.

His flap of hair waved gaily at her.

Any man can be charming, she told herself stoutly. One need only *look*.

"Perhaps it is simply the nature of youth, sir," she suggested carefully. "One can more effectively give advice on whether or not to drive a fast carriage or to gamble and the like if one has suffered the effects of such behavior, and repented."

He looked with sudden delight at her: perhaps the word "repent" had excited him.

"You pose an interesting theory, my dear. Would you care to continue?"

She had the sense he wished to take notes for his book.

And she suddenly thought of Miles Redmond, and the spider rebuilding its broken web to be stronger than before. She knew a perfect analogy.

"Well, do they not say that when a . . . tree is cut, it is stronger than ever where the branches scar over? If you do yourself an injury through"—*having a wonderful time*—"an inordinate amount of frivolity and recklessness, and you truly do regret it and make a choice to repent, does this not mean your soul is stronger than it was before? Does it not take more moral strength to overcome a wicked nature and transform it into a good one than it does to *maintain* one already good?"

She thought of Lady Georgina. That girl would need

to expend no effort at *all* to be good, she thought, half resentfully.

Mr. Goodkind stopped walking abruptly. He turned to her. He seemed speechless. He was, in fact, looking at her as though she was a revelation.

And slowly his face lit with epiphany.

"What I am saying, sir is . . . perhaps there is great merit in being just a little wicked once in a while, Mr. Goodkind."

His head went back in astonishment. He continued to stare at her. His hair swayed to and fro now; the breeze had changed direction.

And then Mr. Goodkind smiled very slowly, and the smile became a laugh, a sort of "Oh *ho!*" sound. A reluctant, if genuine, sound.

And many, many degrees less pompous than previously.

She smiled up at him. His eyes twinkled back at her. His eyes were pale blue, with deep lines etched into the corners, which made his smile appealing.

She clasped her hands piously behind her back. Which, she was fully aware, had the effect of lifting her bosom just . . . so. Just a little movement, just enough to catch the eye of a red-blooded man. It was a test.

Ah. He was a red-blooded man.

His blue gaze flickered back up from her bosom to her face. He didn't blush or even look disconcerted. He looked, in fact, downright cheerful, which reminded her that he'd been a soldier, had known blood and grit and doubtless a camp follower or two.

"May I pay you a compliment, Miss Brightly?"

It was the first time anyone had ever requested *permission* to do such a thing. She was distantly amused. But far be it for her to deny a man an opportunity to compliment her.

"I would be honored to receive a compliment from you,

Mr. Goodkind." She said this somberly. Her eyes were glinting.

"You could tempt a pious man into being wicked."

Oh! *Very* good compliment indeed.

"I shouldn't fear the temptation, Mr. Goodkind. As we've established, a little wickedness is good for the soul."

And at this he laughed genuinely, a hearty sound, and she laughed, too.

Again, she considered the fact that nearly any man could become charming given the right encouragement.

Cynthia returned to the house strangely weary, though she'd done little during the day but misfire a musket, converse with a handsome if pompous man—though granted, she'd convinced him that wickedness was indeed the path to virtue, no mean feat—and have her heart and mind whipsawed by a large, dark man who'd given her a kitten and didn't know why and seemed angry about it.

She wasn't certain any of this constituted progress toward matrimony. And because she was practical, the first thing she did was locate a footman to ask about her mail.

"I'm sorry, Miss Brightly," she was told. "If a letter comes for you, you can be certain I will bring it up to your rooms straight away."

So she went downstairs and spent a dutiful hour in the company of ladies sewing very sedately, but contributed little to the conversation. And then she couldn't bear it, retiring to her room, because she wanted to play with her cat, and she wanted to think, perhaps have a rare restorative wallow in self-pity.

She took off her shoes, sat on her bed and held Spider in her lap, demanding comfort.

Spider didn't wish to cooperate. He squirmed out of her

hands like a silky little bar of soap and attacked her toes. Cynthia gave it her best effort, but she could not be morose when she needed to defend her toes.

By dinnertime she'd recovered her spirits and was ready to renew her campaign.

The men did come home with grouse. And dinner was tasty and filled with talk of shooting, and everyone was well-bred enough not to tell Mr. Goodkind precisely what had struck him in the hat, and he managed to be slightly less insufferable, in large part due to Cynthia's efforts. And Miles was encouraged again to talk about Lacao.

After dinner, Jonathan persuaded Argosy to go with him to the Pig & Thistle to participate in an ongoing dart tournament that Jonathan intended to win. Argosy cast one brief but gratifyingly longing look over his shoulder at Cynthia, who reassured him with a smile but silently made no promises to him, as of course Lord Milthorpe and Mr. Goodkind were present and would remain so all night.

Lady Middlebough wanted to retire early. "The third floor is always my favorite floor in a home," she said. "And my room is *four* doors down from the stairs, and four is my favorite number."

Cynthia once again stared at Lady Middlebough, puzzled. She thought her own favorite number must be twenty-thousand.

As in pounds.

"Where are the family rooms, Violet?" Lady Middlebough wanted to know.

Violet looked baffled, too, but manners made her answer politely. "We're on the third floor, too. But in a different wing. Well, Jonathan and I are. Miles is on the second floor. He has the only family rooms on that floor."

"Must be lonely to be the only one on the second floor."

And with that Lady Middlebough went up to bed.

Violet decided they ought to play card games, so a game was set up out of the remainder of the party. Apart, that was, for Miles and Lady Georgina.

"Perhaps in a few minutes," was all Miles said. "We've ants and lepidoptera to discuss." And he'd deftly steered Georgina to a striped settee, where they now sat talking in low voices. A very respectable distance of settee remained between them.

"Oh, Mr. Redmond! How interesting!" Georgina said softly and predictably moments later.

Cynthia supposed he was as methodical and dutiful in his wooing as he was in all things. Was this all ceremony? The walking and talking with Georgina? How would he know when Georgina was *won*? Or had the decision to mate already been made, and all of this was formality?

She was thinking in terms of insects again.

The cards were dealt, and a halfhearted game of whist began, while Cynthia tried and failed not to listen to the conversation taking place on the settee. She stared over her cards at Georgina and her perfectly round coil of pale blond hair and she felt something devilish welling up.

"Oh, Mr. *Redmond*," she mimicked under her breath. "How very interesting!"

Lady Windermere looked up, surprised. "I beg your pardon, Miss Brightly?"

"Have you noticed—" Cynthia stopped. *Be good*, she told herself sternly. *You'll cause a disaster if you can't* be good. *Everything, your future, hinges on decorum, and wise choices and not* toying *with people.*

She shifted restlessly in her chair. But Lady Windermere

had asked her a question. And it wouldn't be polite to ignore her, would it?

"Have you noticed . . ." In for a penny, in for a pound, she decided. "Well, have you noticed that Lady Georgina says"—she adopted a breathy tone—" 'Oh, Mr. Redmond. How very *interesting!*' rather a good deal?"

"Does she?" This came from Mr. Goodkind with bright interest. He'd reached the point in his visit where anything said by Miss Brightly was interesting. And since Goodkind had taken the marble penis in the hat, everyone was more inclined to behave more charitably toward him. "Listen," Cynthia said, her voice a hush, her eyes downcast.

They all dutifully harked in breathless silence as though waiting for a rare birdcall.

In the low murmur of conversation—Miles Redmond's earnest voice provided the bass notes, a melodic rise and fall of enthusiasm—she heard the word "lepidoptera" and then a chuckle. Perhaps he'd told a butterfly joke.

Cynthia waved her hand like a conductor as on obliging cue Lady Georgina responded in treble:

"Oh, Mr. Redmond. How very *interesting.*"

Chuckles rustled about the table, a sound much like the sound of shuffling cards. Hands of cards went up over mouths to stifle them.

"You're very observant, Miss Brightly," congratulated Mr. Goodkind.

Lord Milthorpe bristled, as he'd missed the opportunity to say something flattering to Cynthia. He settled for agreeing with Mr. Goodkind. "Yes! Very observant, Miss Brightly."

Violet glanced at Cynthia and surreptitiously rolled her eyes.

Men battling for her attention, a naughty idea on the boil: Cynthia was feeling decidedly more herself.

The card players were all now furtively watching Miles Redmond and Lady Georgina over their neglected hands of cards. Miles Redmond's low voice again assumed the cadences of lecturing enthusiasm. He made a sort of crawling gesture in the air with two of his fingers. Then he made a flapping motion with his other hand. He seemed happy.

It appeared to be a monologue.

How *very* like a man.

Lady Georgina's face was a moonbeam of rapt attention. Her body angled toward Miles, as though being pulled into his orbit by the superior force of his intellect, and her lips were parted as though she breathlessly awaited each of his words and enjoyed each one more than the next. They moved a little, too, helping him form his words with the force of her fascination.

Cynthia wondered if Lady Georgina was actually listening to him or whether she was watching—as it was so tempting to do—the light move in the depths of his eyes when he talked, or the shape of his mouth, which was rather mesmerizing, but perhaps that was only because she knew how his mouth tasted, and felt, and—

She jerked her head toward her cards.

Violet seemed a bit skeptical of Cynthia's assertion, and a little disappointed. She leaned toward Cynthia. "Surely she doesn't say it all that oft—"

"Oh, Mr. Redmond," Lady Georgina breathed. "How very *interesting*."

The card players gasped and then laughed quietly in collective astonishment. Cynthia shushed them over her own laughs.

Miles Redmond and Lady Georgina turned in their direction a little bit, smiling at the mirth. Then returned to their conversation. Or rather, to their roles as monologist and audience.

Cynthia felt a twinge of guilt. But *honestly,* even if Lady Georgina *was* genuinely smitten with Miles Redmond, was this any reason to behave like a parrot?

Georgina had tilted her head now to look into Miles Redmond's face. Parrots do that, too, Cynthia thought. When they're curious about something. They have eyes on either side of their head, and not in the front, so they had to tilt their heads in order to see.

See? Never let it be said that I am not knowledgeable about nature.

"Very well. But it can't be as often as you say . . . can it?" Violet was a stickler for specificity, it seemed. Perhaps it was a Redmond trait.

"I've an idea," Cynthia said slowly. She had only heard Violet peripherally, because her mind was at work on a plan. *No, no, no.* Her conscience was a little scolding schoolmaster, stomping its feet. Still, she knew that Violet could be persuaded to mischief. She succumbed to a very unworthy impulse to muss the Redmond perfection.

"Here is my idea. Every time Lady Georgina says . . ." Cynthia lowered her voice. " . . . well, what she *says* . . . we shall all take a drink."

Delighted and appalled silence greeted this suggestion.

"Of tea?" This was from Violet, who, though familiar with myriad kinds of misbehavior, was new to this particular brand of it.

"Good heavens, no, you featherbrain." Lady Windermere turned on Violet with wide-eyed censure, worried that the rules of the game would become corrupted. "Of *sherry.*"

"Pre*cise*ly," Cynthia agreed happily. "And if the sherry runs dry, we shall ask for champagne."

This was optimistically said, as she hadn't the faintest idea whether the Redmonds would countenance opening up champagne for guests outside the occasion of a ball, but she had all the faith in the world in Violet Redmond's ability to persuade her father's staff to do anything.

"Perhaps you would be so kind as to expand the rules to allow the gentlemen to imbibe port or brandy instead," Mr. Goodkind suggested shrewdly, as he was a businessman, and believed every deal could benefit from refinement.

He received a nod of approbation from Milthorpe and a smile of encouragement from Cynthia.

"Done," she said crisply, as though they were indeed engaged in a negotiation, easily accepting the role of rulemaker.

"Who wins the game?" Violet asked.

"The last person upright," Lady Windermere said with relish.

They all looked with pity upon Violet, who they assumed wouldn't make it beyond the first two or three *Oh, Mr. Redmonds!*

"Now—everyone review your glasses. We don't want to miss an opportunity. Quickly now," Cynthia commanded quietly.

Glasses were raised into the light, liquor volumes assessed. Violet clapped her hands, and a blue-and-gold liveried footman appeared in the room with breathtaking instantaneousness and rectified inequalities with splashes from a cut crystal decanter.

Everything had begun to sparkle: eyes, sherry in glasses, moods, smiles.

"Very well, then. Let the games begin. Shall we play another hand?" Cynthia said sweetly, reaching for the deck.

Rain was still being flung sideways by the wind at the windows, only now it was dark, and Miles, as pleasant as he often found speaking nonstop about common blues and Formicidae, or his first look at Reverend William Gould's fascinating *Accounts of English Ants*, was growing restless. He'd given this particular speech in numerous forms before to the Royal Society.

She was a woman. He wanted to *flirt*.

She *was* flirting in a way. With those attentive eyes, and her soft mouth, and the neckline cut to ensure admiration of everything it contained, and he was dutifully and discreetly admiring it. And he supposed innuendos could be made from a discussion of the mating habits if he was so inclined. He was not inclined.

He was *bored*.

He found his mind drifting to the third floor, fourth door from the left. Poor Lady Middlebough. He was reducing her to something approaching obviousness.

He would reduce her to quivering pleasure tonight, he decided firmly.

And he was steadfastly avoiding Cynthia Brightly, because that way lay danger and confusion. But because when she was near, he tended to do the opposite of whatever he intended to do, he of course looked up to see what she was doing.

And when he did, he saw a footman hurrying by.

There was nothing at all unusual about this. Footmen were everywhere in the Redmond house, part of the silent bewigged battalion that kept it passionately clean and smoothly running, along with all the maids.

But as Miles watched this particular footman, he was struck by a peculiar sense of déjà vu.

He officially gave up attempting to listen to Lady Georgina and simply watched.

The footman bore a tray of crystal decanters toward the table in the corner where Cynthia Brightly glowed in pink-faced, burnished splendor, in a champagne-colored satin dress ribboned beneath her breasts in bronze. Other people of course sat round the table, too, including his sister—all of whom were also peculiarly pink-faced.

The footman poured for them—brandy and sherry—and hurried out again.

As he passed, Miles noticed that the servant was a bit pink in the face, too—from exertion. His forehead was a mirror of perspiration. He even huffed a little.

"Don't you think so, Mr. Redmond?" Lady Georgina was saying. "Whereas the ants we have here in Sussex are—"

"Georgina, how many times has the footman passed by in the last hour or so?"

"I . . . goodness, I haven't noticed. Your conversation has been so very interesting."

Like a group of gophers popping up out of holes, every head at the card table pivoted alertly in unison.

"Does that count?" Miles heard someone hiss. It sounded like Mr. Goodkind.

Some sort of earnest sotto voce conference took place among the card players. Their heads were so close together Miles could only see the tops of them. It became heated at one point—a hand waved out from the circle, adamantly.

And then everyone sat back, lifted their glasses in unison and took sips.

Cards were taken up again, a set of glances sent his way, then dropped immediately when they intercepted his steady gaze. He saw the quivering smiles hidden by the lowered faces.

"Lady Georgina. My apologies. Will you excuse me for one moment?" he said grimly.

"Cert—"

Miles was already up and striding away from her toward the game table.

A pair of gas lamps lit the card players—his father loved the modern conveniences, and he was always the first to employ them, and had the money to do it. And thus he was able to ascertain that his sister's eyes were downright glassy.

Everyone turned up faces of cautious greeting.

"Oh, *Milesh*!" Violet cried affectionately. They might have been reunited after eons apart. "I'm sho glad you're here! Where doesh Papa . . ." She paused and frowned. Then she leaned forward and pulled Lady Windermere very familiarly toward her. "What do you think I meant to ashk Milesh?" she whispered.

"Champagne," Lady Windermere prodded on an equally loud whisper.

"Oh!" She beamed. "Milesh, where doesh papa keep the . . . champagne?"

He'd never before seen Violet in her cups, and though part of him—the sibling part of him, the part that Jonathan, who no doubt at this very moment was in his cups at the Pig & Thistle, would have exploited with no compunction—thought it was very, very funny, the other part of him was incensed. He was responsible for her well-being, and she was far better bred than this; she ought to have known better, and he knew, he *knew,* who had encouraged this.

"Why do you ask, Violet?" His voice remained level.

Cynthia Brightly was steadfastly *not* looking at him. She was studying her cards as though they held the secret to her salvation, and biting one side of her lower lip in a vain attempt to keep it from curling up into a smile.

Violet was beckoning him closer with such great waving curls of her hand of cards that everyone could see them. Goodkind and Milthorpe leaned over to have a look.

Against his better judgment, Miles did lean toward his sister.

She caught hold of his coat sleeve, tugged him abruptly down, and whispered confidingly and somewhat regretfully close to his ear: "Becaush we *need* it, Milesh. The champagne. If you're to keep talking with Lady Georgina, we shall need champagne. Becaush the sherry's nearly gone."

Miles gently freed himself from his sister's grip and was upright again just as the footman approached with the sherry decanter.

Only to run into the great seething dark wall of Miles's gaze, turn on his heel and smoothly leave the way he'd come in.

Mr. Goodkind had opened a few buttons on his waistcoat to allow his stomach to billow forth. Milthorpe was scarlet-nosed and brilliantly scarlet veins webbed his cheeks. Lady Windermere was red and blotchy from the clavicle upward. The color clashed badly with her plum-colored gown and matching plumed turban, which for some reason was now listing badly, though it had been most decidedly upright on her head when the evening began. The plume of it now extended horizontally, and whenever she turned her head just a little, it inserted itself into Mr. Goodkind's ear. Mr. Goodkind brushed at his ear and smiled in a faintly pleased but puzzled manner every time it happened, but by the time he managed to turn his head, the plume was gone.

Miles watched this happen twice in the matter of seconds.

"Are you enjoying your evening?" he addressed the entire group. Some mischief in particular was collectively being enjoyed.

He disliked being excluded. He disliked not knowing what was afoot. And he had a strong sense it had something to do with him, and this he of course would ferret out easily enough.

"Oh, yes!" came an angelic chorus from the card players.

Then silence.

"What card game have you been playing?" He directed this pleasantly to Cynthia. He couldn't identify it from the number in their hands or the arrangement of the cards on the table.

Cynthia couldn't answer him, because Violet was speaking.

"Are *you* having a nice time, Milesh?" Her eyes were limpid with poignant concern. "*Are* you? You ought to have a good time every now and then, you know. And not just with *native girls*."

Violet clapped an appalled hand over her mouth and gazed up at him with mock innocence. She removed the hand carefully.

"*Hic,*" she said.

Miles felt his internal barometric pressure dropping to thunderstorm levels. He was furious at Violet, and furious at Cynthia, and furious at his circumstances, and furious because he was bored by Lady Georgina and furious because he was almost *never* furious.

"Forgive me, Miles," Violet apologized sadly. "It was jusht in there, I suppose, and out it came."

Miles turned his head slowly to look at Cynthia Brightly. Suppressed mirth was vibrating her like a leaf in a windstorm. Her eyes were watering and brilliant pink at the edges. Both of her hands were covering her mouth now, overlapping like palm leaves on the roof of a sturdy hut: wonderful for keeping out typhoons, when done properly. Or so he'd learned. She appeared to be attempting to keep a typhoon of laughter *in*.

"*Are* you having a nice time, Milesh?" Violet pressed, sounding a little belligerent now, as he hadn't answered her.

"Yes, Violet. I'm having a very lovely conversation with Lady Georgina. She is speaking to me of ant colonies, and I was sharing a few of my South Sea stories with her."

There was an instant, palpable hush. All those glassy eyes and rosy faces gazed at him for a fraught moment, studying him with unholy glee.

It was Mr. Goodkind who finally said it. In a falsetto, no less:

"Oh, Mr. Redmond. You're so *interesting*!"

The table exploded into laughter so uproarious Miles actually leaped backward.

Cynthia Brightly laid her face on the table sideways, her back jumping with such violent mirth she began to cough from it. Milthorpe sounded like a frantic donkey fleeing from a branding-iron-wielding farmer: *haw haw haw haw haw!* Goodkind's head was thrown back and his mouth was a perfect wide O from which issued long hoots of laughter. He gave the table a series of good hard slaps, which caused Lady Windermere's turban to at last vibrate from her head entirely, sending the plume fluffing into his eyes. His hoots stopped abruptly and he flailed at the plume in terror, then lost his balance and toppled from his chair, dragging down the tablecloth, all the sherry glasses, and finally, Lady Windermere, whose hem he'd seized in desperation on his final descent.

Lady Windermere went pop-eyed with alarm, flung her arms skyward and vanished below the table as though a shark had pulled her underwater.

Her hand cards sprayed up like sea foam then and rained down.

It was the funniest thing Miles had ever seen in his life.

He'd also seldom known such towering anger. Split neatly in half by the two poles of emotion, cleaved as if by lightning, he was speechless.

The rest of the table, however, was still crippled by laughter. Cynthia decided she ought to investigate her toppled comrades, but she began to topple when she bent over.

Miles bent over and began sorting them out. He reached into the melee and carefully seized the proper limbs—arms not legs, because Lady Windermere was involved—and got them upright and propped back into their chairs, where they slumped like marionettes. He was forced to retrieve Lady Windermere's turban as well. The plume had been crushed. Mr. Goodkind's flap of hair was vertical now, too, sitting like a little wall atop his head, a plume of sorts of his own.

"Shinthia is shooooo clever!" Violet said mistily. "God *bless* Shinthia. *Where* ish that footman with the sherry?"

Miles knew the best way to obtain information was to pretend near indifference to it. "*Why* is Miss Brightly clever, Violet?" He got the words out through clenched teeth.

Cynthia Brightly, with her instinct for self-preservation, had abruptly stopped laughing and was now waving her hands at his sister in some sort of frantic warning. But Violet was lost in admiration and eager to give her friend credit where credit was due.

"For thinking of the game."

Chapter 12

Cynthia vanished adroitly moments later when Miles turned briefly away. He would find her later, he thought grimly.

His primary directive was to get everyone more or less packed off to bed, but it took some time and strategy and a bit of negotiation. As it turned out, Milthorpe liked to sing when he was drunk, and Goodkind got a little maudlin and weepy when *he* was drunk. And then Jonathan and Argosy returned from the Pig & Thistle, both in their cups, delighted to find Milthorpe and Goodkind in kindred state, and they all had a sing over billiards.

Goodkind fell asleep with his chin balanced atop his hand atop a billiards cue.

The footmen were enlisted to help get everyone to their rooms; Miles's valet did double duty to pull off boots and pour large men into their beds. Miles instructed the maid to put the chamberpot next to Violet's bed, and knew that his sister deserved every bit of what she would likely feel the next day.

Lady Georgina was given a rote explanation for the rowdiness. She had brothers and a father; she was familiar with these types of events. She indulgently went up to her rooms.

He was about to do the very same as he left the billiard room. And later, he would never be certain why he paused near the library door on the way up to the third floor, fourth door on the left. When his faculties were finally returned to him, he would, of course, speculate in terms of the properties of physics: magnetic attractions, atmospheric disturbances, things of that sort, because analysis was what gave order and meaning to his world.

Regardless, pause he did.

And in that dark room, two things created light: the dying fire, and the shining head of the person bent toward it from a perch on the settee. An *unmistakable* head.

For an instant he went still and admired it the way he might the moon: with a helpless, impartial wonder. All those burnished shades of—

Oh, for God's sake. *Brown*. Her hair was *brown*. Her dress was some shade of *brown*. And the fact that Cynthia Brightly was still wearing it meant that she hadn't yet gone up to bed.

She was perched on a settee, her body curled forward toward the fire, her face cupped in her hands. Something about the pose implied . . . Was she . . . could she . . . could she be *weeping*?

He froze, instantly restless and panicked. He took a step forward.

A step backward.

And then her body slowly curled upright again, as lyrical as a flower blooming, and one hand dropped to her lap, and—

For God's sake. She'd been leaning over to light a damned *cheroot* in the fire.

She balanced it at her lips with a disconcertingly practiced motion and was clearly about to suck it into full flaming life when he spoke.

"Where did you find a cheroot?"

Her head whipped toward him and she launched her cheroot-holding hand the entire length of her arm away from her mouth, looking like a chaste maiden fighting off a zealous suitor. She froze that way, her eyes round and white as eggs.

Miles tried and failed to turn his laughter into a cough.

She reeled her arm back in. "I nearly swallowed this thing whole," she said peevishly. "I searched the house over for it, too."

"You went . . . searching . . . for a cheroot."

She stared at him, her head at a slight tip, dark brows diving toward the bridge of her nose. And then with pointed theatricality she slowly, slowly—*pruriently* slowly—inserted the tiny cigar between her lips, pursed them around it. And sucked until the tip was a tiny, angry red dot.

Miles was undecided as to whether he was fascinated or repelled. Though he was certain he was aroused. Out of genuine curiosity, he waited to see if she would cough or tear.

Instead she sagged elegantly against the generously curved arm of the settee, cast her head back and released a slim geyser of smoke toward the ceiling.

The elegant sagging shifted her bosom in the confines of her bodice, which was suddenly beautifully illuminated by firelight, soft, round, inviting. He stared.

And he was, in just about a thrice, hard as a rock.

"I searched the house over, and at last I found three of them in the humidor in this room. Fortunately this room already smells of cheroots."

"Muskets, sherry, and a room that stinks of tobacco. The stuff of every young lady's dreams."

"I find cheroots relax me."

"I suppose hunting heirs *can* ride roughshod over the nerves."

She rewarded this terse witticism with a duck of her head and held the cigar out before her to study the burning tip reflectively.

"The thing is . . . I find being incessantly . . . *good* . . . and sparkling leaves me strangely depleted. And as I will be allowed no habits at all when I am married—or rather, honor dictates that I continue with the habits I've demonstrated thus far—the urge suddenly overcame me."

Miles was silent. He didn't know which part of this revelation to address.

" 'Honor,' Miss Brightly?" he decided upon.

Her head turned sharply toward him. "I've more notion of honor than many of the people sleeping under this roof tonight, I'd warrant, Mr. Redmond."

She left her gaze level with his. He wondered suddenly whether he was included in the remark. Thinking of Lady Middlebough. Third floor, fourth room from the left. Which is where he should be right now.

She took his silence for the apology it was.

"What precisely was the nature of the game tonight?" he genuinely wanted to know.

"We were all to drink when Lady Georgina said, 'Oh, Mr. Redmond. You're so *interesting.*' "

He was struck. Imagine Cynthia noticing such a thing. And once again he was torn between hilarity and anger.

Georgina did say it rather a lot.

"Perhaps she thinks I'm very interesting." He said this dryly.

"That could very well be," Miss Brightly allowed skeptically.

He couldn't help it. He smiled. She shifted again on the settee, and her dress pulled at the swell of her breasts, and his smile vanished, and he felt that familiar difficulty with his breathing.

"She's very nice," she added. It sounded almost like an accusation.

"That isn't her fault," Miles said quickly.

Which then struck both of them as funny, and they both smiled this time. The smoke she'd released now hovered over them like a net about to drop.

Leave now, you bloody, bloody fool, the voice in Miles's head said.

"Have you considered that you'll spend your entire wedded life 'depleted,' as you say, Miss Brightly?"

She turned to look at him. "Depleted but *rich*," she corrected slowly, deliberately.

He went still.

And then the fury was instant and seemed to come from nowhere and everywhere.

It propelled him into the room and down on his knees next to her so swiftly she didn't have time to gasp: he gained an impression of her wide blue eyes and of the cheroot tip glaring between her fingers like a third accusing eye.

And then he plucked it from her fingers and hurled it into the fire. They stared, astonished, toward where it vanished, devoured with a pop and a hiss.

Silently they sat. Miles watched the flame inexorably reducing the log to ashes, feeling oddly spent. After a time, he became aware of Cynthia's breathing beneath the groans and pops and hisses of the fire. The logs sounded as though they were objecting to being consumed.

He turned slowly. She wasn't staring at the fire.

She was staring at him, and some expression that haunted him fled her eyes when he turned. Shadows of flame leaped and shivered over her throat, as though she herself were being consumed.

As if to test whether this was true, he watched his hand move toward her. His fingers landed softly, softly, beneath her jaw.

Her breath snagged audibly. And so did his.

He couldn't stop.

She didn't stop him.

With two fingers he slowly, purposefully, gently, followed both the clean, fine line of her jaw and the unthinkably soft skin beneath, marveling at this contrast in textures.

Like a vigilant chaperone, he watched his own fingers as he drew them slowly, slowly, down, down, down. Her throat was satiny and hot, frighteningly delicate. Her pulse bumped hard there, sending blood rushing through her veins, flushing her skin with a heat that transferred itself to his own skin. The surface of it felt feverish, every cell of his body alert to, craving, sensation.

Onward his fingers journeyed. They made an almost whimsical figure eight over those bones at the base of her long neck.

"I don't want you," she said. It was a cracked whisper.

Miles, the truth seeker, sought proof of this. Lower, just a little lower, just above the pale round give of her breast, his fingers found again her rapid heartbeat. He paused them there to savor, with vindication, its tempo, and levered his head up to meet her eyes.

It was the only warning he gave her before he eased his forefinger into that alluring crease between her breasts.

Her head jerked back; her lips parted on a silent gasp; her rib cage gave a minute leap.

"I don't want you, either," he whispered, too. It seemed the proper language for the dark, the language to use when touching bare skin.

And at that, she smiled faintly: that was the lies out of the way, then.

And when Miles slowly withdrew his finger from its silken berth, desire dragged a slow, rapier line down his spine, and he was tense and shaking with it.

Ah, but he was a man of method. He retraced his path, lightly up over her chest, her throat, to her face.

And there at last he tipped his fingers up, creating a little cradle for her jaw.

Cynthia turned her cheek into his palm. And as he once suspected, it fit into his hand as though carved for the purpose.

Her eyelids drifted closed.

His thumb ran once over her cheek. Oh, God. There were no words for how soft her skin was.

They were creating something dangerous and foolish that could never end well. *Pleasurably*, perhaps. But not well.

But it felt like gamesmanship. Miles disliked the quality in people; he disliked *strategizing*. It reminded him a bit too much of his father. He resented that Cynthia brought out the quality in him, and he resented the tremble in his hands, because it made him feel foolish, naive, for thinking that anything he'd felt for any other woman before now qualified as desire. He now knew he'd only known . . . appetite before. The one he could satisfy at whim.

This . . . *this* had him at its mercy.

And implicit in surrendering was the fear he would simply never sate himself.

To hell with gamesmanship. He knew how to be direct.

He took his hand abruptly from beneath her cupped chin,

180

fitted it around the back of her neck, and sought with his fingers that column of tiny buttons that closed it up.

In a thrice he had the top one undone.

Shock stiffened Cynthia's spine. He undid another. She possessed a voice, he reminded himself. She could use it if she wanted him to stop. She possessed the ability to fly up off that settee in indignation or deliver a stinging slap.

She showed no signs of doing any of that.

Still, he felt obliged to offer her those options, and did so by raising his brows in a query.

Ah, but she'd turned her head away from him ever so slightly just then. He suspected—no, he knew—it was so she could pretend the choice hadn't been offered. And with this realization, suddenly lust was a riptide. And as for his erection . . . well, it was hardly poetry, but the words "ax handle" sprang to mind.

He easily and quickly thumbed open the remaining tiny buttons; the holes were loose from being done up and undone over and over during two seasons worth of balls and soirees. Those loose buttonholes were a reminder of Cynthia Brightly's straightened circumstances. But he didn't pause to reflect.

He wanted. He wanted.

And then they were open, all of them, and the fabric of her bodice loosened and sagged, and her throat moved in a swallow. He felt her head turn again to watch him. Flickering firelight tended to distort expressions; the glance he cast made him think he saw uncertainty in hers. But he promptly buried his face into the crook of her throat so he wouldn't need to wonder about it.

A few threads of her hair came down to brush his cheek; he breathed her in, sweetness and smoke. He considered then that he ought to have begun by kissing her mouth. In truth he was working his way toward her lips because he now knew he could lose himself entirely there, and the idea of experiencing that sort of vertigo again unnerved him.

He surprised himself by licking her instead.

Given how rigid she went, he wasn't the only one surprised by the licking.

Still, he'd begun, and he felt compelled to commit to it. His tongue continued in a slow line up the cord of her throat. Cynthia remained unnervingly still, tense as a harp string.

He began to feel a trifle uncertain. Was she . . . shocked? Frightened? Horri—

She exploded in a muffled giggle.

Wonderful. She'd been suppressing *hilarity*.

"For heaven's sake, Redmond. You're not a *spaniel*. And I'm not a bone, so you needn't go at me with your tongue like—"

His tongue flicked out to touch, delicately, the lobe of her ear.

Which silenced her instantly.

He knew why: the promise inherent in *that* particular little caress made the point—he knew things about her body she'd never suspected, and how to make her feel things she'd never imagined. And because of the sensations one flick of his tongue against her ear had sent through her body, she was in thrall to possibility.

He followed through on the promise.

He dipped his tongue into her little ear. Delicately. Once, twice. His breath soft and warm there, too. He took her lobe lightly between his lips. Cynthia exhaled a soft breath, sucked in a deeper one, and her body shifted on the settee, her fingers slowly curling and uncurling in the plump velvet in an attempt to accommodate the current of new pleasure he was sending through her body.

He left her ear to blow softly over the path his tongue had traced.

"Oh . . . *oh.*"

One "oh" for comprehension, the last one—the fractured whisper—for arousal.

Cynthia's hand stirred indecisively then on the settee. And then it took slow flight, and came to rest softly on the back of his neck. Her fingers knit up through his hair.

And with this act she was fully complicit.

It also reminded him that he'd been keeping his own hands knotted against his thighs, as if in solidarity with the ax handle cock imprisoned in his trousers. Ridiculously delighted to recall he possessed hands, he freed them to do what he'd intended to do all along: lower that bodice.

Miles devoted himself to kissing her throat now, kisses involving lips and tongue and teeth, the variety intended to dazzle her senses and distract her from the fact that his hands were now peeling the dress away from her shoulders and would have her breasts out in seconds. Her neck arced to abet his kisses; her fingertips glided over the nape of his neck, her nails lightly, lightly scoring his skin, sending threads of lightning through his veins. *Sweet merciful*—

And then at last the dress slipped the rest of the way of its own gravity with a silken sigh of its own. Cynthia Brightly was nude from the waist up, and Miles abruptly stopped kissing, to admire. Her breasts were saucy and luscious and vulnerable, and before the woman who possessed them could become fully aware of how exposed she was, he cupped his fingers beneath the silky curve of one and bent his head to apply his tongue with wonder and skill.

Cynthia made a sound, something between a gasp and a whimper.

The velvety wet heat of his mouth shocked her. The sensation unbearably exquisite in a way she was tempted to battle. It was too much, and too good, and too foreign, and she was frightened.

And she'd told herself she would be *good*.

And still his tongue did slow deliberate things to the stiff peak of her nipple as his fingers feathered along the tender skin beneath her breast, and hot ribbons of sensation unfurled through her body.

"Miles."

She wanted him to stop.

She couldn't bear it if he stopped.

He did stop.

But only long enough to rise up from the floor and in a fluid motion stretch his long body alongside her on the settee. He gently and expertly folded her into his arms as though anticipating no protest or struggle, as if it to cover and protect her, though he was the one who'd exposed her. She offered no protest or struggle. He sought her mouth with his; she gave it to him with hunger and relief.

Her lips parted for him, and his tongue found hers, and she took it greedily. She was new to this sort of kissing, this sort of kissing that led places and meant things, but she didn't care: it became a battling kiss, a hot and graceless tangle, deep and invading, dark and drugging. She learned and refined as she kissed him; she gave back what he took and wanted more.

So it was this she needed: his tongue in her mouth, and now, just now; and then to feel the low moan in his throat vibrating through her.

I did this to him.

But as his tongue plunged and tasted, drove her to depths she didn't know she possessed, dissolved the supports of the world from beneath her, his fingers were gliding so very,

very lightly, reverently, over the surface of her bare back. Skimming the blades of her shoulders, following the line of her spine up to the fine hairs at the nape of her neck, leaving a trail of sparks on her skin. The sensation was like being simultaneously devoured and cherished.

Her eyes felt hot with something nearly like tears.

She broke the kiss abruptly, placed a hand hard against his chest.

"I don't—" she whispered urgently, her voice shredded and frightened.

His hands froze on her; he stared down at her, his dark eyes glittering even in the shadows, nearly obscured by the fall of his hair. What had he done with his spectacles? He must have deftly removed them. His vast shoulders beneath her hands rose and fell hard.

What was he thinking? What was he feeling? She didn't dare ask.

At last she shook her head roughly, unable to say anything or even remember what she'd meant to say. She found her hands on either side of his face, pulling him down to her mouth again.

She was afraid of herself.

She stopped kissing him to reach for his shirt buttons, and she stared at her ten fingers dumbly, as though she could not be held responsible for their actions as they worked open the first one. She felt Miles Redmond's eyes on her face; she ignored him and frowned with concentration, until four of his buttons were open. She gently spread his collar, arced up and until her breasts met his skin.

She felt his belly shift over her as he drew in a sharp breath. His eyes closed. He exhaled at length.

"This," she whispered to herself, surprised and satisfied, as though she'd solved a puzzle.

How did her body know what it wanted? How could she allow it to rule her?

She slipped her hands inside his shirt and pressed them against the sticky heat of his skin, marveling; she found a thudding heartbeat beneath the silky net of hair, beneath that shockingly masculine muscle. The heartbeat proved definitively that Miles was a *man* beneath his scientist's clothes.

And as if to underscore entirely *this* particular point, he seized her wrist.

He placed her hand over his cock. And then dragged her hand slowly, roughly down the length of him. "Like this."

The coarse demand frightened and thrilled her. She obeyed, just as he'd shown her, and he hissed in a breath that was pure pleasure.

Good God, but he was astonishingly hard. Wonder and curiosity took over: Cynthia's hand instinctively sought out the full and alarming contours of him, marveling.

"Again." His raw whisper shook with tension. "Again."

She did, and he shifted, his thighs falling apart to allow her hand to roam freely.

"Mother of *God*." The words were a groan. His hands slid hard down her back to her buttocks and cupped them to lift her roughly against him, and he was so rigid he hurt her, hurt the soft join of her legs. But she wanted him there, and pressed herself closer to him, and she gasped at an unfamiliar bliss. She suddenly felt the air of the room on her calves as he began to furl her dress up in his fingers. Quickly. Her body was bowstring tense, shaking with a need she didn't understand, her limbs stiff and awkward with it. She only knew she needed him closer, closer. She widened her legs, pulled him closer.

She wrapped her arms around his neck, *"Please"* she said, her voice shaking.

She didn't know why, or what she meant, or what she really wanted. It was the voice of her body, not of her mind.

His fingers were touching the backs of her calves now, stroking up.

"Cynthia . . ." His voice was low and dark. He made her name sound both like a warning and a hosanna. "Cynthia . . ."

Her own breath had become a storm in her ears.

His fingers were now on her thighs, above the tops of her stockings. Slipping beneath them to slide over the cool bare skin of her thighs. Closer, closer, to the source of her need.

"God," he groaned. He pulled her more tightly against him. He lifted her thigh to wrap his leg, and he pushed his groin against her.

"Miles . . ." Her voice shook. "I . . ."

"Christ . . ." he murmured. He rocked with her, his arms trembling as he propped himself over her, as he pressed against her, and she clung, whimpering. He reached for his trouser buttons, had two of them open. Stopped.

"Cynthia . . . you can't . . . we can't . . ."

And suddenly with an oath Miles tore himself from her.

They were so entwined, it felt as though her own limbs were being ripped from her when he abruptly sat up and flattened his hands on his thighs. His broad back imitated bellows.

He sat for a moment like that. Breathing in and out, raggedly. Then tipped his forehead on his hand. She watched him struggle with himself, struggle to regain sense, as she lay sprawled, bare, disheveled, bereft. She wanted to touch him. She didn't dare touch him.

He'd done the very right thing.

At last he turned toward her. Stiffly; painfully, nearly. Even in the dark she could see that his expression was amazed and tense with a peculiar anger they seemed to inspire in each other.

"There's more, Miss Brightly."

His words returned sobriety to her as surely as a slap.

He'd known how desperately she wanted; he'd known *what* she wanted, even as she wasn't entirely certain. And he confirmed what she'd suspected.

And left her wanting more. Wondering about more. When they could never, ever, ever have more from each other.

And with sobriety came shame.

She crossed her arms over her breasts, fumbled with awkward hands for the edges of her bodice to tug it up again, as she watched a man apparently do battle with his confusion, and lash out at her because of it.

And she couldn't feel as angry as she wanted to. Because she felt his suffering as surely as her own.

She found his spectacles on the table before the fire. She leaned over, and he was still as she slid them onto his face, a gesture so instinctive, so natural, it surprised both of them.

He made a short sound. Almost a laugh.

They sat in silence; together and apart.

And then suddenly he reached for a cheroot in the humidor, leaned forward and held it coaxingly out to the fire, as if offering a morsel to her kitten. The fire licked it alight.

He held it out to her. "I thought you might need to relax."

She stared at the cheroot dumbly. Then she took it with shaking hands and stared at it as though she'd forgotten the English word for it.

"And it's much more relaxing if you actually *inhale*, Miss Brightly."

She whipped her head toward him. The bloody man had known all along.

He was smiling a little, faintly. Struggling to restore his sanity and hers with lightness.

But did he know *everything*? It struck her suddenly as grossly unfair, the advantage he had over her. This perceptive, probing man.

But then again, she wasn't the only person at the mercy of whatever it was between them.

She wanted to drop her head into her hands, too. To surrender to the impulse to be weak for once. But she wouldn't allow him to see it. Instead her head did the opposite: her chin jerked up. She stared at him.

And after a moment he stood, swiftly and deftly buttoned his shirt, shoving the miles of it down into his trousers, flattening his palms over his hair, which was in astounding disarray.

Fine hair, so soft, and too much of it, she thought, watching him. Her thumb and forefinger slid together absently, as though she could feel it between her fingers.

Miles waited there a moment indecisively. Opened his mouth to say something, shook his head roughly.

And of all things, bowed.

And left her.

Chapter 13

⌒⊂∞⊃⌒

The next day four of them set out to visit the Gypsies. Goodkind shuddered at the idea of having his fortune read, Lady Windermere and Lady Middlebough had gone to visit a Sussex neighbor, and Lord Milthorpe had gone to see another neighbor about a horse he wished to buy.

And Miles Redmond and Lady Georgina stayed behind as well.

Jonathan wagged his eyebrows. "I b'lieve Miles will be leg-shackled ere long."

No one took up this comment. Violet gave a little grunt, as last night's sherry had not been kind to her, and Argosy slid Cynthia a look full of mysterious portent.

Cynthia was boarded into the carriage in the morning, quiet and desolate and utterly absorbed, and doing her best to disguise it, because Argosy was clearly full of admiration for her and enthusiasm for their escapade.

Pennyroyal Green in daylight was charming: the pub named for a farm animal and a weed and the little stone church sat across from each other, as though cheerfully resigned to the fact they shared the same customers. Two enormous trees grew closely together at the very center of the village, and off in the distance, up on a hill, a stately building rose: Miss Endicott's Academy for Young Ladies, not too secretly referred to as the "School for Recalcitrant Girls" by the townspeople. A swath of brilliant, fragile red poppies lead up to it.

"We should have put Violet there many years ago," Jonathan told Cynthia.

"I should have organized a mutiny," Violet said easily. "It would not have been *sensible* to put me there."

"Doubtless you are right," Jonathan agreed, yawning. He'd been awake very, very late over billiards with Milthorpe and Argosy, and he'd had rather more to drink than his sister or Cynthia.

Violet, pale from far too many glasses of sherry during last night's drinking game, had only cast her accounts once, she'd confided proudly to Cynthia. Cynthia's head felt a little woolly, but she was quite accustomed to fast living and had been equal to the sherry. She was subdued for an entirely different reason.

"Well, I'm certain I'll learn from the Gypsies that I shall take a long ocean journey and meet a tall, dark stranger," Violet said.

Jonathan laughed. "I only *wish* you'd take a long ocean journey."

She gave him a little kick.

"Children," Cynthia said.

Still, it fascinated her, and sometimes taunted her to the point of restlessness: this easiness, this playfulness, this taken-for-granted affection and history and money. She wanted it. She wanted it for *her* children.

She *wanted* children. She wanted a family.

Argosy smiled at her warmly. His thigh was but three inches from hers.

She saw her own thighs in an entirely different light now,

191

since she'd had them wide open and dangerously wrapped with Miles Redmond's last night. Her hands curled tightly into her dress to steady herself as the memory washed through her body and made her weak with want.

"*Miles* took a long ocean journey. But he returned," Jonathan said.

"Miles will always return," Violet said contentedly. "No matter what he does. He's quite reliable."

Cynthia had left the quite reliable Miles's arms in a fog of banked desire, said good night to Susan the Spider and Spider the cat, and expected to lie awake in a torment of confusion and desire both banked and thwarted; to doze fitfully, be torn from sleep by her nightmare, and doze off again until the maid arrived to build the fire.

Instead, oddly, there was something protected now about her room, despite Miles. No: *because* of Miles. Because he'd given her a small cat, which vibrated, alternately, on her stomach, her knees, and finally—at least when she awoke— on her head.

She'd slept the night through. Another miracle.

There's more, Miss Brightly. Desire at once arrowed through her, and her breathing hitched.

Argosy smiled secretly, just for her. Why didn't *his* very nearness, his fine features, make her weak? Why didn't she picture melting against his slim body and wrapping her thighs around—

"The Gypsies are here every year?" Cynthia said instantly, to get the word "Miles" out of the carriage and out of the conversation and out of her thoughts.

"Oh, yes. Since I can remember," Jonathan said. "I've known the Heron family for years. We were sometimes allowed to see their entertainments as children. And I like them well enough, thieves and rascals though they are. I wouldn't call them a *bad* sort. But the fortune telling is pure nonsense."

He yawned again.

Cynthia exchanged an indulgent glance with Argosy: we know better, it said.

The carriage horses were pulled to a halt at the edge of a meadow that rolled softly, like a blanket carelessly tossed aside on a bed. There was a rise over which they couldn't see, but intriguing masculine laughter, hoofbeats, and shouted Rom—the Gypsy language—floated from the other side of it.

In the midst of it they heard the word "Samuel" sharply said. And more laughter.

A good dozen or so tents were concentrically pitched about a central campfire that had burned low, now half ash, half glow. A cooking pot swung over it; something savory scented the air. A smooth yellow dog sleeping outside the tent lifted his head questioningly and lowered it again, deciding they were nothing to become excited over. Perhaps it had seen the *gadji* come and go for weeks now, hoping to be told their destinies in their palms.

Curious about the noise, they turned in a sort of idle, tacit agreement to scale the small rise before entering the camp. They looked down.

Cynthia froze, breathless.

A copper-colored horse was stretched out in an easy gallop across the meadow, and this was lovely but hardly shocking. The slim man standing—*standing*—on the back of it was, however. Like a bird riding a current of air, his arms were outstretched and he tipped them now subtly, now deeply, like wings, in rhythm to the horses' rippling muscles and easy gait.

It was as disorienting as if they'd been plunged into a collective dream.

Then they heard deep laughter, and swiveled their heads, noticing the other man: shorter and broader at the shoulder, holding by the halter a restive brown horse sporting four handsome white stockings. He called something to the balancing man in delighted Rom; they heard him say "Samuel" again. It all sounded like approbation. And that the young man's name was Samuel.

Then the broader man swung himself up onto the brown horse and nudged and clucked it into a gallop.

"They're horse acrobats," Jonathan murmured. "They travel the country. They make most of their money at the Cambridge Horse Fair."

The man atop the brown horse man levered himself into a standing position, and the two horses, nudged by the feet, the muscles, the Rom commands of the men, carried their cargoes toward each other at a determined canter.

Violet gripped Cynthia's arm. "What are they *doing*? I can't look!"

But she was, of course, not only looking, but *feasting* on the spectacle. Excitement crackled from her. And Jonathan and Argosy, being men—riveted by anything that appeared dangerous or could kill them, or so it seemed to Cynthia— were motionless, too.

The animals drew abreast, and the men leaped from the horses in unison.

The quartet gasped, and Violet clutched Cynthia's arm.

There was an airborne eternity that in truth lasted only a second as the men sailed past each other. The stocky man landed neatly on the back of Samuel's mount, strong thighs flexing to a crouch, then pushing upward to stand.

The slim man crashed into the side of the brown horse, scrabbled futilely for a grip, then slid ignominiously to land in a heap on the ground.

A burst of laughter escaped Violet before she could clap her hands over her mouth.

The sleeping yellow dog leaped to life, wagging furiously and dashing to lick the prone Gypsy, as if he'd just been waiting for such an opportunity. Samuel struggled to an upright position as the brown horse trotted nonchalantly off. Riderless. Looking for all the world resigned.

The Gypsy called Samuel looked up, shading his eyes, and scowled in Violet's general direction, where the peals of laughter were coming from.

"I am glad I can amuse you, *Gadji*."

"I am glad, too," Violet called cheerfully.

Her brother shot her a warning look—Redmonds did not flirt with Gypsies—which she of course ignored.

"I could have been hurt."

"But you are not," Violet said pragmatically. "Or not very, anyway. Are you?"

"No," he conceded after a moment. He sounded good natured about it.

Samuel rubbed the yellow dog's ears and said something to it in Rom that made it wag all the more vigorously. He said something else that was apparently much less polite to his partner, who threw up his hands and responded with a stream of amused-sounding Rom. His partner was laughing at him, too.

"The *first* part was very nice," Violet called, in an attempt to mollify.

Cynthia gave Violet's arm a squeeze. She wasn't certain whether Violet would interpret it as encouragement or warning.

"Was it, *Gadji*? Perhaps you'd like to give it a try?" It was elegantly sarcastic.

"Could I?"

"Violet," Jonathan warned again. This time the warning had an edge. "Miles will *kill* you."

Samuel whistled to the wandering horse, which was now docilely nipping at meadow grasses. The horse ambled over, and Samuel reached up for its halter and used it to pull himself to his feet.

He led his mount over to the group.

His eyes were remarkable: brilliant, alder-leaf green. An extraordinarily pure color, as though no one in his lineage had ever mated with anyone with eyes of a different color. His nose was narrow with a bit of a hook, and his lips were full, the upper one arching over the bottom to form very nearly the shape of a heart. He'd tucked copper-streaked brown hair behind his ears. His skin was the burnished shade of a copper kettle, a degree lighter than the coat of his horse.

Handsome devil, in other words. Young, slim, exotic.

Cynthia immediately understood the appeal of the exotic. And she was not at all immune to handsome devils.

But he seemed to have eyes only for Violet. Who, to the consternation of her brother, was not at all displeased at being the subject of Gypsy attention and was returning it measure for measure.

"Your have almost Gypsy eyes, *Gadji*," he said to Violet, as though answering a question she had posed. "Nearly as beautiful."

Violet's eyes widened at the boldness. Jonathan and Argosy moved in closer, to sandwich her between them.

The stocky Gypsy said something to Samuel in Rom. It had the distinctive tone of a warning. Samuel gave a start and seemed to take his first very close look at the men.

"It is Mr. Jonathan Redmond!" He bowed low to Jonathan. "Forgive me. I didna recognize you. 'Twas yer 'at, ye

196

see. 'id yer face." He smiled, touched his hand to his forehead, to make it a jest.

Jonathan relaxed his brotherly protective stance somewhat. "How goes it, Samuel? I have not seen you . . ."

"Since two years. I have traveled with my uncle"—he gestured behind him to the stocky man—"to learn the horses."

Silence.

And then all in a rush Jonathan said, "Will you show me how to ride the horses like—"

"Good God, no, *Gadji*, I am not mad, and you are not a Gypsy. We do it for money, not for fun," he said, matter-of-factly. He was amused. "Ye'll break bones. Yer brother will kill me then."

"Gypsies do *everything* for money," Argosy said. He was bristling with jealous fascination.

"Your friend is correct," Samuel said cheerfully. He turned curiously to Lord Argosy.

"Anthony Cordell, Lord Argosy." Jonathan provided the introduction, and Argosy provided the bow, which was a thing of majesty.

Samuel bowed low, too, though his bow looked theatrical and almost mocking.

"And this is my sister, Miss Violet Redmond, and our friend, Miss Cynthia Brightly." Jonathan gave the word "sister" a bit of a warning inflection.

Samuel the Gypsy's eyes widened briefly, and he gave a quick nod. "I've not yet 'ad the pleasure of meeting yer sister." His voice had gone formal. "And 'tis a pleasure indeed . . . Why 'ave you come for a visit, friends? We leave tomorrow." He gestured at the camp, which still looked intact.

"We'd hoped to have our fortunes told," Cynthia told him.

He gave her a dazzling smile, and lingered on her face speculatively. "Ah! Ye'd like someone to dukker for ye, *Gadji*?"

A lethal flirt, this one. Cynthia enjoyed lethal flirts. Argosy stirred beside her, like a young bird of prey ruffling its feathers in warning.

Ah, this was good. But she must be very careful.

Violet was a bit too quiet. She was watching the Gypsy boy raptly. But he seemed to have forgotten her after his initial burst of flirtation, or he was carefully not flirting with the daughter of a Redmond, because he did not want to be skewered on a Redmond pike.

"Very well." Samuel said. "Follow me. It's of a certainty me auntie will dukker—tell your fortune—for ye, if ye've coin fer it."

The four English guests followed the slightly limping Gypsy, who led the brown horse and was followed by the yellow dog.

"Probably stolen," Argosy muttered. "The horse."

"Probably," Samuel said cheerfully over his shoulder. "I canna recall."

Samuel disappeared into the third tent they came to, and emerged followed by a sallow Rom girl dressed in shades of beige and brown. Her somber clothing was almost an apology for the springing abandon of her curls. Cynthia swiftly counted nine hairpins glinting in the mass, but snakes of glossy dark hair bobbed everywhere over her forehead anyway. Her face was spherical and the color of tea mixed with milk; her eyes were a shade darker than harvest moons.

"I shall dukker for ye, *Gadji*," she said. "But I mun see yer coin, first like."

"Martha! Come away."

The scolding voice emerged from another tent, and turned out to belong to a tall handsome woman with a comet tail of silver striping her dark hair. "Ye're not yet ready to dukker, as ye ken. Ye've work to do. Off." Then she said something rapidly in Rom that made Martha's face darken, and the girl vanished with a flounce back into the tent.

The woman sighed, said something sternly to Samuel in Rom. He replied contritely and glanced at Cynthia. The woman nodded.

And then Samuel receded with a waved farewell to the English visitors and a flick of a glance at Violet, who watched him go.

"Come with me, my friends," the woman said pleasantly. "I am Mrs. Leonora Heron. The auntie of Samuel. I mun see the color of yer money before I dukker."

"How much?" This came briskly from Jonathon.

The Gypsy must have assessed her company in an eye-blink: all the shininess apparent—boots and buttons—fabrics spotless, clothing expensive, cut to fit each of them expressly. They were clearly all cared for by servants. They had smooth faces and spotlessly gloved hands.

"Six shillings," was her exorbitant response. She smiled serenely.

Cynthia coughed. It was the price of a stagecoach ride from London to Edinburgh. The woman's nerve was admirable. Her acumen impressive.

Argosy shrugged. He shook six shillings from a purse inside his coat and handed them over to the Gypsy, who gave each one an insultingly close examination.

They passed inspection.

She motioned her aristocratic friends into the tent, which was pungent with the smell of dried herbs and lit by a single large oil lamp, which enclosed them in glow and atmospherically portentous shadows. Cynthia saw their silhouettes thrown against the back wall of the tent, and she thought, as Jonathan and Argosy moved closer together, that their shadows together made one the size of Miles Redmond.

She squared her shoulders and tossed her head. Argosy was handsome, and his purse clinked as though it were nearly bottomless, and here he was, next to her, smiling, eager to be supernaturally persuaded that she would be part of his future.

Miles had slept badly. A carafe of very black coffee and the content of his correspondence revived his mood, however. He'd broken half a dozen seals this morning on letters from members of the Royal Society. Half a dozen brilliant, adventurous men expressing enthusiasm, pledging time and resources for his next expedition.

He savored the thrill quietly; the satisfaction ran bone-deep. Not once had he doubted he would return to Lacao on a grander scale, because he'd always accomplished everything he set out to do.

But it might have taken years to plan, years to amass the proper resources and financing.

And now . . . well, now the dream of returning to Lacao was as far away as his own nuptials. And he imagined the thrill of announcing that the expedition had been fully and neatly financed.

He thought about passion, and the forms it took.

He thought about Cynthia Brightly, enclosed in a carriage with Argosy on the way to visit the Gypsies; there was nothing like an enclosed space to nurture intimacy. She would next be enclosed in a tent with Argosy, if they were to have their fortunes told. Jonathan and Violet would be there, too, of course, and no untoward intimacies would take place. And Argosy was a gentleman.

But the idea of her in dark places, close to another man who would one day have the privilege—the right—to touch her skin whenever he wished it—

He jerked his thoughts roughly back to his other passion, his other world: Lacao, and an expedition, and the girl who was the means to it all, and therefore, he told himself, must be a part of his passion, too. Because his mind had a gift for rationalization, and refused to be subjugated to the mad desires of his body.

Miles stood up quickly and forged the stairs, because he was almost late to meet Lady Georgina to take her for a stroll. He'd set the appointment yesterday, once it had become clear that everyone else would be otherwise occupied. And because he was dutiful.

She stood diffidently in the downstairs drawing room, in muslin striped in pale yellow the precise shade of her hair. He watched her surreptitiously from his peculiarly aerial position. He could see her hands, covered in white gloves, folded tightly, nervously, together; her face was already funneled in a large straw bonnet, decorated with lively silk flowers.

Nothing about Georgina caused his mind to launch into embarrassingly florid superlatives. Nothing about her affected his breathing or his temper. His mind, in fact, functioned just as admirably in her presence as it did in her absence.

He gazed down and tried to picture her standing in his home, greeting their guests, should they marry. He pictured her in bed, his body covering her lush white body, her shy gray eyes gazing up at him, those round breasts—

His mind could gain no purchase on any of the images. They altogether refused to form. Thinking it felt like a betrayal. And this was patently ridiculous and unnerving and confusing.

She admired him fiercely, at least. It was in her eyes, in the light of her face when she heard his footsteps on the stairs as he came down now. This was flattering and inexplicable.

But perhaps an indication that the girl had a certain sensibility after all. She should have been mooning for Jonathan. Or for Argosy. Who was at this moment enclosed in a carriage with—

"Beautiful day for a walk, Georgina."

Why did he always begin with the weather? Because "Platitude" was a language everyone spoke, he supposed.

"Oh, yes!" she agreed.

"Perhaps the lediboptera will be out in force." He was teasing her by getting the word wrong.

"I hope so," she agreed eagerly.

He stifled a sigh. His sense of humor always seemed to alarm her into earnestness. He didn't think Georgina unintelligent. Perhaps once she was filled with someone else's thoughts and opinions they would then transmute into thoughts of her own, like specimens grown under different laboratory conditions.

And then he had a useful but traitorous thought: it would be no sacrifice to leave her behind when he went on an expedition, and perhaps that was reason enough to wed her.

As they strolled by in the garden, and he asked Georgina to tell him of her interests, a common blue flapped by.

He didn't point it out to her. It was something, somehow, he wanted to keep for himself.

Chapter 14

⎯⎯⎯⎯◦⎯⎯⎯⎯

The extravagantly curled Gypsy girl was in the corner of the tent when the quartet entered, rustling and clinking things, adding them to a trunk. As Samuel Heron had said, they were making ready to break camp.

"Sit, please, my friends." Leonora Heron gestured vaguely. There were no chairs.

Violet was always reluctant to muss anything, and she glanced skeptically at the floor of the tent. But it appeared to be spotless, and the place *smelled* very clean, like an apothecary, or a doctor's office.

Her brother gave a long-suffering sigh, produced a handkerchief, and spread it out for her on the ground. She knelt upon it.

They *all* knelt in the circle of light.

"How do you see the future?" Argosy was breathless with eagerness.

He was close to Cynthia. His knee, quite daringly, brushed hers, moved away, brushed again. This contributed to his breathlessness. Cynthia kept her own knee very still. She watched her shadow blend with his and part on the tent wall across from them as they leaned toward Mrs. Heron. She felt a peculiar twinge of oppression.

And then their shadows separated again when he turned to smile at her, that easy, secret smile, those white teeth in his amber-tinted symmetrical face.

"I shall dukker by reading your palms and the leaves, brother," she said. "Martha, bring in the kettle, please."

The girl stood and flounced out of the tent, but not without touching lowered-lashed looks upon all the young men. Jonathan was not immune to this particular look. He smiled.

Argosy, however, was utterly focused on the business at hand. "You will read our palms, and the tea leaves for all of us?"

"Six shillings more to read the leaves," Mrs. Heron said placidly.

"*Mrs.* Heron . . ." Jonathan was alarmed.

Argosy had his purse out and was poking through it. "I can give you three shillings."

"Six shillings for all of you to read the leaves," Mrs. Heron said gently but firmly.

Argosy looked at Jonathan, who shrugged, and turned out his palms to indicate he had nothing.

"Three shillings for just Miss Brightly and myself?" Argosy gave Cynthia one of his little secret smiles.

"Certainly." Mrs. Heron smiled. "It is the cost of tea, you know," she added, by way of apology. "I canna *give* the dukker away."

"All right," Argosy said, sounding bored.

Cynthia doubted that he ever considered the cost of anything. He probably didn't know the cost of tea. But Gypsies were very clever, she thought. The cost of the reading certainly had nothing to do with the cost of tea.

Martha returned with the kettle, hovered in the lamplight to ensure that both Jonathan and Argosy were able to get a good look at her. Leonora Heron said something in Rom, and she handed over the kettle with a pout and retreated reluctantly to the edges of the tent.

Leonora Heron then shook earthy-smelling leaves from a packet into the bottom of two shallow white cups and poured the steaming water over them. Cynthia, half mesmerized, watched the water slowly darken into drinkable tea.

"While it becomes tea I will dukker wi' yer palm. Turn your hand up so, *Gadji*," she said to Jonathan. She demonstrated with her own hand.

With a wry look at his sister, Jonathan extended his hand and gave it to Mrs. Heron.

Argosy watched breathlessly, leaning forward.

"Ye'll 'ave a long, long life . . ." Leonora murmured matter-of-factly, sounding a bit distracted, tracing a finger over his palm. "Ye'll break one heart. It might be your own, I canna say . . ."

"Oh ho!" Jonathan said nervously. Everyone else rustled a little, too.

She peered beneath his little finger. "Ye'll have ten children—"

Jonathan snatched his hand away as though she'd spat in it.

Leonora Heron's eyes widened innocently. Cynthia half-suspected she'd read Jonathan's character correctly, too, that the Gypsy woman had known precisely how he would react to that particular bit of news and saw a way to earn her shillings easily.

"I'm done," Jonathan said simply.

Mrs. Heron shrugged. "Next, Miss Redmond, I will read yours."

Violet extended her hand gracefully, as though bestowing a blessing on a peasant.

Leonora Heron frowned into the hand for a long time. "I see a long ocean voyage." She sounded surprised.

Violet rolled her eyes.

"Aye . . . a journey far from home . . . a tall stranger . . . dark . . ."

"Lavay!" Martha blurted from the back of the tent.

There was sudden, total silence. Everyone swiveled toward the Gypsy girl, astounded.

"What is it, *bibi*?" Her mother said sharply.

Martha didn't come forward. "The word was in my ear, Mama. At least I think it was in my ear." She sounded genuinely surprised, and almost tremulous. "I 'eard it. Just . . . 'Lavay.'"

"Who is Lavay? The tall, dark stranger?" Violet wasn't terribly impressionable, but now she was curious. "Do you know anyone named Lavay?" It was a general sort of question for everyone in the tent.

Everyone shrugged.

"I do not know," Martha said sullenly. "Lavay. That is all." She fell silent.

It was Violet's turn to take her hand nervously, quickly, away from Mrs. Heron. "Perhaps you will read for Lord Argosy now," she said shortly.

And then she folded both of her hands back into her skirt, as though she didn't want anyone else discovering things in them.

Mrs. Heron said something to Martha in Rom, something that had a soothing inflection, and the girl resumed rustling and packing things.

Lord Argosy whipped out his hand eagerly.

The Gypsy took it, gently spread his fingers, and pored over his palm thoughtfully. "This line is yer line o' the 'eart, *Gadji* . . ." She'd chosen to trace a line that nearly bisected his hand. " . . . an' I see 'ere . . ." She paused to examine it. "Why, I think ye'll wed inside two months." She took pains to sound astonished. "I see . . . is it . . ." She clucked thoughtfully. "Why, yes. There is a girl. I see a girl. She is dark. She has light eyes. She is . . . quite charming. Not quiet." She looked up at Argosy. "But ye mun act quickly if ye want 'er. She is desired by many."

Argosy looked alarmed. He swiveled to gaze passionately at Cynthia.

She produced a reassuring smile for him. She felt like producing a kiss for the Gypsy.

Argosy smiled with relief.

"What else do you see?" he asked the Gypsy. As the beginning of all of this had been so promising.

"I see much pleasure and excitement," she said, tracing another line in his palm. She made this almost a purr.

Argosy slid a sidelong glance at Cynthia. The man did enjoy innuendos. He cleared his throat. "I don't suppose, Mrs. Heron, you'd be willing to expound on the nature of the pleas—"

"Duck!" Martha screeched.

Everyone flung themselves forward and hands over their heads.

"What, what?" Leonora Heron frowned and turned to her daughter.

"The duck is . . . empty." Martha trailed off, sounding faintly abashed to be saying something so patently absurd.

There was a stupefied silence.

"Bloody hell," Argosy muttered, managing to sound both astounded and resigned. "I suspected as much."

"What the devil, Argosy?" Jonathan said crossly.

Argosy shook his head, and exchanged a glance with Cynthia, who was nervous now.

Leonora turned and said a stream of something to her daughter in Rom. Her face was troubled.

Martha shrugged in the shadows; there was a flash of her white teeth. She was no longer disconcerted, but rather, enjoying the attention.

But she dutifully returned to packing the trunk. The lid closed with a dull *thunk*; she latched it noisily.

"And ye, *Gadji*?" Mrs. Heron beckoned with little swoops of her hand to Cynthia.

Cynthia gave her palm to the Gypsy, who took and cupped it in her roughened hand and began to use a finger like a compass point to trace lines. Leonora looked at Cynthia's palm for what seemed an inordinately long time.

Then she looked up into her face. And what Cynthia read there was a gently curious, puzzled sympathy.

Cynthia instantly felt panicked. She pled silently, with her eyes.

Leonora Herron met her plea with a firm complicity.

"I see . . ." Leonora began quickly. She hesitated, then said firmly. "A wedding in yer future. Is it *yer* wedding, *gadji*? I think perhaps 'tis." Argosy rustled restlessly; his knee brushed Cynthia's again, more decisively. It was surprisingly knobby; she could feel it through the fine fabric of her skirt and the fabric of his trousers. "I canna quite see whether yer groom is fair or—well, I think he mun be a man of great strength—"

Argosy meltingly met Cynthia's eyes. *Great strength*. She thought of a certain pair of hands. A certain pair of shoulders. Dark eyes behind spectacles.

And she smiled slightly at Argosy. Who warmly, sultrily, returned it with one of his own.

"And I also see—"

Blood! Martha shrieked.

Everyone jumped. Violet clapped her hand over her heart. Cynthia jerked her palm away from Leonora Heron. It was already cold and clammy. The steeping tea toppled and gurgled onto the tent floor.

Leonora gamely attempted to ignore the interruption. "Oh, and see!" she said hurriedly to Lord Argosy. "Here in yer cup, *Gadji*. The leaves 'ave made an 'eart." Tea leaves clung to the side of the cup. They all glanced into it, frowned—the residue might well have been in the shape of a heart—then Argosy turned to look at Martha firmly.

He was an aristocrat, after all. He wanted her to expound, and expected her to comply.

Cynthia began to panic in earnest. The girl really *did* have some sort of horrible, fragmented gift. Martha Heron was petulant chaos on legs. Not ready to dukker yet, *indeed*. Ready to shriek out non sequiturs that might very well spell the ruination of Cynthia's future, more like it.

The Gypsy girl slid dramatically to the ground, put her face in her hands and rocked it.

"Oh! Pistols! They are shooting! 'E falls! Blood! So much blood! It is because of . . ." She looked at Cynthia accusingly, and every head in the tent swiveled toward her and gaped. "She is . . ."

Martha stopped. She studied Cynthia curiously for what seemed a very long time.

Cynthia's stomach was as choppy as the English Channel.

The silence in the tent thickened to palpability. Argosy's breath was clearly held.

"Good *heavens*," Martha finally said admiringly, as though she'd been reviewing Cynthia's history in her head. "Ye're a minx, *gadji*, aren't ye?"

* * *

209

Needless to say, the return carriage ride to Redmond House was an uncomfortable one. Everyone seemed to be holding one-sided conversations. With themselves.

"Ten children!" Jonathan muttered darkly, incensed. "I'll break a *heart*! Hmmph."

"What do you think she meant by Lavay?" Violet said aloud to no one in particular. "Who the devil is Lavay? *What* is Lavay?"

"She knew the duck was *empty*," Argosy mused. His knee was indecisive about touching Cynthia's. Brushing. Moving away. Brushing again. All in all, he'd become a trifle remote and absorbed.

"She said I would be wed, and soon!" Cynthia said cheerily and desperately, hoping to herd everyone into *her* topic. "Mrs. Heron did. She seemed very *sane* about it all. Not like her daughter."

"I don't think I'd mind a long journey," Violet mused. "But I wonder who Lavay is?"

Argosy turned to Cynthia. "Why do you think she called you a minx?" And what did she mean by blood and—"

"Perhaps she had a vision about the statue of David," Jonathan guessed. "Cynthia shot its tender parts off."

Cynthia glanced at him gratefully. It was a *marvelous* theory. Entirely *wrong*, but marvelous.

"And thought it was a *man* being shot?" Argosy said dubiously. "But she mentioned blood. Statues don't bleed."

Jonathan slumped in the seat. "Ten *children*."

And so it went until they were home again.

When they reached the house, everyone spilled out of the carriage and scattered, perhaps to recover from the visit. Cynthia scaled the stairs, hoping to find a safety net in the form of a missive from the unpleasant old woman in Northumberland, waiting for her on her dressing table.

The table was bare.

But Spider the cat was delighted to see her. And so she played with her cat for an hour or two, in this way keeping her fear at bay, before venturing down the stairs again. Wanting to see Miles and not wanting to see Miles.

And the first person she saw when she went downstairs was Miles.

The rest of the day was too sultry for any vigorous outdoor group activities, and inside the house, party guests formed quiet configurations. Goodkind was said to be upstairs in his room, working on his book about behavior. Doubtless he was learning a good deal about the virtues of wickedness from his visit.

Cynthia took the lay of the salon. Argosy and Jonathan were slumped in chairs, long legs outstretched, across from Lady Georgina and Violet, who held in their hands embroidery frames and needles. Lady Windermere and Lady Middlebough faced each other over backgammon at the game table. Milthorpe was the only one who had ventured out, taking a carriage to see a nearby Sussex dog breeder.

Cynthia wondered whether she would be presented with a puppy, or if Milthorpe had decided he only needed for a wife the kind of woman who could shoot an apple even with a spaniel nose in her bum.

Near the doorway, near her, sat Miles, seated at a petite escritoire facing a window with a view of a leaf-heavy tree. He was bent over correspondence. His too-long hair nearly touched his collar, was swept sideways over his forehead; it gleamed against his pale skin. She'd wanted to know its texture; she now knew just how soft it was. The quill scratched rapidly back and forth over the foolscap.

He looked up sharply from his work. He'd sensed her standing near, of course. Seemed arrested momentarily by her face.

Then he looked away slowly. His hands were at once still. The quill, which had moved like a living thing in his hand, seemed unnaturally motionless now.

"Good afternoon, Miss Brightly." He said it almost gingerly. He still didn't look at her.

"Good afternoon, Mr. Redmond."

More innocuous words were never spoken between two people.

Well, what language should she use now to speak to him? After she'd brushed her nipples against his and greedily twined her tongue with his?

And then the slightest of rueful smiles turned up one corner of his mouth, which made her smile a little, too, because as usual he seemed to know her thoughts.

"Are you attending to correspondence?" Well, this was inane. She might well have said, *Are you attending to breathing?*

"Yes. I shall be meeting a fellow member of the Royal Society this evening to attempt to persuade him to come along on my expedition. Brilliant scientist. From Sussex. I truly hope he agrees to come along. I'm just sending a message off to tell him I'll be there."

She hesitated. "Are you eager to go? Back to Lacao?"

He leaned back a little in the chair. He breathed out a little. "Oh. If you only knew. There's so much *more* to see there. It's remarkable. I've only just begun to skim the surface. I could be forever discovering it. If only you could see how . . ." He trailed off, fanned his fingers in the air at the enormity of it, the magnificence of it.

"I should love to see it," she said fervently.

He looked up at her wonderingly. "Would you truly want to visit a place where plants eat meat?"

She smiled. "Good heavens, yes. I've never been anywhere at all outside of England. It sounds so beautiful and . . . *different*. Endlessly exciting. I should like to see a whole new world."

He was watching her talk as if her mouth was a miracle. And then a ghost of a smile touched his own mouth: he knew every word she said was true. She was no stranger to excitement or privation or exploration, and liked all of it.

Save the privation part.

Say it, she thought suddenly, desperately, irrationally. *Say one day I'll go to Lacao. With you. Say it, Miles.*

She looked down at him, at his strong throat, the silky dark hair falling to touch his neck. She was suddenly fascinated by the lobes of his ears. She wanted to lick the place below them, where his pulse beat. It suddenly occurred to her that there must be secret little places just like this everywhere on his body: corners, curves, softness and strength that could be explored like Lacao.

How could this man possibly marry someone like Lady Georgina?

"When will you go?" she asked softly.

He hesitated. "I just need to secure funding, and then I'll be able to complete the planning. Inside a year, I hope."

"Will the Mercury Club fund the expedition? Or your father?"

He looked up, surprised. "You know about the Merc—Ah."

Of course she did. An association with the Mercury Club meant a man *had* money. And Cynthia of course would know this. She shrugged. She wouldn't deny it.

"My father . . . well, my *father* won't countenance financing the expedition. He patently doesn't understand the reasons

213

for it, and he won't present it to the investment group. But Lady Georgina's father is an avid amateur naturalist. And if her father becomes a member of the Mercury Club . . ."

He said this with peculiar hesitation, and a gentleness that sent a warning prickle along the back of her neck.

An instant later she understood with a painfully blinding clarity.

"Lady Georgina's father will fund the expedition. If you're a member of his family."

His silence told her everything. He tried to hold her eyes. His were enigmatic, his jaw tense. He looked away, dropped his chin to his chest briefly. Then looked out at the tree.

How like falling and falling that moment felt. The plummet was sickening. And for an instant she couldn't speak through the pain, which seemed everywhere. She breathed in.

"I shall need to know about Goodkind." Her cool tone gave her strength, even as the words were faint.

They both had their objectives, after all. Despite what their bodies might desire.

Miles's gaze remained fixed upon that leafy view. And then a wry and not very pleasant smile touched his lips. When he turned back to look at her, he said flatly, quietly, tautly, "Don't you trust your own ability to charm, as it were, Miss Brightly? You've two men on the dangle. Shouldn't that be enough for any woman?"

Only two *men on the dangle?* She was oh, so tempted to say it. She thought it unwise to test his temper simply because her own had been kindled.

"It's important."

It was. She'd felt confident enough, she felt she had *momentum,* until Argosy was spooked by that deuced Gypsy girl, and then she disappointed Milthorpe with her skill as an outdoorswoman, and she still had no letter from Northumberland . . .

Miles studied her intently. Her face gave him nothing.

Then he touched a look upon Lady Georgina bent over her embroidery hoop, as if to remind himself of his own passions, his own objective, to solidify his resolve. Or perhaps to clear his head the way a gentle, smooth landscape soothed one's soul.

Cynthia knew *she* certainly brought him no peace.

He finally gave a humorless laugh. "Well, what do you know about him?"

"I know what you've told me and what he has shared with me: that he was a soldier, and now he considers himself a man of God. He is writing a book of essays about proper behavior for young men and women."

"*Is* he?" Miles's eyes brightened at this; a delighted smile slowly spread. "Did he happen to read to you from it, Miss Brightly, when you apologized to him yesterday? Hoping to reform you?"

His amusement was contagious, damn him. "Do you recall what you said about the spider's web when Milthorpe broke through it? That when it's torn, the spider can rebuild it, and it will be stronger than even before?"

Humor flashed across his face. "I recall every word I ever say, Miss Brightly, and it's flattering to hear that you're listening to me. I'm anxious to hear how this applies to Mr. Goodkind's book of essays."

"I said that exposure to wickedness helped to strengthen the soul, because it requires more fortitude to overcome a wicked nature and become good than it does to *stay* good when one is never tempted to be otherwise. So indulging in wickedness can ultimately only strengthen the soul."

Miles stared at her. "Good *heavens*. Diabolical logic."

"Thank you."

"Is that why he got foxed on brandy?" He was genuinely pleased and wondering.

She basked in his admiration. "I do take credit for that. That, and I do believe he was a little bored."

"Interesting." Miles tapped the quill thoughtfully; the feathers trembled when he did. She wasn't used to seeing him fidget; it interested her. "You might not make a terrible naturalist, Miss Brightly, should the predilection ever strike. And to think Goodkind is an ass, typically."

"Perhaps 'ass' is strong, don't you think? He can be charming. Any man can be charming, given incentive."

And at this Miles froze. He stared at her incredulously. He opened his mouth briefly. Closed again.

And then he put the quill down so sharply that his hand all but slapped the desk. She flinched.

His voice was low and quick and fiercely exasperated. "*No*, Cynthia. Milthorpe is a blustery rustic, Goodkind is a pompous ass, and Argosy is an unfinished, arrogant twig. Not a one of them is actually *charming*. It's *you*—*you* make them charming. You spoke of spiderwebs to Goodkind? I'll tell you of chemical reactions."

She was completely taken aback. "I . . . I beg your—"

"You are the . . . the . . . *compound* that makes them effervesce. You transform them, Cynthia. *You*. With your . . . *efforts*. You listen, you smile, you coax, you include. Otherwise, those men are *precisely as I describe them*."

These last words were delivered with ferocious weight. As though he'd been storing them for quite some time.

Cynthia's face went hot. She glanced toward where Violet and Argosy—the "arrogant twig"—and Jonathan and Georgina sat. At least no one was overtly staring at them.

"I believe I heard the word 'depleted' from you recently." Miles's voice was still quietly fierce.

Cynthia jerked her head back as though he'd struck her. "Recently," of course, meant the night before. Last night, in the dark, by firelight, in a smooth motion he'd slid his long, warm body up next to hers, folded her half-nude body in his arms and took savage kisses, and his big hands had filled with her breasts, and he'd closed his beautiful mouth over her—

He had no right to lash her with that memory. No *right.*

"Rich," she reminded him evenly, coldly. "Depleted but *rich.*"

He turned slowly away from her, toward the window. Great bushels of teardrop-shaped leaves made nearly the entire view green.

"They aren't as awful as that. They aren't," she insisted in a whisper, almost desperately. She needed to believe that they weren't. She wanted to persuade him. She wanted him to reassure her.

He didn't. He was silent a moment longer.

"Very well," he said evenly instead. "Here's what we know of Goodkind. We know he's wealthy, pious, pompous. And persuadable." This he added somewhat wryly. "He's a widower. Has two children. He *has* an heir. Wouldn't be averse to a spare. Was a good soldier. *Cannot* hold his liquor, or so I've learned. But . . ." He hesitated curiously. "Well, should I assume you are interested in peccadilloes you could . . . shall we say . . . exploit?"

"Explore," she corrected primly, "is a better word."

"If you wish." He picked up the quill and absently, gently, ran his long fingers along it, as if soothing it after slapping it down impassionedly. "I hadn't wanted to mention this . . . as it might remove him altogether from your

217

consideration. And I comprehend you wish to consider multiple options." Dryly said, that. "And this is something *very* few know. Perhaps myself and . . . one or two other people."

This was worrying. "Is he . . . depraved in some way?" Well, that was a very general guess. It just seemed so *unlikely*.

"It all depends on how you define 'depraved.' "

Worse and worse. "You'd best just tell me."

"Let us just say that I have it on good authority from . . . shall we say . . . a female acquaintance of mine who works for a house of, er, *certain* repute . . . that Mr. Goodkind . . ."

He paused.

"Just *tell* me," she hissed.

" . . . likes to dress in women's clothing every now and then. He finds it erotic."

Cynthia was dumbstruck.

"I find women's clothing erotic, too," Miles confessed cheerily. "I just don't like to *dress* in it. I like to remove women's clothing from women. Piece . . . by . . . piece."

He watched her closely. Cynthia knew her face had gone cerise, because the temperature was burning her eyes. She surreptitiously pressed two fingers against her pulse in her wrist, and found it pecking with desperate speed in there. Trepidation about Goodkind and a great whoosh of lust had conspired to make a roiling caldron of her stomach.

She took a deep breath.

"He doesn't . . . he doesn't . . . not in public?" she stammered. Wondering if she should pretend to be worldlier than she in fact was. Trying to find the silver lining.

"Of course not. Absolutely in private. And he doesn't do it all the time." As if this was reassuring. "It's only upon whim."

There was a silence.

And now . . . well, now she was curious. "What manner of women's clothing?" *Please not slippers and evening gowns.*

"Oh, stockings. Garters. Gloves if he can get them. Once a bonnet. So I'm told." He said all of this matter-of-factly. Miles Redmond had seen and heard all manner of strange things in his life, including plants that ate meat and people who ate people; apparently this hardly registered as such.

She pictured it. She was quiet. And then . . .

"Oh . . . good . . . heavens." It had to be said.

Cynthia hadn't decided whether she was appalled. Garters. Gloves. Bonnets. They seemed small, harmless things, when taken separately. But on *Goodkind*? When engaged in . . . intimacies?

Intimacies such as she'd been engaged in . . . last night?

"Does this remove him from the running, Cynthia?" Miles simply sounded curious.

God help her. She could simply not afford to remove anyone from the running. And again . . . taken separately . . . garters, gloves, bonnets . . .

"Well, he doesn't do it all of the time, does he?" She was trying to convince herself. "Doubtless he'd like an understanding wife. With a versatile wardrobe." She said this somewhat desperately. But firmly.

Miles stared at her for some time, and she saw the light of incredulity in his eyes. She refused to look away, and she refused to be ashamed. Miles would *never* know what it was like to be her. He could use the money provided by his future wife's father to send himself into exotic danger and beauty, he could seek out risk and danger and study it at *whim*.

He didn't live on the very edge of survival as she did. He hadn't been *born* on the edge of survival.

He dropped his head to look at his foolscap. He looked at that lifeless quill.

She was quite, quite sorry she'd asked about Goodkind's peccadillo. But then again, perhaps forewarned was fore-armed. And perhaps she could present herself to Goodkind as sympathetic somehow.

Miles looked up again. "How is Spider the cat?"

This was her favorite subject. "Savage. Fearless. Affectionate. He sleeps on my head."

He smiled. But his eyes didn't fully participate in it. They'd gone abstracted; they weren't warm. He glanced away from her. He gripped his quill and studied the feather pattern. "You don't have blue beneath your eyes. Are you sleeping at night now?"

She was stunned breathless. Her fingers flew to touch beneath her eyes, self-conscious.

Of course this man would notice that she'd not been sleeping well. She turned away briefly. Was this why he'd given her a cat?

Oh, God. What was the man *doing* to her?

"I . . ." she stammered. She was entirely unused to someone looking out for her welfare, and it knocked the breath from her. Her equilibrium wobbled. "Did *you* . . . sleep well . . . last night?" she asked hesitantly.

She did *not* want to care. About anything he said or did.

She cared about every minute motion he made. His every breath and word.

His gaze had slid elsewhere very briefly; she caught it just as he was returning it to her. And when it did, his face had gone closed.

"No," he said simply, finally. He looked her evenly in the eyes. There was no accusation or warmth in the word. But he presented it to her as if she'd know what to do with it, or what it meant.

She didn't know.

There's more, he'd said last night. And she'd deprived him of it.

"I'm . . . I'm sorry." She didn't know why she'd said it. Mostly she was sorry she didn't understand his mood. And she was sorry they both seemed to be suffering, but she could not have said why they were.

Her eyes followed the trajectory of his glance then. Lady Georgina wasn't on the end of it.

It was lady Middlebough. Whose glance was now still slowly retreating from Miles, like a partner in a reel: sidelong, subtle. Meaningful. The lovely brunette matron's expression hadn't changed. And Lady Windermere, her partner in backgammon, didn't seem to have noticed a thing.

It was such a small exchange. So quickly, subtly done. One would have easily missed it.

And she thought now of all of Lady Middlebough's little comments. The absence of her husband, due to return in a day or so. The explicit, absurd directions to her chambers she'd announced the other night.

Cynthia's heart, warmed a moment earlier by Miles's concern, closed into a cold, tight fist.

After a silence during which he met her eyes and during which her face went hot, he motioned with his hand to his foolscap and his quill. Widened his eyes a little. Said nothing else.

Cynthia understood she was being politely dismissed in favor of his work.

She gave him a small social smile and offered a shallow curtsy.

And then she drifted over to where Georgina and Violet sat across from each other, engaged in the reassuringly feminine activity of embroidery.

Stabbing needles in and out of fabric seemed a soothing pastime at the moment.

Creating something with measured stitches seemed meditative, too.

Like a spider. Weaving and reweaving a web.

All the younger people smiled and greeted her, and Argosy stood and bowed and smiled. And she chose a chair near him, which made him glow, and the glow eased her mind just a little.

He stretched his limbs again. A form of preen she understood and appreciated. And this was reassuring, too. She exhaled. She hadn't realized she'd gone tight in the chest until she did exhale.

"She *was* a looby," Jonathan said darkly. "Ten children! Of all the . . . !"

Ah. They were still talking about the Gypsies. And Jonathan was still incensed.

"A looby!" Cynthia leaped upon the explanation with relief. She wished to encourage it. "I really was rather frightened by her."

"I still can't decide what she meant by pistols and blood." Argosy was shrewder than that. "She called you a minx. I wasn't pleased."

Cynthia was worried about the particular reason he wasn't pleased. But then she glanced at his face and he looked very masculine and protective, and she remembered he had five sisters, and decided it was gallantry on his part.

She smiled at this, and he gave her one of his sultry smiles in return.

She wasn't certain she was entirely out of the woods with regards to Argosy, however.

"We must be charitable if she has a disease of the mind," she said gently, while silently, mentally, apologizing to the gifted if obnoxious Gypsy girl. "How awful it must be for her."

"How awful, indeed!" Georgina contributed, though she hadn't been present for the event. "To just blurt things without being able to stop yourself!"

"I just think she is a spoiled girl who wished to cause controversy." This was Violet's opinion.

"You ought to know," Jonathan said.

Violet wrinkled her nose at him, and then stopped herself, as she never wished to encourage wrinkles. She settled for trying to kick him again. He languidly moved out of the way.

"She was correct about the duck," Argosy insisted. He'd sat up more stiffly, as though reliving and reworking the episode in his mind.

He was giving this an uncomfortable amount of thought, Cynthia noted. And the last thing she needed or wanted was for him to begin researching the matter of *her*.

She wondered how much Jonathan knew. She exchanged a glance with him. There was something reassuring in it. For reasons of his own, Jonathan liked her, and there was a hint of his brother in him. His first instinct—well, his second instinct, after having a wonderful time—was to be protective.

"I still believe it was just a coincidence," Cynthia said. This was another thing she meant to encourage. She accompanied this reiteration with a warm smile.

"But an *empty duck*?" Argosy said.

Everyone looked confused, but he looked at Cynthia meaningfully. She was apparently the only one he'd told about the empty duck. She did feel a bit honored.

"Perhaps she simply reads your concerns from your mind. I've heard of that sort of skill."

"Ah!" His eyes widened. He nodded sagely. "As have I. As have I. You may have a point, Cynthia."

She smiled at him again.

"I wonder what it is like to travel the way they do? The Gypsies?" Violet wondered this. Her voice was dreamy. "They are forever on the move. Seeing every part of England. Seeing people everywhere. She said I would go on a long journey across the ocean. I'm not certain I would mind."

"You need to sleep in a tent when you're a Gypsy," her brother told her. "Tents can be dirty. And you would need to sit on the ground to eat around the fire."

"Like a picnic," Lady Georgina contributed brightly.

"Hardly." Argosy was laconic.

Georgina looked chastened.

"But the Gypsy *boys* make up for that," Cynthia said. "Such green eyes . . ." She sent a sidelong look at Violet.

Argosy bristled. A little jealousy was healthy, she decided.

Jonathan looked at Cynthia, eyes wide. Gave his head a little shake: *don't encourage her.*

It was too late. "Why shouldn't I admire a Gypsy boy?" Violet asked."When he was in the tropics, *Miles* knew any number of exotic wo—" She stopped, remembering Georgina.

Cynthia looked over at the man who'd allegedly known any number of exotic women. He'd stopped writing altogether. He was staring out of the window, broad shoulders motionless.

She jerked her head back to present company.

The subject was changed when Jonathan began to discuss the horse acrobats with Argosy, and soon they were arguing, half seriously, over who might be the better acrobat based on their current riding skills.

"The Gypsies leave tomorrow," she whispered to Violet moments later. "As does that boy. What I wouldn't give to run off with them just for a little while!"

And then out of the corner of her eye, Cynthia watched Miles put down his quill and walk toward the doorway just as Lady Middlebough stood casually up from her backgammon game.

Their paths convened in the middle of the large room. They paused to exchange a few quiet words, and the tone, at least, was *disinterested*, polite and almost bored.

But Cynthia heard—because she was desperately interested, and desperately listening, and her hearing was good—a few words in that swift exchange.

They were: "tomorrow" and "midnight" . . . "Shall I bring a dead fly?" and "I'll find *you*."

The last was punctuated by Lady Middlebough's low laughter.

Then they parted, seconds later, as though it had all been happenstance, and went their separate ways.

Chapter 15

The following morning's activities had been unscheduled, but a stroll in the gardens had been discussed before everyone retired the previous evening, with a gardener as a guide to explain the plants growing in the greenhouse, none of which, they'd all been informed regretfully, ate meat. Cynthia had just gotten her walking dress buttoned up and her feet into her slippers in preparation for going down to breakfast when a sharp rap sounded on her chamber door.

The kitten darted under the bed.

"Mr. Miles Redmond would like to have a word with you straight away, Miss Brightly," the maid told her when Cynthia opened the door. "He's in the library. He said you'd know where it was."

She certainly did know where the library was. She'd smoked a cheroot there—well, nearly—and had writhed in his arms there.

And tonight *he'd* be writhing in the arms of Lady Middlebough. On the third floor, behind the fourth door from the left.

If she had gauged that conversation correctly, that was.

Her spine stiffened. She felt cold and rebellious and disinclined to obey his summons. But judging from the expression on the maid's face, she had not been dispatched on her errand by a cheerful man. *Straight away*, she'd said.

And so Cynthia went.

It still smelled of cheroot, she noticed, sniffing. Miles, standing very still in the center of the room, turned and saw her. He didn't bother with a greeting.

"Violet is missing."

Something was very wrong. His voice was . . . *too* calm. The little hairs on the back of her neck stirred in warning. If she were a small rodent, she would have taken shelter in preparation for a storm.

Miles's face was peculiarly pale. He'd likely returned late from his meeting with the Sussex scientist, but this wasn't the white of fatigue.

"Violet is missing?" she repeated dumbly She had an uneasy suspicion why. "What do you mean by—"

"Gone, Miss Brightly," continued that calm, calm voice. "She has not been seen since dinner yesterday evening."

She studied him carefully. "You've looked every—"

"It has been determined through a series of discreet inquiries made by myself and my brother Jonathon that she is nowhere on the property. We have searched. She is gone."

Well, then. So Violet had done it. She'd run off with the Gypsies. Violet was quite, quite mad, Cynthia thought half admiringly. Despite her increasing trepidation at the large man advancing upon her.

And he *was* advancing.

She struggled to hold her ground even as he brought his anger with him.

"I wonder whether you might have any idea where Violet might have gone?" It came off him in waves, the anger.

Cynthia's throat had tightened. Her lungs had congealed. She finally, airlessly managed, "I think there is a possibility she went to the Gypsy camp . . . there was a boy who—"

The look on Miles's face was so murderous it killed the rest of her sentence completely.

"Why," he repeated, with a patience so weighty it might have mowed down a less stalwart soul, "do you think she returned to the Gypsy camp?"

"We . . . I may have mentioned that Gypsies do a good deal of traveling . . . when she mentioned she might like to travel . . . that she often feels restless, and . . . the boy . . . I didn't know she would . . ."

"You didn't *know*?" And now his voice was raised. He gave a short, unpleasant, incredulous laugh. "I don't believe for an *instant* that you didn't know precisely what you were doing. Violet *acts*, Miss Brightly. She's impulsive. And you know this because you *see* people, you know how to *play* with them, you *understand* consequences. And yet you encouraged her *anyway*. What kind of friend *are* you?"

By the time he'd reached the end of his sentence, his words snapped at her like sparks struck from an anvil. His fury had sucked the air from the room.

Fury. That explained the white face. That, and fear. He was terrified for his sister.

Oh, she hated him in that moment. Still, she wanted to go to him, lay a hand on him, take away some of his fear, if only she could. But he was *right*. He was right about *her*. In a sense, she'd known precisely what she was doing when she'd suggested Gypsies to Violet.

Bloody man was always *right*.

But in the interest of fairness, she would not take all the blame, and his own anger provided wonderful fuel for hers.

She advanced on *him*.

He took a startled step back.

"I know you're afraid for her, Miles. But she's *bored*. She's intelligent and energetic and spoiled and *bored*. She hasn't the faintest idea what to do with herself. She does these reckless things for all of those reasons. *And* I think she misses her brother."

All at once the fury animating him was snuffed as surely as though she'd thrust a fist between his ribs.

And now she saw pain.

Ah, Lyon: the Achilles' heel of this family. She had forgotten about Lyon, and about disappearing Redmonds. And how Miles could never, ever be Lyon. And how it must have felt to Miles to think that yet another Redmond had disappeared.

Oh, God. She was a terrible, *terrible* person.

She desperately looked her apology at him. And together they were silent. As if Miles was abashed to have revealed his weakness.

When he spoke again, the snapping energy of fury was gone. But a weary implacability remained.

"But we have a *responsibility*, Miss Brightly. When we know more, see more, understand more than the others we care for. We have a responsibility to look after them. *Do you understand me*?"

Cynthia suddenly became aware that her fingers were cramped. They'd been gripping a fold of her skirt. She absently flexed them as she met his gaze. He willed her to understand him with those dark, endless eyes of his that could, like night, show and hide so many things all at once.

We, he'd said.

Including her in this alleged legion of stronger people, people who saw more, knew more. Inadvertently acknowledging, perhaps, the most powerful similarity between them:

They were both *strong*. Stronger than everyone around them. By nature. And by necessity.

The realization that he viewed her that way took her breath away. She stared at him.

She had never quite viewed herself in that light: strong. She'd simply tried to survive. She looked after herself, and always had.

But who looked after Miles?

Yesterday she'd witnessed him arrange an assignation with a married woman. He would buy his own future as surely as she wanted to buy hers.

She would have taken him in her arms right then, anyway, and waited until he was no longer pale with fear, and no longer tense with fury. She would have done anything in that moment to take away his pain and fear and frustration.

They were quiet together for a moment. As if the confession had made him feel raw. He turned away. The man of fact and purpose and courage was vulnerable after all.

Oh, how they undid each other.

"In a way, Miles . . . this is . . . wonderful."

He jerked his gaze back toward her. His jaw actually dropped. "*Wonder*—" He nearly spluttered. "What in God's name are you talking about?"

"This." She turned her hand up almost impatiently in a gesture meant to encompass his bloody willful missing sister, his display of temper, and his scathingly honest but undeniably accurate assessment of her own character. "All of this. You care very much for Violet, don't you?"

He frowned blackly, impatiently. "I would do anything for her."

She looked at this man, a faint smile on her face, and said it gently. "Precisely."

She turned away from him idly just as she said it, toward

the window. So he couldn't look at her expression just then, because she didn't trust that he wouldn't see regret.

And then she squared her shoulders.

Silence followed. Well, then. She'd struck him utterly dumb. She turned back to find him motionless, watching her.

"I'm sorry if I had anything at all to do with this, Miles. Truly."

He nodded shortly, still staring at her, his face abstracted.

"I'm sorry I lost my temper," he said stiffly.

She'd noticed that he didn't apologize for saying any of the things he'd said during his outburst. He wasn't about to insult her with such an apology, either. Everything he'd said about her was, in fact, true, and she knew it.

"I'm not entirely certain you *are* sorry you lost your temper. I'm not sorry you did." And she smiled at him.

He looked startled, but she didn't allow him time to ask questions. "I should visit the Gypsy encampment, Mr. Redmond," she urged gently. "They intended to leave this morning."

He opened his mouth, then closed it and frowned. He bit his lip.

Clearly he wanted to say something, but she sensed he couldn't put it into words.

She knew a peculiar tenderness again, and a great satisfaction that she'd robbed the clever man of speech and clarity.

"Thank you," was what he finally did say.

He spun and quickly left her.

When Miles galloped into the encampment, he saw it was being disassembled with organized alacrity. Another town would look forward to horse acrobats and fortune-tellers and healers. The Gypsies would return to their comfortable Sussex encampment in a year's time, or a month's time; one never knew. But they were as much a part of the scenery, the history of the town, now, as the pub, the church, and Miss Endicott's academy on the hill.

It was impossible to miss Violet: she was perched on a large rock in the middle of all the activity. Miles dismounted and tethered Ramsay's reins to a low-hanging branch of an ash tree, then strode forward to confront her, relief warring with anger.

They regarded each other for a moment in silence.

His knew his sister was considered a diamond of the first water and all that. But he simply saw her as Violet: he saw her as a child with tangled dark curls and bright eyes, all laughter and mischief and offhanded cleverness and falling down and following him and his brothers. Someone he'd played with and teased and looked after and loved his entire life.

"I imagine it's not as simple to run away with Gypsies as one might think," he offered finally, conversationally.

"They won't take me," she confessed glumly.

"Imagine that."

"I might have been of *some* use," she groused.

Miles saw the healer Leonora Heron cast him a look and heard her mutter something in Rom. It sounded to him like a vehement disagreement.

"Did you stay here all night?"

"No. I arrived this morning," Violet told him. "Mrs. Heron kept me in her tent for a time."

Miles turned to the Gypsy woman. "Thank you for looking after her, Mrs. Heron."

"You are welcome, Mr. Redmond. I have one of my own,

you see." She sent him a long-suffering look. Commiserating about recalcitrant girls.

Behind them, a cluster of bright Gypsy horses tossed their heads, approving of the breeze, seemingly approving of the fact that they would be off again soon, entertaining other pockets of England, men riding their backs the way birds bobbed ocean swells. Horses who lived with Gypsies became Gypsies, too, Miles supposed.

He saw the direction of Violet's gaze: Samuel Heron, who was a now a grown man and handsome, and clearly reveling in being both. Samuel glanced toward Violet warmly, but gave a start when he encountered Miles's ferocious unblinking stare. As effective as a spiked wall.

Samuel hastened toward the horses.

"Did you know Gypsies consider the *gadji* unclean?" Miles offered mildly. "It isn't personal, really. It's simply a cultural belief."

Violet watched Samuel go. "Ironic," she said glumly, "given that I am so very clean."

Miles lowered his long frame and sat down on the ground next to his subdued sister. He whipped his coat out behind him, leaned back on his hands and sighed."Why?" he asked simply.

When it came to Violet, *Why?* was nearly always a rhetorical question, but asking it had become a tradition of sorts between them.

"Why?" She turned to him, a picture of wide-eyed innocence. "Whatever do you mean by—"

"Enough, Violet." He said it so firmly it nearly qualified as snapping. She blinked in astonishment. "Tell me the *real* reason you ran away. Do you even know? Was it Samuel Heron?"

Violet opened her mouth to speak, then paused, looked

into his face, and frowned. Then caught herself frowning and the frown eased away. She was always careful about inviting lines to etch themselves upon her lovely visage.

"You look weary, Miles."

He cast a baleful glance at her. But her surprise sounded genuine, not a diversionary tactic.

Late nights with Cynthia Brightly. "I wonder if it has anything to do with my sister disappearing."

She flinched. The word "disappear" had an unpleasant connotation in their family.

They were quiet again.

"No," she said finally. "It had naught to do with Samuel Heron. Not entirely. Though he *is* handsome. He's different. *You* should know about different." Her sidelong glance was accusing but it lacked conviction. "He's . . ." She sighed. Pushed a wayward strand of hair out of her eyes. "It had naught to do with him. I'm not sure I know why I did it, Miles. That's the truth."

Miles was tempted to give her a hard shake.

"Violet . . . let's suppose you *had* left with the Gypsies. Had just . . . vanished into the night, and we never saw you again. Do you have any idea what that would have done to Mother and Father? To . . . all of us? Do you honestly mean to tell me that this doesn't *matter* to you?"

She began to cry. Quietly at first, so he wouldn't know it, and because Violet hated to be messy about things, and she wasn't sentimental. But they were genuine tears. And they soon became the messy sort, replete with sniffing and gurgled sobs.

He suffered along with her. He'd never been able to bear her tears, from the moment she was born. But he didn't "There, there" her, or pat her back, or hug her. It was good for Violet to cry tears that weren't meant to be anything but tears. Tears that merely meant genuine grief and frustration, not a means to make someone—usually a man—so uncomfortable he would do absolutely anything she wanted.

So he let her cry. And felt every single one of those tears as surely as if they were his own.

And eventually she pulled out one of her spotless handkerchiefs and dabbed daintily at her eyes. Violet was invariably, astoundingly, crisply neat. He wondered how she did it, as she was active enough.

"I'm sorry to worry you, Miles."

"I know," he said gently.

"It's just . . . I miss him."

Him being Lyon.

"I miss him, too."

"I hate him for leaving. I hate *her*"—Violet had managed to thoroughly demonize Olivia Eversea, and refused to even utter her name, as though its mere utterance would conjure a devil—"for making him leave. Everything was lovely, and now everything is ruined. Ruined and quite odd."

Miles didn't know about ruined. They had all managed to stagger on somehow; Redmond life continued in all its forms, mundane and profound. Laughter and arguments and feuding and the making of money continued. But he did agree with the "quite odd." And he didn't know whether his brother had *left* or whether something had befallen him, and he wasn't certain whom to blame. It was an odd sensation, this not knowing, like falling and falling and falling and never knowing where or when or if one might land. A different sort of gravity seemed to apply to their family now.

"We don't know what really happened, Violet." He said this to her again though he'd said this so many times it had begun to lose all meaning and sound strange to his own ears, the way any word might if you stare at it for too long. There were moments, he confessed to himself, when he hated Lyon, too.

But he was tired of humoring Violet; thanks to a certain house party guest, he'd acquired a taste for bald honesty. His sister's recklessness took place against a backdrop of entirely taken-for-granted love and protection. She *expected* to be scolded, rescued, punished, and pampered no matter what she did, and not once had her brothers or her parents disappointed her. Her recklessness required no real courage, as such. And it was, as Cynthia had pointed out, an indulgence of a bored and willful girl who didn't have the faintest idea how to channel her energies.

And it was an expression . . . of loss. Loss of family, loss of certainty, of equilibrium.

"Do you truly think Olivia Eversea could actually *make* Lyon do anything, Violet? *Lyon?* You know Lyon."

"She broke his heart." Violet made this sound like the most sinister of crimes, and as though a broken heart was the sort of debilitation excusing all manner of behavior.

"We don't know this, either. It's all conjecture." He'd said this a thousand times before, too.

They watched the Gypsies, including Samuel Heron, cluck to the horses, begin saddling the ones they would ride out of camp and settling harnesses over others. Rolls and trunks were being lifted into wagons. The tents would come down next, like flowers blooming in reverse.

"Miles . . ." Violet said this with uncharacteristic trepidation. She took a breath. "It's just . . . sometimes I don't think it's enough."

This was a faintly alarming statement. He swiveled toward her. "*What* isn't enough?"

She went abruptly quiet. As though saying those words

aloud had unnerved her. As though she hoped he would forget about them.

He halfsuspected he knew what she meant. It was just as Cynthia had said: Violet was intelligent and bored and restless, and nothing in Sussex, or even London, would satisfy her.

He simply didn't know what to tell her. She was a woman. And a Redmond. This rather firmly delineated her options.

"I do miss Lyon, too, Violet. But he isn't here. And I know I am *not* him. I can never be him. I wish I could, but I know I can never make up for the fact that he's—"

She'd turned sharply and was looking up at him in such blank astonishment that he stopped speaking.

"What is it?" he asked irritably.

"Miles, don't you know that we would fly apart without you?" She looked truly bemused.

"We?"

"The *Redmonds*," she said, as though he were slow-witted child. And no one had *ever* spoken to him that way. "All of us."

"Well, I suppose I'm now the . . . Heir *Regent*, if you will. Given Lyon's absence, my role has changed and I'll be expected to—"

"*No*, Miles." She was genuinely impatient now. "For heaven's sake. It was *always* you. I recall . . . well, there is something boring and scientific you tried to explain to me once . . . a theory about a certain force that keeps the moon up in the sky and hugging close to the earth rather than flying off into space?"

"Well, that would be gravity, I suppose, for a beginning," he supplied wryly. Wondering where she was headed with this.

"If you say so," she allowed dubiously. "But that's you,

237

Miles. You've always been that. If you had been the one to leave, we would all go flying apart, cartwheeling off through the solar system. Papa is so absorbed in making money and hating Everseas and *impressing* everyone. Mama cares only for us and for the house and for the things she buys. It's enough for her. And I love both of them, I do. Lyon was so busy being *wonderful*, being the heir, you know, learning the business, making everyone proud. And Jonathon is *Jonathon*, and—well, what I mean to say is that Lyon might be the sun in all of this, but you're the earth. You allow all of us to be who we are, because of who *you* are. Solid. Looking out for us. We can *count* on you. We all know it, you know. I think even Father does. And then you went off to the South Seas, which seemed very exotic, but even that was so scrupulously planned, and we knew you were going . . . but I never doubted for an *instant* that you would return to us. Not one instant. Because that's who you are."

Miles went still. He was immensely discomfited. Imagine *Violet,* of all people, arriving at such a conclusion. He wasn't certain what to make of it. He wasn't certain he entirely liked what he'd heard, either. He shifted with uncharacteristic restlessness.

"Did the Gypsies teach you profundity overnight, Violet?"

"Ah, see, I've embarrassed you." She was quite pleased. She smoothed her dress over her knees and smiled. Getting the better of Miles happened so seldom.

They were quiet together.

"How did you find me?" she asked.

"I asked discreetly, in case you were concerned. In other words, the entire party of guests does not know you attempted to run off with the Gypsies. In case that matters to you. Miss Brightly suggested I might find you here."

Violet nodded almost approvingly.

"I like her." She said this almost defiantly. Deliberately, as though she'd expected to provoke him with the observation. "I do. Cynthia."

"Why do you like her?" and Miles sounded once again like a scientist. Even-toned, genuinely curious. But his heart thumped peculiarly. He wanted to hear someone else talk about her.

Violet thought about this. "She's very clever, you know. She's very . . . *alive*. She's quite pretty. She's a good deal of fun. I do believe she's fearless. And our parents most decidedly do not like her. Those are the reasons." Violet smiled wickedly.

He suppressed a smile. No mention of kindness, or goodness, all the other fashionable attributes young ladies were supposed to admire in one other.

All the qualities Lady Georgina radiated. All the qualities he appreciated, too.

But there was no mention, either, of honesty. Or passion. Or true courage. Or complexity. Or . . . kindness.

He supposed it wouldn't have mattered what words Violet used. He knew now that language was insufficient to describe what happened to him when he was near Cynthia Brightly.

Violet turned to him.

"You don't like her, either, do you?" she pressed. "You should see your face even now. You've gone so *dark*. You're so *thunderous* when she's about. And it's so unlike you to be rude. I saw you speaking with her yesterday, Miles. You looked . . . *impatient*. I have never in my life seen you like that. She *is* my guest. She cannot help that she has no family at all. We must be kind to her."

Imagine Violet observing *this*. And sounding reproving about it.

Unbidden came the image of a pair of shoulders almost imperceptibly squaring against the light of a window. As if adjusting a burden that had just awkwardly shifted.

He felt again that peculiar pierce in the vicinity of his breastbone, that familiar restlessness.

Who looked after Cynthia Brightly? Cynthia Brightly.

He didn't think she was fearless. And this is what made her courageous.

And then he thought of what she might be doing now: doubtless toting up the assets of each of the guests in order to decide where to fully direct her charm in order to gain what she wanted. He'd been right from the very beginning: the two of them were not so very different in that regard. They would each do what they needed to do in order to get what they wanted.

"I haven't yet decided what I think of her," he said shortly.

This wasn't a lie. And as this sounded very like something Miles would say, Violet accepted it with a one-shouldered shrug.

"I like Georgina, too," she said, generously. "She's very nice. Always has been. You're going to marry her, aren't you, Miles? She'd suit you." She said this conciliatorily. "And that would certainly please Papa."

Miles felt a pressure, an irritation, welling. An irritation encompassing every woman he currently knew, including Lady Middlebough, who'd been extraordinarily patient, and whom, *by God*, he would see—in her glorious bare entirety—tonight.

He ignored his sister's question and pushed himself to a standing position.

"Well, then, Violet. Will you please think before you set off to do something rash?"

"I don't think that I can promise that, Miles. Thinking takes a good deal of time. You do more than enough of that for all of us."

She was flippant, entertained by herself. She expected him to laugh.

And suddenly he was *furious*.

"For God's sake, Violet. Do you want to break my heart?" The words were out of his mouth before he could reconsider them.

His sister's mouth dropped wide. Her eyes bulged with shock.

"*What* . . . what a thing to say, Miles! I've—I've never heard you speak of broken hearts before."

Ah, poetry had other uses then: shocking his recalcitrant sister into stammering. It was admittedly very funny, but beneath his amusement sizzled irritation. *I've a heart, too,* he wanted to say. *I'm not just gravity. I can be furious. I could do something rash. I could suffer torments.*

Violet remained speechless. She'd leaned back a little and was squinting at him, as if to draw him into focus. To ascertain that it was actually *Miles* speaking to her.

"Just think again before you do something, Violet. You've a brain, for God's sake, and when you display evidence of it, I am equally shocked. Please recall your brain *can* be used for something other than preventing the wind from making a whistling noise through your ears. In other words: *think*."

"Or I'll . . . or I'll 'break your *heart?*'" She sounded as though she was quoting him, and she still sounded incredulous.

He sighed. Miles could not for the life of him imagine the man who could possibly manage Violet, or turn her into the woman he liked to think she could become. She had all the finest qualities of the Redmonds, magnified and run amuck.

"Very well," he said finally. "Yes. You very well might break my heart the next time you do something rash. Would you like my broken heart upon your conscience?"

She continued staring at him, and suddenly produced a frown. Perhaps she was attempting to picture him as a broken man, he thought, stumbling about in a state of internal chaos she'd caused. As she stared, she almost unconsciously raised her hand to smooth the frown dents out from between her eyes.

She exhaled finally, resignedly, and turned away again, looking toward the horizon. "Very well, Miles. I shall endeavor to *think*. But only for you." Her wryness was intended to disguise the fact that she meant it.

My bloody maddening sister loves me despite herself. He disguised a smile.

"Oh, wait, Miles." Violet peered at him. "Look at that. One of the buttons on your coat is loose." She reached over and gave the dangling silver button a flick with two fingers. "You should have your valet see to it. Isn't that a Weston coat? They normally sew buttons on with steel. What have you been doing to it?"

Writhing on settees with maddening, cheroot-smoking female guests.

Violet *would* notice his loose button. In some ways, her vision, her way of approaching the world, was like his own: precise, detailed. But channeled, obviously, in very different ways.

"Thank you for pointing it out. I'll see to it, lest I offend your sartorial senses."

She smiled a little, but the smile faded as trepidation set in. She cleared her throat. "You won't tell Papa about . . . this?"

"No. And Jonathon probably won't tell Father, either, of course. Do realize, however, that he will *know* you've tried to run off with the Gypsies, which means he now has something new with which to blackmail you."

Violet snorted. "Jonathan hasn't nearly as much on me as I have on him."

This was interesting, and one day he might want to press his sister for details. Not today, however.

Miles stood and brushed at the back of his coat. He'd grown chilled simply sitting for a short time. He reached down, seized Violet's hands and hauled her to her feet unceremoniously. Then he waited for her to shake out her skirt, took her hands back in his and rubbed them hard. They were very cold.

And then he released them, exasperated.

"How *did* you get here, Violet?"

"I walked for a time, then I paid a farmer going north a shilling to take me the rest of the way. I didn't want to take a horse, you see, as I knew the Gypsies would make it their own soon enough, and Papa would have fits and have everyone quietly arrested. You rode, did you not?" Violet looked hopefully toward Ramsay. Then gazed eloquently off toward the long, long distance where the house presided, and limpidly back at him.

He rolled his eyes. He had to admire the attempt, but he wasn't Lyon or his father.

"I certainly did ride. You, however, will be walking all the way back, while *I* ride. The walk ought to warm you up nicely. I'll ride next to you. We'll discuss gravity and other planetary properties the entire way home."

In the end, he knew best how to punish Violet.

Chapter 16

A subdued day had followed. Violet was chastened and quiet for a few hours, then emerged from her room and wanted to go on a walk in the garden, and all the females decided to accompany her to sketch follies and flowers and the like.

Cynthia's skill in this regard was modest, at best, and she felt impatient, thought her time more constructively spent charming men, all of whom accompanied them out to the parklands.

All, that was, except for Miles. He'd made himself scarce for the entire afternoon to see to business about the property and to attend to correspondence. At least this was the excuse he gave.

Eventually, in the laughter and flirtation of the day, Cynthia almost forgot her time here was growing shorter, her shoes and purse growing thinner, that no letter had yet arrived from Northumberland, and that Miles Redmond would allegedly be making love to Lady Middlebough this very evening.

Lady Middlebough sketched very well. If with an excess of passion.

But in the dark, after she'd retired from the evening, Cynthia had great difficulty forgetting all of these things.

A particular impulse gathered momentum, became unbearable.

She finally surrendered to it. She slid out of bed, because she had to see for herself. And she had directions, after all.

If he were completely honest, Miles realized, he half-wished that Lady Middlebough had departed from sheer exasperation.

But now making love to her seemed a matter of honor, for heaven's sake. So he waited, and held the image of her in his mind, and pictured what he might like to do to her and what she might like to do to him, and finally began to look forward to it *greatly*. To lose himself, exhaust himself, in mindless, obligation-free pleasure was very likely precisely what he needed to restore his peace of mind. Or so his formidable mind told him.

When the appointed hour arrived, he opened, very slowly, the door of his chambers to peer down the hall. In case Lady Middlebough knocked upon the wrong door.

"What the *devil*?"

Cynthia Brightly was standing in the hall outside his room. Right where anyone strolling by—or rather, *slinking* by on the way to an assignation—might see her.

He seized her by the wrist and pulled her through the doorway before she could squeak. He stood looking at her, standing on the carpet, toes bare, and—

Wait—he couldn't have her in his *room*, for God's sake.

He reflexively furled her right back out into the hall so quickly her hair sailed behind her like a kite.

Good God. Such a *lot* of long, thick hair.

He left his hand indecisively curled around her wrist because she was bright as a ghost in her nightdress in the dimly lit hall, that hair pouring down the front of her managing to give off a gleam even in the dark. Lady Middle-bough would appear nearly any second, and see her standing there, and—

Miles gave a tug and spooled her back into the room.

It occurred to him then that they were engaged in the world's most absurd reel.

"Are *you* enjoying this, Mr. Redmond?" Cynthia whispered conversationally.

He made the mistake of looking into her face. The fire-light made her nightrail nearly transparent.

"Bloody woman." He furled her decisively back out into the hall again.

He didn't yet let go.

It occurred to him that perhaps he *couldn't* let go. Her wrist was narrow and so soft and cold in his fingers, and if he began to think of how soft her skin was—

He wouldn't think of her skin.

"What the devil are you doing here?" he hissed finally.

"Why? Are you expecting another guest?" As innocent as blossom, those words. Her eyes, no doubt, danced pure deviltry, but he couldn't see it in the dark.

He let his long, incredulous silence serve as an emphatic yes.

"Lady Middlebough?" she pressed on a whisper.

"What"—and he made the whispered word a veritable monument to sarcasm—"do you *think*, Miss Brightly?"

She was silent for a time. Apparently his waves of fury and exasperation and the sheer size of him were finally driving his message home.

"I should leave," she suggested faintly.

"Oh, you should definitely leave," he agreed grimly. He threw a nervous look past her down the hall.

But she remained standing where she was. Paralyzed with

nerves now, and by his presence. Which somehow contrived to make her feel like an insect trapped in amber.

Miles muttered one final oath, pulled her into the room once more, released her wrist, closed the door as quietly as he was able, and slid the bolt.

It was perhaps the most final sound either of them had heard.

"Will you plead a *mal à la tête*, Mr. Redmond, to Lady Middlebough, when she arrives?"

He slowly turned about to look at her. "I do not at the moment find you *witty*, Cynthia."

Looking at her was a mistake. His eyes felt quite at home now ravishing her in the firelit dark, and it tempted his body closer and closer, and his entire being protested fiercely when he forced himself to look away.

He took five steps to the other side of the room. As if somehow those five steps would protect him from his inconvenient desires.

This is what he would do: he would wait for Lady Middlebough to arrive, he would send her away with sincere whispered regrets and promises of another evening in the *ton* one day, and then he would give Miss Brightly an earnest push from his room and bolt it against *all* women this evening.

"We'll wait until she taps at the door, I'll extend my regrets, and then I'll send you away," he said firmly. Still not trusting himself to look at her.

Cynthia said nothing. She was looking around his room with avid curiosity.

He'd thought to feel bolder in her presence. After all, he'd demystified her somewhat: he knew the texture and temperature and scent of her skin, the sweet hot taste of her mouth. He'd felt the chafe of her hard nipples arched against his chest, and her fingertips dragging over his scalp, and—

Desire cleaved him. He curled his hand around the bedpost as though it were shipwreck flotsam and he the lone survivor bobbing on the sea. Or perhaps a spear he could hurl into the gaping maw of the frustrating *everything* that was his desire for Miss Brightly.

Bloody *metaphors*. Here they were, of course. Unleashed by Miss Brightly, whose name itself was virtually an absurd simile.

She was quicksand. The more he struggled away from her, the deeper he sank.

Now, if Lady Middlebough had entered the room, he would have welcomed her with a warm kiss, plied her with brandy, undressed her with alacrity, and they would at this moment be mutually, enthusiastically, discovering each other's charms. He would have been proving to her that everything she'd heard about him was true.

But now, instead, he stood hiding in the shadows. And Cynthia stood before the fire with her arms wrapped around her like a shawl.

He'd left his coat on the chair near the bed for his valet to look after later. He reached for it—it was a long reach—but walking toward it felt like he'd be relinquishing his position of safety.

"Put this on."

He tossed it to her. It flapped across the room like a great bird, and she plucked it from the air before it could settle on her head. Gracefully, with a certain amount of aplomb, she arranged it over her own shoulders. And sent a bemused look in his direction.

"Thank you," she said softly, uncertainly.

"Don't talk," he whispered irritably.

This for some reason made her smile.

There was silence. He wondered what she thought of his room: simple, dark colors, chairs enormous and comfortable and well-used, a carpet plush as a meadow, a bed that could comfortably fit an entire family. Miles was large. He liked large furniture, and he generally employed the entire bed when he slept.

"Isn't Lady Middlebough married?"

It sounded dangerously as though she intended to make some sort of point, which did nothing to blunt the edge of his irritation.

He broke his own rule about talking. "She's a grown woman. She can do as she wishes. She knows precisely what she's doing. She wants only one thing, as do I."

There was a pause.

"I wouldn't," she said softly. "I wouldn't do it."

He sighed with weighty patience. "We are two adults, she and I. And how do you *know*, Cynthia? How on earth can you possibly know what you will or won't do once you're mar—"

Three little taps sounded against the doorframe. He froze.

He truly did despise lying. He was terrible at it, really. However, if he claimed to be woefully indisposed, he wouldn't be far wrong in this instance.

Emerging from the shadows, he slid the bolt and opened the door two inches. He saw in the dark a pair of dewy glowing eyes and the slow beginnings of what promised to be a sultry smile when it was completed. Sadly, what he was about to say would put an end to it.

"Victoria . . . please don't despise me." He was all soft contrition. The smile froze midway up. "I find that I'm feeling terribly . . . indisposed. I fear that I might . . . I might not be able to . . ."

He left his sentence incomplete, in what he hoped was a meaningful manner. He prayed she would be merciful.

"I can change that," whispered the surprisingly confident Lady Middlebough. Without a second's hesitation.

This gave him pause. But only for a moment.

"I fear it's a very—" He cleared his throat discreetly, searched for a deterring sort of word. "—unpleasant . . . sort of indisposed."

Absolute silence ensued.

His words hovered like a miasma, accumulating mystery and vileness in proportion to the length the silence stretched.

He and Lady Middlebough regarded each other through the space in his door. Miles realized then that his cheeks were actually *burning*.

He silently, floridly, juicily cursed Cynthia

"I do hope your health improves soon," was what Lady Middlebough finally chose to say, with all the exquisite politeness born of her breeding.

He wondered what she would choose to say to the *ton's* other widows.

"Thank you for your understanding, Victoria." His voice was a silken apology. "And no one is more abashed or more regretful than I, given that you will be leaving in the morning. Please do promise me . . . another time?"

This at least was heartfelt, and Lady Middlebough knew it. She gave him a somewhat uncertain smile, but then touched her fingers to her lips in a gesture of a blown kiss, which he made a show of snatching from the air.

She backed away, then turned and headed back toward her chambers, her footsteps light, her posture slumped and thwarted, taking all of her luscious charms with her.

Miles waited until she turned the corridor corner. Then closed the door, slid the bolt, and whirled glowering on Cynthia.

"Perhaps you should have been more specific about your complaint from the very beginning." She was struggling not to laugh. "You would not have then had to debate it."

"*You* are my complaint," he hissed.

"I—" she began to protest. Her voice rose in pitch.

He thrust his finger forbiddingly against his lips and frowned darkly. *Shhh*. "I'll tell you when to go." His whisper was vehement.

It was silent for a time.

"I wouldn't," she whispered, haltingly, as though they were resuming a conversation interrupted by his *invited* guest, "because it isn't something I would ever take for granted. If I am fortunate enough to marry well, *I* will behave honorably."

"Again: how on earth do you know what you would do? Perhaps it's much more difficult than you can possibly imagine."

"But isn't that what makes it honorable? The difficulty?"

A sizzle of anger almost made him dismiss her for a naive fool. But he was honest enough with himself to concede that he was angry in part because her point was excellent.

And that in truth, he didn't think he could have gone through with it with Lady Middlebough. And not necessarily because of honor.

"Perhaps it's just that everyone expends so much effort upon making excellent matches without thought to the *suitability* of the pairing, and therefore much unhappiness is perpetuated."

"Ah. And so you are a *philanthropist* to the likes of Lady

Middlebough in that you ease, shall we say . . . unhappiness?" she asked politely.

Miles thought of Lady Georgina's earnest gray eyes then. He wondered if she would have an affair with one of his friends or some other blood in the ton should they marry.

Doubtless *he* would. Have an affair, that was. The thought brought a peculiar desolation.

"Why are you here? To make a point, or to stop me?" He said it curtly.

"I thought . . . I thought you were a man of fact and truth." It wasn't an accusation. It was as though she was gently reminding him of who he was, because the essence of who he was mattered to her. He heard hurt, faint bewilderment in her voice.

"There has only been the one married woman," he said softly, after a moment. "And not yet. And you just saw her leave." The confession cost him. But her face eased, and somehow this was all that mattered in that moment.

"Would you . . . " she swallowed. "Would you have . . . if I hadn't come?"

He waited. In the end, he of course answered truthfully, though it unnerved him.

"I don't know," he said softly. And the admission was a gift to her. Because the answer would have most certainly been an unequivocal "yes" only days ago.

Cynthia's eyes widened, then she quickly dropped her gaze. Ah. So she understood.

Take for granted, she said. He studied her. Oh, God. It struck him that there was no end to the way she could fascinate him. Her hair . . . her hair seemed a universe of colors. He'd seen her in an iridescent dress he'd confused with the wings of a tropical butterfly, and in a perfectly lovely, demure green dress that had somehow made him think of Tudor prostitutes, and now she was in her nightdress, which was large and loose and free of frills, but revealed a swoop of pale skin above the gathered neckline, between where her hands clutched his coat closed. He wanted to land his hands there, touch his tongue to the indentation between those fine bones at the base of her throat—

"All right, you should go now," he said instantly.

Her presence and the conversation combined made him feel cornered. He could skillfully negotiate with *cannibals*, but this girl overwhelmed him because she intruded upon places in him he'd never dreamed existed, showed him undreamed of desires, raised uncomfortable questions his analytical mind could not dissect. He had no idea how to prevent her from doing it.

Or how to defend himself.

And there was one thing Miles Redmond hated more than anything in the world: not *knowing*.

He took two quick strides forward to take his coat from her. Something in his face must have told her he was quite serious about evicting her. She shifted the coat from her shoulders into her hands.

He meant to take it from her. Instead, it dropped to the floor.

And he watched his hand sink into her hair slowly, wonderingly.

What the bloody hell was the matter with him? A few nights ago he'd licked her like a spaniel, and he'd begun this evening by flinging her in and out of his chambers as though she were a bandalore.

Now he was pulling her hair.

Well, perhaps he wasn't *pulling* her hair. But he did have his hand rather emphatically in it, and he was loath to take it back out again. The dense silkiness mesmerized him, and again, the sheer force of his wonder infuriated him even as it weakened him. He lifted his handful slowly up, let its weight waterfall down through his fingers, watching the dozens of subtle colors sparking in it: fire reds and coppers threaded through glossy mink brown. Combed his fingers back through it.

She was still. Either captivated by his wonder or, once again, utterly surprised by what the mad Miles Redmond had chosen to do to her. But then his coat slipped from her fingers and fell to the carpet, and he looked into her eyes. They'd gone hazy and soft, pupils large and dark, lids heavier now.

He slid his other hand through the other side of her hair, hair that now made her his prisoner. He gave a gentle tug upon it to tip her head back into his hands.

And softly, softly, he brushed his mouth over hers.

Her breath sighed out against his lips. Relief, or resignation? Or something of both?

Her eyes drifted all the way closed. And he could see in her throat the quick thump of her heart.

He touched his tongue to the corner of her mouth, to that surprising, sensitive little place, to remind her that he knew secrets about women and therefore about her. And then he made the kiss a real but leisurely one: gentle, drawing the carnal pillow of her lower lip between his own. Slowly, slowly, savoring the generous give of it, taking just a quick tantalizing taste of her mouth. Dark, sweet, rich as exotic fruit.

And just like that he was drugged. Drugged from one kiss.

He ended it as slowly as he'd begun it. Still, his lips hovered above hers. Loath to leave her.

"What do you want, Cynthia?" he whispered a scant inch from her mouth.

It wasn't a demand, though he'd meant it to be. He was in fact no less angry or confused than he'd been moments earlier. But somehow the words emerged gently, because he was genuinely curious. He *genuinely* wanted her insight. Perhaps if *she* knew what she wanted, or why she was here, or what they did to each other or truly wanted from each other, they could be done with it. They could solve this for the both of them, and then he could resume the more or less peaceful life he'd enjoyed before her.

Her lids fluttered up in languid stages, as though she'd grown unaccustomed to the weight of her own eyelashes. Her pupils were nearly indistinguishable from that rich blue. It was like looking into midnight.

She met his eyes, her own dark, enigmatic, helpless, as though she would speak . . . if only she could. The uneven tempo of her breath breezed against his lips.

Excitement built upon excitement. His, hers.

"I don't think it's me you want," he surmised relentlessly, punishing himself with his own logic and his own words, his voice a murmur, his fingers leisurely dragging his hands all the way down through that shining sheet of hair, down her back, to her buttocks. Through it his fingertips brushed the muslin nightdress; it was worn nearly as smooth as her skin, partly chilled from her sojourn down the hall, partly warm from the fire. God. So many glorious sensations belonged to this one woman.

"I think I've inadvertently shown you what your *nature* wants," he said, "and you think there's something in particular you've missed. And . . ." His voice became a hush. " . . . you think I'll show you what this is. That I'll show you what you want to know. What you now *need*

255

to know. And you think that I'm . . ." And now his voice was a whisper:

" . . . safe."

It had begun as a word, but he ended it as a kiss. As soft as the whisper itself.

Chapter 17

A s nearly chaste as the kiss was, it burned Cynthia's lips.

He'd fashioned a net of his voice, that voice of raw silk and midnight. *Safe?* she felt about as safe as any netted creature. She wished he would stop speaking, for it seemed unfair for only one of them to have the use of words, and she could say nothing.

She existed only to be touched, and everything else—speaking, breathing—was superfluous at the moment. Why didn't he realize this?

She closed her eyes again. A vain attempt to keep him from reading her thoughts.

This large-nosed, broad-shouldered, warm-skinned, probingly subtle, bespectacled man was too clever. He was entirely right, of course, about her. Had always been. She felt exposed; she ought to feel resentful.

But now, his large hands were warm on the small of her back, spanning her waist entirely, and she was impatient to feel them on her skin. And surely this was a dangerous, *dangerous* way to feel.

Why then was she here? When her entire future was at

stake? When all she had to offer a man was beauty, charm, and virtue?

And suddenly the hands were gone, his warmth was gone, his breath against her lips was gone.

He was gone.

She realized her knees had turned to water when she swayed forward and nearly stumbled.

Why? Where . . . ?

She opened her eyes, disoriented. She saw that Miles had stepped back from her and was sitting in a chair near the fire. He gave it his weight with relief, pressed his back against it; it was, in fact, very nearly a sprawl. He squeezed his eyes closed briefly; tipped his head back. His fingers gripped the arms of the chair. This was the only sign of tension in the man.

He didn't fidget, or tap a foot, or hum. No: whatever storms took place in Miles were given expression only when he touched her.

Or when he touched the likes of Lady Middlebough?

Was it the same for him with other women? Was it *always* the same for him? How could it possibly be? Surely if it was, it would have killed him by now.

It occurred to Cynthia to wonder whether perhaps *his* knees had turned to water, too, which was why he'd sought out a chair.

And now his eyes were open and hot, and his face was taut with whatever decision he was attempting to forge in that formidable mind of his. Silence elongated, but the fire had been recently built—the flames brilliant, lively and leaping—and the room was growing warmer and warmer still.

At least, she preferred to blame the fire for how much warmer she was feeling.

"Very well. I'll show you, Miss Brightly."

She nearly jumped.

His voice was soft and husky, hesitant; it seemed to come from somewhere inside her when he spoke. Oddly, he sounded . . . resigned. It sounded like a verdict he'd been reluctant to deliver, as he was uncertain of her reaction. Or even of the wisdom of delivering it.

Thus having delivered it, his mouth quirked at the corner. He was awaiting *her* verdict.

Thank God, was what she felt like saying. She couldn't yet speak.

He must have seen this in her face, because he gave a short low laugh: the sound of rueful desire.

"Come stand before me, Cynthia."

She was tempted to disobey, simply to prove to herself that she still possessed free will.

Her body wasn't interested in disobedience, however: she drifted over as surely as if he'd tugged her by a string.

She stood before him, looking down, her knees just shy of touching his, her heart thudding in her chest

Miles looked up at her, and she floated in the dark, hot, enigmatic world of his eyes for a long moment. She only became aware that his hands had moved away from the arms of the chair when she felt the air of the room sigh against the backs of her calves. And then, over the pop and spit of the fire, she heard the hushed slide of the nightdress being drawn upward in his hands.

On its way up it left behind a trail of gooseflesh, brushed over the very fine golden hairs of her thighs, turning her spine to liquid. Absently she considered the irony that her own nightdress could be used as a tool of seduction.

Ah, but this was not to be a seduction, she reminded herself. She could never allow it to be fully that.

I'll show you, he'd said.

There's more, he'd said.

And now she stood before him, scarcely able to draw a proper breath, as her blood seemed to have been replaced with fire itself.

She stood looking down, her nightdress gathered in Venetian folds at her hips in the hands of a man she'd known only a few days, her thighs bare and vulnerable, shockingly pale to her own eyes in the shadowy room, and wondered why it was only then that she considered herself stark raving mad for allowing this moment to happen.

Safe, he'd said. Did she *truly* think this?

How had he known?

She trusted him. Then again, everyone seemed to trust Miles Redmond.

Reason began to invade her delicious torpor, and she tensed. Miles sensed it, of course, doubtless the way he would sense tension in any warm-blooded animal within his control. One of his eyebrows arced in question. He was allowing her a moment to decide. She felt the slight tremble in his fingers, too; heard the uneven in-and-out of his breathing—nerves or desire? And understood how difficult this was for him.

Safe. She supposed she was safe with him.

And admitting this to herself, Cynthia slowly closed her eyes, and with that invited more sensation.

He wasted no time: his fingers began feathering, slowly, slowly, toward the tender insides of her thighs. Those warm fingers, coaxing them apart. They needed little coaxing.

"So soft," he whispered, and there was a peculiar pain, an agony of want in the voice, that was erotic as his touch.

His hands slid beneath her buttocks and he gently pulled her forward. Until his knees were quite between her legs.

"Sit," he whispered.

"Sit? On—"

"Me," he completed easily. Softly. Making it sound altogether reasonable.

So she did.

She eased onto his lap, straddling his thighs. She felt the jump of his chest as his breath caught; saw the dark flare of his pupils, the taut cords of his throat, as their bodies slowly met. And through the confines of his trousers she could feel, she could see, the shockingly hard length of his erection.

Desire gave a great unladylike thump as she found herself groin-to-groin with him. She was weak, weak from it.

Even so, his hands remained downright decorous. Rested lightly at her hips, right at the point where he'd gathered up her nightdress. Even as his chest moved unevenly, swiftly.

"Why don't you lower your nightdress, Cynthia?"

Again, it was a suggestion, silkily delivered. But it was also shot through with implacability, and hopelessly compelling for that reason.

And so her hands, just as much a slave to his voice as the rest of her body seemed to be, found the neckline of her nightdress. Her eyes couldn't leave his face, so she fumbled for the limp ribbon that held it snugly closed about her throat.

Miles waited. Riveted. His hands motionless on her hips. Breathing in and out, the heat from his body all but burning her bare thighs even though his trousers.

She plucked at the ribbon until it gave way, releasing her neckline. It loosened, then sagged, and she felt the air in the room meet her skin. All the while savoring the searing fixity of his gaze.

She waited, testing her power over him, testing his patience.

Then suddenly feeling shy, she ducked her eyes from his as she shrugged her shoulders. The top of her nightdress dropped.

But not far enough to suit Miles. She felt a small triumph as impatience won over him, and his hands were on it, drawing it effortlessly down.

And in the next instant, it seemed, his hands were filled with her breasts. His hands were hot, roughened from riding, from the outdoors, from simply being who he was. They were urgent. His thumbs dragged hard over nipples already peaked.

"God."

He took her gasped oath into his mouth because his lips were already there for a kiss. She feasted on this kiss with relief, welcoming his searching, hot tongue as his hands became thoroughly reacquainted with her breasts.

His mouth traveled her throat, to her ear, and ducked beneath to lick the tender hidden place there. She turned her head to abet him, to allow him access to every angle and valley, pleasure shivering through her, from lips, his tongue, his hands.

She'd been very ill with a fever once, as a child. So odd. It hadn't been entirely unpleasant, living in a world created only of heat.

And this . . . this was a fever. She thought she could live in this world forever.

When his mouth returned home to her mouth, it was hot and open and savage, and she fell into the kiss, reveling in the clash of teeth, the sinewy darting tongue. He took his lips away from her briefly and raised two fingers to drag them across her mouth for her to suck them.

He drew his fingers away wet.

And without preamble he slid his kiss-dampened fingers between her legs.

"Oh." She jerked. The intimacy shocked her.

And she could not have possibly described the sensation, unless with one word:

More.

"I'm going to make you come, Cynthia." The words were coarse and fascinating and unbearably erotic. "Because I do believe that's what you came here for."

His fingers slid forward over her again, through her damp curls, her cleft, her—

Dear God . . . incredible . . .

"I—" she choked. What could she possibly say? Very well, then?

He locked eyes with her. She saw triumph and determination and a soft sympathy in his: he understood her suffering; he was the source, and succor.

His fingers slid again. She was drenched and hot and how did he *know* precisely where to touch her?

Her lips parted on a gasp; her breath came roughly now.

"How?" That whisper again. "How do you want me to touch you?"

Her head had tipped back helplessly. She pushed her body against his hand. *Touch me again.*

"I don't *know* . . ." The words were shredded, airless gasps. She was angry to be asked. He *knew*, she thought; why didn't he simply *give* to her? "Just . . . please . . . more . . ." She shifted against his hand.

"How?" He insisted on that brutally silky murmur. "*How* do you want me to touch you?"

She swallowed. She despised him for making her think, for making her form words. "Harder . . ."

How did she know that?

He stroked, deliberately, precisely . . . harder.

Lightning forked through her body. Her head jerked back on a sob of pleasure.

"Ah," he murmured, pleased with this discovery.

"Again," she suggested breathlessly, her head rocking back limply, then against his chin, where his own harsh breath fell hot on her ears. She moved her body against his fingers. "Please . . . again . . ."

She was distantly aware of his faint smile.

"Now we know *how*." His voice was low and taut. "Show me precisely where. With your body. Your body knows."

"Please just—again—" she nearly wept. She ached with the need. "Please . . . like this . . ." She moved against him, asking, begging.

"All right, all right. It's all right, love," a cracked whisper.

Glory of glories, he touched her again precisely the way she wanted to be touched, dragging his fingers harder over her. Circling deliberately.

A moan spiraled out of her. Guttural and primal. The sound of bliss through the ages. She hadn't known herself capable of such a sound. It wasn't enough.

He ducked his head against her throat, as seemingly moved as she was.

She felt his breath against her skin, cooling it; it was how she knew she was drenched in perspiration now.

She didn't know how she could bear this. She should stop him. Stop him now. She was afraid; it was too new, too unknown, and she didn't know where it was leading. She hooked her arms around his neck, stroked her fingers up through his hair, held his head fast.

She placed her mouth next to his ear. "Please don't stop."

She felt his chest leap in what might have been a short laugh.

Miles found her mouth again with his. He demanded a kiss, and he thrust and stroked with his tongue while his talented, insistent, obliging fingers made good on his promise, stroking, circling, and oh God, once, sliding deeply into the depths of her. Instinct guided her. She moved with him in a rhythm at first tentative, then deliberate, and then swift and abandoned as the pleasure swelled to something almost indistinguishable from agony.

She jerked her head, took her lips from him, buried her face in the crook of his neck.

"Miles . . . please—I want—"

It wanted something from her, this pleasure, or she wanted something from it, and she didn't know whether to fight it or rush toward it, or how to do either. And still he stroked, insistently, a torturously exquisite rhythm, faster now. *He* knew.

"Trust me," he whispered.

She had no choice: she abandoned herself to him. They rocked swiftly together, and then all at once white heat rushed over her skin; the mingled roar of their breathing beat in her ears like waves. She could feel, distantly, her nightdress fused to her shoulder blades with sweat.

"Miles. . ."

A conflagration ripped through her; his name emerged a soundless scream.

The release arced her like a bowstring, shook her body, rocked her forward and back, and he held onto her as it wracked her with wave after wave of indescribable bliss.

And in that moment, nothing else mattered, not him, not herself.

Pleasure owned her.

And then it was done with her. Leaving her limp, at peace.

265

She was aware now that Miles's hands were resting lightly at her hips. His chin resting lightly against the top of her head. Her eyes were level with a wedge of burnished skin showing where his shirt was unbuttoned. He glistened with sweat; he smelled male. His chest rose and fell, rose and fell. She found she couldn't yet meet his eyes.

And then she did.

He lifted a hand to stroke her hair from her face; his hand dropped heavily again. She saw some expression fleeing from his face. Something that made her catch her breath. She might have called it pain, but it wasn't that.

How do you know? he'd said with exaggerated patience, when she loftily claimed that she would not be slinking through corridors once she was wed. He might as well have laughed at her; she would have deserved it. She'd always understood the power of attraction and the attraction of power; she'd made good use of it, and responded to both.

But now she understood why people would risk a good deal for this kind of pleasure. Behave ridiculously, embarrassingly, dangerously.

She'd thought herself worldly. She'd been outrageously naive.

But she knew she would hold herself to it. She had nothing else in the world but her own particular form of honor. She was tired, tired of games.

If she never knew this kind of pleasure again, she would have this: this moment, this man, this knowledge.

She said nothing. Then she just looked up at him, and he must have read everything in her face—the wonder, the gratitude, the awe, the embarrassment—because the corner of his mouth lifted.

She breathed in to steady herself. And reached for his trouser buttons.

He placed his hand abruptly on hers. "You'd best not." His voice was low and hoarse, startled. It contained an unmistakable warning.

"But—"

"No." Firmly.

"Why?" she demanded.

He drew in another long impatient breath, exhaled. And when he spoke, his quiet voice was a whip crack.

"Cynthia, for God's sake. Do you understand what you're asking of me? You might think I'm in control of my every action, but I'm a man. And so very, very little stops me from throwing you down right now and plowing you senseless. Not a moment has passed since we've met where I haven't wanted to do precisely that. Don't be a bloody fool. For the love of God, don't test me."

He was furious; this was evident.

But it wasn't directed precisely at her; it was more directed at the circumstances. It was fury born of fear.

She knew him so well now.

And suddenly she knew why.

He'd seen *her* vulnerable and abandoned and utterly at his mercy. He'd begun and ended every moment of their encounters. He'd always been in control.

She suspected that he was afraid to be vulnerable. He was *afraid* to relinquish control. And perhaps, in particular, he was afraid to be at *her* mercy. Because he'd been to some extent at her mercy from the moment they'd met.

"It's all right to lose control," she said softly. "You're safe with me."

His eyes flared hotly in surprise. "Cynthia—"

She met his eyes. "Stop me."

And before he could, she dragged her palm over the hard length of him curving toward his belly. She could feel the smooth round head of his cock even through his trousers; her fingers lingered there.

His head went back hard; he hissed in a breath. "Sweet *holy . . .*"

He followed these words with a stream of much more shocking, gratifying words.

She did it again, and he shifted beneath her, his chest. Her deft fingers swiftly opened his trouser buttons.

"So show me," she whispered. "How do you want to be touched?"

"Cynthia," he whispered hoarsely. "I swear to you, it won't require much . . . *dear God.*"

His cock leaped free, bare, from his trousers, and her fingers instantly traced the hot length of him. He was enormous and thick; the sensation of him in her palm was powerful and strange and more than dangerous.

She looked down. It was foreign and frightening, ugly and beautiful, for all of that.

He swallowed hard. His hands gripped the arms of the chair.

"How?" she whispered. "Show me."

She stroked him again.

He seized her hand in his and held it fast in his for a moment, his eyes burning into hers, his mouth a taut line. His breath gusted hot against her throat. A bead of perspiration traced his temple, traveled his jaw. The tension in him thrummed through her body, and where moments earlier she had been exhausted, the excitement began to build in her again, in tandem with fear.

The suppressed force of the man was palpable. She suddenly had no idea of his intentions. And this, too, was part of the excitement.

Curse her for being a gambler.

And then he moved. Deliberately, he guided her fingers to wrap around his cock.

He held her hand there for a moment.

And then, his warm hand over hers, he dragged it slowly and hard down around the head of it. Then up again. Hard. His eyes never leaving hers.

He took his hand slowly away.

"And for the love of God don't stop," he growled.

Cynthia knew triumph, but fear lingered.

She drew her hand down. Hard. And up again. He struggled for control; his chest rose and fell with swift breaths, his fingers curling whitely into the arms of the chair.

She stroked again. And again. Feeling the enormous swell of him grow thicker, tauter, in her fist.

His hands lifted, slowly, to languidly twist, then tangle in her hair. As if he needed her for balance. His head rocked back, the lids of his eyes lowered to slits. The cords of his neck were taut. Watching him struggle to withstand this pleasure was extraordinary; knowing she was the source of it sent a wash of awe through her.

"Cynthia . . ." His voice was a choke of near disbelief. "God help me . . . I want you . . ."

Throw you down and plow you, he'd said. In that moment, *she* wanted nothing more.

And this would mean the end of everything for her—of all her hopes. Because virtue was one of the very few things she had to offer anyone who married her.

This, surely, was why he'd warned her. *Do you know what you're asking of me?*

How reckless she'd been to take for granted his control. How foolhardy, how selfish, to impose the need for such control upon him.

Still, she couldn't find it in herself to regret it. Not yet. She'd never felt more powerful in her life.

Miles pressed his back against the chair; his head tipped back; his throat moved in a swallow as she stroked him. His breath came in harsh bursts now between narrowly parted lips; he thrust his hips sharply up into her fist. *Faster.* She shifted her weight upon his thighs and complied with her fist, and together they found the rhythm he wanted.

"Cynthia. . ."Her name was a raw gasp. " . . . so . . . *good . . .*"

And moments later his head jerked forward as if he'd been brutally lashed, his body bucking sharply beneath her.

Peace followed. He eased back against the chair and was still, as though some demon in him had at last been exorcised. He was still, that was, apart from the bellows of his breathing.

His eyes were closed. His hands loosened, slipped from her.

Cynthia glanced wonderingly into her palm, warm and damp where he'd spilled into it. Her cheeks burned.

She watched him struggle to even his breath, head pressed back against that generous chair, perspiration gleaming on his temples. The dark brush of his eyelashes lay still against his skin. His jaw was darkening with the beginnings of the beard he or his valet would scrape off with a razor in the morning. She knew an impulse to brush her hand against his skin, to follow with her finger the uncompromisingly defined lines of his face, as if she could learn why he was put together precisely the way he was. To push that silky dark hair away from his eyes.

He looked like a boy, free of the weight of his thoughts for the moment, free of the weight of his life, and suddenly he was new. And a stranger.

She almost wanted to cry like a confused child.

What were they creating here? It had no beginning or end she could trace; there was no possibility she would be able to make sense of it or control it. It had no part in her life.

It could not end well.

It needed to end now.

These thoughts frightened her in the way this physical intimacy had not. She tensed. Her eyes sought the door: escape. His eyes opened then; he looked into her face. Seemed to drink her in, to sense what she was thinking.

Then he looked down at her hands. His expression didn't change. But he shifted in the chair and found in his trouser pocket a handkerchief.

Wordlessly, gently, he took her hands in his, matter-of-factly rubbed them clean.

She had no precedent for what to say under these circumstances, and the usual tools at her disposal—charm and beauty, insight and wit—were thoroughly unequal to the occasion, sitting on the lap of a man who had just made her scream silently with untold pleasure.

And for whom she'd returned the favor.

She did it almost unconsciously, as though it was a substitute for words: she raised her hand and rested the backs of her fingers to his cheek. She dropped her hand swiftly again along with her gaze, because the enigmatic flare in his eyes unnerved her.

She slid from his lap, suddenly eager to leave him. And just as reluctant to go.

She straightened her nightdress; he assembled himself behind her. She heard the rustle of it.

He turned to her and looked at her for a long time, seemed to consider what to say. When he decided, he looked away to speak.

"Not again," he said finally, very softly and firmly. "This can't happen again."

He'd been measuring, weighing, examining those words in the laboratory of his mind before delivering them. She almost smiled; if she had, it would have been a decidedly bittersweet smile.

Miles Redmond didn't say things he didn't mean.

He turned back to her then. He was asking for her complicity, she thought, for he didn't trust himself. He was asking her not to test him again.

She simply nodded.

She was, in fact, in wholehearted, fervent agreement. Because she had assumed there was nothing she couldn't understand, and she was afraid now in a way that felt peculiarly like the opposite of fear.

Her impulse, in fact, was to bolt. And she had never before run from any challenge.

She didn't know the protocol for parting in the aftermath of . . . what they'd just done. Miles didn't, either, clearly. He bent toward her awkwardly, then straightened again just as she leaned in. She leaned back again as he leaned in again.

And thus two people known for their social grace spent a few seconds feinting ridiculously at each other.

But then Miles took in a breath and stood before her—planted himself before her—in a way that caused Cynthia to go very still. He'd made another decision. He leaned in very slowly, or so it seemed to her—that time grew thick and elastic—and there was first his warm breath, then the fall of a strand of his dark hair, then the graze of his lips against her cheek. And for a moment his cheek rested against hers.

Her heart kicked once, sharply. She closed her eyes: his skin was still feverishly warm; his whiskers chafed her. She breathed; in came sweat and clean linen, tobacco and soap, the lingering faint musk of his desire. *Their* desire.

Slowly, slowly, as one emerges from torpor, he lifted his head; the warmth of his cheek faded from hers. He stepped back. His fingers reached up to the bridge of his nose; his spectacles weren't there. He dropped his fingers again.

Later, in her chambers, she couldn't remember leaving him. She didn't remember the feel of the cold hall marble against her feet, either; she didn't notice the candles burnt to nubs in the rows of sconces, or the length of the shadows thrown by moonlight through the long narrow windows. Her senses were given over to reliving the feel of Miles Redmond's cheek against hers, to the image of him slowly, slowly, stepping back from her, as if it had required every bit of strength he possessed to allow her to go.

Chapter 18

Cynthia awoke with a cat on her head, and knew a peculiar bright happiness. It was that moment before memory sifts entirely into place.

Which is when she remembered that today was an ending and a beginning.

She plucked her furry, yawning feline hat from her head and kissed it good morning. She slid from the bed. She raised her nightdress to lift it over her head, to bath her face, her torso, from the lavender scented basin water.

She stopped abruptly, the nightdress half over her head. She could still smell him. His skin, his sweat. On her nightdress. On her own skin. She took great, dizzying breaths of him.

And then realized it wouldn't do for the maid to find her with the nightdress half over her head and her sniffing it.

With a sense of ceremony, she pulled it all the way off over her head, laid it gently aside, as if she were indeed shedding him.

And with the same sense of ceremony, she washed her face, her skin.

This can't happen again, he'd said. No, it most definitely could not. She would ensure that it didn't. They needed distance from each other, and Cynthia told herself that her instinct for self-preservation would ensure it, and she would be here only one week more.

Only one more week.

The backs of her hands iced.

She opened up the wardrobe and gave her slim purse a shake. In one week this house party would end. She would have three pounds. A trunk full of wilted clothing. One cat.

And nowhere at all to go.

She sat down hard on the bed, because suddenly her nightmare of falling and falling was a waking one. She looked in the mirror, and the girl who looked back at her wasn't someone she wanted to know: who would want to dance with that tense, frightened girl?

Though she was admittedly still *pretty*.

This amused her. She had beauty. She had pride. She was clever. She was resourceful. She was suited for absolutely *nothing*.

Apart from what she was doing now.

This last thought made her laugh at herself, and she kissed her cat again, squared her shoulders and went down to breakfast.

But today she couldn't quite bring an appetite with her. Nerves made rather a whirlpool of her stomach.

Everyone was at the sunny table but Miles, and for this she was grateful. She scooped eggs and kippers she would not be eating onto her plate and amused herself by arranging them in artful heaps, and looked up at Mr. Goodkind.

She stared at him. Offered a tentative smile. Tried not to picture him in a bonnet, a great satin bow tied beneath his chin.

Blue would be his color, regardless.

He smiled. He *did* have a nice smile, she conceded again. And quite fine eyes, though they looked a trifle bleary this morning. He also had a good deal of forehead, but this was to be expected in a man his age.

"Miss Brightly," he said suddenly, "I wonder if you might like to stroll in the garden with me. I could use your unique insight into my work."

His voice was a bit cottony. Jonathan and Argosy must have been keeping him up nights.

Violet, none too subtly, winked. Cynthia gave her a kick in the ankle under the table. Georgina looked encouraging, which made her want to kick Georgina, too, for an entirely different reason.

Lady Windermere seemed puzzled. She glanced at Argosy.

Whose fine jaw looked quite set. When would he understand that feigned casualness had its consequences? Cynthia wondered, giving him a conciliatory smile that softened his jaw.

She had an objective. To the victor goes the spoils, she thought firmly. Rather disliking the word "spoils" at the moment, and wishing she could tell Argosy he had but a week to press his suit, before Cinderella became a charwoman again.

She didn't touch her breakfast at all.

But off she resignedly went for a stroll near the roses with Mr. Goodkind, because they both agreed they enjoyed the roses.

A gardener had just come out to see to them, and began working up the row, clipping great blown, crisped heads and dropping them into a basket. They heard the snicking of scissors behind them as they strolled. A soothing, summery sound.

"Well, how goes your work, Mr. Goodkind? Are you finding inspiration in your surroundings?"

"Oh, Miss Brightly. I must thank you. You have helped to add a new dimension to my work."

Upon closer inspection, she saw that his poor hair lay splayed on his scalp, greasy and exhausted. She peered closer still: no, it wasn't the light filtered through the trees. His skin really did have a bit of a green cast to it.

He correctly interpreted her peering.

"Mr. Jonathan Redmond and Lord Argosy persuaded me to billiards last night. I believe I lost a good deal of money and drank a good deal of brandy."

"Did you ask the housekeeper for a headache powder, Mr. Goodkind?" she asked solicitously.

"Oh, no. I think it helps to suffer the consequences of my own forays into wickedness in order to effectively repent, and then write passionately about them." The look he sent her held something of an innuendo. "*You* look no worse for wear."

It was part compliment, part accusation. He paused at a bench as if to say, *Shall we?*

"Ah. Perhaps you are more accustomed to such evenings," he said after they seated themselves.

"Perhaps," she said carefully. He suddenly glanced down at her hands. She wondered if he was admiring her gloves.

She felt a slight crawling sensation at the back of her neck. He looked so *ordinary*, really.

Apart from the green skin, that was.

"You've some familiarity with various *varieties* of wickedness, Miss Brightly?"

She gave a start. She wasn't certain whether he was flirting. It certainly sounded like the beginnings of flirtation. Or perhaps . . .

Perhaps he'd begun to gingerly fish about for her degree

of tolerance to various kinds of wickedness? Did dressing in women's clothes count as wickedness for a man like Mr. Goodkind?

It had never been explicitly addressed in one of the vicar's sermons, to her recollection.

Perhaps Mr. Goodkind suffered a good deal over his urges.

She looked into his pale blue eyes. *Would* he gravitate to blue? Bonnets with blue linings? Gloves of pale blue kid?

"I've experience with a great variety of . . . needs and behaviors," she began carefully.

"Do you?" His eyes widened. Then he winced, as the widened eyes allowed in more light than was comfortable. And apparently wincing hurt, too. "Perhaps we should discuss them, Miss Brightly."

This sounded like an invitation to engage in innuendo.

"Well . . . for example, I've come to understand that certain gentlemen have . . . idiosyncratic needs."

Goodkind eyed her with some fascination. "N-needs?"

He'd relaxed his body somewhat and his knee just shy of touching hers, in that accidental way that was entirely purposeful. She could smell him now over the tired roses: mostly he smelled clean. Shaving soap. With an infinitesimal series of glances, he took in her bosom outlined in white muslin, then her lips. And then his eyes went to her hands, gloved in white. They lingered there. His hand crept closer to hers on the bench.

Speaking of needs, she suspected she would need to go gingerly here lest she find herself needing to fight off Mr. Goodkind in the garden.

She reached out and touched a rose nodding over the top of the bench. He followed her hand very closely with his eyes. *It is the gloves.*

She turned to him. "But then, don't we *all* have particular needs? And should we not be forgiving of differences in others?"

"Miss Brightly," he breathed. "You have a truly revolutionary way of thinking."

She was encouraged. "And two people with different or unique needs can find a way to live comfortably together."

This confused him a little. "I suppose you are correct," he agreed carefully.

"For instance . . . I am quite a fair seamstress. Which means I could discreetly sew a very large garter." She sent him a sidelong glance. "The kind that might even fit . . . a masculine thigh."

Goodkind froze.

For a brief moment there was no sound apart from the snick of scissors lopping roses.

"Are we still discussing . . . unique needs, Miss Brightly?" He said this gingerly.

"Oh, yes," she assured him gently.

He frowned slightly. Then his mouth opened. He began to point with his finger in what appeared to be the beginnings of a fervent comment. Then he stopped, as frowning seemed to make him feel queasy.

"And I believe very strongly in sharing," she added, prompting him.

"Well . . . sharing is admirable." He began to brighten a little.

"I shouldn't mind at all sharing my bonnets. For instance . . ." She took a deep breath, in preparation for the plunge. "I have one that I think would look very well on you. It would suit the shape of your face."

Goodkin recoiled. His blue eyes bulged.

"It has a blue lining," she added encouragingly, but hesitantly.

He stared at her. Then he stood very, very slowly, straightening very, very slowly, as one crippled.

"A den," he muttered darkly, sounding amazed.

"I beg your pardon, Mr. Goodkind?" She was nervous now.

"A den!" he roared to her, to the sky. He was upright now. She heard a distant little yelp. He'd frightened the gardener. Cynthia scrambled backward on the bench.

"This place is a *den* of iniquity! First you encourage me to drink myself into foolishness, and then young Redmond and that lordling *rob* me blind with wagering on billiards, and *now* you tempt me with your pretty face and your talk of *needs*—and you want me to wear a garter and bonnet to satisfy *your* unique needs? You are depraved, Miss Brightly. Irreparably damaged by your time in the ton."

"Mr. Goodkind—"

He shook his head sadly. "I shall pray for your soul, Miss Brightly. But I do thank you. You are the devil in a beautiful disguise. I have seen temptation, and I have shown that I can conquer temptation, but my writing will be the better for it. I need no longer remain in this den of iniquity, and I will not wear a garter. For anyone! I will depart."

He turned to stalk off. He'd gone a few yards when he turned to her.

"Don't forget to buy my book this fall," he added, on a slightly less aggrieved note.

And then he turned and strode righteously to the house.

"Garters," she heard him muttering.

* * *

Miles had just swung his body down from Ramsay and was getting ready to hand the reins off to a stable boy, when a voice made him whirl.

"Mr. Redmond?"

It was Cynthia. He wasn't certain whether he was happy to hear it, because he'd spent the morning attempting to drum her from his mind and body with a hard ride and rigorous planning.

Yet something about the tone was portentous. He turned slowly.

Her face inside her bonnet was rosy from heat and from a lengthy walk from the house. She pushed the bonnet impatiently from her face then, and it dangled down her back, and dark dampened streamers of hair clung to her temples. She must have made a *point* to track him down. She must have asked *where* he would be.

Why did he feel a trifle . . . uneasy?

"Good afternoon, Miss Brightly," he said, matching her formal tone cautiously, as stable boys lurked nearby, awaiting orders from him, and eager to eavesdrop if he gave them an opportunity.

But he couldn't help it. No matter what: it was wonderful to see her, and his voice was soft. "Was there something I could help you—"

"It seems, Mr. Redmond, something I said to Mr. Goodkind *greatly* offended him."

Oh, dear.

"Is that so?" It was a brilliant bit of nonchalance. "Would you, er, care to *share* what you said to Mr. Goodkind?"

There was a pause. "No." One crisp, inscrutable little syllable. "I would not."

He waited. He cleared his throat. "What makes you think he didn't like—"

Cynthia swiftly moved very quickly toward him, stood so close to him he could have counted her eyelashes. Her eyes were ablaze, and two spots of deep color sat on her cheeks.

Well, then. It's safe to say she's angry.

"Mr. Goodkind *has,* in fact, ordered his trunks packed and has departed in one of your family's carriages for saner climes. Specifically *because* of something I said."

"He did?" Miles said stupidly. He was stalling now. He made frantic shooing motions at the stable boys, who wisely fled across the yard, sensing that an uproar was about to ensue.

"You lied, didn't you? About his alleged peccadillo? About the women's clothing?"

"Well . . ." He was still picturing Goodkind storming off, and then he imagined the content of the conversation . . . and it was nearly impossible not to smile. *What*, precisely, had she said? "I might have . . . *invented*—"

He stopped. Because she looked stunned.

"That wasn't fair," she whispered. "What you did . . . it wasn't . . . it wasn't cricket."

"Cricket?" It seemed an odd word. He couldn't quite gauge her mood.

She was breathing heavier now. "This is not a *game*." Her voice was shaking a little.

"Not a *game*?" He gave a short laugh. " 'Oh, Mr. Red-mond,' " he falsettoed. " 'You're so *inter*—' "

She flew at him before he could dodge and thumped one of her fists against his chest. "It's not a *game* for *me*!"

"Christ! Cynthia—"

"It's not a *game*!" She hit him again. A good one. The third time she tried it, he captured her hands and held her fast and it was like holding a trapped wild creature. She was remarkably strong for someone so small.

"You—You with your money and your bloody grandeur and your family and history. It's all very well for you and Violet to *play* at romance. It will all be all right in the end, of course. But I've none of that. None. I've *no one*. And you've gone and played dice with *my* future. Why shouldn't I have what Violet will have? What *you* will have so easily? Why shouldn't I? You bloody . . . bloody . . . *snob*." She could have chosen a different word, a much more scathing word, and somehow he didn't doubt that she knew words like that; still, the one she'd chosen stung.

She tried to kick him in the shins; he dodged.

"Cynthia! Please! Just—"

She looked up at him, attempted to tug her wrists free. At least she wasn't biting.

Yet.

"I know what you think of me, Miles. I know what you-*have* thought of me. But I have a heart. I do have a *heart*. I just cannot afford to *use* it. Don't you see? Why can't you see this? Whereas *you*—may play at all of this as much as you like. There will always be someone for you. And that is the difference: I cannot *afford* to use my heart. And you— you *choose* not to use yours."

Stunned, he kept his grip on her wrists. And could say nothing at all.

Her voice cracked a little. "I have a heart," she repeated very softly, wearily, as though some invisible audience had accused her otherwise and had been dunking her over and over again for a witch. As though confessing a fatal debility of which she was ashamed.

She turned her head away from him and gave a half-hearted attempt at freeing her hands.

He maintained his grip. Such fragile wrists. Her skin was hot, as though her anger, her fear, permeated her skin.

"Cynthia . . ." he said firmly. "Do you have any money at *all*? Anywhere at all to go that isn't here?"

She turned away from him. Still breathing hard. She refused to look at him.

She had no family, no money, the rumors had said. He'd always thought it figurative, a means of social dismissal, social ranking.

"Tell me," he demanded.

"I'll be penniless within a week or so. And no. I have no place to go when this party is over. I have no one."

He'd given her a kitten, he'd given her bliss with his hands and tongue, he'd known bliss at her hands. *Playing at romance.*

She was mercenary because she was *terrified.*

His stomach knotted in fear for her. Oh, God. He'd been an ass.

"I liked him," she said again, finally, and he could still hear the thwarted, fear-tinged exhaustion in her voice. "Goodkind. He was pompous and he wasn't interesting, but he was kind enough and wealthy and he liked me and it would have been . . ." She shook her head. "It would have been safe."

He pictured this sensual starburst of a woman standing before him married to a "kind enough" man. Would she end up creeping through hallways in the dark toward assignations? Running away with Gypsies?

No: she wanted safety. She'd never known it. She'd told him that she would be loyal.

He didn't doubt it at all. She had that kind of fortitude.

He kept his hand tightly round her wrist, as if holding onto her to prevent her from drifting away. Her fist was still a small white knot at the end of it, and her whole body trembled slightly; hectic color stained her face.

"Tell me what happened in London, Cynthia," he ordered softly. "What went wrong?"

She sighed.

He waited.

"I'm not good," she finally said, softly.

This was an intriguing beginning. "No?"

"No. Someone was nearly killed because of me."

"Ah." His head went back sharply, then came down in comprehension. "Why don't you tell me the story?"

They were quiet for a time. Around them was the powerful, comforting smell of horse and hay and leather.

"It was so wonderful," she began, faltering. "If only you know what it meant to me, that season in London. It was a miracle; I could scarcely believe I was there. I was so *popular.*"

"I recall. Diamond of the first water, and all that."

She made a sound. It was a bleak cousin to a laugh. "And all that."

"And?"

She sighed. "It was marvelous. Nothing so marvelous had ever happened to me in my entire life. I could have—there was a time during the season when I *genuinely* could have taken my pick of the men, Miles. I was *shocked.* A brief moment in time where little mattered but that I was charming and beautiful and original."

It is fashionable to be in love with her, Albemarle had told him then. And yet no one had ever truly known her, he realized. She hadn't allowed it.

"And then?" he encouraged softly.

"And then . . . well, Courtland . . . Courtland proposed."

This is what Miles knew of Courtland: young, arrogant. Had all of his limbs, even features, splendid manners. Owned fine cattle. Could hold his liquor, could shoot tolerably well.

He knew, in short, the things most men knew about other men of a similar station.

He knew nothing of the man's character. He was inclined to think well of him for not abandoning Cynthia because of her lack of pedigree. "I know of Courtland."

"I want you to understand, if you can. But I'm not certain you can. Because you . . . you've hundreds of years of family. Family simply *everywhere*. And for me . . . well, Courtland was the ending of the story, you see. I never sensed I belonged to anyone or anything. My own family history is hazy at best. So I thought: *I* will have a happy ending. I will have a family. Why shouldn't I?"

"Why not, indeed?" He said it easily, to calm her, but he felt the depth of the loneliness she carried with her in the pit of his stomach. There wasn't a soul to help her bear it. He stopped himself from putting his arms around her, because he would have done it as much to comfort himself as her. He squelched a directionless anger, because it wouldn't help her now.

"Well, the Standshaws are from Little Roxbury. And Liza was my friend, and Liza and I made the right friends. I had barely enough money for a season's worth of dresses, so I took the gamble and I bought them and then . . . and well, they *fought* over me. The men in the *ton*." She still sounded breathless, bemused.

"I heard about it." Endlessly.

"I found it exhilarating. And Miles, I *did* play one off another. I can't tell you why, precisely. Part of it was the pure pleasure of being *wanted*. For the first time ever in my life someone—everyone!—*wanted* me. And the other part was that I couldn't seem to stop testing them, to see if the magic would last. I didn't trust it. And so I tested it again and again, and it lasted and lasted. Until. . ."

"What finally happened?" Behind him Ramsay whickered, his way of clearing his throat: *Ahem. I'm still saddled.* Ramsay would have to wait.

"Well, I truly thought it was all drama and silliness— the bets, the bristling, the arguments over who would fetch punch for me, the jealousy. All manly posturing. But Courtland truly *was* jealous. He had a temper." She gave a short, wondering laugh.

There really was no end to the way men could be stupid, particularly over women.

"So there was a duel?"

She inhaled resignedly. Looked up at him more calmly now. "You should know I cared for him," she said evenly. "I did. Or thought I did. But someone who managed to . . . kiss me in the garden . . . just a *little* kiss . . ." She said this cautiously. She knew all about kisses that weren't little now, but he wasn't eager to hear about anyone else kissing her. "I told Courtland about it. To test him, you see. Courtland called him out."

She tensed again as the memory rippled through her. He stroked, lightly, the insides of her wrists with his fingers.

"He would hear nothing of reason. Bloody *pride*. And so they dueled. He was . . ." She cleared her throat. "He was shot," she said baldly. "In the shoulder. Gravely injured. He almost died—it was a very near thing, I'm told—I'm *told*, because they would never let me see him when he was carried off, and I . . . I haven't seen him since." Her voice had gone thin. "His parents brilliantly hushed it up. It's not as though dueling is *legal*." She said this with admirable irony. "And they somehow made certain I was dropped. Completely. By *everyone*. I was poison. He broke it off with me with a letter." She gave a short wondering laugh here, too. It was only a little bitter. "And I can't say that I didn't deserve it. And all of this mystery about my sudden loss of status, of course, intrigued Violet. And she invited me here. I've always been more fortunate than I deserve." This she found ironically amusing.

Fortunate. It wasn't the word he would have chosen.

"So, you see, though I didn't pull the trigger, I did play with his life. And he paid for it. So I'm not good."

Suddenly he *was* angry.

"Cynthia. Enough self-flagellation. I cannot tell you what 'good' means. Perhaps it simply means one hasn't the imagination or character to think of being *wicked*, as you once convinced Goodkind. I don't admire what you did, but I understand it. And Courtland, the bloody fool, had free *will*. He got *himself* shot. But it's a measure of your heart that you would suffer at all over what would make Milthorpe happy, or over Courtland. It's a measure of your heart that anyone would want to help you or be your friend. It's *you*, Cynthia. Don't you see? You don't *feel* kind or good because you don't like what you're doing to them or to yourself. People like you because you *are* good. But mostly you're *you*, and that's worth . . ." his voice nearly broke. "That's worth everything."

She was staring up at him, eyes wide. Mouth parted in astonishment. Listening raptly.

"But this doesn't mean you can *use people* simply because you're afraid. And that means Milthorpe, or Argosy, or Goodkind, or anyone. Your fear doesn't justify it."

Her head jerked back; her eyes wide. "I'm *not* afraid."

"You *are*," he corrected firmly. "And you've every right to be. Anyone would be in your position." He said this relentlessly. "You're so afraid, in fact, you're willing to deny *every* other part of yourself in order to ease your fear. You're hurting yourself, don't you see? And by God, you're *proud*."

His anger had infected her. "Proud! Interesting thing to say to a kettle, Mr. Pot."

This was so nearly whimsical he stopped speechifying at once.

"What about Lady Georgina, Miles? Do you think you will be happier with her than I would be with Goodkind? Or with Milthorpe? *You've* just had the convenience of having all the work done for you. Your father chose her, didn't he? Brought her right to your door. And with her comes all of your dreams."

"I've centuries of family honor and a missing brother and a duty to people who *need me*. I can't just abandon it."

"I do understand. I do. I don't begrudge you any of it, I swear to you. But it doesn't make what I said less correct. It doesn't make you better than me."

He conceded this with abrupt silence.

"What would you have me do?" Her voice was harder now. "I *shall* have what you or Violet has. I want it. Why shouldn't I have a *good* marriage, and money, and a home? I'm suited for nothing else. I won't take money from you, Miles, so don't offer it. I want a *life*. A family. What would you have me do instead?"

Stay with me forever. Be my mistress. Make love to me every night as long as we're able.

She read it in his eyes, and he read in hers that she was tempted.

"Don't say it," she said softly.

He sighed. "I wouldn't ask it of you," he assured her softly.

They let a silence go by. Animals in stalls shifted their hooves, and somewhere a bird sang out its joy in sunshine.

"Just . . . see people, Cynthia, first in terms of *who* they are. And then in terms of what they have. Not as twenty thousand pounds. Or a dour second son."

It was out of him before he could stop himself.

She froze.

And then:

"Oh." It was a gasp. Her face went blank with the sort of astonishment that arrives with a sudden blow to the stomach. "Now I . . . Oh, Miles. You heard me. At the ball. When you first saw me. Malverney's. My blue dress. My . . . face. You heard me talking to Liza. About you."

"Ah. So you do remember what you said." He said this lightly.

Her face went closed and stoic. She said nothing for a moment. "As I said, I'm not good."

"But I understand now why you said it."

She was finding it difficult to meet his eyes. "It . . . wasn't a nice thing to say."

"I won't disagree with that." He said it with gentle irony.

"How you must have hated me."

"I have never," he said with quiet fervor, "*ever*, hated you."

She looked up at him then, searching his face again like a jeweler with a loupe, ensuring that she saw every gradation of meaning in his words, deciding he wasn't angry.

"You weren't meant to hear it," she offered.

"Somehow that doesn't surprise me," he said dryly.

A ghost of a smile touched her mouth.

Another moment of silence.

"I didn't mean it," she tried.

"You *did* mean it."

She sighed. "Very well. I did mean it."

And they were quiet together, remembering that evening.

She asked the question he'd already once asked himself. That terrible question: "And if we had danced that evening Miles . . . if we had spoken, or been introduced?"

"This is what I know now, Cynthia," he said decisively, because he did know it, and she sounded so afraid. "It would not have made one bit of difference. Even if we had danced, you would not have truly seen me. And I would not have truly seen you. We were different people then, and we are different people now"

Because of each other, he didn't say.

Her gaze dropped. He noticed worn toes on her slippers as well as worn heels. Her circumstances touched chill fingers to the back of his neck, and made him feel restless.

He wanted her eyes back on his face, so he said, "You're correct, Cynthia. I suppose I am proud. The Redmond heritage, and all that. I imagine I didn't enjoy being overlooked. And I suppose my pride is in part what made me lie to you about Goodkind. I wanted to prove a point."

She looked up again. Blue, blue eyes. My heart is blue, he thought absurdly.

"But your pride is what made you kiss me the very first day of my stay here," she said softly.

Ah, clever girl.

The word "kiss" arrived, like a waft of opium. They both drifted on possibility for a moment. He could close the inches between them by simply bending his head, touching his lips to her soft lips. He'd cup her beautiful kitten's face in his hands, and with his mouth and tongue and hands, he would make her forget everything. He would slide his lips to her throat, drag his hands around to cup her soft breasts inside that soft and warm muslin . . .

"Are you sorry that I did?" he asked, his voice hoarse with emotion now.

His grip tightened on her. He saw her pulse beating in her throat, felt it beating in her wrists. She looked stricken.

He didn't know why he'd asked the question. No answer could possibly satisfy either of them.

So he gently released her wrists. Slowly.

She took them back as if he'd given her a gift. She touched her fingers absently to where he'd touched her.

"Did I hurt you?" Her hand went out as she asked, as if to smooth his chest where she'd thumped her fist; she stopped it before it could touch him. It was an echo of the first time he'd kissed her. That hovering uncertainty. He remembered the wrenching pain that came with thinking she might push him away.

Her hand dropped back to her side.

"You did," he said, bemused. "A little." He put his hand over where his heart beat for her. Because she couldn't touch him. Because she wouldn't now, and shouldn't now.

The corner of her mouth twitched. "Good."

They were quiet together. Standing just a foot, but now an eternity, apart.

"Cynthia. I'm sorry about Goodkind. I swear to you I'll make it right."

"Well, it's rather too late to make it right with regards to Mr. Goodkind," she said practically. "He . . . said things . . . and fled. Don't smile," she warned.

"You really aren't going to tell me what you said?"

She sighed. "Oh, very well. I might have said something about how I am sympathetic to dramatic differences between people in physical *needs*, shall we say, and that I was not averse to sharing my wardrobe with a man, should he take a fancy to something in it. I might have mentioned that I would happily sew a large garter. You may smile now."

Miles already was. "Did you mean it?"

"Why shouldn't I be sympathetic, provided he's discreet?" she said, sounding puzzled.

He paused. "Of course. Why shouldn't you?" he repeated softly. She probably *would* have been sympathetic. Or at the very least, pragmatic. She wasn't the sort to collapse in the fit of the vapors if she caught her husband attempting to slide one of her satin garters up his own thigh or trying on one of her bonnets. They would have sat down and discussed it.

A tropical jungle would pose no real challenge for Miss Brightly.

"If you must know, it was very funny," she conceded. "I wouldn't have thought you capable of the inspiration."

He gave a shallow nod. "You were my muse."

She smiled genuinely at this. Color of the healthy sort was returning to her face.

Oh, but *he* was in hell. Discussing the men who would have her for the rest of her days seemed too much to ask of him. His hands had gone cold and numb; in the pit of his stomach was a strangely familiar hollow feeling.

She wasn't to know it. He would never let her know it. He would do anything to take away her fear, to restore the color to her face, to ensure that she slept peacefully at night and never wanted for anything for the rest of her days. And he wouldn't allow her to regret it.

"Argosy!" Fear crept back into her voice. "Have you— did you—"

"No. No. I swear to you. I've not tampered with the facts there," he told her. "Everything I've said about him is true."

"But the Gypsy girl told Argosy I was a minx, and shouted something about pistols and blood. And ever since then I think he's been uncertain about me."

"Hard to see why."

She laughed. "She's unnerving. Martha, her name is. Her mother, Leonora . . . now, *she* said I'd marry very soon."

"Helpful of her."

"I thought so."

"If you had to choose between Milthorpe and Argosy, Cynthia, who would it be?"

He managed to say this calmly. It was like swallowing knives.

Her hands twisted nervously in her skirt. "Argosy, I suppose."

"Consider it done."

"Miles—"

"You know you can trust me." The words brought back the night before. He'd meant them to, which was unfair, but it was how she knew she *could* trust him.

She jerked back and stared up at him.

"Trust me, Cynthia," he repeated softly, when she remained silent, her cheeks hot, her eyes dark with memory. "I have *never* in my life failed to do what I set out to do."

"Very well. I trust you."

The words were a gift: her trust.

And there was nothing else to say, and yet there was everything. And Miles found he couldn't allow her to leave just yet, because there was something he needed to say. And yet he had no vocabulary for what had happened to him since he'd met her. He faltered; he tried.

"I want you to know . . . that you're wrong on one count, Cynthia. I *have* a heart. I have only . . . recently discovered this. Ironic, isn't it? Given that I've made rather a life out of discovery. And I wish to God I had a choice. I wish to God I could . . . because if I could . . ."

"Don't." She bit off the word. She backed away from him. Her face was white again. "That . . . *that* . . . isn't cricket. And you know it."

She turned so quickly her dress whipped her ankles, and she was rushing from the stables on her worn slippers.

Chapter 19

Miles made it right.

    Cynthia might have said that this—the business of snaring a husband—wasn't a game to her. But viewing it as a game was the *only* way he could make good on his promise to make it right. It ensured that his intellect was fully engaged. It gave him permission to bluff or lie.

And to do all of this, he reminded himself that he was a man who could view with fascinated detachment a rodent-eating plant the height of his younger brother. He would wonder at its genus, its history, its diet, and draw it, in detail and never fear it or exalt it. Everything, he reminded himself—awe, fear—had component parts and an origin. Could be understood when examined, demystified.

Feelings needn't enter into the equation at all.

No one need ever learn that he'd discovered he had a heart. He wasn't about to deliver a paper to the Royal Society about that particular discovery, after all.

No objective in his life ever felt more urgent, and he had scarcely a week to accomplish it.

Then again, as he'd said before, there was nothing he had failed to do once he set out to do it.

He started his campaign that very evening.

"Didn't you have your fortunes told by the Rom while they were here?" he asked Jonathan and Argosy idly over billiards.

They were surprised, but pleased enough, to have him about.

"Why, yes, we did," Argosy told him. "*Eerie*, it was. They know things, those Gypsies."

Jonathan snorted. "Ten children!" he muttered resentfully. "Poppycock. A man would have to be *mad*. I paid good money for that dukkering, too."

"*I* paid good money for that," Argosy corrected idly. "Take your shot, Redmond."

"You're going to have ten children, Jonathan?" Miles was genuinely surprised by this.

"*No!*" His brother was appalled.

"Was Mrs. Heron's looby of a daughter present?" Miles asked as he stood by the table, waiting for his brother to shoot.

Argosy turned to him a bit defensively. Then again, Miles was something of an authority on all things as far as the younger men were concerned, and so he hesitated to object too strongly.

"I'm not certain at all she was a looby, old man. She seemed to know a good deal that seemed true."

Miles snorted. "Oh? Tell me, did she happen to shout something about a 'duck'?"

Argosy's face was a wonder to behold. Brilliant with astonishment. "How did you *hear*? Did someone tell you?"

Miles was all amusement. "She *always* bellows that when her mother reads fortunes. From what I've heard from those in Pennyroyal Green, anyway. I'm not certain she can control the impulse. It's something that comes right out of her. She's touched in the head."

"*Does* she always shout that?" Argosy was both disappointed and relieved. "'Duck,' is it? But she said the duck was *empty*." He made an emphatic gesture with the last word. This seemed to be meaningful to Argosy.

Cynthia had said nothing about an empty duck. Miles realized he would have to improvise.

"Precisely," he said, and took his shot, a clean and true one.

The ball smacked so hard Jonathan and Argosy winced.

"An empty duck," he continued. "When I first heard her say it, I thought it had something to do with a hunting decoy. Very odd. But then one must be sympathetic to the ravings of a madwoman. Her mother, on the other hand . . . her mother sends chills up my spine with the accuracy of her readings."

Jonathan was staring at his brother as though *he* was the looby.

"How much have you had to drink, Miles?" he asked suspiciously. Dukkering wasn't something that would interest Miles at all, apart from its potential to be mocked, or its anthropological appeal. "And haven't you known Mrs. Heron and her daughter for years?"

"I've naught to drink." Miles yawned indolently. "Which reminds me. Where is the brandy, anyway? What did Mrs. Heron tell you, Argosy? Now, anything *she* might say I would entertain quite seriously. She told me I'd go on a long voyage."

She'd done nothing of the sort, but this impressed Argosy. As Miles most certainly had gone on a long voyage.

"She told me that I would be wed soon. To a charming girl with many admirers. And that I . . . I'd best act quickly lest I miss my destiny." He actually flushed.

He feels something for Cynthia, Miles thought suddenly.

For some reason, the realization struck him like a billiard cue in the solar plexus.

But why shouldn't he feel for her? She was remarkable. Argosy just would never be able to truly *know* her.

"*Int*eresting." Miles enunciated every syllable drawlingly. He fixed Argosy with his see-everything look.

And then he found the brandy decanter, turned his back and poured. "Where's Milthorpe got to?" he said while his back was turned. "I wanted to have a word with him about my next expedition."

"Sorry. Couldn't say, old man," Argosy said idly.

There was a *pock* as a shot was taken. "Ah. Now I recall." Miles held up a finger in recollection. "He is having a chat with Miss Brightly in the salon. I believe they have come to a decision regarding what manner of dog she might have. I do think Milthorpe might want to have his palm read as well. I believe I heard he was looking for a wife. Seems everyone is in the market for a wife. Most of us at the house party, anyhow."

Argosy went rigid with alarm.He had probably never seriously entertained Milthorpe as a rival, and was suddenly reviewing him in a different light entirely.

"She'll be gone from Sussex in a few days, too. Miss Brightly. So I'm told. By Milthorpe."

Argosy was distracted from that point on and lost badly at billiards, which meant Jonathan and Miles won a good deal of money from him.

Trust me, he'd said.

Cynthia had decided she would. And the day after he'd asked her to do precisely that, Argosy had become ardency personified. A miraculous evolution, indeed. It required a bit of adjustment, but she was nothing if not resilient, and allowed herself to savor just the tiniest bit of ease, and to enjoy the attention, and to try not to feel guilty.

She only shook her reticule once that day.

And she, like Miles, refused to think of anything that had happened before, refused to think of what could not be. She focused on the needs of the present.

Two days later something extraordinary happened while she waited in the salon for Argosy, who had begged permission to take her walking—alone!— in the garden.

"Miss Brightly, I wonder if I may beg a word?"

Cynthia turned very slowly.

It was Lady Georgina. Sun blazed in the big windows of the salon, and on the shady end of it, Violet sat with Jonathan and Lady Windermere. The safety of other people seemed acres away.

Bloody hell. No escape.

Cynthia eyed Georgina cautiously. She hadn't *sounded* accusatory. She had sounded . . . diffident. In fact, as though she were indeed *begging* a word.

"Of course," Cynthia said warmly. Meaning precisely the opposite.

Cynthia settled into the chair next to Georgina, and the bright daylight pouring in the window contrived to wash Georgina nearly free of color entirely, apart from her hair, which was, as usual, wound up smoothly and neatly and glowed like a halo.

"I don't quite know how to begin . . ." Georgina's hands worked nervously together.

Again, Cynthia studied the girl for signs of irony or innuendo. "Please feel free to be open with me, Georgina," she said kindly, though her stomach felt as though it were turning on a spit.

Georgina whirled on her impulsively. "Very well! It's this. Well, you're so very charming."

"Am . . . am I?" Cynthia was suddenly very nervous.

"Yes. Everyone can see it, you know. You quite *sparkle*," she insisted.

It was tremendously odd to hear these words from Lady Georgina. She'd never dreamed flattery could also be strangely terrifying. And yet, she reminded herself, Lady Georgina communicated primarily by admiring people, and didn't need to isolate her specifically to compliment her.

She really *is* a nice person, Cynthia thought desperately. And I'm horrible, *horrible*.

"You're too kind, Georgina." Which was at least the proper response to most compliments.

Georgina's hands went still in her lap. Pretty, smooth hands. Nary a freckle, kitten scratch, or scar.

She cleared her throat. "Here is the thing, Miss Brightly. I wonder if . . . I wonder if you might know what it is I ought to be doing to charm Miles Redmond?"

Cynthia couldn't help it. She felt her mouth drop open. She closed it quickly, but not before Georgina had gone scarlet in the face.

But the girl straightened her spine, and added in a determined rush, "Since you know how to charm people, and since I cannot quite seem to do it. I can't charm him, anyway."

"Since I know how to . . . charm?" Cynthia was baffled.

"Everyone is quite taken with you."

Ah. Now this sounded like something of an accusation. Though it was true.

"Mr. Redmond likes you very much, Lady Georgina," Cynthia offered. Well, he *liked* her, anyhow.

"Do you think so?" Georgina sounded desperate. "He is

so very kind, and he teases me sometimes, which is pleasant, but I never know quite what to say, so I become very shy and he must ever carry the burden of conversation. I feel so *gauche* around him Miss Brightly, and I *ought* not, as I am well out of the schoolroom, and I am an heiress, for heaven's sake. And yet he is . . ." She paused, picturing Miles, perhaps. Tiny white teeth sank into her neat lower lip. "I feel he is somewhere else when he speaks to me. I do not engage his interest. And I think that *you* know how to engage the interest of a man."

The generalization was a trifle uncomfortable. Imagine *Lady Georgina* arriving at these conclusions.

Cynthia studied her face for signs of subtle meanings, or warnings. No: she meant it. Georgina thought, somehow, that she could impart the secret of charm.

Charm, my dear, Cynthia wanted to tell her, *is not learned, it is innate. And it is honed by desperation and need and sharpened by application. If you want the truth, that is.*

It might be entertaining to confuse and unnerve the girl by saying those things, but she knew it would be unkind.

"You are fond of Mr. Redmond, then?" Cynthia said slowly, her voice a little faint.

"I have been in love with Mr. Redmond since I was eight years old."

Cynthia froze.

Georgina's intonation had been fervent and factual, and her expression scarcely changed, which might be the fault of her pale lashes and brows. But her eyes held misty torments.

"You are in . . . in *love* with Mr. Redmond?"

"He is *beautiful*. Don't you think? So very quiet and calm! So large and dark and wise. His eyes . . . his . . ."

301

Words clearly failed her. "He has always been so pleasant to me."

Cynthia couldn't stop gaping at Georgina. *Pleasant?* And this was love?

Probably Lady Georgina could not put into words the things she felt. The sum of love, and of Miles Redmond, would be impossible to put into words.

And despite how she would have *preferred* to feel, suddenly Cynthia found herself begrudgingly respecting this girl. For Georgina had the good sense to fall in love with the quiet Redmond long ago.

How in God's name could she tell this girl how to make Miles Redmond fall in love with her?

"Well, a place to begin," she faltered, "is to share his interests, Georgina."

"Oh, I have tried. But Miss Brightly . . . I have a confession to make."

Cynthia braced herself. "Y-Yes?"

"I *loathe* spiders and insects!" Georgina was all passionate despair. "They frighten me." She gave a shudder. "I hate them. Hate them *all.*"

Cynthia was shocked speechless. Her words emerged stammered. "But spiders are so—"

"Repellent," Georgina moaned. "It is all I can do to *look* at one."

"But—But—you think ants are—"

"—disgusting, tiny, busy things, eating carcasses and the like." She gave another shudder. "I care naught for their societies, or that they have queens, or *anything* about them, and yet I am an expert on the ants of Sussex only because I care for Mr. Redmond. And so I have tried and *tried* to take an interest in his interests. Why does he have to *like* these things?"

It was all very dramatic, and admittedly fascinating to see Lady Georgina in the throes of such romantic pain: the *pressure* the girl had been under to pretend to enjoy the things Miles Redmond enjoyed. She'd held up admirably.

Ironic to discover that she had rather more in common with Georgina than she'd ever dreamed.

Cynthia considered the moment. There were myriad things she could have done or could have said. Myriad things she was *tempted* to say or do right now.

But here was the woman Miles Redmond was compelled to marry, would spend the rest of his life with, would see and talk to and . . .

Cynthia closed her eyes for a moment. She needed to breathe through the sudden sharp pain as her heart kicked a protest over what she was about to do.

"Have you considered that these things—Mr. Redmond's interests—are a reflection of who he truly is?" she said carefully.

"All these many-legged crawling things?" Georgina whispered, aghast. Her hands went up to cover her face, briefly. "Surely not. Surely it's just a diversion of some sort. A . . . *boy* type of thing. Surely once he's wed he'll take an interest in the Redmond business and the Mercury Club and his . . . his children." The scarlet color that had begun to ebb from her face rushed in again.

"But he wants to return to Lacao. He wants to take an expedition there." Cynthia was aghast.

"I'll refuse to go."

"But, Georgina!" Cynthia was suddenly terribly afraid for Miles. "Perhaps it's . . . perhaps he's interested in *all* living things. In learning and discovering them. And how they live among us, and the worlds within worlds, and . . ."

But she could be days explaining Miles. And if she did explain, go on and on, she would only betray herself.

She thought of Miles married to someone who would never truly know him. Who was incapable of seeing him. She felt the howling loneliness of his future in the pit of her stomach, and her palms felt damp, and she thought:

I need to do for him what he is doing for me.

"Do you truly care for him, Georgina?"

"Oh, yes."

Georgina, at least, *thought* she meant it.

Cynthia took a deep breath, pressed her damp palms against her knees, and chose her words carefully, feeling as though Miles's entire future rested upon her shoulders.

"Then you *must* learn to understand why he likes the things he likes, because then you will know him. Those things will cease to repel you, if you understand them. And once you understand them, then you will be able to truly charm him."

Lady Georgina seemed to consider this. "I was hoping you could simply tell me how to charm him," she said stubbornly.

Cynthia sat for a moment in quiet, bemused irony and gazed at this girl who was her same age, but such a babe in so many ways. What a gulf Miles would need to cross.

And here was another person who thought love could be *managed*. Why is it we want things that are not right for us? She wondered. Why is it we want things we cannot have? What is the *point*?

She imagined these were age-old questions, and she was not of a sentimental bent, and not one to wallow, and she doubted it was the sort of mystery even Miles Redmond could solve, as he was at the mercy of it, too.

"I *have* told you how to charm him," she said to Georgina. "You *must* do what I say. You must try. Please try."

304

And then she stood and walked quickly away, so Georgina didn't see her squeeze her eyes closed, or see the flush of color on her face.

And so there passed three more days, days both peaceful and also hollow, where Miles scarcely saw Cynthia at all, except from a distance, across the great green spread of Redmond land. He would see her burnished, shining—*brown* hair, her hair was *brown*—alongside Argosy in conversation.

What on earth did they talk about? He supposed it didn't matter, as it was Cynthia after all, and she would make the conversation effervesce, take shape somehow. She would take an interest, and Argosy would feel even more interesting than he *already* felt, and this would be the life Cynthia would lead for the rest of her life.

And during the evenings, over cards, when they socialized, or during dinners, part of him participated while the whole of him was entirely on edge and vigilant, and though he and Cynthia scarcely exchanged words beyond banalities, because this was part of their agreement, too—the only way they would ever accomplish this—they were both intensely aware of each other as conspirators.

Miles watched the circumstances carefully, like the scientist he was, or like one of the Gypsy acrobats balancing atop the rippling back of a horse. Ready to calibrate with just the right word here, a subtle action there, or a nice juicy lie, if it looked as though Argosy's ardency was ebbing or his intentions wavering from Miss Brightly.

But Argosy showed every sign of worship. Cynthia showed every sign of fondness. And soon their attachment was much taken for granted.

Jonathan was amused. Violet bemused. And Milthorpe,

perhaps sensing he'd been edged out by a younger stallion and giving up hope that Isaiah Redmond would be home very soon, decided to depart to buy the greyhound puppy he'd told Cynthia about during the picnic.

And soon even Lady Windermere, who stalwartly hoped for the return of her friend Mrs. Redmond so she might get in a juicy bout of gossip, spoke in the not quite innuendos so beloved of those who'd been married and bore children and lived to see others do the same.

And when the servants dutifully began polishing silver and beating carpets and getting in supplies for the second and final of the dinner parties—the dinner party that would conclude the house party and see everyone disperse—the air at Redmond House began to shimmer in portent.

"We'll have a wedding ere long," Lady Windermere predicted, with a finger alongside her nose. "I always think dinner parties are wonderful places to announce engagements."

And as for Miles, he took walks in the garden with Lady Georgina. One walk per day.

For all the world as if she were a pet.

And he reminded himself, all the while they were walking, of the reason he was doing it.

Who are *you?* he'd wanted to ask her. They never got beyond Sussex and their families and flora and fauna.

He was a brave man, but he didn't have the courage to ask her that question.

His thoughts were too full, and one day the silence had stretched too long, and he'd been mentally planning his overseas expedition, the passion remaining to him, the passion he nurtured.

When she startled him with precisely that sort of question.

"Why do you like the things you like, Mr. Redmond?" she'd asked him. Hesitantly. She sounded as desperate as he felt.

He turned to her, astounded. He stared at her. Looked down into her gray eyes.

"Miles," he said to her.

Aware that his name was a metaphor for the distance they would need to cross to know each other. But the fact that she had asked the question at all meant, perhaps, there was a glimmer of hope.

And he tried to explain those things to her. But he didn't know where to start, as those things had no real beginning or end. So he stopped. It was so much harder to explain it to her when another woman had simply *known* it from the moment they'd met.

Well, from the moment they'd truly *seen* each other.

Quietly, bets were taken below- and abovestairs: Lord Argosy would propose to Miss Brightly the day of the dinner party, was the popular guess. No two people had been better matched for beauty or youth or spirit, it was thought, and dancing at a ready-made celebration seemed ideal.

Mr. Miles Redmond was expected to make his proposal soon enough, though less certainty seemed to surround this, as he had appeared so different from himself of late.

"Return of the fever," it was whispered sympathetically.

Miles felt the tension as surely as a drawn-back bow. Two more days remained.

But Cynthia, who had progressed to allowing Argosy to touch her hand and call her "Cynthia" warmly, began to feel more confident.

She told Spider the cat as much when she went to bed at night. And as a token of her faith in Miles Redmond, she'd left her reticule untouched for one entire day.

Two nights before the dinner party, Jonathan and Argosy went off to the Pig & Thistle for an evening, because Jonathan was about to win the darts tournament.

Jonathan returned home triumphant. He'd been given a small trophy, which he cherished inordinately.

Argosy, on the other hand, returned distracted, morose, and utterly, terrifyingly silent.

Which they all only discovered the following day. When he refused to talk to Cynthia over breakfast. He in fact left the room when she entered it.

And then left yet another room when she entered that.

His mood was in fact so black and impenetrable it deterred people from pressing the issue beyond, "Are you feeling quite well?"

He confided in no one. He instead indulged in the most thorough, bitterly profound sulk anyone had ever before witnessed.

Blasted pup, Miles thought. He felt a strange impulse to shake Argosy hard.

He pulled Jonathan aside. "What in God's name is troubling the man? What *happened* at the Pig & Thistle? Who did you see there? Did he stop drinking? Perhaps he should begin again."

"He won't tell me, Miles. And I was busy winning the tournament. Didn't see what Argosy got up to. But whatever happened to him started there, I'll tell you that much. And whatever it is, it's clearly all about Cynthia."

The brothers exchanged a look. Somehow Cynthia's past had made its way to Pennyroyal Green by way of the Pig & Thistle.

Miles intended to find out how. There was no way in hell he wouldn't keep his vow to Cynthia to make it right.

Inside of a day Argosy's mood had blanketed the atmosphere inside the Redmond House like a grim layer of London soot, even as the house itself became cleaner and cleaner and cleaner, until every stick of furniture and piece of silver and china gleamed blindingly, and the delicious smells of cooking for the nearly thirty people invited rose up from the kitchen to fill the upper floors.

Just before three in the afternoon, carriages began to roll into the drive, spilling out neighbors expecting to be entertained, and they came pouring happily into the house, their gaiety jarring.

And still no bloody letter from Mrs. Mundi-Dixon in Northumberland.

Cynthia entertained the possibility that Mrs. Mundi-Dickson might have died of meanness, or been murdered, at last, by one of her companions. If so, the timing could not have been worse.

What had *happened* to Anthony—which was how she now referred to Argosy—since they'd become so very intimate, so very *attached*?

With shaking hands, and no idea where to get the bravado she would need to bring with her to the tea party in order to face or, indeed, charm away the impressive aristocratic snit Lord Argosy was indulging in, she got herself into her green dress with the net overlay.

There was a small tear at the hem where it had been trod upon at some point. It suddenly seemed significant beyond all reason.

Her life was unraveling.

On impulse, heart hammering, she crossed to the window and peered up into the corner, half dreading what she might find. She exhaled: The web was still intact. Susan was perched up in the corner of it, quietly waiting for her next meal to fly into it. And somehow this seemed a more significant sign than anything a Gypsy might read in her palm or in the leaves of tea. Cynthia closed her eyes and heard his voice again, saw his eyes, felt his hands on her wrists.

I'll make it right.

A smile began to tug up the corner of her mouth, and she felt the beginning of ease in her chest.

She gently detached her kitten from the hem before he turned it into streamers, then made her way downstairs, shoulders squared.

By three o'clock in the afternoon a good many of the guests had arrived and were milling happily about in the grand salon, partaking of tea and little cakes, the crumbs of which would be ground into the carpets and keep the maids busy for days.

Miles greeted all of them—from Pennyroyal Green, the vicar had been invited, as well as Mrs. Notterley, a local widow who loved gossip as much as his mother and seemed to know it before anyone else. He held entire attentive conversations with a half dozen or so people without remembering a word afterward. And then, when he'd done his duty, he could bear it no longer.

He brought a glass of brandy to Argosy, who had slumped gloomily in a chair in the corner, oblivious to gazes both admiring and curious from all the guests.

He stood there, holding it out, until Argosy's hand came up listlessly to take it.

Argosy, old man . . . is aught amiss? Of late it has been

such a pleasure to witness your happiness, and I was so certain I would be able to congratulate you on the same milestone *I* soon hope to reach. And here you have a festive occasion and a crowd of friends with which to share it. Perhaps you can confide in me."

The younger man's flawless features tightened with righteous anger and he stood suddenly.

"Very well, Redmond. *I'll* tell you. I saw Lord Cavill at the Pig & Thistle, Jonathan and I. He was on his way through to take his daughter to Miss Endicott's academy."

Ah. Another recalcitrant girl for the school, Miles thought. Miss Endicott did rather a brisk business in that. But the name . . . Cavill . . . Cavill . . .

"He's a dear friend of the Earl of Courtland."

Oh, Christ. Miles felt the backs of his hands go cold.

Involuntarily, he glanced toward Cynthia. Her face was too white above the dark green of her gown, her smile forced. She was talking with Violet, or rather, Violet was talking and Cynthia was merely actively wearing that horrible smile. Probably only he realized was false.

"How *is* Lord Cavill?" he asked calmly.

Argosy was puffed with wounded fury. "I'll tell you how he is. I shared with him my happy news—that I hoped to be a married man soon, that I was in love—" His voice broke here. Argosy really *had* thought he was in love. "—and I told him about . . ." It seemed Argosy couldn't get the name out now. "I told him about Cynthia." He made her name sound like the blackest evil, synonymous with betrayal.

Miles instantly felt his temperature changing. A blaze of heat raced over his skin, making it difficult to breathe. He was aware of a peculiar metallic taste in his mouth, and tightness in his stomach, like a coiled spring. He listened.

Argosy went on, his voice low and bitter. "He pulled me aside, and quite in confidence, said he'd *heard* of Cynthia Brightly." He gave an incredulous laugh. "He told me story after story about her, all the things that went on during the season I was on the Continent. All the betting book wagers, the races, the fights, the duels, her playing men off of one another. Rumors of kisses in gardens. And a *duel*? By God, man! The girl's a *doxie,* from the sound of things!"

Miles's vision, peculiarly, began to blur. Every muscle in his body seemed to bunch.

"And you saw how she played all the poor fools here, Redmond. *I* was played for a fool. I would have *married* her. I count myself lucky to have seen Cavill. And If Cavill's correct, the girl must have kissed at least a half dozen—"

Later, he remembered the impressions coming at him swiftly, and all out of order:

First, the windstorm of gasps.

The numb and stinging fist he'd instinctively wrapped in his other hand.

Then he followed the general direction of all the heads in the parlor. The heads of a dozen or so of his Sussex neighbors, people he'd known all his life.

All eyes were on the floor.

Which is where Lord Argosy lay stretched out heaving like a fish, eyes bulging up with disbelief. Which is when Miles fully realized he'd thrown his fist like a shot put at the man.

Clearly, Argosy had gone down like ninepin.

Fortunately, he landed on one of his father's thick Savonncrie carpets and not the marble floor, so his golden head lolled against an expensive cushion of antique wool.

And then in unison all the heads of all the partygoers lifted up from Argosy and swung toward Miles. A hush thick as that Savonnerie carpet blanketed the room. Shock was palpable and unanimous.

Miles Redmond—calm, elegant, reliable, renowned Miles Redmond—had just thrown his fist at a guest in his own home during a *party*. Knocked him *flat*.

In front of an *audience*.

And of all the things he probably *ought* to have felt in that moment, the first thing that reached Miles through his ebbing tide of fury was immense and inappropriate satisfaction at meting out justice.

He'd felt Argosy's words as viscerally as an attack upon someone he love—

He dodged that thought as though it were a fist aimed for his head. He jerked his gaze up from Argosy. Like a compass finding north, his eyes immediately found a particular pair of blue eyes in the group of aghast faces.

Her face was white apart from a blaze of pink spots on each cheekbone; her eyes were brilliant. She wasn't looking down at the floor in concern.

She was looking at him.

And she was quite clearly *furious*.

Because no doubt she thought the two of them were going to shoot each other now.

Well, then. He'd promised to make it right, and as usually was the case when it concerned her, he'd done the opposite of what he'd intended to do, and instead put it spectacularly *wrong*.

And here she was, again at the center of yet another controversy.

Miles uncurled his fingers from their fist shape and fanned them out in front of him, over and over, bemused at how quickly one could make a hash of things.

Reflexively, he reached his now benign but still stinging hand down to assist Argosy to his feet, as everyone else seemed far too stupefied to do anything but stare at the fallen man.

When he did this, murmurs began to rustle like the wings of a released hundred moths.

Argosy ignored the proffered hand, touched his fingers to his inflating lip, and continued to glare from the floor. His dark eyes were impressively, aristocratically, flinty.

Miles silently revised his plans for the following day to include the possibility of a duel.

He nodded, as though accepting a verdict. "If you'd like to speak with me, Argosy, I'll be in my father's second-floor study."

The room in which everything of consequence to Redmond history had taken place.

Miles bowed, turned with something approximating his usual dignity, and left the congregation to their gaping.

Chapter 20

I need my own home, Miles thought, resenting this room suddenly and irrationally. He'd been traveling so much, so often, he hadn't established a home other than his rooms in London.

He wondered dismally if Argosy would manage to recruit seconds from among the guests. He hadn't the faintest idea of the protocol involved in challenging one's host to a duel, but doubtless there was precedent. If there was anything he had learned from the books surrounding him now, it was this: regardless of how appalling the behavior, some human had already done it.

The thought cheered him perversely.

What he was about to do was the most difficult thing he'd ever done. Grimly, he thought: Goodkind would think this kind of sacrifice will purify my soul.

And then there was Georgina . . .

He hadn't thought once of Georgina, hadn't sought her eyes out in the crowd.

Again: quite the hash he'd made.

Two vicious raps sounded at the library door.

He was on his feet instantly, but Argosy didn't wait for admittance: he threw the door open as though it had been

315

put there deliberately to thwart him and flung it shut again with an impressive amount of wounded drama.

He planted himself before Miles and looked up. "Redmond, name your sec—"

"Argosy," he said evenly. "I apologize. I was an ass."

"—onds . . ." Argosy stuttered to a halt. "I beg your pardon, Redmond?"

"I apologize. What I did was unforgivable, Argosy, but perhaps you'll at least understand if you know why I did it. I beg an opportunity to explain my atrocious behavior."

Words like "atrocious" were apparently balm to Argosy. He enjoyed hearing his attacker denigrate himself. His feathers visibly settled.

"Firstly, Cavill is wrong. He's fortunate he wasn't here, because I might have been tempted to call him out. The rumors about Miss Brightly were a result of jealousy in the *ton*, nothing more. I greatly dislike hearing Miss Brightly disparaged; it is a *personal* affront to hear her name at the center of rumors, and to hear them repeated beneath my roof. For Miss Brightly's character is without question a . . ." He cleared his throat. " . . . a very fine one."

He paused; Argosy was watching him, a bit puzzled, but drinking up the words. And it occurred to Miles again that Argosy genuinely cared for Cynthia, as much as he could care about someone. It was disorienting. It was painful. It was a very good thing.

He forged on.

"She is, like Violet, spirited, true, but she is very . . ." Such a homely word. Such a right word. " . . . dear."

"She's dear?" Argosy was confused now. Given that this was Argosy, he probably thought he meant "expensive."

"Rather, I should say, she is a dear friend to this family. And as such, though I am certain you were not aware or else, as a gentleman, you never would have slurred her character"—Argosy stirred a little resentfully; perhaps there was potential in him—"we care very much for her welfare, and slurs to her reputation are felt personally. I am as protective of her as I am of Violet."

Argosy smiled slightly when he said "Violet." Her name generally elicited rueful smiles in males.

"I should say that despite her obvious *enjoyment* of life, she possesses a level head and a soundness of character that would do credit to anyone who associates with her. Regardless, my action was unconscionable and uncharacteristic, and though I do not regret defending her honor—as I'm sure you would do for any of your five sisters . . . " He paused to allow Argosy to give a short, manly nod. " . . . I deeply regret the manner in which I did it. I hope you will find it in your heart to forgive me, and to not think unwell of Miss Brightly for an action I am certain she would *never* have condoned."

Argosy said nothing for a time. A rivulet of blood slanted from the corner of his mouth and had begun to congeal.

"It is clear Miss Brightly inspires strong emotions in those that know her," he finally replied, his words beginning to thicken along with the size of his lip. "It is just that my emotions were so very strongly engaged, and I was terribly upset at the betrayal. What I *thought* was betrayal," he added hurriedly.

Miles could only nod. He did feel a twinge of guilt about obfuscating to the man. But no matter what Cynthia had ever done or not done, Argosy was clearly getting the best part of the bargain.

"You see . . . I'd intended to propose to her," Argosy confided hesitantly. "Yesterday. I wanted to so badly. You must know that we have formed an attachment. I fear we have been obvious of late. My passions do run quite deep"—this was interesting news to Miles, and rather sounded like a line of poetry Argosy might have read—"and the Fates seem to decree the match . . . I cannot imagine enjoying another female more than I enjoy her. I am quite in love. I suppose I was gravely, gravely disappointed to hear what Cavill said about her. Her family is a bit of a question mark, I do know that. It matters not to me. But I do know my father would prefer me to bring home a bride whose character has never been called into—"

Miles straightened his spine to full commanding height. And lied.

"Miss Brightly is a fine young woman," he said, his voice nearly stentorian. "And I can assure you that she enjoys the *abiding* friendship and respect of this family. I speak for my entire family when I say that anyone who questions the quality of her character questions the judgment of the Redmond family." He allowed this particularly subtle threat to penetrate; it would never, ever do to alienate the Redmonds. "And it is our belief that any family, no matter how ancient or noble, would be improved by her. And *any* man free to do so would be—" He stopped. His heart closed over his words like a fist, as though attempting to prevent him from saying what he was about to say. He was forced to turn away, toward the window, as if to turn his back on his own heart. "—would be blessed indeed to wed her, should Miss Brightly accept him. And that includes you, Argosy."

By the time he reached the end of the sentence, his voice had turned to gravel.

Argosy was impressed into somber dignity.

"My father would of course prefer an aristocratic bride. But as I am his only son, he finds it difficult to deny me the things that I want. And I do feel destiny has decreed that

Miss Brightly and I forge a future together. After all, Mrs. Heron predicted it."

"So she did."

"And given your defense of her, I congratulate myself that my initial judgment was correct. And I want her."

He said this very simply. The words of a man who had never before been denied something he wanted. They weren't combative or defiant. They were breathtakingly straightforward.

Miles found that he could not dislike Argosy. And yet the fact that he did not *dislike* him was not quite a strong enough reason to like him. The man was simply unfinished, and might never become more than that. Character, he knew, was shaped through resistance and trial.

Then again, Cynthia Brightly for a wife might just prove resistance and trial enough for any man.

And then, realizing that his strength was failing him, it occurred to Miles that this moment was almost too much to ask of any man. Of all the myriad little agonies he'd endured in his day, this one had required everything of him.

But it was almost over. All of it. This entire episode of his life. Almost over.

These were the same words he'd used as he escaped cannibals, as his strength returned to him when the fever finally gave way.

"Miles," Argosy said impulsively, with charming earnestness, "you are forgiven. Please accept *my* apologies for my careless and unwitting slur against your dear friend and mine." He was having a bit of difficulty enunciating his *s*'s, as his lip, before Miles's wondering eyes, was growing enormous. "I shall endeavor to behave as reflects my breeding in the future."

There was ruefulness in this, which Miles liked, and

a hint of censure, which he deserved. As it was hardly as though he himself had behaved in a manner that reflected his breeding. "I disliked feeling fooled, you see," Argosy went on, "and as I said, I was quite disappointed. I should have known the Redmonds would not have welcomed Miss Brightly into their home as a guest if all of the things said about her were true."

Well, not *all* of the things said about her were true. It didn't mean that some of the things said about her weren't true.

"I am glad we are friends again, Argosy," was all he said.

"As am I." The man tried to smile. His lip, however, was inflating, and would not curve.

Miles still could not find it in himself to feel guilty about that lip. Perhaps later.

He extended his hand, and Argosy took it and gave it a good pumping.

They backed away from each other, and a silence ensued.

And then Argosy looked toward the window and fidgeted a bit. He turned back toward Miles, his face alight.

"Well, old man, I find I'm nervous as a cat now." He tried the smile again; it became a wince. Miles offered him a handkerchief; Argosy took it with something of distracted charm. "I knew I would wed one day, but I never dreamed 'twould be so soon. But I find I am eager for it. I will ask Miss Brightly for her hand tomorrow, and should fortune smile upon me—and as I say, I do believe fortune means for us to be together—she will be my wife within a fortnight. I cannot imagine waiting longer than that to get her into—" The words had a momentum of relish, but he saw Miles's face and halted abruptly. "May I assume that I have your blessing, as a member of the Redmond family, and your approval when I ask for her hand?" he said humbly.

Well. And now it was done.

Miles could not help but acknowledge the irony of it all: he had done what he'd set out to do. He'd promised her he would make it right, and he had.

And now he realized he'd known this particular feeling before: when he first heard of Cynthia Brightly's engagement to the heir to the Earl of Courtland. She'd had nothing at all to do with him or his life then, apart from an appalling moment of wounded pride in a ballroom. The peculiar, sharp knell of grief had puzzled him.

He knew now that's precisely what it had been: grief. Something in him had known even then what she meant to him.

So the place in his chest where his heart used to beat was empty. And Argosy's words rang in there like the clapper of a bell.

"You do have my blessing, Argosy. I wish you great joy in your marriage."

And with a sense of something right, and something terribly wrong, he saw the future light up the other man's face. As though Miles had transferred all of his own happiness to him.

"You'll want to see the kitchen about your lip," Miles said.

And that's where Argosy went.

While Miles went to find Cynthia.

The drawing room had cleared as surely as though he'd fired a pistol into it. Hitting a guest in the jaw was a surefire way to dampen festivities, he supposed.

"Has everyone departed?" he asked a footman.

The blessedly bland face, in the blessedly familiar blue and gold livery his mother had spent a decent amount of his father's fortune upon, said, "Yes sir."

As though this was a reasonable question, and Miles Redmond hadn't just behaved in an entirely unreasonable way.

"Have you seen Miss Cynthia Brightly?"

"I believe she went out to the garden, sir. The other young people decided to do so, anyway."

Cynthia sat alone in the garden, near the maimed statue of David and the drooping roses. She'd surreptitiously fled while Miles and Argosy were behind closed doors hashing out the rest of her life, wondering which one of them would wind up dead. And she'd been watching clouds, inhaling the heavy scent of the flowers, and holding herself very still, as though her past could not catch up and destroy her if she didn't make any false moves. Her heart was a stone in her chest.

She heard his footsteps behind her. Saw his shadow fall at her feet.

She didn't turn just yet. She'd seen Miles shoot, and he did it as easily as he did everything else: it was Argosy who would most definitely die.

Oh, God. He'd knocked Argosy to the ground with one blow.

What had *happened*?

She looked up at him then. And he must have seen something terrible in her face, because he immediately sat next to her and said without preamble:

"I shan't be aiming a pistol at anyone at dawn, nor will anyone be aiming a pistol in my direction. I, in fact, made a very impressive speech during which I buried your reputation and character to a high luster and issued an apology for my behavior, which quite dented my pride, and I believe I have assured you of a proposal."

They were silent together for a bit.

And then Cynthia slowly released the breath she'd been holding. And closed her eyes.

"Your pride, his jaw," she mused after a moment.

Miles looked at her questioningly.

"Both dented," she clarified.

He smiled faintly at this. "I think you'll find his looks untarnished once the . . . well, once the swelling diminishes. He did rather go down like a matchstick, didn't he? And doesn't he already have something of a dent—in his chin?" He fingered his own.

"I believe it's called a dimple."

"Ah." Miles nodded, appreciating the specificity.

Another silence.

"I'm . . . sorry," he said. He sounded utterly bemused. As though he hadn't the faintest idea what had come over him.

"Miles . . ." She hesitated to ask the question. "I assume the fact that you needed to buff my reputation to a high luster meant you were defending my honor when you . . . hit him in the face?"

"Defending your honor rather reflexively, as it turns out," he confirmed ruefully.

This made her smile a little. "What did he say?"

"Among other things, he said something about you having kissed a half dozen or so men in the ton."

"A half dozen?" She was appalled. "Who on earth would have said such a thing? I don't think I've kissed more than two, or three at the most. I've only—"

"Cynthia. I'm not certain it's necessary to enumerate," he said dryly, quickly. "And I assure you, I have taken care of it. It's as though your past never happened. I told him they were all lies."

A small fat bird landed with a sudden splash in the bird-bath near them and began to bathe exuberantly.

"Thank you," she whispered. Half wondering.

Thoughtful silence ensued.

"That must be why you like him. The dimple. God knows it isn't his intelligence."

Was he was teasing her? If so, the attempt was woefully limp. His voice was distracted and hollow.

"The dimple?" She pretended to consider this. "Perhaps. Well, he has three altogether. The one in his chin, one on this side of his mouth, the other—"

"Cynthia?" Miles interjected with sudden strength and urgency.

He hadn't been listening to her at all. His gaze was aimed gazebo-ward.

"Yes?" She turned, surprised. And her heart stepped livelier.

He said nothing for a moment. She knew him well enough by now to suspect it was because he was deciding precisely what to say. And that when he said it, it would be irrevocable.

"You . . . do like him?"

The question surprised her. "Argosy?" she replied stupidly, because of course this was whom he meant. "Yes," she added. Then realizing this sounded rather pallid, she added stoutly, if not with complete fervor, "Of course."

If Argosy was prepared to offer for her, she was prepared to be grateful to him for the rest of her days. She would like him for that alone. He would have her loyalty. She liked him enough to try to make him happy. But he was not . . . he was not . . .

"Because . . ." Miles stopped again. He pulled in a long breath. Sucking in courage from the Sussex air, it seemed; all the brio from his Saxon ancestors permeating Pennyroyal Green.

Then he exhaled and turned to her decisively.

"Because I cannot bear thinking you will spend the rest of your days with someone you do not . . . you do not at least *truly* like. Your happiness, quite simply, is my happiness."

Cynthia slowly closed her eyes against the look in his.

Cannot bear.

The words swelled in her chest. She let them sit there, let the meaning penetrate, and she gave a short, ironic laugh. Almost a moan. Oh, at last, the joke was on the two of them, wasn't it? For a moment she couldn't speak at all. She lowered her head when her eyes began to burn.

"I like him," she told him gently at last. It hurt to speak; her throat seemed swollen; the words had jagged edges. She knew it was important for Miles to know it, even if she was uncertain. "Truly. Thank you. I . . . Thank you."

The last words contained all of her heart, encompassed everything that had happened during this fortnight, and were barely audible.

They sat in a little pocket of silent surprise, these two people who'd been so certain love was unnecessary when they set out to get what they wanted. How peculiar it was that this moment of realization and total happiness should be indistinguishable from anguish.

Cynthia risked opening her eyes. The striped muslin covering her knees now swam before them. Bloody *tears*. She never wept. Weeping, over the years, had become a luxury. No one had ever been about to hear her do it, or to care. Ah, but now . . . but now . . .

How like tears to take gross advantage of the circumstance. Now that here was someone who cared, and who would do anything at all he could for her.

Through the moist blur she noticed a tiny pale green insect sitting on her knee. The sun had turned the minuscule wings it wore into miniature rainbows. Well, then. She held very still for it. Interesting that she could be a place of rest between bouts of flight in its brief life.

Bloody Miles Redmond. She was certain she would think of him for the rest of her life whenever she saw any crawling or flying thing, and of course crawling and flying things were simply everywhere. And then there was Spider the cat.

A tear splashed free of her eye. It surprised both Cynthia and the insect: its wee wings whirred invisibly and it was gone.

She dismally watched the tiny damp spot darken her knee. She half hoped it would stain; she wanted the reminder of the moment. She breathed in, and squared her shoulders.

So be it: this interlude in her life was to be as brief and brilliant as that little winged creature. She envied it the speed at which it had disappeared.

Still, she had never been one to flee. And she wouldn't do it now.

Distantly, voices and laughter came to them. Violet, Argosy, Jonathan, she picked them out from the bright tangle of conversation, and the polite, amused tones of a gardener pressed into answering frivolous questions. The whole crowd of them would happen upon Miles and her and their little tableau of misery-edged bliss at any moment, as they were obscured only by that veritable vat of a birdbath, in which three birds were now hedonistically wallowing, and a robustly green, aggressively uniform hedgerow. Keeping Redmond house, and Miles, in his place.

She lifted her head, knowing her eyes were damp and ringed in red and that the tip of her nose was likely scarlet from efforts to suppress the tears. She had never been a graceful weeper. This was as stripped bare as Miles would ever see her; he might as well have a good look. She brushed a knuckle at one of her eyes almost defiantly, sending tears scattering like brilliant pinheads from her eyelashes.

He did look. And the *way* he looked . . .

It was as though he knew this moment would need to last him a lifetime.

And then he slowly turned away from her to look out over the Redmond parkland that unfurled nearly to the sea, and despite the fact that anyone could happen upon them at any minute, Miles slowly, purposefully, gently, defiantly, slid his fingers through hers until their hands were woven into a single knot.

Their entwined hands rested between them on the bench.

It was more shattering, in its way, than that moment of release. It was gratitude and apology; it was acknowledgment of all there was between them that would never be spoken. It was reassurance and farewell.

And given the voices coming upon them, it was a grave risk.

Cynthia clung to him. They didn't look at each other. She fancied she could feel his heart pulsing in his palm, but more likely she was simply marshaling all of her senses to remember forever the feel of his skin against her, and the beat of her own heart echoing resoundingly through her veins. If she closed her eyes, she could imagine his hand was his body, his long fingers his limbs twined with hers, and this was what she did. For this was the very last time she would touch him, and her imagination was greedy.

Together they sat as though riveted by the scenery that spread in abandon ahead of them. Neither saw a thing.

Then Violet's voice rose up, startlingly closer now.

Miles drew his hand away from hers, inexorably, until just the tips of his fingers touched hers. They lingered against hers for a brief second, like a kiss.

Then he stood, and with no bow or word, just a single, enigmatic glance back at her, gracefully made himself scarce in the hedgerow.

Seconds later Violet came bounding forward, turned to call out something. "Jonathan, you really must stop behaving like an ar—"

She stopped comically abruptly, dumbstruck at the sight of a red-eyed, red-nosed Cynthia sitting alone on the bench.

Violet mercifully and instantly misinterpreted the red eyes and nose and rushed to Cynthia, reaching for her hand. Cynthia almost snatched it away from her. She felt proprietary about that hand now. She'd wanted the warmth of Miles's touch to linger.

But Violet wouldn't release it. "Oh, Cynthia," she whispered excitedly. "Dry your eyes, goose! All is well. Miles has apologized and Argosy is mostly unhurt and quite in love with you, and he intends to propose tomorrow! I do believe he meant to surprise you, but I thought I should tell you now."

"Tomorrow?" Cynthia repeated numbly.

"Yes!" Violet repeated triumphantly. "Tomorrow! He shall ask you to go for a walk in the garden, and do it then."

"But . . . why tomorrow?"

"Violet!" came a male voice from the distance, sounding faintly irritable.

Violet looked a bit puzzled by Cynthia's response. She ignored the voice and lowered her own. "Well, he won't do it today. He's having a bit of trouble getting out his *s*'s and *f*'s, as his lip is rather large—Miles quite laid him out, didn't he? I wonder what on earth got *into* him. He should see a doctor, I'm really quite concerned. Anyhow, Argosy is a trifle sensitive about it. He thought a day might be time enough for the swelling to recede, but if not, he needs time to phrase his proposal properly. The sentence, 'Will you consent to be my wife?' contains too many difficult consonants given his swollen lips. 'I would be honored if you should spend the rest of your days with me' is scarcely better. We've been trying to help him decide upon just the right one. 'Will you be my mate?' is easier, but it does sound like something Miles would produce."

Cynthia was paralyzed by a wave of conflicting emotions. She was battered by hilarity and grief and relief. She couldn't find a single word that encompassed any of those things.

A worried look settled over Violet's face when Cynthia seemed unable to speak. "I thought I should tell you straight away, regardless. It was just that when I came upon you just now, I thought you looked so very . . . so very . . . *heartbroken*." She sounded in awe of the word.

Cynthia took a deep, resigned breath. It felt portentous, that first breath taken in a world without Miles in it.

She would have to keep breathing, regardless of whom her future contained. She was fortunate, indeed, to have a future.

She longed for a handkerchief. She began to make do with patting gently at her eyes with her cool fingers when Violet produced one. Its spotlessness was startling; her initials, V.R., were stitched in blue near the hem. Cynthia took it and blotted the corners of her eyes. Then gave her nose a discreet little toot into it.

"My goodness! Cynthia! It is a lovely day for a stroll, isn't it?" Violet suddenly all but bellowed.

Cynthia jumped, whirled on her in amazement.

Violet whispered, "It's just that I'm certain you wouldn't want Argosy to see you like this, and I know for a fact he wouldn't want you to see his lip just yet. He hopes very much for the swelling to ease, as I do believe he might want to kiss you after you accept his proposal. 'Tis customary, you know," she added sagely. As though she were in expert in such things. Cynthia had never asked Violet what sort of knowledge she might possess of such matters. How many proposals *had* she received?

No doubt she deflected them with her sheer Violetness.

Cynthia began to hand the handkerchief back to Violet, who waved at her to keep it.

On the far horizon, foamy clouds were forming. They would make their sluggish, woolly way across the sky and pour their contents down over Sussex toward the end of the day, most likely.

"You've a kind heart, Violet," Cynthia said finally.

Violet, who had never been accused of such a thing before, looked at first taken aback, and then pleased. Cynthia watched her friend silently add it to her mental inventory of virtues.

Suddenly Violet glanced down. She froze; her expression went peculiarly alert. She bent over and swiftly plucked up something, examined it, frowned, then stopped the frown from forming.

Cynthia saw a glint of silver before whatever it was vanished into Violet's apron pocket. A coin? Violet hardly wanted for spending money.

And then Violet returned her eyes to the clouds.

"Cynthia, was I wrong to tell you about Argosy's proposal in advance?"

Lifting her lips was a Herculean effort, but Cynthia was reasonably certain what she produced could pass for a smile. She at last gently wormed her hand free from Violet's grip.

"No. You did . . . absolutely the right thing, Violet. The very best thing you could have done."

Chapter 21

O ver dinner it became clear that the ranks of the soon-to-be-unforgettable Redmond house party had thinned so considerably it scarcely qualified anymore as a party. Neither Lord Argosy nor Miles Redmond were present at the table, the one taking a meal of cold soup in his chamber and the other said to be visiting with a Dr. Price of the Royal Society, who lived a few miles away. He was expected to return later in the evening, weather permitting the horseback ride.

To her astonishment, Violet seemed to have become by default the lady of the house and therefore the official hostess of the event. The footman could not entirely disguise his trepidation. His voice had a bit of a quaver in it as he dutifully delivered his message, knowing Violet would reach this conclusion by the end of it.

Fortunately for him, an air of sobriety was laid over the entire dinner when word was sent ahead from the inn in West Chiverley: Mr. and Mrs. Isaiah Redmond would be home the following morning.

Cynthia disconsolately, distractedly, devoted more energy to stirring her soup than drinking it. And then she pleaded a headache in order to escape the need to eat at all.

"It must be all the excitement of the past few days," she told Violet apologetically, though compared with the life she had lived in London, the last few days in Sussex hardly constituted excitement.

Violet stared at her accusingly. Then her face brightened.

"You shall want to look your freshest in the morning," she said meaningfully.

"Yes," Cynthia agreed. Thinking, given what her plans were, it was hardly likely.

When she returned to her room, she found a letter from Northumberland on her bureau. She stared at it, then with trembling hands rushed to slit it open, and read.

She lay it gently down again.

She scooped up Spider the kitten and kissed him between the eyes, causing a rumble. She peered up into the corner of the window; the web was still there. Susan the spider must be asleep. She was nowhere to be seen.

She slipped quickly out of her dinner dress and hung it lovingly in the wardrobe, slipped into her nightdress, then climbed beneath the counterpane and wrapped it around her shoulders, her feet tucked beneath her, Spider playing within her nightdress as though it were a tent, pouncing on her toes to encourage her to move them. She waited for warmth and watched the fire, hoping to find answers in it the way the Gypsy woman found the future in the leaves of tea left at the bottom of cups. Looking for just the right shape.

He'd given her character depth and dimension now. Her focus had been single-minded before, born of fear and ambition. But now she knew what she needed to do. *Light* had flooded into her life.

She decided that was sign enough.

"Be a good boy," she told Spider, and placed him, fruitlessly, in his basket in front of the fire. He wasn't quite ready to go to bed yet; he leaped out and began to attack the fringe on the carpet.

And Cynthia left the room.

She tried the handle and found that his chamber door wasn't bolted, so she gripped the doorknob and turned it slowly, then eased the door open just a few inches—enough for her to slip into the room. It didn't creak as it opened, nor did the bolt squeak or protest when she turned and slowly slid it to lock it. Of course it wouldn't: it was a *Redmond* bolt, after all. It was maintained as scrupulously as the rest of the house.

The dark in this room was as dense and velvety as his eyes; the fire was lowering; shadows and chill encroached. And for a moment she wasn't certain he was there at all.

But then she could hear him rhythmically breathing in that vast . . . *schooner* of a walnut bed.

She waited for the shadowy shapes to come more into focus as things she recognized before she thought it safe to travel deeper into the room, for it wouldn't do to crash into furniture. When she was oriented, she placed one bare foot carefully in front of the other, slowly, as though walking a high wire, as though conscious of the danger and beauty of what she was doing. The thick carpet silenced her footsteps.

The bed was before her, and Miles, asleep, mounded beneath his blankets. Breathing steady, rhythmic, deep.

Slowly, slowly, she crept forward and perched upon the edge of the bed. The mattress didn't creak so much as sigh; it was thick and she was small. Slowly, slowly, she swung her legs up.

His arm lashed out and held her arm fast. "Who the devil are you?" he snarled.

334

Ah. So he'd simply been *pretending* to be asleep.

Angry breathing filled the next few seconds.

"Ouch," she said softly. She made it sound like an endearment.

Miles's hand flew from her and he rolled away. With a rustle, a clink, and an oath, he had the bedside lamp lit, and then he fumbled to place the globe atop the candle. A soft, small canopy of light swelled over the two of them.

He was sitting bolt upright now. His hair was in disarray, standing up behind him, falling down over his eyes—well, it was everywhere, really. He pushed a hand self-consciously through it, improving matters not at all.

For a moment it seemed he couldn't speak. He simply gazed dumbly at her.

"Cynthia." His voice was hoarse. She heard the astonishment in it. And, oh yes, the yearning, too, because she suspected it was the only way he would be able to say her name from now on, and the only way she could say his. "What the devil—you can't—"

She leaned forward and abruptly placed her fingers over his mouth.

He glared at her, almost comically, over the tops of her fingertips.

It was then that she became fully aware that the bedclothes had slipped from him and he was bare at least from the waist up.

Whoosh, just like that, she lost her ability to pull air into her lungs.

She'd taken his beauty in before, in fragments: that wedge of burnished skin through an open shirt, for instance; and she knew the feel of his skin against hers, because wanton that she was, she'd sought it out.

But Miles entirely bare seemed to demand everything of

her senses; weakened, her fingers slid from his lips to lie in her lap.

She drew in a steadying breath. Viewed from this distance, his bare shoulders loomed; muscle both ridged and elegantly curved met in a torso that tapered to a narrow waist that was . . .

Sadly, at this moment draped in rumpled sheets, and hidden from her view.

That fine dark hair she'd curled her fingers into before, had brushed her breasts against before, trailed from a flat belly upward, from where it began.

Beneath the sheets.

He was at once magnificent and so unutterably *male,* she felt bashful and peculiarly unequal to him and the occasion.

And yet he was somehow vulnerable, too, because this beautiful bare person was Miles Redmond, rumpled from sleeping, confused, yearning. And she knew him. She knew him. Odd that in this very moment she should feel protective of a man who could probably lift her by the scruff and toss her from the room. But she would go at anyone with her fists for him.

As he had done for her.

He saw her expression; his own instantly reflected hers, she suspected. The awe, the heat, the immeasurable desire, the futility of resistance.

"Why?" He sounded bemused. He'd whispered the word.

She supposed he meant: why are you here? Because her mind answered with: *Because I love you, and damn you for it. You have both made my life worth living and utterly ruined it, and I'm grateful that you did.*

She smiled faintly. She would never say it.

She reached out a shaking hand instead, and dragged the bedclothes entirely away from him.

Why, yes: in answer to her question, he *was* completely nude. He coughed a surprised laugh. His erection was already curving quite impressively toward his belly.

Reflexively, she drew a proprietary finger along it. How utterly brazen she'd become.

He closed his hand around her wrist to stop her.

And like that, he held her, for the time it took the two of them to breathe in and breathe out. Then gently, slowly, he uncurled his fingers from her wrist. And with both hands he reached for the hem of her nightdress, draped around her feet.

Thus with those two gestures he told her: *I will lead every moment of this.*

Her heart bucked

She never seemed to have any choice where he was concerned: she gave herself up into his hands.

Now, she slowly raised her arms so Miles could divest her of the nightdress, which he did with a minimum of ceremony. It was going well enough until it snagged on her chin, necessitating a grunt and a decisive tug from him.

So this wasn't to be a flawless seduction.

He folded the nightdress neatly in his hands and placed it aside on the bed as carefully as if it were a living thing.

She was suddenly *profoundly* aware that she was entirely nude; the air of the room chilled her skin. She fought the urge to cross her arms over her breasts.

But there was no need; his arms were already wrapping her bare back gently, his warm hands sliding firmly along either side of her spine, just as her hands went around his neck. She knew she would forever remember the moment they were finally folded tightly together, skin against skin.

Cradled in his arms, he tipped her back against the bed; her head seemed to sink for slow miles into the feathers of his pillow.

And there were his eyes above her, burning, his beautiful mouth a solemn line.

She was afraid, and a little frantic, and shivering with desire. Frantic because she wanted to touch him everywhere, to know and memorize every inch of him, to *become* him, and this seemed impossible in the time they had, because every inch of his skin seemed precious, desirable, interesting, a *universe*. A lifetime would be required. Her hands unlocked from their grip around his neck, slid urgently down to smooth over the hard ridge of his collarbone, the taut swell of his chest, to discover again the texture of his flat nipples.

He allowed her to explore. But she felt the impatience in him. "God help me and forgive me, Cynthia, I don't think I can be slow." He said it ruefully; a slight smile came with the words, but his eyes contained a warning.

She'd thought herself unable to speak. But when she opened her mouth, out the words haltingly came, like something imprisoned too long, unsure of its welcome: "I want you *now*."

Well, she might as well have handed him her raw and beating heart along with a knife with which to carve off a piece.

But Miles closed his eyes, as if to protect her from the searing emotion flaring in his. He gave a short laugh, and then his lips moved in a silent hosanna.

Ah, but she'd seen his eyes before he closed them: white hot joy. And it was as though the sun lived in her chest, rose and set there.

His hands pulled her hard against him now, and rearing against the soft place between her legs was the enormous, meaningful swell of his cock. The pleasure nearly blackened her vision. Her entire body instinctively opened toward him: her arms pulled him closer; her legs wrapped his thighs, found them warm and thick and hairy; her mouth took his tongue when he bent his head for a kiss.

His hands were swift as he smoothed over the nip of her waist, the rise of her hip, to the round white swell of her arse, setting her nerve endings aflame, until she was arching and rippling for his touch. It was difficult to distinguish where his body ended and hers began; it didn't matter, as his pleasure was hers.

And the motion seemed natural and inevitable when he pressed her flat, raising her arms above her head, and covered her body with the heavy hot length of his. She pulled her knees higher to cradle his groin with hers; he raised himself on trembling arms to fit himself to her. His desire quivered in the muscles of his body; his sweat slicked over her body.

Her thighs gripped his waist, and he dipped and dragged, just once, his cock against where she was wet and aching for him. Her body leaped up eagerly; she moaned softly.

Miles didn't ask, *Are you certain?* He knew there would be no niceties, only this joining. It might very well be the first and last time he used his body for its truest purpose. For why else had the species been given this capacity to give and take pleasure unless to express the vastness of what he felt?

Her breath was hot and quick against his throat, her eyes hazy with want, with trepidation.

"Hold on to me, Cynthia," he told her softly. Thrilled, afraid, she obeyed: her fingers gripped his shoulders. And he thrust into her hard.

She gasped, her chin tipped back, her teeth in her lips; her belly leaped up. Of a certain he'd hurt her a little.

He comforted himself that her pain would ease. And he would make certain her pleasure was incendiary.

He sank slowly, deeply into her. Withdrew and thrust again slowly. *Christ.* The pleasure . . . so sweet . . . it all but blinded him. It rushed over his skin with a breath robbing white heat.

"Cynthia . . . I don't know if I . . . I can't wait . . ."

He wanted to drive himself into her until the two of them were senseless, to indulge an animal need. And then again, he wanted it to last forever, to be forever. He opened his eyes to find her gazing up at him through heavy lids. Her chest rose and fell hard in tandem with his. Together they had created a storm of breathing.

She pulled him closer with her thighs, locked her legs around his taut buttocks. She drew her fingertips down his shoulders, tracing the muscle there. "Please," she whispered. "Take me now."

He didn't need to be asked twice, yet at first he attempted finesse. Attempted to angle his thrusts to give pleasure to her, and when she hissed in a breath and released it as a moan, he knew he'd succeeded. Her head thrashed back; her body arced to meet his.

The rhythm of their joining remained nearly languid for a brief time, their hot skin meeting as he sank himself into her; but a wild building bliss urged him on, faster, harder. It cost him everything he had not to obey it: sweat beaded, gathered, on his chest. Cynthia's skin was sheened in the firelight.

He would die, die, if he couldn't just drive himself home.

"Miles . . ." She writhed upward, taking him more deeply still, as he drove into her yet again.

He knew triumph. But he wanted her bucking with pleasure beneath him when her release came. He dipped to take her nipple in his mouth, he bit lightly; she gasped an oath of pleasure so raw he smiled. And he sank into her clinging heat again.

Her nails dragged his skin. Delicious pain. And the pleasure mauled him.

He sank into her again and again, and she shifted her body to take him deeper still, rose up hard to meet him, arms and legs clinging to him, murmuring urging things in his ear, words he hadn't the faintest idea she knew, spurring him on. He was dimly aware of the sounds of their bodies meeting hard, of the slide of sweat between them, their hands slipping from each other, clinging, nails dragging.

And then he was at the mercy of the drum of his own hips and the ecstasy driving him. And then Cynthia bowed hard upward, whipsawed by her own release. Her cries rang in his ear, and she pulsed around his cock as he drove mercilessly home toward a completion he'd needed since he laid eyes on this woman.

He heard his own voice, a raw scraped sound forming her name, echoing in the dark of the room, as a violent pleasure tore him out of his body, wracked him like no fever ever could. He surrendered to it. Eased himself down over her on shaking arms. Tucked his face in the crook of her throat, where her soft dark hair cradled his cheek.

He floated on peace.

Cynthia couldn't yet open her eyes; her lids were far, far too exhausted. Every bit of her body seemed to have participated in and thoroughly enjoyed this bout of lovemaking with Miles Redmond, and she needed to marshal all of her resources to lift her eyelids. Not yet, not just yet.

She felt him gently withdraw from her body and lower himself next to her; he pulled her into his arms, and she went with a contented sigh, as though she had no muscles or bones. *Warm again*. His body was home. She listened to his breathing and smiled. He sounded as though he was recovering from running a mile or two. It soothed her, the life gusting through him rhythmically.

She finally got her eyes open, curious to see what Miles Redmond looked like in the aftermath of ferocious coupling.

He lifted his head to look at her. He was smiling. He looked amused at her languor and—

"Smug," she murmured. "You look smug."

He seemed to think about this. "That's one of the things I feel," he concurred, his murmur as languid as hers. He continued to smile.

She raised a hand and pushed his sweat-dampened hair back so she could see his eyes and those straight dark brows and his eyelashes and nostrils and . . . Every bit of him, every hair and scar, seemed important. Every bit of him comprised the topography of her heart.

She traced that smile with her finger, slowly. Beautiful, gifted mouth. It seemed permanent, his smile. He kissed her finger. She rested it on his sandpapery chin.

"Wonderful," she murmured, almost to herself. She didn't know why she'd said it, but it rather summarized everything.

And for a moment he seemed mesmerized. Gazing down at her, not blinking at all, as his smile slowly faded. "Yes," he said. The word was faintly surprised and soft as cobwebs. And full of his heart.

She turned her head and slowly bit his shoulder shoulder, savored the salty, musky taste of him.

He laughed. "Savage."

"I learned it from Spider."

She turned to laugh up at him but he surprised her with a kiss. He'd meant it to be tender and brief, she knew. But once his lips pressed hers, they lingered, as though he couldn't bring himself to leave her unless he'd thoroughly tasted her. And minx that she was, she parted her lips, inviting him in, touched her tongue to his. He sighed deeply and happily against her mouth and surrendered.

And thus their mouths began again to blend, to tease, and of course to arouse. The kiss became purposeful, hungry and deep and greedy, and soon their hands were roaming each other in feverish objective, limbs tangling to pull each other closer and closer still, a vain attempt to all but fuse. Cynthia loved and was a little afraid of the sheer size and hard strength of him; there was great relief in surrender, great safety in those strong arms and great hard hairy thighs, and a dizzy sense of falling, pleasure and terror in allowing him to do what he would with her.

He drew her upward to her knees before him, her shoulder blades against his chest, his arms wrapping her waist. He ducked his head, whiskers chafing her chin.

"Look," he whispered directly into her ear. "Look in the mirror."

In the oval cheval glass across the room she could see two shadowy people, pale and clinging and abandoned. She watched in the mirror as Miles's pale, shadowed hands traveled her moonbeam white belly, saw the flat of his hand slide over the furred triangle between his legs, saw his fingers disappearing into that shadowy valley. She saw her head loll back against his shoulder as his fingers moved over her, slipped easily inside her, sent bolts of nearly intolerable pleasure through her that made her groan and move with him. Saw herself arcing back against him, moving her body against his hand, abetting

343

him, telling him precisely how to touch her. And watching this was incomparable; it was almost as though two men were making love to her. Her every sense now engaged, every sensation doubled.

She watched Miles's dark head duck to gently nip the place where her neck and shoulders joined, then his mouth traveling upward again to whisper in her ear.

"God, how I want you."

He sat back against the headboard and pulled her slowly, slowly, backward until she was in his lap, her legs nearly straddling his, and like this he eased his cock into her again.

He took in a breath, a sharp hiss of pleasure.

The surprise and pleasure at being filled by him again was extraordinary; she leaned back against him.

And for a moment they were still together, savoring the wonder of being joined, the sway of each other's breathing. And then, mesmerized, Cynthia watched the shadowy Miles in the mirror fill his hands with her breasts, and his fingers explored them until her ribs leaped and fell with tattered breaths. His hand slid down to stroke between her legs, where he joined her.

"Oh God. . ."

In her own ears, her wondering moan sounded like a plea for mercy, but it was in truth a plea for more. More. The kinds of pleasure that could be had from him seemed endless. She raised her arms, latched her hands behind his head, pressed back against him, and lost herself in the play of his fingers over her.

"Like this, Cynthia," he demanded on a whisper. He braced his hands on her hips and urged her up and then down over his cock.

She learned: she slid languidly along him at first, purposely teasing, loving her control. And then she all but unconsciously took her cues from him: from the heat of his body, the slick sweat and damp curls of his chest hair chafing her back, the tempo of his breathing, from muttered oaths and soft groans of disbelieving bliss.

And as she teased his desire into a conflagration, he did the same to her own, and they played each other as intuitively as two musicians in an orchestra, moving together.

She saw two abandoned people in the mirror out of the corner of her eye, and in the haze of her lust she thought, it looks like love and it looks like violence. It looked like a capture and surrender and bliss and torture. It was all of those things, and it was beautiful, beautiful.

And then Miles was begging her with her name, the syllables of it a ragged gasp against the crook of her neck. "Cynthia . . . faster . . . Oh, God . . . please."

His body tensed, and even as he cried out his release with hers and she felt it inside her, her own came from everywhere and nowhere, white heat roaring along her skin, incinerating her with astounding bliss. Shaking her violently. His arms wrapped her tightly, and she surrendered to it, until she was limp in those arms.

They lolled for a time without speaking, enclosed in a peace in which they were alone with their thoughts. Until Miles brushed a finger against her arm and found it pricking up in gooseflesh, which was how they became aware of how long they'd been still, simply being together. The fire had officially ceased throwing off heat.

He reached for the blankets, slid down with her in his arms and cocooned the two of them in blankets. They burrowed into the pillow, and soon Cynthia was warm and drowsy, and growing drowsier, lulled by his soft snoring.

For he was asleep almost instantly, and in this he mimicked the proverbial log: he moved not at all, nor did she think she could budge him.

She experimented by moving just a little out of his grasp; his arms were slack, and they released her easily.

She smiled. They'd worn each other out.

She liked excitement—well, she liked it rather less now than she had a few years ago, but nevertheless—she deplored melodrama. And she feared what she was about to do would be interpreted as such. But it was nearly dawn, and she intended to leave before it was officially daylight to avoid explanations and uproar and hurt feelings and confusion. There was no telling whom she might encounter in the house in the early morning hours, and she was certain she could persuade one of the stable boys to drive her to the coaching inn, where she could pay for a stagecoach to Northumberland.

She saw no other choice. She'd known as much from the moment she made her decision to come to him tonight. Her sense of honor, such as it was, meant she couldn't marry Argosy, both for Argosy's sake and because she'd made the choice to give herself to Miles.

Perhaps one day she'd see this moment as a sacrifice, she thought, with all the martyred drama the word implied. But now, instead, she felt . . . rather pleased with herself.

It was not quite the happy ending she'd envisioned. But it was one, nevertheless. Both happy, and an ending.

She inched her way out of his arms, and felt a peace and happiness and a lightness she hadn't known was possible. It was the peace of having done the right thing, the *truest* thing she'd ever done. She knew what it was like to love; he'd shown her. And she also knew love simply demanded to be given away. She'd given him all that she could of herself. But it didn't strike her as sacrificial; it was something she'd done as much for herself as for Miles.

She knew with a bone deep certainty that she would never regret it, no matter how long those days with the woman in the bath chair should prove to be. For she'd been offered employment.

He'd broken her heart open like an egg, but inside was . . . the whole world. And as she looked back at him, she felt the serrated edges of her heart in her chest. But also a sort of dizzying vastness: she could face anything now. Loving and being loved had given her that kind of strength, and a sort of permanent safety she could carry with her forever.

So she would not be spending her life with him. Life was not fair: that's what made it interesting.

And she had probably been much luckier, in her day, than anyone had a right to expect.

She had three pounds to her name, one of which would pay her way to Mrs. Mundi-Dickson's home by stagecoach, a small trunk of tired clothes, a tiny cat, and, though he'd never said it, she knew she had Miles Redmond's love. She was the richest woman in the world.

She slipped the final way out of his arms and placed a light kiss on the hard curve of his biceps.

And after all, she *was* Cynthia Brightly. She squared her shoulders.

Miles stirred as she slipped out of the room; the sheets sighed. He murmured. But he didn't wake, and she was glad.

Because despite her own grand inner talk, she didn't quite trust her own resolve.

Chapter 22

Miles awoke to the sound of a maid building up the fire. He stirred, remembered, shot upright, alarming the maid, who had not expected to find Mr. Redmond half bare in a bed that looked as though the sheets had been frappéd.

He slid a hand over to where Cynthia had slept. The other side of the bed was cold.

So she'd been gone for some time. Sensibly, perhaps, slipped out during the night. He supposed he was relieved.

He couldn't have said what last night meant for their futures. It occurred to him that he ought to have asked her. He dressed, a peculiar unease making him hurry. He looked in the mirror, saw the beard darkening his jaw, decided to leave it until at least after breakfast, because of his urgency to see her. He looked *thoroughly* rested. He grinned wickedly at his reflection.

He found his sister alone at the breakfast table, her chin propped on her fist. She looked up, saw him, frowned—perhaps at the beard—and gave him a baldly succinct report.

"Cynthia has gone." She sounded subdued and, truth be

told, a trifle envious. "She's nowhere. Argosy is in a bit of a state. She left him a note. Jonathan is comforting him. Georgina has not yet come down to breakfast, as I am earlier than usual. Oh, and Mama and Papa are home."

And at first it was like the angels had descended to sing a celestial chorus. The day was brilliant. Cynthia *wasn't* engaged! She wouldn't marry Argosy! She—

His heart skidded to a sickening halt. "Gone?" he repeated with near funereal calm.

"She left a letter for him. Slid under his door! It said, 'I'm sorry.' He's feeling quite thwarted." Violet was wry. And disconsolate. "He's having his valet pack his things."

"Gone?" Miles had forgotten every other word he knew.

No note or letter for *him*? "Gone" meant not knowing where she would be, or with whom she would be, or whether she was safe and well. Gone meant possibly never seeing her again.

Gone might mean gone in the way Lyon was gone. He knew a moment of complete paralysis.

"Miles . . ." Violet was scrutinizing him in that way she had that wasn't entirely sympathetic. "Why are *you* in a state?"

"I'm not in a state." The denial was a reflex. Repeating her words saved him from having to think of other words to say.

Violet tipped her head. "I do believe you are," she persisted.

He ignored her. "Where do you suppose she went?"

He'd hoped the words sounded casual. Unfortunately, they emerged sounding like a military command.

His sister was frowning darkly now. Her hand went up to smooth it out. The frown remained. "Why do *you* want to know?" she demanded.

"For the love of God, Violet," he said very, very slowly—
punishingly slowly, as though she were a backward child.
"Do you know where she went?"

His sister froze, eyes round as wagon wheels. Her mouth
dropped, brows dipped. And for a beat she stared at him,
just like that, and did nothing to prevent a frown from
encroaching.

"Miles!" Her gasp nearly blew back his hair. "Oh, good
heavens! You! Cynthia Brightly!"

"Violet—" He growled the word. He was pacing. It was
as if he kept moving, he would somehow get closer to where
Cynthia might have gone. *"Please."*

"You and Cynthia Brightly! Cynthia Brightly! You!"

Oh, now he'd done it. He'd addled Violet, and for the rest
of her days she'd repeat those two things like a demented
parrot.

He stopped pacing. "Do you want me to shake you by
the scruff, Violet? Is that what you want? I can still do
it, and I have no compunctions about it. Tell me where
she might have gone . . . that is, please," he added as an
afterthought, an absurd attempt to return the conversation
to normality.

"You haven't been rude and strange because you were
feeling *ill*. You were feeling . . . *Cynthia*!"

"Oh, God. Violet. You must stop."

Clearly Violet's fascination was buffering her from the
very real threat of being shaken or boxed about the ears. She
was still staring at her brother in a way that had begun to
make him feel distinctly exposed.

And then her expression softened into awe.

"Good heavens, Miles. How very sweet that you—
you!—have a *tendre* for Cynthia Brightly and oh dear God
in heaven Papa *will disown you*!"

A sentence that had begun in wonderment ended in shrill alarm.

"He won't disown me." Miles said this rather by rote, as he wasn't at all convinced of it. He was, in fact, certain the consequences would be grave.

"No. Miles, you cannot do it," Violet said firmly. "You cannot go after her. I can't bear losing you, too, Miles, and Papa will cast you out. He nearly made a meal of Lyon. Surely whatever you think you feel for Cynthia is only—"

"It's not 'only,' Violet."

He said it quietly, but with such Miles-like finality that it stopped her as surely as though he'd clapped a hand over her mouth.

He gave a short, humorless laugh at her stunned expression.

"Nothing about Cynthia is 'only.'" He hated confessing this. Nothing had ever made him feel more . . . foolish. More vulnerable.

More human.

Violet was quiet now. In her world, Miles behaved in certain ways, always. He held their worlds together. And what could it mean if Miles, of all people, were just as human as the rest of them?

He wasn't certain what to expect: a tantrum? Storming from the room? More stubborn silence?

She dipped her hand into the pocket of her pelisse, fished around a bit, extended her palm. Something glinted from the center of it.

"This is yours, isn't it?"

He looked down at his missing silver button.

Then looked up at Violet, the answer on his face.

"I found it near the bench yesterday. Where I found

351

Cynthia in the garden. She was sitting alone and she looked . . . quite pink in the face." Violet touched her nose by way of illustration. "She'd been crying. I told her she looked . . ." Violet paused. Just as she'd stumbled across Cynthia yesterday, she was stumbling across a realization now. " . . . she looked heartbroken. Miles . . . Oh. She *was* heartbroken. She wanted you. She wanted *you*."

Her hand went up to her mouth. Violet's face went pale and pinched, as surely as though she felt the heartbreak herself.

Miles thought of Cynthia yesterday: weeping and trying to disguise it. He'd known how that must have felt for her. Then turning her face up to him, so he would know for certain everything she felt.

Last night. Her generosity and beauty and oh God . . . her gift for passion.

It had been a blessed interlude of forgetting, a reckless respite from thought and sense. It had seemed terribly right, terribly necessary.

He, so like a man, simply hadn't considered what the morning might bring.

"I just . . . I just never imagined she'd leave."

He was barely conscious of having said the words aloud; the sentence was a finish to the run of his thoughts. He never suspected there was pain in his voice. He didn't hear it.

But his sister heard it.

Violet watched him, trying not to frown. She rubbed his silver button between her fingers thoughtfully, because he hadn't taken it from her.

Poor Violet. Once again she was confronting upheaval and change and realization, but perhaps she needed to. The Redmond family, so serene and elegant and dignified and impenetrable on the surface, buffeted this way and that by that capricious thing called love, shaped by it despite the fact that they would prefer to be above it. Shaped by it the way the elements shape mountains and valleys.

He wouldn't blame Violet if she decided to retire to a convent.

The very idea of this—the havoc she would immediately wreak in any convent—distracted him, and almost cheered him up.

"Miles?" She made his name sound like a question. Interestingly, she also sounded like their father: coolly in command of what she was about to say. She'd come to some conclusion, then. "I cannot bear the thought of losing you. But I also find the idea of you with a broken heart makes me dreadfully unhappy. And I have decided that I should like you to be happy more than anything."

He managed a faint smile at this. "How very mature of you, Violet."

"I invited her to the party. It's all my fault."

"Oh, no," he said, smiling a little ruefully. "It most certainly is not all your fault, as much as I would like to credit you with it."

She was quiet—for Violet, anyhow—and subdued for a moment.

"Violet, I promise you this: you will never lose me. Never. No matter what happens."

Implying, of course, that *something* was about to happen.

Neither he nor Violet had any idea how he would be able to keep that promise. For that matter, neither he nor Violet had any way of predicting what their father might do, only that it was a certainty he would do something.

But the force of Miles's conviction seemed to cheer Violet, as it always had.

She simply sighed.

"No matter what, Violet, you should know that I will do anything at all to find her. It doesn't matter whether you tell me or not."

"She said something about an irritable old woman in a bath chair. Mrs. Mundi-Dickson. In Northumberland. She will be a companion."

This seemed an entirely unlikely occupation for Cynthia Brightly. He wondered what manner of trouble she would manage to get into as the paid companion to an irritable woman in a bath chair.

"Where?" he demanded.

"I don't know. Northumberland is all I know."

It was enough. Really, a single fact posed no difficulty for Miles, who was trained to follow facts to wherever they might lead next, to ruthlessly unravel mysteries.

He turned swiftly to leave. He hesitated.

"Did you tell Argosy about Mrs. Mundi-Dickson?"

"Well, no, but—"

"Tell him," Miles said. "I want him to know."

Because no matter what, he wanted Cynthia to be able to choose. Despite what he thought he knew about how she felt and what she wanted, he wanted to be *chosen*.

And if Argosy had sufficient wherewithal, if Argosy was driven by need and passion to track her down, then he ought to have the right to do it.

Miles wanted everything to be cricket.

He seized his sister and kissed her on both cheeks, surprising her perhaps permanently speechless.

He would find Cynthia. But there was something he needed to do first, because Miles Redmond always strove to do the right thing.

With the enthusiasm with which he'd landed on an

island populated by cannibals, he went in search of his father.

His father was having a perfectly pleasant, ordinary morning, from the looks of things. He was replacing a book on a shelf in his great meeting room, and turned when Miles entered.

"Miles. How did the house party—"

"Good morning, sir. I thought I should tell you that I intend to propose to Miss Cynthia Brightly."

His father's entire body—his face, his hands, everything—went *alarmingly* still.

Miles waited. He wondered whether this what it looked like when one's internal organs congealed in shock.

He was about to step forward to touch his father, to make sure he was still alive and not just about to tip over face first onto the carpet, when Isaiah suddenly moved. Quite fluidly, as though the alarming frozen second had never occurred.

He'd absorbed the shock and formulated a response. His breathing resumed. His father was extraordinary, really.

"Well, this wasn't precisely what we'd planned, is it, Miles?"

Cold, wry and detached, calculated to intimidate: ah, the Redmond aplomb. They all had it in one form or another, but no one demonstrated it more profoundly than his father. He'd had decades to hone it. "What of Lady Georgina? The daughter of a very wealthy man and dear friend of this family? The man who will happily fund your expedition?"

"I shall find my own funding for the expedition. I imagine Lady Georgina is taking breakfast at this very moment. She's a lovely girl."

He'd done very badly by Georgina. Still, they never would have suited. He would find it in himself to feel ashamed later.

Other things seemed urgent now.

"She is that. And yet you . . . you couldn't manage . . ." His father couldn't finish the sentence.

Miles was resolved. "I should like you to know that I don't take any particular pleasure in shocking or disappointing you, sir."

"*Such* a relief to hear." No alteration in tone accompanied those words.

"I have no choice with regards to Miss Brightly."

"You have no *choice*?" Isaiah's voice was contemptuous and incredulous now. "For God's sake, Miles. Did you get the wench with child? Are you doing this out of *honor*? She scarcely warrants such extremity of reaction. A little money ought to—"

"Not a wench."

Quiet, implacable, sinister as a garrote, his words. Miles had never felt such black anger.

Isaiah's head went back a little with the force of the shock. *No one* ever spoke to him that way.

He studied his son. Green eyes glass hard.

"I beg your pardon, Miles?" the words were silky and dangerous.

Miles got the words out through a jaw that threatened to lock from tension.

"To clarify, Father: I must insist that you never again refer to Cynthia as a 'wench.' I intend to make her my wife."

"You're . . . insisting?" His father's voice had gone deadly. The *s*'s hissed with impressive snakelike sibilance.

Interestingly, his father's disdain merely gave Miles strength. It banked his anger and resolve. "Yes. I'm insisting. I intend to make her a Redmond. As such, I cannot allow *anyone* to refer to her with anything other than respect in my presence, and I best not hear of anyone referring to her with anything other than respect *outside* of my presence. Are we understood?"

His father's stare was arctic. And then he smiled, and the smile was miniature and nasty.

He said nothing for a time.

"Where is the . . ." The pause was deliberately insulting, implying that if he couldn't call her a wench, there were simply no other words available to describe her. " . . . *she* . . . now?"

"Gone," Miles said simply.

His father clearly hadn't expected this answer. He watched Miles. "Why?" he asked after a moment.

Miles thought about this. "Honor, I believe."

Isaiah gave his head a shake. This clarified nothing. "Where did she go?"

"I don't know." Miles felt pressure welling in his chest, urging him to be off, to go. The longer this conversation took, the longer she would be gone.

"Then how are you going to—"

He stopped when Miles made an impatient noise.

He stared at his son, puzzled. "Didn't she have Lord Argosy on the line?"

Well, then. Imagine his father knowing such a thing. More likely, he'd been informed, by his mother, who had probably been informed by a servant. His mother loved almost nothing more than gossip, unless it was fashion and her children.

Miles was silent. He wondered what Argosy's lip looked like today.

"She sank her line for a lord, and came up with a Redmond instead?" His father's voice was still quietly contemptuous. "Is that what you mean by honor? She decided to leave because she cuckolded Argosy?"

He supposed he'd learned cold, cold silence from his father. But he was only now learning how very effective it was. And it prevented him from doing the unthinkable, and losing his temper with his father.

Isaiah was finding Miles's silence difficult to penetrate. It was rather like doing battle with one's reflection.

"And what will you do now? Go after her?" He made this sound like Miles intended to mount a broomstick and fly, or spin straw from gold: as though it were ridiculous and fanciful.

His father was brilliantly testing him. Little did Isaiah know that Miles was enjoying his own fury and finding it downright nourishing.

"Yes." A clipped word. Miles gave it no intonation. "I have accomplished every single thing I've ever set out to do. I can't imagine how this will pose any difficulty."

Miles noticed then that his father was holding his own body very still.

He *had* been dealt a blow, Miles reminded himself. And Isaiah Redmond was attempting to come to terms with it. But he was still coping with the consequences. His father wasn't young.

"What *happened*, Miles?"

It was Miles's turn to greet his father with incredulous, furious silence.

"Oh, for God's sake. That isn't what I meant. I don't want *details*. I've seen the girl. It's not as though she hasn't the goods to cause any red-blooded—"

"You'd best not finish that sentence. . . sir."

His father wasn't the only one who could make a point with an insulting, insinuating pause.

A fleeting, black fury darkened his father's face, and his hand twitched, as though he would have enjoyed laying the flat of it against his son's cheek. But Miles had to admire the control. It was gone then, the emotion. Isaiah's face cleared again.

And then he looked at his son.

Really looked at his son. Green eyes studying him.

There was another silence. If he could have fallen in love with Lady Georgina, Miles thought, he would have willingly done it. If he'd never met Cynthia Brightly, his life would be different today. But he knew he could not undo anything.

He'd spoken truly: he took no pleasure in disappointing his father. He took no pleasure in creating a fissure. He suffered. But he knew what was right. And now that he knew what love was, what it did to his world, he could never, never give it up.

Miles quieted his voice.

"I understand your anger, Father. I don't question your right to it, and I don't take pleasure or pride in it. I can assure you this is something I never set out to do, but I have never in my life done anything rashly. I speak truly: I feel I have no choice. But I can also assure you that if you come to know her, you'll see that Miss Brightly will only be a credit to the family. She has spine and wit and intelligence and pride and integrity and . . ."

When he was young, his father routinely used his brilliant green eyes as flints to strike fear from the hearts of his misbehaving children. Miles was used to the stare; he'd found it quite effective when he was younger, and had never been on the receiving end of it as an adult.

But it wasn't the stare that gave him pause.

It was the fact that at some point his father had stopped listening to his words. And was instead absorbing all that his words contained.

And before Miles's eyes, something seemed to ease out of his father's posture. Out of his face, out of his eyes. And he saw there something like . . . peace?

"All of that, is she?" His father's voice was inexplicably gentle. He sounded amused. And—if he wasn't mistaken— Relieved?

The expression on his father's face was, in fact, reminiscent of Violet's a few moments ago.

Miles now felt *officially* disconcerted. Deprived of his anger, of his righteousness, he was suddenly at a loss.

Isaiah Redmond strolled over to the table near the window. He used a finger to slowly trace the complex whorls of the polished wood. Perhaps he was using its polished surface to scry his future, the future of his son and heir. Or tracing it like the road he would have preferred Miles to travel.

Miles waited. He'd said all he meant to say.

Isaiah turned around to face him again. "There are three things I'd like you to know, Miles. Are you listening?"

"Yes, sir."

"First: I simply cannot and do not condone a match between a Redmond, any Redmond, and Miss Cynthia Brightly. This means you will *not* receive another shilling from me while I'm alive should you choose to marry Miss Brightly. You will, however, be welcomed in our home by your mother and me; the rest of the family will be free to receive you as well. But you and your . . . may not live in Redmond House. You are not welcome at the Mercury Club. You will not become a member. I will not fund any of your endeavors. I shall not revoke this. Are we understood?"

The punishment was severe; Miles was certain Isaiah meant every word, and would be inflexible in enforcing it.

But it was not as severe as Isaiah was capable of meting. It was, he supposed, just.

He would have time to absorb what it meant to him later, or if it would mean anything at all to him. Nothing mattered at the moment but Cynthia.

Miles inhaled, nodded.

"The second thing?" he urged his father curtly.

"The second thing is this . . . "

Miles watched in fresh amazement as his father's lips drifted upward into a smile that bordered on the rueful. It was, in fact, very nearly affectionate. It was decidedly *amused*.

"It's not absurd, is it, son?"

It took a moment, and then Miles remembered.

Miles was difficult to stun. He was stunned now.

What did his father know about love? Was his mother the love of his life? Had he correctly interpreted that look his father had sent Isolde Eversea so many years ago?

And . . . no. Love might be humbling, miraculous, hilarious, and necessary, transcending. It required everything of him. In fact it was . . . everything.

Everything, that is, except absurd.

"No, sir," he conceded firmly. "It is not."

And then his own mouth rebelled: it twitched up into a crooked smile. The other side of his mouth wouldn't commit to the smile.

But he supposed that was a place to begin knowing his father: this tentative exchange of smiles after a cold battle of words.

And all of this was Cynthia's fault. Miles contemplated all the many ways in which Cynthia Brightly had managed to upend his life, split him open, show him vistas he'd never dreamed existed—he who had wended his way through jungles, sweated through fevers, peered through microscopes, and tasted exotic pleasures of the flesh.

The real frontier, apparently, was inside him . . . and in front of him. In the form of his family. In the form of his father.

In the form of his future with Cynthia.

He was now free to spend the rest of his life in discovery. This was interesting. And of course, he loved "interesting" more than anything in the world.

His father gave a crisp nod of satisfaction.

A silence bordering on awkward ensued. The only other awkward moment involving his father that Miles could recall was when Isaiah Redmond had shouted out "*Son of a* bitch!" when Colin Eversea hadn't been hung as scheduled.

To this day Miles wondered why Isaiah had been at *all* surprised. Colin was an Eversea, after all.

"The third thing, Father?" he asked gently. He struggled to keep impatience from his voice.

Miles wondered if the long pause that followed indicated his father's indecision about what he might say. But in the end, Isaiah finally said it:

"I admire you, Miles."

The mild surprise and reluctance with which he delivered the words were hardly flattering. But the words stopped Miles's breath. Not: *I'm proud of you, Miles.* But the infinitely better, *I admire you.*

Isaiah had carefully chosen the words to acknowledge that he deserved no credit for who Miles had become, and to ensure that Miles knew another formidable man—a man Miles admired—found him worthy of admiration.

What *specifically do you admire?* he suddenly wanted to know. *My achievements? Or my choices? My ability to make them irrevocably? To risk everything I know for the one thing I need?*

For now he simply gave a short nod.

His father smiled to himself.

Isaiah Redmond was deliberately offhand. "If any weddings do take place, I should be happy to see them held at the church here in Pennyroyal Green. I believe the Everseas are one nuptial ahead of us in terms of recent weddings. And we simply can't have that."

Miles was in absolute concurrence with this. "Yes, sir."

His father's brow made a steep upward arch by way of dismissal, and his body slowly rotated back toward the window.

As if one day Lyon would come home over the green.

Miles bowed, wanting to make the gesture of respect whether or not his father would see it.

And he turned and strode from the room, shoulders straight, dignity intact.

He paused in the hall outside of his father's study as the peculiar enormity of the conversation broke over him. He allowed himself just one moment of stillness, of wonderment; he placed one hand on the shining curve of the banister for balance, to reorient himself, to connect with all that was Redmond.

Then he used the banister to launch himself down the stairs.

He all but flew down those marble steps, hand burning from the speed with which it traveled the banister, boot heels slamming down hard on the marble, taking three steps at a time. These were stairs he had traveled countless times before in his life; they would never be part of his home again.

He would have his own home.

For now, the only thing that mattered was locating an ill-tempered old woman in a bath chair.

In truth, this posed no challenge.

In his experience, a single clue often was the portal to an entire universe. One only need know how to look.

Chapter 23

"Miss Brightly. The demmed wicked cat is in my yarn again! It ought to be drowned for a rat!"

Mrs. Mundi-Dickson's voice could have chiseled facets from cold stone: screeching, operatic, and impressively healthy of volume for one who claimed to be unhealthy. There was nothing wrong with Mrs. Mundi-Dickson unless it was age—and age, to Cynthia's way of thinking, was *not* in and of itself an infirmity. Mrs. Mundi-Dickson had simply decided years ago to be bored and unhappy, had enthroned herself in her bath chair and had proceeded to make a reputation from her unhappiness. At least she kept legions of girls employed as they passed in and out of her service. In this way she provided a service, Cynthia told herself with dark amusement.

It was a rather remote area of Northumberland. Escape would be challenging. Cynthia spent every conscious moment thinking of it, and she'd been there for four days only.

"I'll fetch him, Mrs. Mundi-Dickson."

"I never said you could bring a demmed *cat*," her employer sopranoed from the sitting room.

"You never said I couldn't," Cynthia sang in return. She

went in to fetch Spider, extricated him from the yarn, in which he was genuinely, complexly entwined, took some time removing him from proximity to Mrs. Mundi-Dickson's knitting needles, and returned to the foyer because she thought she'd heard the door open.

As it turned out, she had. Apparently Miles Redmond had let himself in.

"Oh." The breath left Cynthia in a gasp. She almost dropped the cat.

She managed to slowly put Spider down at her feet.

Miles watched her every movement carefully, following it with his head. As if everything she did was unutterably important.

The kitten flung itself bodily at Miles's boot in a splayed attack. It then flew off in the opposite direction down the hall, tail a puff.

They stood and faced each other in utter silence.

She breathed. "But how did you—"

"I knocked. But then I decided to let myself in, as no one else seemed inclined to." He sounded calm.

They stared another moment.

She felt herself began to smile.

"You *left*." He sounded irritable. She knew this meant he was feeling awkward. And as her departure was rather self-evident, and she was finding it difficult to precisely gauge his mood, she said nothing.

She just gazed at him. She seemed to feel him everywhere, on her skin, in the swelling of her heart in her chest. It very much wanted to leap out to be with him.

"Well, I thought it best to—" she began softly.

"Before *dawn*." He accused her of this almost triumphantly, his voice gaining tension. As though she'd begun to argue the point.

"Well. Yes, I did," she humored tenderly.

He could rail at her all he wanted. He could shout epithets, shake his fist, fling his arms up in the air, pace, do whatever he wanted to relieve himself of the fear of losing her, of the fear for her safety, of the fear of his loving her.

She would wait it out, and stand there and love him. And open her arms when he was done.

"*Miss* Brightly!" The yodel came from the next room. "I want my demmed tea! Now!"

They both ignored Mrs. Mundi-Dickson.

Miles pulled in a long breath. He was holding his hat in one hand and he'd begun to tap it against the other, almost as if attempting to shake something out of it.

Good heavens. Miles Redmond was *fidgeting*.

"How . . . how did you find me?" She was tremendously impressed at the *speed* with which he had found her.

"Violet," he said shortly. His voice was still very soft. "She knew something about an old woman in a bath chair in Northumberland. It was a simple enough thing to ask questions. Seems Mrs. Mundi-Dickson is rather well known in these parts."

"Miss Brightly!" bellowed the old woman in the bath chair from the next room. "I *want* my *tea*. T-E-A. *Tea*. And if you don't bring it straight away I'll take a cane to—"

Miles whirled abruptly. "*If . . . you . . . please,*" he snarled.

Shocked silence rippled out of the other room.

Cynthia had *never* known such delight.

Miles turned to look at Cynthia looking just as composed as if he'd never said a word.

"I've come to ask something of you, Cynthia," he continued softly. "And before you answer, I should tell you that I have spoken with my father and he doesn't approve of . . .

what I'm about to ask of you. In the event you are amenable to . . . what I am about to ask of you, you should know that we will live on my income only. Which means we will live modestly in comparison to how my family currently lives. And Lord Argosy could at this very moment be in pursuit of you, as Violet told him where to find you as well. And as you know, Argosy is a man of not inconsiderable means. But we will be allowed to see my family. You will *have* a *family*."

Her heart stopped mid-leap. What of . . . all of his dreams, the things that made him who he was . . . He was to give them up? For her? For this?

"Miles. I cannot . . . I cannot allow . . . what of all your dreams? Lacao! I cannot allow—"

"*You* are my dream, Cynthia," he clarified simply. He didn't add *you fool,* though it was nearly implied in his tone.

She stopped abruptly. Ah, she'd been silly. She knew that Miles Redmond never did anything he hadn't carefully considered. He knew *precisely* what he was doing.

He'd chosen love. He'd chosen her.

Her heart launched itself skyward like coins flung in the wake of a wedding.

He read her face correctly. And one of those slow smiles—the ones that heated her inside and out and seemed to stop time—began to spread over his face.

He took a step forward. She took a step forward. Still, a gulf of foyer remained between them.

"Cynthia, here . . . here is the thing." He frowned darkly at his hat and placed it gingerly on the entry table, as if it was the hat's fault he'd been tempted to fidget with it. "I've loved you from the moment I laid eyes on you. From the *very* moment I saw your blue dress out of the corner of my eye. My heart knew and my soul knew, but my mind is an arrogant thing and thought it had a say in the matter, and my pride is apparently . . . shall we say, formidable. As you well know. And it happened all out of order—the loving you. It made no sense to me. I tried to make sense of it in the only way I knew, and . . . well, no science is a match for love. Our bodies knew first." And he produced a smile that made her unbearably randy. "And then . . ." He stopped.

"And then?" she encouraged. She could never, never hear enough of Miles Redmond telling her how much he loved her, and she was enjoying this speech.

"Well, *wanting* you is how I was able to see that I love you. But the funny thing is . . . I did know right away that you are meant to be part of me, and do you know why? I stopped breathing when I first saw you. But the irony is you, when I'm with you, I feel like every breath is my first one, and . . . I was never really alive until I touched you. So clearly, in order to continue living, to keep breathing, I need to be with you."

It was the most extraordinary speech she had ever heard, or would forever in her life hear again. Count on Miles Redmond to find a way to entwine love with science and to add a dash of irony.

"It's a matter of biology, is it?" she said softly.

"Well, that, and I would happily die for you."

She didn't doubt it for a moment.

"I'll try to arrange it so that will never become necessary."

This made him smile.

"I *love* you, Miles." She sounded so surprised that he gave a short laugh.

"It *is* strange, isn't it?" said the man who had never before been daunted by anything strange.

It was as though they'd both assumed "love" was a mythical place akin to El Dorado, but they'd gone and stumbled across it and were now abashed. Both for attempting to evade it—for who were *they* to attempt to subjugate something so extraordinary to their petty human objectives?—and by the very fact of its existence.

Love was really more like Lacao. Beautiful and terrifying and strange. They could be forever discovering all it could offer them.

"Miles. I love you. You. I *love* you. I am sorry if Argosy is hurt, but I cannot feel *too* sorry with you standing here. But I will go anywhere with *you*."

"Oh," he said softly. "Very good, then."

He took another step forward.

She took another step forward.

"We'll find a way to go back to Lacao," she promised him fervently.

"Of course we will." He still sounded distracted. Spider the cat skittered back into the room and sat on his boot for an instant before darting off again.

"Which brings me to my question. Cynthia . . ." He took a sustaining breath. " . . . will you do me the honor of being my wife?" The words came out in a rush.

Oh.

Everything had gone blurry and moist. Like the tropics, perhaps. She brushed a hand back across her eyes, as she needed to see his face when she answered him.

"I should be honored to be your wife, Mr. Redmond." She'd said it with a dignity that would do honor to any Redmond. Or, rather, she *tried* to say it with dignity. Her voice did break a little.

Miles cast a glance skyward—in gratitude, perhaps—and then his eyes were on hers, and his face was brilliant.

Cynthia wondered how *anyone* could withstand this sort of happiness.

But no doubt no one had ever before been as happy as she was at this moment, so there couldn't possibly be any precedent. She would have to show them all how to do it by surviving it and marrying Miles Redmond and living to a ripe old age.

Suddenly bashful, suddenly equal, they regarded each other across the stretch of Mrs. Mundi-Dickson's foyer.

Mrs. Mundi-Dickson, shockingly, had said nothing more. They heard stirrings and thumps in the other room. She sounded as though she were pouring her own tea. Imagine that. The moment was simply filled with miracles.

Then Miles was before her in a final long, startling stride, his big hands cradling her face, and his mouth touched hers almost tentatively. As though he could hardly believe she was real.

So she assured him that she was: she looped her arms around his neck and held him fast, so he would know she wasn't going anywhere ever again. She reached up and kissed his beautiful mouth fiercely. Kissed his jaw. Turned her cheek to feel the scrape of his whiskers. Murmured to him nonsense, which is the language of love, inhaled the heat of his skin, the sweat from his mad galloping rush to find her.

And as his arms went around her back, folding her close to him, where she belonged, she leaned back in his arms and gently plucked his spectacles from his face because they'd misted over a bit. She rubbed them against her bodice, and replaced them on his face, because it was her job to take care of him from now on.

He was amused. "The better to see you with, my dear," he murmured.

And then his lips touched her, and he proceeded to make a thorough job of tasting her.

New York Times bestselling author Julia Quinn

The Bridgerton Novels

On the Way to the Wedding
978-0-06-053125-6

Gregory Bridgerton must thwart Lucy Abernathy's upcoming wedding and convince her to marry him instead.

It's In His Kiss
978-0-06-053124-9

To Hyacinth Bridgerton, Gareth St. Clair's every word seems a dare.

When He Was Wicked
978-0-06-053123-2

To Sir Phillip, With Love
978-0-380-82085-6

Romancing Mister Bridgerton
978-0-380-82084-9

An Offer From a Gentleman
978-0-380-81558-6

The Viscount Who Loved Me
978-0-380-81557-9

The Duke and I
978-0-380-80082-7